Square Spirits
The Shops on Wolf Creek Square

Gini Athey

Enjoy,
Gini Athey

Editing: Brittiany Koren/Written Dreams
Cover art design/Layout: Ed Vincent/ENC Graphic Services
Front cover photographs moon: © kostins/Shutterstock.com;
storefronts: © LanaN/Shutterstock.com;
candlestick: © Babich Alexander/ Shutterstock.com.;
wine bottles: © Valentyn Volkov/Shutterstock.com

Map illustration by Logan Stefonek/Stefonek Illustration &
Design.

Category: Women's Fiction/Romance

First Print Edition May 2016.
0 1 2 3 4 5 6 7 8 9

Wolf Creek Square Series

Book 1 – Quilts Galore

Book 2 – Country Law

Book 3 – Rainbow Gardens

Book 4 – Square Spirits

*To Kate B. – my first trip to your house for a writing seminar began my journey to becoming an author.
Thank you.*

*To Helene F. – we live in two different countries, but our friendship has no border.
Love you.*

Note to Readers

Welcome to Wolf Creek!

Square Spirits, Book 4 of my Wolf Creek Square Series, brings a new resident to this ever-growing tight-knit community. Zoe Miller has worked hard for two years to recover from a devastating divorce, and she's ready to open her New Age shop among the traditional established businesses on the Square.

Zoe becomes friends with the residents and shopkeepers from *Quilts Galore* (Book 1), *Country Law* (Book 2), and *Rainbow Gardens* (Book 3). These new people in her life are her guides to the Square's annual activities and events that keep shoppers returning year after year.

Nestled in rich farm land, Wolf Creek is a small fictional town west of Green Bay, Wisconsin. Unique to the town is Wolf Creek Square, a pedestrian-only area where historical buildings surround a picnic area, a stage used for concerts and festivals, flower gardens and walkways. The Square is a beautiful place year-round and is rapidly becoming a four season destination in Northeastern Wisconsin.

Zoe guards her ability as a practicing psychic, even after buying the building on the corner that for many decades has been rumored to be haunted. Zoe has seen the spirits of the two young girls that reside in the building, but keeps their presence to herself, even as she learns more about the fires that caused their death.

Reluctantly, Zoe admits that Eli Reynolds shifts her energy, but she's committed to her independence, even as their paths continually cross. Zoe slowly realizes that on some level, Eli is a kindred spirit.

While Zoe is new to Wolf Creek Square, many of her colleagues and friends can trace their family history to the early days of the town. More of the history of the town can be found in the other books in the series.

I invite you to enjoy the comings and goings of this lively community, then visit my website, www.giniathey.com, to sign up for my newsletter. You never know what will happen next on Wolf Creek Square.

Gini Athey
2016

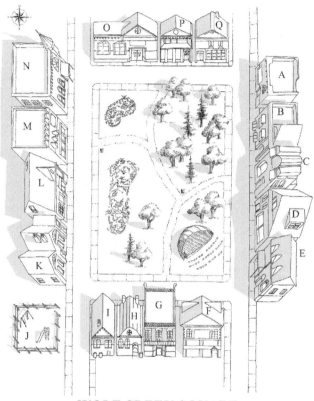

WOLF CREEK SQUARE

A-Farmer Foods
B-The Fiber Barn
C-Rainbow Gardens
D-Clayton's
E-Country Law
F-Art&Son Jewelry
G-Quilts Galore
H-Vacant
I-Pages and Toys

J-Fenced Playground
K-Styles by Knight and Day
L-Vacant
M-Biscuits and Brew
N-Inn on the Square
O-Museum
P-Mayor's Office
Q-Square Spirits

"Spirits make me smile
Ghosts make me shiver."

—Author Unknown

~~~~~~~~~~~

"As fine as wisps of smoke
Spirits travel through the air
To places far and near.

Ever present, young and old,
Gems we need not fear."

—Author Unknown

November

1

Seeing the girls' faces in the upstairs window clinched my decision. That same day I made an offer on the building, and when it was accepted, my two years of searching came to an end. But even better, my life sparkled with all the possibilities of a new beginning.

It hadn't taken long to get a special feeling for Wolf Creek, Wisconsin, specifically the southeast corner of what was known as the Square. Not just an ordinary town square, this location was bustling and vital, and the primary attraction for locals and tourists alike. I sensed deep within me it was exactly the place where I'd achieve the inner peace I sought, along with the excitement of the new creative challenges I'd longed for.

Even before buying the building, I knew I was especially sensitive to the energy in my newfound space. Not surprisingly, everything fell into place quickly after the girls showed me their faces. Of course, I told no one about their presence. I also was under no illusions about these spirits. I had my eyes wide open, and one way or another, these girls would have to be dealt with at some point in the future.

The building itself was not such a daunting challenge. I'd have my retail business on the first floor and an apartment above it. Both areas had been newly renovated, and the shop was outfitted with almost everything I'd need to fling the doors wide open and greet the shoppers on Wolf Creek Square.

Early one morning, I stood in the middle of the shop, with

rays of sunlight coming through the window in the door. I was filled with gratitude that the first day of my new life was as bright and shiny as the key to the front door I turned over in my palm. Born and raised in Northeastern Wisconsin, I was well aware that the first of November could be cold and rainy, downright miserable. Even snow was not unheard of. But rather than think of what the day could have been, I focused on what it was, bright and cheerful.

It had taken two men, cousins Nolan and Reed Crawford, working hard and fast to get my store ready to open. Their part was almost done, but my job had barely begun. First, though, a solo celebration. I raised my arms to my sides and made a quick turn all the way around, laughing to myself. I'd had a vision and what I saw exactly matched it. Not that I hadn't bumped up against a bit of resistance, namely Reed and Nolan's skepticism about the color scheme for the walls. I felt cocooned in the colors I'd imagined, starting with the deep plum at the baseboards, progressively lightening to violet, and then blending to sky blue where the walls met the ceiling.

Nolan, the older of the two cousins, seemed to have had a better sense of the atmosphere I wanted to create, and surprised me with a sunburst in the center of the ceiling, done in a soft yellow-gold. He offered to paint over it if I didn't want it. Not a chance.

Although the renovation work and the trial and error involved in designing the store itself went smoothly, the building still held its secrets. Fortunately, what might put off other people were exactly the elements that attracted me.

Early on, Nolan and Reed were thrown by the odd air currents circulating through both floors. Nolan had opened up about the dilemma after we'd discussed the wiring updates needed in the shop and the apartment.

"Well, uh…you see, Zoe, we can't explain it," he said, "but sometimes it's cold up there. The kind of cold where I need to grab my jacket. But then, it's suddenly so hot I almost can't breathe."

Suppressing a smile, I'd stuck my hand in the pocket of my slacks and rolled the familiar amethyst point between my thumb and index finger. It centered me, but also served as a reminder that sometimes staying quiet about what I knew was more effective than simply blurting out the truth. I was also relieved Reed and Nolan hadn't found something as dramatic as scorched timbers when they tore out old wiring and plaster. Over my nearly 50 years, I'd learned to hold back explanations about what I knew—and experienced—because I wasn't sure others were ready to hear what I had to say.

I had yet to learn how much the local people understood about this building, other than being aware it had been vacant for many years. Most people in town had heard idle speculation about the building being haunted. *Strange happenings*, some said. Even the mayor of Wolf Creek, Sarah Hutchinson, had been surprised I had bought the place so quickly and without reservation.

So, rather than alarming Nolan and Reed, maybe scaring them off, I played it safe and muttered something about calling the furnace guys to check it out. I assured them I'd see to it, and besides, the problem was likely easily fixed by HVAC techs. That wasn't true, but the explanation would settle the matter with Nolan and Reed, at least for the time being.

In reality, the shift in air currents was only odd or scary to those who didn't know about the two young spirits living in the building. Who they were when they'd been *living* girls I couldn't say, so I gave them names that popped into my head and seemed to fit: Grace, the cool one, and Rose, the hot entity.

My unwillingness to explain the situation to the two men was part of my resolve to tread carefully in my new town. I didn't want Nolan and Reed spreading the word that I was a bit of an eccentric, even a bit of a nutty fortuneteller. I'd have a failed business on my hands before I could welcome the first customer.

I had to face facts. Taking on the persona of Madame Zoe, an amusing fortuneteller, at the Square's Labor Day Celebration was one thing, an acceptable label for an event that also featured face painting for the kids and grilled hot dogs and burgers for sale. But having an actual psychic in their midst, one who *saw spirits*? No, that likely would be something else entirely in my new community.

I'd questioned my judgment about allowing myself to be anything other than Zoe Miller, psychic medium, but somehow, I hadn't seen the harm in being the slightly exotic Madame Zoe for the day. Besides, the Square's festival had been a turning point for me. First, I'd managed to convince Eli Reynolds, an attractive man, but kind of a grouch, to alter the arrangement of the festival's booths in order to give me the exact spot on the Square where the energy was most suitable for me. No matter that the spot happened to be in front of Farmer Foods, a store he and his twin brother owned. Second, I noted immediately that my own spirit quieted in this little town. A sense of peace washed over me—at long last—and I breezed through my day as a festival fortuneteller. Everything flowed from that event, including finding my new home and starting the business I'd dreamed of for a long time.

Granted the wisdom of being Madame Zoe for a day was an open question. Nonetheless, there I was, only weeks later, standing in my very own shop, Square Spirits, spontaneously taking another 360 degree turn to embrace the energy in the space.

The buzzer on the back door rang and interrupted my train of thought. That was okay, because I had mountains of work ahead of me.

***

Twenty minutes after propping open the back door, I said goodbye to the delivery truck driver and watched him pull away. When I locked the door behind me, I turned to stare at the two dozen boxes stacked in piles of twos and threes around the room. I longed to grab my handy pocket knife and dive into the cartons and get my hands on every item I'd ordered. Just thinking about the contents of the cartons brought the sense of excitement I'd felt the day I placed the order. I had looked forward to my Grand Opening Party, the grand opening of the boxes, that is.

I took a deep breath. *Slow down, Zoe, first things first.* The glass shelving and display cases, and even the floor, needed preparation. Nothing, not even one crystal could be placed and displayed until I rid my shop of the last bit of telltale dust left behind from the new construction.

I grabbed the handy-vac and got started on the glass shelves, all the while basking in my vision of the kind of shop Square Spirits would be. I'd open the doors the next day, if all went well. The name had been blissfully easy to come up with for my new shop. Square because of the location, and Spirits because I'd sell candles, different varieties of polished stones, crystal jewelry, pendulums, note cards, blank journals, calendars, books, and other items that fit the definition of a New Age shop. But Spirits had another meaning, too, because my family owned DmZ Winery, located south of Green Bay.

As I prepared to open my shop I also polished the wooden wine racks Nolan and Reed had installed where I'd stock selected varieties of the best DmZ wine.

I hadn't been all that enthusiastic about selling the family's wines, but it was a peace offering to my older brother, Devin. He'd expected me to stay and help him run the winery now that congestive heart failure had slowed down our dad and diminished his vitality. My biggest challenge with my family dynamics was trying to get Devin to understand that creating a new life in Wolf Creek wasn't about abandoning him or our parents and the winery.

I checked my watch. I'd made reservations for dinner for the four of us at Crossroads, the restaurant inside the Inn on the Square. I knew full well Devin might make a statement and refuse to come along, and we'd be three at dinner. I mentally went back and forth between hoping he'd come and wishing Devin would stay away and spare me his attitude. He'd been so unpredictable lately, one day grudgingly accepting of my impending move, the next openly hostile.

But family conflict aside, even if my parents arrived alone, I wanted them to see me busy settling in, excited and happy. With the cleanup done, it was time for my reward, namely, sorting through the boxes, starting with the one with the fat invoice envelope taped to the outside.

As I pulled out my knife, a sense of déjà vu washed over me, but there was nothing otherworldly about it. I'd opened hundreds, thousands, of cartons of supplies when I'd taken on the position of office manager for Tyler's clinic. Tyler Goodman, ex-husband. My business mind had been forged as I'd thrown myself into the work that would eventually bring him, and his partners and best friends, great success. By association, of course, I'd enjoyed that success, too. I used to joke that my job at the clinic was to handle all those little details Tyler and his partners and the other doctors they'd hired hadn't wanted to bother with.

At the beginning that included unpacking equipment and supplies and developing systems to keep track of what came in and what went out. Eventually, our hired staff took that over, but I oversaw their training, including the various computer programs I'd had customized to keep the ever-growing clinic running like a well-calibrated machine.

Now, acting on my own behalf, I needed to compare the invoice list with the items in the boxes. Slow and steady. I laughed to myself. I'd recovered from my divorce slowly, and *almost* steadily. It had taken a full two years to find myself this new life, but here it was.

I took a deep breath and sliced the blade through the tape on the box, and pulled out the shredded paper packing material, which soon scattered around my feet. The faint aroma of lavender wafted up from one of the larger cartons. Not surprising, since I'd chosen lavender as a theme for my shop. That's why I'd wanted the walls to gradually change from the deepest shades of purple to light lavender, mirroring the variety of shades of amethyst, my signature stone. I lifted lavender candles, some square, some round, from their individual nests in the box and arranged them on a low glass shelf.

As if the candles and their colors solidified my presence in the shop, with new vigor I unpacked the smaller boxes of stones, pendants, and other shapes, sizes, and colors of candles from the large shipping boxes, along with crystal and amethyst necklaces and earrings. I dug another carton until I found the CDs I was looking for. Nolan and Reed had wired speakers, giving me the ability to play music from my computer, but I was also selling CDs. I chose one that I knew was a lively combination of Celtic fiddle and drums, and put it in the player behind the counter. As I hummed along with the music, I arranged the collection of CDs on the shelf I set aside for them.

With candles and stones, journals and CDs in place, I stepped back to breathe in the peace and beauty I'd created with my first displays. I had a long way to go, but I was off to a great start. Any lingering apprehension about the challenges ahead had vanished.

Lost in having so much fun, I startled at the knock on my front door. Since I'd told my family to come to the back entrance with the truck, the Square being designated as pedestrian only, I was curious about who would be paying me a visit.

Looking through the glass window, I recognized Eli Reynolds' sister. I couldn't recall her name, though, but I swung the door open wide. "Come in, come in. Excuse the mess. I'm unpacking my inventory."

She stood in the doorway, a slight frown forming between her brows. It occurred to me she was afraid to come inside. *The girls.* No surprise. She probably wondered if the building truly was haunted. Not the word I'd have used. Grace and Rose hadn't made themselves known the last few days, what with all of the commotion of Reed and Nolan finishing the last details of the remodeling.

I reached out to touch my visitor and coaxed her inside like I would a young child. "Come on in."

The woman held a bouquet of flowers tight to her body, but then stretched her arm to hand the vase to me when she crossed the threshold.

"Thank you. These are beautiful." I set the vase on the glass counter. The vibrant colors of gold and rust and burgundy mums added another bright spot to the space that was still three-quarters bare.

"You're welcome." She moved tentatively about the room, touching a candle here, a pendulum there, running her hands over the wooden shelf on the wine side of the shop. As she walked around, she relaxed and accepted my invitation to sit in the lone chair in the room. The small table and chairs I'd ordered hadn't been delivered yet.

"It's soothing in here." She sat back into the chair and closed her eyes.

"The colors…" I stopped myself from explaining the effect colors have on mood. Eli's sister was a florist, so she knew a thing or two about color and mood. It was nearing the point when I'd be forced to ask her name if she didn't offer it first.

"It's more than that. The whole atmosphere is soothing." Opening her eyes, she spread her arms wide, as I'd done earlier, as if embracing the energy. "When I need a break from Rainbow Gardens, I'll stop by."

"You're welcome to come anytime," I said, meaning it. "Maybe we can have a cup of tea together sometime." I waved to the back. "A table and chairs will be delivered soon." I laughed. "Then I'll be able to entertain, if you know what I mean."

She nodded and walked to the front door. "I almost forgot to introduce myself. I'm Megan Reynolds. You met so many people when you were our fortuneteller last fall that you couldn't possibly remember everyone. Of course, you worked with my brother Eli, since he was in charge of the booths."

Megan, of course. "Oh, yes, I remember Eli. He was so accommodating. And Sarah was, too. It was a fun day. I'm glad to meet you…again."

"Hurry with your unpacking. Take it from me, you'll have customers knocking on your door before you're ready."

When she opened the door, a cool gust of November air sent the bits of packing paper skittering across the floor. But Megan seemed not to notice. Instead, she reached up and tapped the corner of the door. "Oh, one quick thing. Be sure to have Nolan install a bell for you. Every shop has one."

"I see." I recalled Sarah saying the same thing, but it had

slipped my mind. "I'll get on that."

"Good. Your shop sounds lonely without it."

I smiled at her characterization, thinking of my invisible partners, Grace and Rose. I watched Megan go on her way across the Square. When I closed the door and turned back to look into my shop, the sight of the bouquet, my first "Welcome to the Square" gift, sent a ripple of excitement through me.

If Megan's prediction of customers descending on me turned out to be right, I needed to get moving. I bypassed boxes on the floor and went to the storage cabinet near the back door and pulled out the small cash register and credit card supplies. So different from the old-style hefty machines that ate up space on retail store counters. My shop might be filled with ancient symbols, but its technology was as updated as I could manage. I also grabbed a supply of different sized Square Spirits bags and gift boxes, and arranged the small boxes and tissue paper reserved for packaging pendants and pendulums.

I spent the next few hours sorting what I'd display now and what inventory I'd stash in the basement or in the back room to bring out as needed. I hoped I could enlist my brother to help with that. If not, I'd haul the boxes downstairs myself and organize and label them later. I wanted to be sure I could get my hands on chunks of green or orange calcite or amethyst points or scented candles without rummaging through every carton.

With only three more boxes to go, I uncovered my crown jewel, the single display piece that was not for sale. Its purpose was to inspire a little awe, and attract a shopper's eye to the smaller pieces on the surrounding shelves. A large amethyst geode, cave-like and sparkling inside, it took both hands to carry the heavy stone to the glass shelf. Since I was almost six feet tall, I didn't need a ladder or even low stool to put it exactly where I wanted it in the middle of the wall. After making sure the stone was secure, I adjusted the overhead spotlight to enhance the sparkling purple stone.

I made quick work of the remaining boxes of cards and artistically designed blank journals and a small number of books with spiritual themes. I would wait to order more titles until I learned what the bookshop on the Square stocked. It would do me no good to unintentionally start out as a competitor with a colleague.

With my family due any minute, I whisked away the remaining unpacked shipping boxes and stashed them at the back of the store. If Megan was right, I could have customers surprise me and I wanted them to have plenty of room to wander around. I broke down the empty cartons and hauled them out the back door and across the alleyway. I was struggling to keep the lid of the recycling bin open with one hand and stuff in the cartons with the other when Eli stepped out of the back door of Sarah's office. I stutter-stepped when I saw him.

"Hi, Eli." My mind went blank. I had no follow up. Not the best way to begin a neighborly conversation.

"Need some help here, Zoe?" He lifted the lid of the recycle container and held it open while I threw in the rest of the boxes I'd stacked alongside. "Any more inside?"

I hadn't expected Eli's openness and willingness to help. At the festival he'd avoided me, but had he thought I wouldn't notice the furtive glances he cast my way the whole weekend? Eli was a serious skeptic. I didn't need to be a psychic to see that he thought Madame Zoe was a fake.

"No more empties for now, but thank you."

"Okay then." He hesitated. "I… I…"

That was as far as it got. He waved and hurried off in the direction of Farmer Foods, kitty corner in the Square from Square Spirits.

I was about to enter the back door when the beep of a car horn stopped me. I spun around and saw my mom driving the winery's shiny silver truck. Wow! I'd have a selection of wine to get started. No Devin, though, so the bulk of it would have to be delivered later.

Knowing Mom would have made the selection of what to bring in the truck, I was eager to see the combinations she'd put together. Probably everything from the driest table reds and whites to the sweetest and most popular of the DmZ fruit wines.

Hugs all around got us started on solid footing. We'd stay congenial as long as we didn't bring up Devin's absence.

"I brought the dolly," Dad said, "so it shouldn't be too hard for you to load up the cartons and bring them inside."

"And I'll help arrange everything," Mom said.

Of course, this was her way to ease past the fact that Devin wouldn't be around to help out, and Dad was certainly no longer able to do this kind of physical work. With them following me, I went inside the shop and pointed to the chair for Dad.

I propped open the back door and stacked the first three cartons on the dolly and after bringing them inside, I unloaded them next to the wine racks. It took two more trips before all nine cartons were inside. Dad started opening them while Mom went off to park the truck in the lot behind the Square. He insisted on helping me fill the racks, but left me to arrange the single-bottle displays. Dad never claimed to have an eye for design, at least not to the level of Mom's and Devin's skills. He always said he was a wine-maker, not a wine salesman. Devin and Mom had a good portion of each skill, with Mom being the expert label designer and wine shop keeper. During the past two years, I helped out where I was most needed, usually handling displays and inventory, not unlike the way I'd spent my day.

When Mom came back, I asked her to do a walk-through of the shop and give me her opinion of the way I'd organized it. I still had time to tweak here and there, to add more visual appeal to the items I stocked. And as of that moment, I was now in the business of selling the family's wine. Devin or no Devin, it was exciting.

Mom tapped my arm to get my attention. She gestured toward the shelves of candles and glass bowls of stones, the calendars and journals accessible in small bins. "Shall I start putting price labels on the wine? You seem to have everything else in the shop displayed beautifully."

"Thanks," I said, grinning with pleasure. Her good opinion of the look of the shop meant a lot to me. I reached into a drawer under the counter and took out the labels I'd written up. "Despite the computer programs, I have a hunch customers will like those price stickers on everything I sell. They can easily keep track of what they're spending, and when I slash the prices for a sale, they'll see that, too."

"That's what we found at the wine tasting parties," Mom said. "In fact, once I started putting prices on the wine—and the glasses—I sold more of them."

A light knock on the front door diverted my attention from Mom and the wine. Because I'd forgotten to unlock the door, Sarah and Nolan were waiting outside. Secretly, I'd hoped for customers to make my launch official, but it was just as well no one showed up. A locked door wouldn't have conveyed a warm invitation.

I hurried to let them in, noting Sarah looking beyond me at Mom working at the racks. On alert as usual, Sarah no doubt wanted to see for herself what kinds of items I'd be selling.

"A lot of activity out back." Sarah absently patted the silver tray where Mom had arranged blush and white wine. "I want to make sure you have everything you need."

Nolan lifted a small bell and shook it so it jingled. "Megan called a little bit ago and said you needed a bell—pronto. That's how she put it. So here I am."

Was everyone always so meddlesome? I liked Megan and Sarah, but really, I could have managed a silly bell.

But this was not the time to rock the boat, so I swallowed my irritation and thanked them all for coming by. "I'm glad you have a chance to meet my family." I made formal introductions and then waved Sarah deeper into the shop to what I considered the heart of what I offered. It was where I envisioned shoppers clustered around the stones and candles and pendants, browsing through books and calendars that prominently featured the phases of the moon, deep space images, and inspirational quotes.

Sarah wasted no time launching into her description of how sensational the holiday season was for the shop owners and visitors. When my mother came up behind me, Sarah handed both of us a welcome brochure she'd written and designed. "This explains a little about the history of the Square and our town. I think Zoe's business will add something unique and special."

"I agree, Sarah. And it's nice to see Zoe happy again, too." Mom put her hand on my shoulder and gave me a quick squeeze.

Again? I winced against the implication. No one here knew my personal history and I intended to keep it that way. Mom made me sound like a problem case—not to mention about ten years old. Meanwhile, Dad sat in the chair by the wine racks taking it all in, including, I'm sure, my grimace as I turned away.

Time to change the subject and put someone else in the spotlight. I called out to Nolan and waved him over to where Mom, Sarah, and I stood. I pointed to the ceiling. "Nolan painted the sunburst on the ceiling. What do you think?"

"It's gorgeous," Mom said.

"I can't even take credit for the idea. It was all Nolan's."

Grinning self-consciously, Nolan asked what else he could do to help.

I led him to the back and chatted with him about additional display space I'd need in the future. In his usual affable way, he said I only needed to give him the signal to start. Then he took off out the back door at the exact time the delivery truck pulled up.

"Must be some furniture arriving," I said.

Nolan and I went out to the alleyway as the driver and his sidekick unloaded the two tables. I led the men back inside to point out where I wanted them. "The small table goes in the front window area, and the larger one near the back." I had to wait a few more days for the chairs.

The delivery guys went back to the truck to get the items for my apartment, and Nolan clomped up the stairs to assemble the pieces. Mom joined Dad at the wine racks, and when Sarah's phone rang, she said her goodbyes.

Comings and goings through the front and back all day it seemed. And it happened again. Barely a minute after Sarah left across the Square, the delivery men hauled a couple of empty cartons out with them through the back, and my first customers came in through the front door—to the pleasant jingle of the newly installed bell.

2

"Are you open?" A group of three young women stood behind a fourth, the one who asked the question.

My body began to tingle as I shifted into saleswoman mode. "Yes, I'm open," I said, "as of right now." I swept my arm in a big "come on in" gesture. "*You* are my first customers."

Their faces lit up in surprise, and I responded with a delighted sigh. "As you can see, I'm still putting out inventory, and unpacking and arranging the shop, but please, come in and look around."

I pointed to my mother and explained that we'd finished stocking my family's wine only a few minutes earlier. "Judith and Russ Miller, my parents, owners of DmZ Winery, are even here to answer questions."

I spotted an empty wine carton and whisked it away as the quartet of customers headed in different directions.

Dad stood and slowly walked to the back of the shop as Mom followed with the folding chair. I listened to the ripple of "ohs" and "ahs." Music to my ears.

Trying to look casual, I ambled over to the register and squared the piles of shopping bags stacked on the shelf below the counter. Then I took out the small business card holder and cards I'd had printed just in time. If customers were ready to buy, I was ready to sell.

And buy they did.

"We're Christmas shopping early," one said, as I used padded recycled paper to wrap one of my prized rose quartz stones, exactly the size to sit comfortably in my palm. I placed it at the bottom of a small shopping bag and handed it to a young woman, in her early twenties or so. Tall like me, and with thick dark brown hair flowing down her back, just like mine, she could have been my daughter. Right down to the dark brown eyes. An auspicious sign? That my first customer so closely resembled me? That's how I chose to see it.

"And as a grand opening gift," I said, "here's a complimentary lavender-scented votive candle. I hope you visit again soon."

The woman grinned broadly as she glanced around. "And that won't be long. I could get into a lot of trouble in a store like this."

Her companions laughed with her and nodded. Each had a small item, a candle, a tiny crystal, and for the third woman, a pocket mirror about the size of a silver dollar with a collaged peace dove illustration encased in glass on the back. "Ah, I see you found these. I was afraid their basket would be lost in the shuffle."

"I spotted them right away," the woman said. "By the way, my friends and I like to come out here for Black Friday sales and Small Business Saturday events on the Square. You'll be part of it, won't you?"

"You bet I will," I said. "I hear that weekend is really something. And I'll have more stock, lots of new items."

"Well, those are the days we do our major shopping." The woman patted the side of the shopping bag holding the rose quartz. "I already have my sister's gift. She's crazy for rose quartz." Glancing around, she said, "Hmm...I see a store filled with girlfriend gifts."

Her three companions laughed, and I joined in, but I also filed that remark away. Of course! Stones and candles and journals and note cards were exactly the kind of small gifts women bought for each other. I fought off a heavy wave of sadness. For all kinds of reasons, I lacked the pleasure of close women friends. That was no one's fault but mine, although I'd blamed the demands of the lifestyle Tyler wanted as a reason I hadn't carved out more of a life of my own.

Gini Athey

"Whenever the shops on the Square are open, Square Spirits will be, too," I said, bringing my attention back to the women.

The shopper who had discovered the pocket mirror had wandered back to the wine racks and I picked up enough of the conversation to hear Mom describe the array of weekend activities at the winery. She was a born saleswoman, with an infectious smile. Although I had to develop a style for myself, one that fit the energy in the shop, I'd learned the basics from the best.

"So, a bottle of pinot noir to go with your mirror," I said when the wine shopper approached the counter for the second time. I finished the transaction and double-checked to be sure each woman had a lavender votive, and off they went.

I stood at the counter and closed my eyes, concentrating on the hazy glow that cloaked me from head to toe. I'd organized my shop, opened the door, was freely handed a new marketing idea, and made my first sale. First *four* sales. *Thank you!*

As soon as the door closed, it opened again. Sarah had returned. "Shoppers already? Terrific!"

Her boisterous voice brought me back to earth. "Ah, yes, my first customers." Still lightheaded, I tried to think of something clever to say, but came up empty.

Sarah had a folder in her hand and put it on the counter. "I came back because I wanted you to see the ad we're going to run. We're promoting your shop as our newest attraction."

"Really? That's fantastic. When will it be printed?"

"Thanksgiving weekend and the weekend before. Can't do a better setup for a new shop than that." Sarah opened the folder and turned it toward me so I could see it.

Glancing down, I checked the spelling of Square Spirits, and my contact information, including my Facebook page. Although I was featured prominently, the ad was inclusive and listed every shop on the Square, including the coffee shop, Biscuits and Brew, which everyone called B and B. The restaurant, Crossroads, was also highlighted, along with all the retail stores. Country Law, a law firm on the

Square, was the only non-retail business in the colorful ad.

"Thanks so much," I said. "I can honestly say that I've never felt more welcomed anywhere than I have here on the Square."

"Good. That's the way we like it." She handed me a schedule of business association meetings for November and December, explaining that she always added notes about tour buses and other groups of visitors arriving, usually on the weekends during the holidays, and almost every day in the summer. I noticed that a community shopping tour bus would be coming through on Saturday.

"I'll be ready," I said confidently.

The sound of heavy boots on the stairs distracted both Sarah and me. Nolan! I'd nearly forgotten about him. He ambled over to the counter to join Sarah and me there. "So, we put the legs on the table and set the bed up."

"Hey, home and business, ready to go," I said with a laugh.

Nolan frowned. "Uh, has the furnace been checked? I'm still feeling those hot and cold spots up there. *Weird*."

Sarah's upper body pulled back, putting distance between us.

This building had a certain reputation, and Sarah knew the rumors.

I nodded to her to communicate my understanding of the situation. But I waved off Nolan. "The heating guys are coming next week to check it out."

Before the conversation went any further, Mom called from across the shop to tell me she had a question about the wine. Sarah and Nolan took advantage of an opportunity to leave and get on with their day.

"What's wrong with the furnace?" Mom asked in a pointed tone.

Mom's intuitive powers were stronger than mine, and she was never shy about using them when it came to her family. Ironically, both Mom and I could accurately read many situations, but we weren't always so good at assessing situations affecting those close to us.

"Russ?" She went around the wine racks and headed to

27

the back, where Dad sat reading a magazine. "Do you feel well enough to get us coffee from that place, you know, the one they call B and B?"

She wants him out of earshot. She knows something.

Dad stood and stretched his arms over his head. "I sure do. Much rather do something useful than sit here all day."

He grabbed his jacket and took our coffee order and left, with Mom and me standing by the window watching the Square. Keeping my tone low, acknowledging not just the secrecy, but the calm I wanted to maintain when I talked about it, I told Mom about seeing the fire and the girls I'd named Grace and Rose screaming in the upstairs windows.

"Then and there, I decided to buy the building," I said, "and I made an offer later that day."

Mom only nodded. "I see."

She'd have added more if something meaningful came to her. Of that I was sure. "I understand the shifting air currents, but unsuspecting Nolan thinks the furnace is seriously flawed."

Later, we finished our coffee as daylight faded. I turned on the shop lights and tested the strategically placed spotlights. I liked what I saw. Every area of the shop sparkled, from the crystals and amethyst to the gold and silver trays under the wine bottles. Every surface seemed to reflect the light, adding extra illumination to everything in the room.

Mom had put one of Devin's award-winning wines on a shelf in front of a mirror. The spotlight highlighted the award medallion she'd hung on the neck of the bottle. The display made its own statement about the quality of the DmZ Winery.

"Gorgeous," Mom said.

I nodded, but my reaction ran along the lines of *almost*. As I scanned the room, the wine side of the shop felt heavy with the wooden shelves and the dark bottles of red wine, at least compared to the glass shelves and progressive shades of lavender walls. My first impulse was to balance the room by adding focal points using royal purple velvet cloth under some of my stone and pendant displays, but I held back, choosing to leave well enough alone. I could make changes tomorrow or next week. My body felt lighter knowing that for the first time in many years, no one else had a voice in the decisions I made, big or small.

Dad had bought a local newspaper and went to the table in the back, along with Mom. She could tell I needed to be alone and quiet amidst my displays. But I wouldn't be alone for long. As I straightened up my wrapping supplies, a couple with a small boy came inside and sent the bell jingling.

I stepped out from behind the counter. "Welcome to Square Spirits."

"Welcome to *you*." The man extended his hand. "I'm Nathan Connor, from Country Law. My wife, Lily, and son, Toby."

"Doris Parker and I own Pages and Toys," Lily said, "on the opposite corner of the Square."

"Oh, yes, when I was here before, I noticed your clever windows. I'm glad you stopped in. Not only am I open for business, I had my first customers today."

"There you go, starting off with a bang," Nathan said, grinning.

"How wonderful for you." Lily squeezed Toby's shoulders. "Always exciting around here, huh?"

A blurry, almost fuzzy feeling came over me, and I reached out to touch the corner of the counter to keep my balance. I knew the feeling well and couldn't will it away. Even if I'd wanted to. And I didn't.

Storm clouds broke apart and allowed sunlight to shine through. Both Nathan and Lily had come through awful times, even before they met. More troubles followed, but they enjoyed some good fortune now—and the little boy...

Nathan's deep male voice broke into the vision. "We're on our way to Crossroads to pick up hamburger platters for dinner." He ruffled the young boy's hair. "Toby got to choose tonight's supper."

"Boy, lucky you, Toby. I'm going to Crossroads tonight, too, with *my* mom and dad."

Grinning, but obviously not overly impressed with that news, Toby said, "Come on, Dad. I'm hungry."

Lily laughed. "You're always hungry." She turned her attention to me. "I'll come back on my own to do some serious shopping."

I took in a couple of deep breaths as the three moved to the front of the shop and out the door. Looking out the window, I watched as they flanked Toby, each taking a hand as they walked away.

By the time we finished unpacking, Mom and Dad were ready to head home. I'd noticed Dad fading and offering a rain check for a Crossroads dinner made sense. When I walked them to their truck and hugged them goodbye, I realized I was so much better than okay. I decided one of those burger platters little Toby mentioned sounded good to me, and I was in high spirits when I left for Crossroads to put in my takeout order. I was ready to fling open the door to my new life and invite in whatever the fates had in store for me.

3

Later that night, too excited to sleep, I honored the urge I had to go downstairs and take a last look at my not-quite-finished shop. I took deep breaths as I walked around the space, the atmosphere serene as midnight approached. I touched the counter and the glass shelves guided only by the light from the antique lamp posts in the Square. The subtle fragrance from the lavender candles lined up in their bins teased my nostrils. I'd have liked to light one, but I instinctively knew Grace and Rose would never allow an open flame, and I wouldn't want to terrorize them. Fortunately, they tolerated candles, as long as no one lit one. The battery run luminaries were a nice substitute.

I meandered through the shop, sifting my fingers through the small gemstones in their bowls, rearranging the journals, and straightening the fringed silk scarves, hand-dyed with various types of angel images. Talk about a wonderful girlfriend gift. In my shop, though, I decided that I'd refer to these items as *girl gifts*, a more up-to-date term.

Sarah and Megan had agreed I was launching Square Spirits at the perfect time. I had the holiday season until the end of the year to see what flew off my shelves and into my Square Spirits bags. I'd soon know if customers showed greater interest in gemstones and candles than the solar system calendars. Would my New Age greeting card collection attract any attention at all? Perhaps the blank journals and the scarves would be among my best gift items. Whatever they wanted, I would be sure to match their demand.

I went upstairs and poured a half a glass of red wine and sat at my new table to go over what was ahead in the coming days. I first scanned the written guide for shop owners Sarah had given me, and noted that she'd highlighted the business association meetings for November and December. I was not only welcome, I was expected to attend. And then there was the day-long bus tour arriving the weekend before Thanksgiving. She'd even handwritten "Be prepared" in the margin.

Looking at it, my first reaction was to laugh, because Megan had said the same thing, and not in her usual airy, almost carefree tone. *Forewarned is forearmed.* These bus tours must be quite the happening. I made my own note to make sure I had more shelves filled with inventory between now and that weekend.

From where I sat, I could see most of my open-space apartment. Only the bedroom and the bathroom were separate rooms. Granted, the space looked nearly empty, but that was okay. So much of this move was a shift away from the old and walking into the new. A giggle escaped. New life and all that aside, psychic abilities or not, I still needed to eat. My food stores included a bottle of wine. It was time for a trip to Farmer Foods before opening time in the morning. Like B and B, Farmer Foods turned on its lights no later than 7:00. And I'd likely see Eli there.

And why would I want to see Eli?

Curiosity, I told myself. Simple curiosity. That was all. Besides, other than appearing at my side to help me stuff broken down cartons into the recycle bin, I hadn't run into him. I was still pondering the mystery of Eli when the lavender aroma coming from the electric diffuser worked its magic and sent me off to bed. I was asleep within seconds of pulling the comforter around my chin.

If only the morning had started off as well. First, I slept later than I'd planned, and when I stumbled into the kitchen and reached into the cabinet I expected to find coffee. But no, all I found was an unopened box of green tea. But green tea didn't cut it for the morning. Freshly brewed coffee was my essential morning drink.

I quickly dressed in jeans and my favorite Irish knit sweater. I pulled my comfy black suede ankle boots out of a bag of shoes I hadn't yet unpacked. After running a brush through my hair, I headed to B and B for coffee. Food shopping was second in line.

I opened the door to a cacophony of voices, laughter, and the ear-piercing whine of the espresso machine. Sarah waved and pointed to an open chair next to her.

Above the noise I heard Eli's voice, "Yeah, she's the fortune teller."

My blood boiled at his biting sarcasm. Surely the man knew I was *not* a fortuneteller, much as he liked to hang that term on me. *Be honest, Zoe, you hung it on yourself.*

True enough. But didn't everyone know that fortunetellers were part of carnivals and magic shows? How ignorant was the man, anyway? Didn't he understand that I was an established psychic, able to gather impressions of past or future events for other people? Not that I was *ever* able to predict my own future. So frustrating.

I ordered my coffee and reached into my handbag. But Stephanie—Steph—offered to open an account, billing me once a month for anything I bought. She went on to say she did that for all the Square's shopkeepers and their employees.

The chair Sarah pulled out for me was at the women's table. Of course. I suppressed a smile. They so reminded me of Mom and Dad and their contemporaries, but when in Rome and all that. As I slid into my seat, I had a clear view of the men's table, especially Eli, whose head was turned so I saw only his profile, but that was enough.

The image of a young man with his face pinched in pain. Such a big loss.

The thought, the vision, crossed my mind, but disappeared just as fast. The sense of loss surrounding Eli remained, though.

Attempting to shake off those images, I swallowed a big mouthful of coffee and turned away to focus on the women talking about the busy days ahead.

I came in on the conversation just as Sarah said, "Let's

not forget these are magical days on the Square, not just hectic ones. We'll be lighting our tree soon, and putting up our unique collection of wreaths." She stretched her arms out. "These tables could soon start filling up with shoppers arriving early and coming here for breakfast."

"Wow," I said. "Sometimes I wonder how you all do it!"

Marianna, the quilt shop owner, chuckled at my remark. "You know, Zoe, I've never forgotten my first Thanksgiving on the Square. I'd moved here in the spring with Rachel, my step-daughter, and her son, Thomas. Quilts Galore was open and thriving, but without any warning, Rachel's estranged mother rushed into the shop with an officer from the Sheriff's Department, talking about getting legal custody of Thomas."

"That sounds awful," I said, feeling a rush of panicky emotion around the incident, even without knowing the facts. Others shifted in their seats as she continued.

"The whole thing was absurd," Marianna said, "because Rachel was well on her way to her eighteenth birthday, and she knew her rights. Still she took Thomas and hid, while I called Jack Pearson of Country Law. He and his wife, Liz, are my oldest friends."

"Since the whole incident was public," Sarah interjected, "it created quite a stir."

Marianna nodded. "That's for sure, and within minutes, many of the owners had left their shops and stood right at my open door, like a support system. They showed up even before they knew the sad truth about Rachel and her mother."

I clutched the edge of the table, lightheaded. I didn't need to know the facts, because I knew in my gut that Rachel was better off with Marianna than with a mother who rejected her.

"Well, Jack straightened the whole thing out, and I basically threw the woman into the street. And what stands out in my mind the most was the sight of Sarah and Art and Mimi and Elliot and Eli, and all the rest lined up outside to show their support."

Surprising tears pooled in my eyes. I knew little about

the individuals she mentioned except their names. That didn't matter. The stirring in my solar plexus told me that despite whatever petty differences and even hurts this group experienced among themselves, they cared deeply about each other.

"Oh, one more thing," Marianna said, tipping her cup toward me. "Don't even think about making big plans for Thanksgiving. We stay open late on Wednesday evening, and then we open an hour early on Friday. And then it's off and running until New Year's Eve."

"Is this supposed to make me feel better?" I asked with a groan. "Like I said, I don't how you all manage. But I expect I'll learn."

"One customer at a time," Marianna said. "That's all you can do."

I laughed when Sarah's watch beeped and like trained troops, everyone stood in unison and busily cleared the tables and rearranged the chairs they'd moved around. I added my pair of hands to the mix, feeling curiously like one of the crowd.

As we filed out the door into a sunny, brisk day and we all wished each other a good day, I stole a glance at Eli, who caught me staring. He gave me a single subtle nod before walking toward Farmer Foods.

I hurried home and grabbed my grocery list off the kitchen table, and by the time I arrived at the door, the store had been open for several hours.

As I walked down the aisles, I caught a glimpse of Eli moving boxes of produce. I fought the urge to tap him on the shoulder and give him my best lecture about the difference between a fortuneteller and a psychic.

How ridiculous.

Even if Eli would listen, and I doubted he would, the middle of his store was not the place to have the conversation. I quickly grabbed what I needed, including a two-pound bag of B and B coffee, and left. Psychic Ability 101 would have to wait.

***

With the groceries stored, the front door unlocked, and the process of inventory control underway, the day had begun. While I was streamlining my systems, my thoughts wandered all over the place, taking dips into the past and creating new visions for my future. I was interrupted only once, and that conversation was a curiosity in itself. A woman came in simply to see what I was selling. She herself even called it "scouting the area."

"I'm planning day trips for family coming for their annual Thanksgiving weekend," she said. "Since I always bring the women over to the Square, I thought I'd come to see what's new."

I encouraged her to take her time wandering through the shop, and she did. It seemed she picked up every piece of amethyst and rose quartz, calcite and jasper, before examining each pendant and pendulum hanging in a row across a metal bar. I think she sniffed every candle, as if assessing every item for sale.

"Well, my family will love this place. I'll be back." With that, she left without buying so much as a single candle.

I would have thought it odd, but Megan had mentioned that prior to big festival weekends and the launch of the holiday season she often had an uptick in browsers in Rainbow Gardens, but few buyers. "Some people like to come in and get the lay of the land," she'd said, "and then they come back when the festival or holiday specials are going on."

I still had a lot to learn. Admittedly, I'd been dazzled by my first sales, but I reminded myself a few times that miracles didn't happen overnight. When Tyler had blown up our lives so abruptly, my self-confidence had been badly shaken. I hadn't seen his desire to end our marriage coming—hadn't felt the slightest hint that anything was wrong. After all, we'd been married for years. We worked together, and up until the moment everything fell apart, we'd always made decisions together. Tyler got his dream when he and his partners, friends from medical school, opened their clinic, and I made his dream my own, working alongside him managing the office and training new staff, while also doing graduate work in psychology.

Led by my passions, I veered my studies in the direction of the paranormal. I soaked up information, practiced my intuitive abilities, eventually attracting private clients. What wonderful years those were. I was happier than I'd ever been, and that's what blinded me and allowed me to foolishly think Tyler was happy, too. We were a team. Or so I'd thought.

Then, one autumn night, the time of year when Wisconsin bursts with the joy of changing colors, Tyler came home and without preamble, opened his briefcase and tossed an assortment of papers my way. Among them was a check for my share of the practice and our other assets. The house, he said, would sell quickly. He'd already investigated that.

"But, but, but..." Those were the only words I could come up with as he went on to tell me, in as few words as possible, that he'd sold his share of the practice to his partners and had liquidated our other assets and divided them. Finally, he got to the reason for all of this upheaval, not another woman, as I might have guessed by then, but another dream. The next morning, he left for Port-au-Prince, his destination a newly formed medical mission that needed doctors. Haiti was still recovering from the earthquake that had devastated the country, and Tyler's new dream was to make his life there. Without me.

How long had he been nurturing this dream?

Over a year, as it turned out.

A year?

It took far less time to finalize everything. Yes, the house sold, and I rid myself of most everything in it. Lawyers, real estate agents, and banks handled everything. I walked away with little except my own name. I'd grown up a Miller, and I was a Miller once again. Other than my favorite clothes, I took only one piece of furniture, an antique desk I'd bought the first year we were married, along with a couple of handmade rugs that meant something to me.

Through it all, Tyler had been clear that a clean break was needed. A period at the end of the sentence of our relationship. True to his word, I never heard from him again.

Tyler would never grasp that his stark rejection had shaken my belief in myself, right down to my core. Nor would he understand the degree to which his last words would ultimately fuel my own motivations. As he sifted through the documents he'd tossed on the desk, he'd thumped his finger on the brokerage house checks and said, "It's not a fortune, but it's enough for you to find your next dream and make it happen."

I never forgot those words.

Two years later, with fall colors fading, I was standing in *my* shop below *my* apartment, prepared to take even more steps to make *my* dream come true. Following the principle of "seek and ye shall find," I'd searched and I'd found. With confidence in my intuition on the rise, I still hoped the strong hunch that brought me to Wolf Creek was not mere wishful thinking.

I sighed to myself as I rearranged some stones on a glass shelf. Time would tell.

Enough with the introspection!

I walked to the front window and looked down the Square, a sight that coaxed a smile to my face. Scarecrows, along with pots of purple, orange, and magenta mums were scatted around the gardens and walkways. Pumpkins and gourds were arranged atop and around bales of straw, and the rich gold and red leaves of the maple trees contrasted with the dark green of the pines. The light breeze swirled small tornadoes of leaves. I slipped my hand in my pocket and touched the amethyst stone and drew air deep into my lungs.

Centered and content, but hungry, I hurried upstairs to fill a plate from the cartons of deli salads I'd bought at Farmer Foods. Back downstairs I settled at the table in the back to eat lunch. Few shoppers were out that afternoon, but I knew that could change in a matter of minutes. After I finished my lunch, I put on the haunting Native American flute music I enjoyed. Using lavender fusion sticks set on a corner shelf, I let my favorite scent permeate the shop, but not overwhelm the more sensitive noses.

I was still taking little jaunts into the future, imagining

the shop exactly as I wanted it, when my phone rang. It was exciting to answer it with, "Square Spirits. May I help you?"

"Sarah here," the clipped voice said. "I know it's last minute, but a bus tour is coming through tomorrow. If you need help, call me."

"Thanks. For the notice and the off—"

Silence.

She was gone before I could finish the sentence. Busy lady. But as Dad often said, she had "places to go and people to see."

I'd never experienced a bus tour on the Square, last minute or otherwise, so I didn't know what to expect, other than piecing together the tidbits others had filled in. Megan laughed about the frenzy, and joked that her now-fiancée, Clayton, had been blown away by the numbers of people who crowded inside his gallery. Marianna Spencer had nodded along with her, so I considered myself warned.

I went to my basement storage and brought up a second box of candles and an assortment of candle holders, from small glass votives to a special ceramic design for larger candles. They were festive and fun. After adding a few more pieces to the bowls that held my small stones, I stood back and let my gaze settle on the amethyst geode, once again admiring the piece that never failed to draw my eye and send a ripple of energy through me.

As it began to turn dark and it was time to close, a small wave of worry washed over me. A tour bus tomorrow was all well and good, but I hadn't made even one sale that day. I pushed the worry away, literally imagining the palm of one hand inside my head gently, always gently, pushing fretful, intrusive energy out. I smiled to myself. How many years ago had a psychology professor of mine suggested that? He'd called it a trick, because all it did was refocus thoughts. True, but I gave it a little more power than he had.

I turned off the window lights and gave the glass shelving a quick once over with the lamb's wool duster. I made my way around the shop to wooden shelves on the wine side, but I stopped abruptly at the end of the first row. The air was cool there, almost chilly.

Grace had made her first visit downstairs while I was present.

"Hello, Grace," I whispered. "I'm glad you've come to have a look around my shop. You're welcome anytime."

The cool air swirled around me then faded away, and the temperature returned to normal.

As I turned off the lights inside the shop, those in the front windows came back on.

"Are you playing?" I asked.

The lights flickered, and then the room went dark.

"Good night, Grace."

As I walked up the stairs to my apartment it dawned on me that I didn't know the real names of the two girls, the girls who'd lived in the very space where I was trying to make my home now. The day I had the vision of them in the burning building, I had a strong sense of them. For now, they'd remain Grace and Rose. But, moving into the building meant I needed to find out more about the fire, and before too long, figure out their real names.

4

The next morning I swallowed the last of my freshly brewed mug of coffee and tried to calm the excitement building within me. A bus tour—and not just any bus tour. *My first*. I'd soon participate in the first of many special occasions on the Square. Now I'd see what all the fuss was about. Or would I? I hoped, even assumed, shoppers would come inside Square Spirits. But what if they passed me by? What if they were only browsing? Would they want to come back?

Motivated, but more than mildly jittery, I didn't trust my gut feeling that Square Spirits was going to do just fine. Maybe it was a crisis of confidence, but I felt a touch of fear, not something I experienced often. It came in the form of "what ifs," the biggest being: *What if I'd made a mistake thinking that a New Age type of store would be a fit among the more traditional ones on the Square?*

I dressed in black ankle pants and my low-cut boots, comfortable as well as professional. My favorite deep purple sweater matched the color of some of the darkest purple amethyst stones lined up on my shelves. Because I wanted to surround myself with things I liked, I chose my new dangling silver and amethyst earrings I bought for myself the day I closed on the building. Finally, I put my amethyst touchstone in my pocket, ready when I needed it to help me refocus my energy in the moment.

As I walked down the steps into the shop a warm glow enveloped me, acting like a cocoon that had come right along with me into the shop.

"Morning, Rose," I said, unlocking the door and flipping the light switches. "Isn't it a beautiful day? Cold outside, but warm in here."

The lights flickered twice. I smiled, taking that as a greeting. "I like the way you communicate, Rose, but it's business hours now. No flicking these lights on and off."

One flicker.

"I'm taking that as a yes," I said.

Over the years, I'd read a great deal about the effect spirits could have on electricity. But the flickering lights were the first time I'd experienced it for myself. Sidney, a friend of mine with an affinity for communicating with spirits, told a good story about her toaster refusing to behave, popping up two or three times while she tried to make a couple of pieces of toast. Even her doorbell would ring at inopportune times, like the middle of the night. By comparison, flickering lights were small intrusions.

For now, I could take on Grace's and Rose's antics with good humor. On the other hand, from my reading and of what others had told me, an angry spirit was a mighty force not to be taken lightly. It comforted me that so far, neither of the girls had shown any sign of anger about me, a newcomer, being in the building. But judging from the way others behaved, including Megan's and Sarah's wariness and hesitation, Rose and Grace hadn't always been so welcoming. Until I'd arrived, the girls had successfully kept anyone from buying and occupying the building.

At the jingle of the bell, the warmth surrounding me dissipated. Rose had left and I went to greet my first customer of the day, a young woman with the biggest gold hoop earrings and the brightest green eye shadow I'd ever seen. Almost my height and a blonde, she carried it off like few women could. She browsed a bit, then began looping long necklaces of various gemstones around her wrists, while she balanced candles in her palms. Somehow, though, she then managed to quickly choose a bottle of cabernet from shelves on the wine side. I saw her struggle trying to hold everything and rushed to lift the wine from her hand before it slipped to the floor.

Oops, I needed baskets for shoppers to use. How fast could I get them? How could I have forgotten that detail?

"Do you have gift boxes for these items?" she asked.

"I sure do," I said, "and they're quite nice." True, but they were plain white because an order with an embossed logo took a few extra days. My plan was to reorder with my logo featured prominently. I'd do the same for the tall bags I needed for the wine, along with a few gift bags, too.

I rang up the sale, reveling in the simple pleasure of wrapping the jewelry and the candles in light violet tissue paper. But, oops, why hadn't I thought about shopping baskets?

She left satisfied, and I quickly went online to order various supplies, including the customized gift boxes and wine bags. On to baskets. I found handsome canvas shopping baskets big enough for wine but small enough for the gemstones and jewelry. They'd be delivered in only a few days, but I needed something for the bus tour arriving on the Square within the hour.

As two women held blank journals and greeting cards in the crook of one arm while they browsed for wine, an idea came to me, namely the attractive bread baskets I'd seen on the tables at Crossroads the other night while I waited for my takeout order. It wouldn't hurt to ask Melanie, the manager at the restaurant, if she had some extras she could loan me.

I called the restaurant, and Melanie herself answered. I quickly explained my predicament.

"Now this is a first," she said, chuckling. "I've been asked to do some quick catering, but I don't recall ever being asked to loan out the bread baskets. Give me ten minutes. I'll bring them myself or I'll send someone over."

The two women left with their journals and wine just as Melanie came in with the baskets stacked in a paper grocery bag.

Melanie took a quick look around the shop before she gave the counter a light slap. "Gotta run, but good luck. It's looking great in here."

"Oh, thanks."

She grinned as she closed the door to the jingle of the bell.

I quickly arranged the baskets in two stacks on the table near the window. And just in time. Within minutes the shop filled with women, some already carrying bags with logos from other shops on the Square. It seemed the little bell on the door never stopped jingling. Since the women were all wearing the same kind of nametag, I assumed the tour bus had arrived.

I came out from behind the counter to see if anyone needed help at the wine bins. Minutes later I heard a voice from across the shop.

"Can someone help me?"

"I have a question, too," someone said from the corner where I'd arranged larger pieces of amethyst and rose quartz.

A woman nearing the counter said, "I'd like to pay for these items."

Panic set in. And panic was not my style. But my words became jumbled as I half-answered one question on my way behind the counter.

"Do you run this store?" another woman asked, her tone bordering on sharp.

"I do." Fortunately my words came out calmly, even though the muscles in my back and shoulders remained tense.

"I see. I thought you were a customer," she responded.

Message received. I'd noted that other owners and employees identified themselves as such. Marianna had her apron, Megan her Rainbow Gardens smock. It was obvious that aprons and smocks were not right for my business, but I needed to identify myself in some way. I'd have to think of something unique, something that fit the image of Square Spirits. One more decision!

What was that Marianna had said? Something on the order of handling periods of frenzy one customer at a time. I turned to the woman next to me and answered her questions, and then quickly packaged another customer's three candles. They were three of the six jumbo size round candles I had out. A couple of cartons, each holding eight, sat in the basement. Why hadn't I moved more stock into the back room, my shop office and one day, when I was ready, the place I'd do readings? I'd designed it with that future in mind. But until that happened, I needed to designate a corner of it as a stockroom, so I could easily fill the holes in my stock displays between rushes.

No time for that at the moment. I had stones to wrap for another customer and a pendulum for the one after, and a single small crystal for the woman next in line. A couple of shoppers picked out scarves while they were waiting in line, and my basket of sachets attracted attention, too. Fortunately, the atmosphere eased and the women began chatting with each other as they waited patiently for their turn.

And then they were gone.

I dashed downstairs and carried up a carton of large candles and balanced a smaller box of scented tea-lights on top. Maybe because the cool weather was setting in, candles seemed to top my list of quick sales.

I didn't need to print a full inventory report to assess what stock was diminishing more quickly than I imagined. The candles and the smallest of crystals and rose quartz and amethyst pieces would last no more than a month if sales continued at today's pace. To say nothing of it being enough to carry me to the end of the year, as I'd planned. How wonderful to be wrong.

I wrote another note and slipped it into my pocket—*Call Julia*. I needed help!

In passing, Mom had mentioned that my cousin Julia had been working part-time at the winery, but she needed another job to fill in until the wine-making end of the business picked up again. Julia and I had grown up in each other's homes when our families lived next door to each other, but as adults we'd never been close. Still, it wouldn't hurt to ask Julia if she'd like to help me through the holidays.

At some point in the afternoon, I managed a few bites of my deli salad lunch, but I barely tasted any of it. The day ended with another flurry of shoppers. A few minutes before closing time I stood at the front window as sunshine faded behind the shops to the west, casting long shadows onto the walkways up and down and across the Square. What a day.

I had no plans for supper, but since eating alone at Crossroads wasn't appealing, I decided to replenish my supply of food from the hot food bar at Farmer Foods. The place was convenient, making it way too easy to pick up hot entrees, sandwiches, and salads to last for another couple of days. Maybe, I'd even see Eli. I still couldn't say why he came to mind, but I knew he was part of what drew me to that store. It wasn't only the food. Tired and hungry, but thrilled with my day, I went upstairs to get my wallet and my shopping tote.

As I walked inside Farmer Foods, I spotted Eli at the checkout counter helping with the end of the day rush. I nodded to him and continued to the produce department, where I picked out a few apples, oranges, and bananas before I added containers of meatloaf slices, a hot pasta dish, and roasted vegetables, along with two sandwiches. I would not go hungry. I was ready to go after I'd filled a container with a green salad, and grabbed a loaf of French bread at the end of the counter.

Eli was still by the register when I was ready to check out.

"Hi, Eli," I said, letting my enthusiasm over the day show, as I put the items on the moving belt. "Such a busy day on the Square today, huh?"

Eli grinned. "I bet you saw that coming, Madame Zoe."

I groaned. "And I bet you think you're the first person to ever say that to me."

"Nah, I just couldn't resist," he said grinning. "But if you want to see crowds you wait 'til Thanksgiving weekend. That one will really wear you out." He shook his head. "Crowds all over the place, even here at Farmer Foods. I can't keep enough of the homemade jams and pickles on the shelves."

"Busier than today?" Eli was chattier than usual, I mused. Maybe being around people in his store brought out the more social side of him.

He began loading items into my bag. "You remember Labor Day, don't you?"

"Like that?" I couldn't keep my surprise from changing my voice.

He gave me a pointed look, followed by a hearty laugh.

I returned a look of my own. Apparently he'd found himself too amusing for words, because he kept on laughing even after I'd left the counter, my full tote in one hand and a paper bag in the other.

Why did he rile me so? I growled to myself all the way home.

5

My first Wolf Creek Square Business Association meeting was due to start in a couple of minutes. As I stepped into the large private dining room at Crossroads, I reminded myself that everyone I'd met so far had gone out of their way to make me feel welcome. But I still had the kind of butterflies in my stomach typical of a kid on her first day in a new school.

Art Carlson, apparently in charge of handing out copies of the agenda, greeted me at the door. I took a seat just as Sarah tapped on the microphone to settle the room. Somehow, being there, nodding to people I was getting to know, curious about the few I'd never seen before, gave me a sense that another detail of my vision for my shop—and my new life—was coming to fruition.

I was amused when Eli came in late and had to take the only empty chair next to mine. I hadn't seen him since my shopping trip in Farmer Foods, and he turned a little red when he nodded to me. Maybe he was embarrassed, not by only his mild "Madame Zoe" teasing, but his full-throated laughter at my surprise over the crowds on the Square. I might have found a way to tease him back, but Sarah called the meeting to order with authority in her voice.

"So, Eli, since you're acquainted with Zoe," Sarah said, "please introduce her to the rest of the room. There could be a few people here she hasn't met."

Eli's face became even redder, if that were possible, as all six-feet-plus of him got to his feet. He motioned for me to rise, too. Then he cleared his throat a couple of times.

"Um. Well, everyone, meet Zoe Miller. You probably heard she bought the haunted building. She named her new store, Square Spirits, and now sells those crystal rocks and candles and other stuff lots of people around here like." He gestured to me, and then almost as an afterthought he added, "Oh, and she's selling wine from her family's winery."

Not bad, Eli. He'd done much better than I expected. Maybe Sarah had given him fair warning. Then, again, maybe my gut instinct was right and there really was more to Eli Reynolds than I'd first thought. I offered a quick wave to the group assembled.

Sarah continued with her agenda, but I didn't hear much. I was still thinking about Eli, speculating about him, more curious about the man than I expected. But then I heard Sarah mention advertising, and focused on her again.

"Remember people, we've had three new shops open on the Square since last year. With that in mind, I've prepared an extensive ad campaign for Thanksgiving weekend," she said. "The ads will be run on local TV and radio stations and printed in all the visitors' guides. Be prepared. Unless the weather becomes an issue, we'll be busy Friday, Saturday, and Sunday. We'll keep our traditional holiday hours on Friday and Saturday, opening our doors one hour early at 9:00 and staying open an hour later, locking up at 7:00. Back to regular hours on Sunday."

All these seasoned owners had survived summer and holiday shopping seasons before, and so would I.

"Any questions or comments?" Sarah waited a beat. "Since Melanie has put out wine and snacks in the back of the room, we'll have a little celebration of our own. So, go have fun, and if you don't know Zoe, be sure to introduce yourself."

Suddenly I was out of business mode and expected to socialize. Oddly, I felt like a stranger all over again. And that feeling originated inside me. The people on the Square had been nothing but generous and kind to me. I put my hand inside my pocket and touched the amethyst stone. It didn't completely take away my sudden unease, but it helped.

"Why don't you come over and say hello to my brother,"

Eli suggested. "I don't know that you've been formally introduced. You probably already know Georgia from your mornings at B and B."

His suggestion calmed me immediately, as if he knew I'd feel awkward wandering around the room alone. "You're right. I've met Georgia, but haven't really spoken to Elliot. Lead the way."

His fingers lightly touched the middle of my back, sending a whole new sensation racing through my body.

He's lonely.

It was the surest of messages. What left me nearly breathless was not that I cared, but how much. For two years I struggled to recover from the pain of losing Tyler, and I had no plans to become involved with *any* man anytime soon. In the last year or so, I'd come to cherish and protect my new found independence. I wouldn't do anything to compromise it.

The old saying, "the best laid plans…" popped into my mind.

No, no, no.

Eli took charge of introductions to new people, mostly employees of the shop owners I'd already met. I'd heard about Marianna's step-daughter, Rachel, and Art's son, Alan, who looked like kids, but had an aura of maturity around them that made them seem older than their years—in a good way. They walked with Eli and me to the snack table where Rachel and I talked about Crossroads food while Alan and Eli made a plan to fix a problem with the lighting arrangement on the Square. I never got to talk to Elliot because after a quick introduction, he and Georgia begged off staying for the snacks and quietly slipped away.

It seemed to fit into the natural flow of the evening that Eli and I left together, right behind Jessica and Mimi, who were deep in conversation with Megan and Clayton. As Eli walked me across the Square, he told me, in a matter-of-fact tone, that his family had deep roots in Wolf Creek and he had no plans to leave. "I like it here," he said, "and I think you will, too."

Having had such a strong reaction to him, I found myself

with little inclination to speak, unusual for me. And he, usually tongue tied and quiet, kept up a stream of impersonal small talk. But that was okay, because I found myself with nothing much to say. We said goodnight and he waited while I relocked the front door before waving and walking away. It was late and tomorrow was another day.

Once upstairs, I poured myself a glass of blackberry merlot and sat at my front window. Despite trying to divert my thoughts, I ended up struggling to figure out why Eli had become important to me, and so quickly. When I reacted that strongly and swiftly to a person's energy, I always learned the reason. I couldn't deny the way I responded to Eli. As tired as I was, it was after midnight before I gave up trying to figure out why and crawled into bed. But without question, the man had a surprising effect on me.

***

The next morning I wrapped my hands around my warm coffee mug and took it to my front window. I smiled with a mix of surprise and pleasure at the dusting of snow that had fallen on the Square during the night. A couple of days of strong winds had blown off any remaining leaves, giving me a clear view of the other end of the Square.

Although it was still early, a few people milled about. Marianna stopped at the steps of the bookstore, where seconds later Doris joined her. They continued down the side of the Square to B and B. Seeing Doris reminded me that I hadn't yet gone to Pages and Toys to take a look at her selection of New Age books. I had to remedy that. No time like the present.

I swallowed a mouthful of coffee and quickly got ready to start the day. I chose a soft turtleneck sweater in one of my favorite colors, a deep, rich mauve. Instead of a coat, I wore my heavy black wool poncho, which I affectionately referred to as "starry night," because the bottom edges were lined with constellations sewn in white yarn. Before I left, I placed my amethyst stone right where it belonged, inside my pocket, and rolled it between my thumb and index finger.

I liked knowing it was there, like a silent friend.

As I walked across the Square to join Doris and Marianna at B and B, the snow melted under the sunny sky. But just the sight of it that morning foretold the weather to come. There would be days in the future when weather would keep shoppers away.

Marianna and Doris were the only women at the table until I joined them with my cup of hazelnut coffee.

Pulling out the chair next to her, Marianna said, "Morning, neighbor. Glad you're joining us." She looked me over head to foot. "Cool poncho."

"Thanks. I bought it at an art fair in Green Bay years ago, and every fall I look forward to wearing it." I sipped my coffee, noting how much better it was than the unflavored variety I had at home. Why didn't I just get myself some? It was simple enough.

"The snow is kind of a surprise," I said, "but the sky is bright now."

"Puts everyone in the mood for the holidays," Doris said, her voice what my dad would call chipper. "Lots of buyers, lots of sales."

"Speaking of sales, would this morning be a good time for me to stop by and see what New Age books you stock. I haven't put in a full book order yet, but I need to. It shouldn't take too long."

"Sure. Probably not many shoppers until later, anyway. North of here, they got a little more snow, and it will hang around longer."

Doris seemed friendlier and more cooperative this morning than she had last week. Maybe having three new shops and an increase in traffic on the Square had changed her outlook. Maybe. I'd tried to read Doris and saw all kinds of conflicted emotions. I didn't like thinking it, but I also saw confusion. Still, whatever was going on with her, I knew for sure there was far more to Doris than met the eye. *Like Eli.*

Doris and Marianna entertained me with stories about the last holiday season on the Square and the rush of shoppers that started on Black Friday. Marianna laughed when she told us that her first year on the Square, she'd pondered not being open at all on Christmas Eve day. But she'd changed her mind fast when she'd heard the other owners talk about the number of last minute shoppers who flooded the Square from early morning to at least mid-afternoon. Doris described buyers standing shoulder-to-shoulder at her bin of wall calendars, thinning her stock to next to nothing by the end of the day. "And I sold the rest of them on New Year's Eve," she said with a laugh.

"Square Spirits will certainly attract a lot of attention," Marianna said. "Candles, wine, gemstones...somehow, your shop radiates romance and fun."

Coming from Marianna, who was respected as well as liked, those words meant a lot. As we bantered back and forth, Marianna confirmed my conclusion that she and I were close in age. I thought of her as a role model of sorts, because she'd made a big change from professional quilter to successful shop owner. Hearing her story steeled my resolve to make a successful transition myself. She'd had more to cope with, since she'd been forced to work through some drama with her stepdaughter, Rachel, and a newborn, Thomas, all while establishing Quilts Galore.

If she could do it, so could I.

None of the other women on the Square had joined us so we left early and walked to Pages and Toys. When we passed Styles, Marianna and I simultaneously pointed to the same magenta pantsuit on a mannequin in the window.

"Uh oh," Marianna said, laughing. "I buy most of my clothes here—I wouldn't be surprised if we like the same kinds of things. I wear muted colors in my shop, so the fabrics will stand out, but I like bright shades when I'm out and about."

"Maybe because New Age stores and psychics seem exotic," I said, "you know, perhaps a little too colorful, I keep my style simple—no turbans and granny dresses, if you know what I mean. But in the shop I'll wear mostly shades of violet to purple, matched with nondescript gray or black. But, I'm like you. I like to let loose with other colors at times, too."

Marianna grinned. "Well, then, we may end up seeing each other coming and going."

"Not a chance," Doris said, waving at Mimi, who was dressing a window model. "Mimi and Jessica are careful about selling one of each item to owners and employees on the Square. They don't want unhappy colleagues, so you won't show up in the same clothes. Guaranteed."

"Good to know," I said, gazing into the window and smiling at Mimi. "They sure do know how to dress a window. And everything they stock looks unique. No wonder they do such a good tourist business. Some women must come out here only to shop for clothes."

"You're right. They do," Marianna said. "Lucky us."

With that, the three of us continued walking, saying goodbye to Marianna when we came to Pages and Toys. The first thing I noticed when Doris and I stepped inside the shop was how well stocked it was. She'd added much more since Labor Day weekend, the last time I'd visited. Books and toys were intermingled throughout, clearly paired to sell together.

"Very clever display idea," I said. "I need to figure out something similar at Square Spirits. For some reason, I put the candle holders too far away from the candles! Now why would I do that?"

"Guess you have some to work to do," Doris said, a grin tugging at the corners of her mouth. "I'd like to take credit, but these pairings were Lily's doing. She's always trying new and trendy selling techniques. I admit to being a bit skeptical at first, but the increase in sales is the proof in the pudding."

I imagined that for Doris, skeptical probably looked and sounded a lot like crotchety. But laughing, I said, "I haven't heard that phrase about proofs and puddings in years. My grandmother used to say that all the time."

I browsed the shelves, noting the many titles reflecting Wisconsin's history, mystery series, children's books, and cookbooks by many local authors. She stocked a large collection of Native American history and art originating in the region, plus books of photography and painting featuring famous Midwest artists. She had the latest bestsellers, and novels by well-known authors, local and national. Almost an entire shelf was devoted to books about the natural history of the Great Lakes and even some about its infamous shipwrecks. Other than a handful of books about haunted houses in Wisconsin, which didn't really count as New Age titles, she had almost nothing that would compete with titles I'd order.

"So, it looks like we won't be duplicating stock at all," I said. I mentioned the names of two or three prominent authors of books about spirit guides, energy healing, and aromatherapy, but she barely reacted.

When she said, "I have only so much room," I detected a defensive tone.

"I'm going to put in a book order today." I picked up a spiral bound appointment book for the coming year. Its front cover was a colorful sunrise over a farm field, and the back cover showed a sunset over a lake. Gorgeous.

"I'm not passing this up," I said, reaching into my handbag for cash. "The outside is wonderful, but I also like that it's designed for making lists and planning. I stock blank journals, but not address books or day planners. I ordered a few wall calendars, but they don't feature landscapes or local photography. And my note cards are geared to the New Age buyer, too."

"Good," Doris said, first giving me the change from my purchase, and then reaching into the painted box on her counter. "Here, take these business cards. If someone asks for a certain kind of book, send 'em down to me. I'll do the same."

"Wonderful! I'll bring some cards by. I still have many details to deal with, but I do have business cards."

Doris waved me off. "You aren't the first who's opened without every last detail in place."

I found it amusing that Doris hadn't put herself in that category. Heavens no. She wouldn't be caught unprepared. I smiled to myself. What a character.

As I made my way across the Square, I spotted a woman sitting on the steps to my shop. I broke into a jog to go the last distance before she gave up on me and left. As I got closer, I was happy to see Georgia Reynolds. I plunked myself down on the step next to her to catch my breath.

"Been shopping?" she asked, nodding to the Pages and Toys bag in my hand.

"A handy appointment book to start fresh in January," I said. "But I wanted to visit Doris' shop so I would know what kinds of books she stocks. I don't want to compete with Doris and Lily, but now I can put in a substantial book order."

"That was wise. All the retailers are careful about not competing with each other." She paused, a thoughtful look crossing her face. "Pages and Toys has changed some in the last couple of years. For the good. Doris and her husband started the bookstore years ago, and it was really Ralph's baby. When he died, we all more or less assumed she'd sell the store and leave. But she didn't."

Georgia grinned in a pointed kind of way. "As you may have noticed, she's not shy about speaking her mind. Doris keeps us all on our toes. Lily has been good for her. Her young energy has made Doris a little friendlier and less disapproving than she used to be."

I listened to Georgia's rundown, a little gossipy, but nevertheless, I enjoyed hearing her take on Doris. But it wasn't long before shoppers began entering the Square. I needed to get my door open and look ready to greet whoever wandered in. At the same time, I didn't want Georgia to feel like I was pushing her away. A fine line to walk, I concluded. Finally, I decided to change the subject of other shops and focus on my own. "Was there something special you were looking for in the shop this morning?"

Georgia stood, and I got to my feet, too. "Well, um, I don't want to butt into your private business, but knowing the shops will be opening early on Friday and we'll be going strong all weekend, I was wondering what you were doing for Thanksgiving."

Huh? I'd barely considered it. "To tell you the truth, I haven't given it a thought. My cousin, Julia, is coming to help me in the shop, but she'll be going home Wednesday after closing and coming back Friday morning."

Georgia flashed a broad smile. "Good. Then you can join us at the farmhouse for an old-fashion turkey celebration."

"Oh, that's very kind, but I don't want to impose on your family."

"Nonsense," she said firmly. "Our first Thanksgiving together at the farm will be a lot like our wedding. Open door, everyone's welcome, and casual is the theme of the day." She laughed, almost shyly. "Well, gratitude is a theme, too, especially given the special year I've had."

"So I hear," I teased.

With a group of three women approaching, I made a quick decision and said yes. "And why don't I bring some wine."

"That would be wonderful. I'm so glad you're joining us." She glanced at her watch. "Oops, I've got to run. But welcome to the Square, Zoe. I'll call you later with directions to the farm." She hurried away.

I greeted the trio of shoppers and invited them inside. I felt a bit like I'd just been had. No wonder the women at morning coffee kept saying Georgia should have been a lawyer. My supposedly loose plans for a quiet day alone in my new apartment had been tightened up, and likely wouldn't be so quiet after all. I was content to change my plan and accept an invitation for a gathering where I'd be a relative stranger, where I'd have a chance to get to know Georgia and Elliot a little better. And Eli. There he was again, suddenly appearing in my head at inopportune times.

So long, Eli. I have work to do.

I traveled around the displays to the back of the shop and switched on the overhead lights and the spotlights, along with the power button for the CD player. I chose lively, wake-up-the-spirit music to start the day, so the sounds of Celtic fiddles and drums soon filled the room.

The women didn't stay long. They were clearly browsers, even explaining that they'd be back on either Friday or Saturday, depending...

Depending on what? Was it about finding better pricing elsewhere, or wanting to search for different items? Whatever it was, I swallowed back irrational disappointment that they hadn't looked around a little longer. I reminded myself about the nature of the retail business. Not everyone who came into my shop—or any shop—would buy something.

I busied myself straightening up the displays and checking the stock I'd stashed in the reading room, and then it was on to the book order. I switched the CD to my favorite harp music and scrolled through computer files until I came up with the list I had started months before of two dozen or so titles I wanted available in the shop.

I placed the order with the same distributor I used for journals and note cards. The order started out large and got even bigger when I added a dozen more titles. Filled with optimism, I chose several journal varieties and small, nicely packaged card collections of inspirational quotes. The Square Spirits version of a stocking stuffer.

As I clicked to place the order, I was conscious of not being alone. My girls, as I had begun to think of Grace and Rose, periodically floated through the shop. I took this opportunity to tell them all about Julia. I needed her to be comfortable in the shop and upstairs, since she'd be staying overnight. Because I had no idea what their reaction would be to another person in the building, I thought it best to be clear about what I wanted from them.

A flurry of air currents circled me. I understood.

"No. I won't tell Julia you're here. As long as you're polite." I grinned. "So, please, be on your best behavior."

My right side became cool and my left, warm. *A spirit hug.* Of course, they knew how it touched my heart. The hug was the first of what I hoped would be many.

"What do you think about my going out to see Georgia, Elliot, and Eli for Thanksgiving?"

Again, cool and warm surrounded me.

"Thank you." I knew perfectly well that I didn't have to speak aloud to spirits—they're mind readers, after all. Still, it felt good to let the sound of my voice mingle with the harp music and know these girls were okay with my presence.

As much as I enjoyed knowing the girls could envelope me in their energy, I had work to do and it demanded focus. I started with checking the selection of wine I'd stock for the weekend, picking out an assortment of six bottles to take with me to the farm, dry and sweet, red and white. I wondered what new people I would meet out at the Reynolds' home. The more I thought about it, the more I anticipated the pleasure of being included in their circle of family and friends. I don't know that I'd ever felt so welcome anywhere. And then, there was Eli, who, like me, wouldn't be alone on the holiday, either.

***

When Julia arrived mid-afternoon on Monday, she triggered a steady flow of conversation—sort of. She talked, I listened. She started with the traffic, moved to the forecaster's dismal weather prediction for the upcoming weekend, and then moved on to chatting about the shop. She insisted on familiarizing herself with every item. She wasn't worried about the wines, though, since she'd worked at the winery over the summer.

Julia wasn't a real cousin, not in a blood relative sort of way, but everyone in the family referred to her that way. She'd come to stay with my aunt and uncle after her parents left her alone and hightailed it out of town one step ahead of the law. With no other family to turn to, she moved in with them and never left. And she became, for all purposes, part of the family. Listening to her ask questions all day, I began to understand why I'd once heard my aunt refer to Julia as "spirited."

Her steam ran out after our post-dinner second walk through the shop. When we went back upstairs, I made up the couch for myself and made sure she had everything she needed in my small bedroom. I loved the open urban loft-like design of my apartment, but the downside of the arrangement was the lack of a second bedroom. On the other hand, my long couch was as comfortable as a bed, so I didn't mind giving Julia the privacy of my room.

Truthfully, after such a chatty day, what I wanted more than anything was a quiet night. Had I made a mistake asking her to help me out over the holiday weekend? Only time would tell, but I hadn't expected to need help, not so soon, anyway. An incorrect assumption, as it turned out, but I'd made no alternate plans. Besides, Mom had assured me that Julia was good with people. Maybe so, but I found her energy a little overbearing.

By Wednesday afternoon, what I considered a rocky start with Julia had turned around and I had changed my mind. Yes, Mom was right, Julia was quite the talker, but she was also friendly and outgoing. I frequently heard laughter coming from her and the shoppers she was helping. I slowly began to relax and enjoy what she offered to the atmosphere in Square Spirits.

Knowing her limitations, Julia deferred to me when customers asked specific questions about a particular stone or crystal. She didn't have a working knowledge of the lore about certain stones or what healing properties they were said to possess. Fortunately, I never heard Julia try to bluff her way through those questions. She noted, as I had, that many of the Square Spirits customers were already fairly knowledgeable about gemstones.

Just before closing on Wednesday, I said goodbye to Julia and told her I'd see her early on Friday morning.

"Be prepared," I warned, sounding a little like Sarah. "From what I hear it's going to be a whirlwind day."

"I'll be ready," she said. With that, she took off.

Alone that evening, a bout of unexpected anxiety broke my usual peaceful enjoyment of solitude. I was restless, at loose ends. But I couldn't identify anything wrong, like a bad day of sales. Quite the contrary. A ton of stock had arrived, and Julia had handled the unpacking and pricing.

Then my phone rang. The screen told me it was Eli.

After a few halting attempts, he got to the reason for the call. "Georgia had the idea that it made sense if I bring you to the farmhouse tomorrow in my truck. You know, rather than each of us driving separately. Kind of a waste of gas doing it that way." He paused, but not for long. "Or, maybe you'd rather drive yourself. I mean, you'd have your car. That's okay, too. I can give you directions."

He'd given me choices. The man was confused, but I

wasn't. I'd keep it simple. "I'd *like* to go with *you*, Eli."

Was that true? Yes.

Silence.

"Eli? I hope that's okay. And by the way, I'm bringing wine."

"Uh, yes. Wine. That's good. Georgia said we're eating around 2:00. I'll pick you up at the back of your shop at 1:30. Okay?"

"I'll be waiting, ready to go."

"Well, hope you like football."

He ended the call. And that was that.

With the plans settled, I poured a glass of wine and sat down with a notebook and pen and mapped out a plan for Thanksgiving morning, an opportunity to spend time getting ready for Friday. That's why I'd been okay with locking up after Julia left and heading upstairs with the shop still in minor disarray. Even before I'd opened, I'd known that the stone displays would inevitably become undone quickly. They were appealing attention-grabbers and their presence encouraged even casual browsers to stop and take a closer look. I'd noticed so many people picked out stones, held them to the light, and often handled a dozen or more before choosing one or two to buy. Other people simply moved on to something else. Fortunately, the stones were easy to organize again.

New varieties of stones had arrived in that day's order, so now I had glacial-blue celestite to add to both blue and green aventurine and blue-lace agate. I wanted to showcase them on Friday and expand the impression of what shoppers could count on finding at Square Spirits.

Later, after I'd curled up on my side in bed, I thought about what I'd wear to Georgia's house. She'd described the dinner as casual. Good. My closet was mostly casual, and it didn't take long to settle on khakis and a red sweater, with one of my moonstone pendants. A change from the purple and lavender pieces I wore in the shop. My mind took a detour into the past and a life that seemed so long ago. At one time, I'd had quite the array of formal dresses and expensive jewelry to go with them. But they'd gone by the wayside after my divorce. And without regret, because they represented a part of my life with Tyler I hadn't much cared for. I would never again be on Tyler's arm at medical conferences or charity events wearing symbols of *his* success. What a relief.

A big breakfast the next morning carried me through my work in the shop. I happily experimented with displays and felt the presence of Grace and Rose. The store was where I felt most at home. The apartment still had a sparse, half-settled feel to it, but I didn't mind. With my mind so intensely focused on Square Spirits, I didn't feel the absence of anything in my life. That's why the apartment could easily wait for a less pressured time.

As I brushed my hair a final time, letting it fall loose down my back, I wondered if Eli and Elliot's farmhouse still had the look and feel of two single brothers living there, or if Georgia had already put her stamp on it. And, in passing, I wondered where Eli lived now. How far was he coming to pick me up?

I was ready to go when the buzzer on my back door rang, and when I opened the door, Eli nodded stiffly. I picked up the Square Spirits cloth tote, in which I'd arranged six bottles of wine. Without a word, Eli took it out of my hand and stowed it behind his seat in the truck. Boy, this was likely to be one long, silent ride. Why had I agreed to this? For a couple of seconds, I regretted accepting the invitation at all. But despite all my second-guessing, I wanted to be with Eli.

As we drove along the back roads, Eli answered my semi-probing questions about living in Wolf Creek all his life and not having any desire to move away. I didn't want to intrude on his privacy and appear nosy. But as we passed farms and homes, he initiated an ongoing commentary about the families, past and present, that lived in the houses. He told me that since becoming mayor, Sarah had begun writing a history of the town and the Square.

"You should ask her about reading it," he suggested.

"Sounds interesting." I kept my voice neutral, but I'd already planned to quietly find out more about the history of the building I'd bought. Sarah's history might be the best place to start.

"There's a lot going on with the town, especially the Square," Eli said. "Clayton's mother, Sadie Winston is working with the new Alexander foundation to get the renovation project at the museum underway. That museum is so outdated, I'm glad almost nobody goes inside. Nothing much to see and it doesn't showcase the town very well."

Whew! I needn't have worried about the ride. Eli was almost as chatty as Julia, and he put more words together than I'd heard from him before. But, my intuition told me why. He didn't want to leave room for me to ask him questions.

When we pulled into the driveway to the farmhouse, I noticed all the cars and trucks parked on the gravel and the adjacent grass. Many more cars than I expected. Wolf Creek was turning out to be much richer in spirit than I'd first assumed.

"Wow, looks like a big crowd," I said, after Eli parked his truck and turned off the engine. "Good thing I brought half a dozen bottles of wine, huh?"

"Guess so," he said. He looked amused, as if on the verge of teasing me about something, probably one of his fortuneteller jokes.

Before he climbed out of the truck, I touched his arm to hold him back. "Thanks so much for the ride. I learned a lot just listening to you talk about Wolf Creek."

"You're welcome," Eli said, "Always happy to talk about Wolf Creek."

A simple response, but I filed away my reaction to touching him. The current of energy was different, more positive. The sense of acute loneliness was weaker, although I knew feeling alone was a chronic issue for him.

Maybe he just needs someone to talk to. He senses I care.

Eli led the way into the house through what my grandparents would have considered the back door. Front or back, it didn't matter. People stood in clusters all through the house, and another group came in behind Eli and me.

The house was filled with the kind of noise typical of a

big family gathering. I followed Eli deeper into the house, where guests were laughing and talking as they grazed at a table laden with dips and chips, cut vegetables, and beverages. Eli put my tote in one of the few empty spots on the long kitchen counters.

A robust round of greetings welcomed him, and by association, me. In the midst of the crowd and noise, I withdrew into myself, an automatic—involuntary—response typical of me in these situations. It wasn't about disliking my surroundings, but rather protecting myself from being overwhelmed by the mix of energies.

When Eli's hand lightly touched my back, I knew that on some level, he understood my way of adjusting to a new environment. His touch sent a signal of safety and security, making me hyper-aware of how long it had been since a man's touch made me feel secure.

But then he was gone, weaving his way through the groups of people in the direction of a different kind of noise coming from somewhere. Shouts and groans mixed together. Of course, some guests were watching a game on TV, probably around the corner in what I guessed was the living room. Most likely, Eli had gone off to see what was going on.

I put my hand in my pocket and touched the amethyst, which in that moment served as a reminder to take a deep breath, and so I did. Then I glanced around as I decided what to do next. That's when I saw Elliot lifting the wine bottles from the tote and setting them out on the table. Megan showed up at his side with two corkscrews and without any conversation between them, the two started opening the bottles.

As if sensing someone was watching her, Megan turned in my direction. Along with sending a bright smile my way, she said, "I can assure you, none of this will go to waste. So, what can I get for you? Red, white, blush?"

I nodded to the bottle of blush she held in her hand. She picked up a good-size wine glass and filled it to the brim. "Here you go," she said, handing it to me. "Enjoy it. You're not driving."

"If I'd known there'd be this many people, I'd have filled a second tote."

She laughed. "No problem. Seems like we finish all we have, no matter how much or little there is. And some of the others brought beer and soft drinks. I'm sure Georgia and Elliot have a stash of wine around somewhere."

"Is there something I can do to help?" I made the offer, although it was clear most of the work had been done already.

"Nah. Georgia's been cooking for three days and the rest of us brought our contributions, just like you did." Megan stretched her arms to the side to encompass the room. "I think she invited the whole Square."

"It's generous of her—and Elliot—to include so many people." Why did I have a strong sense that Georgia hadn't always been so happy? Just the opposite, in fact. I shook off that thought. I didn't want to read energies. I was there to share a day with new acquaintances, some of whom could become friends one day. I didn't intend to be jolted into mood swings in the midst of a swirl of competing energies.

"It's like her wedding," Megan said. "You weren't there, but the big tent was right in the middle of the Square on a busy Saturday and everyone—including the shoppers— were invited to help themselves to the grilled hotdogs and burgers and Stephanie's potato salad. A giant cookout!"

Listening to Megan talk, I felt myself relaxing. Of all the men and women I'd met on the Square, she exuded the greatest degree of uncomplicated happiness, but even more enduring, contentment. "I recall Georgia mentioning that you were her wedding planner. That must have been quite a job, considering you have a shop."

I didn't anticipate ever needing a wedding planner, but it was a light topic of conversation and helped me move comfortably into the atmosphere at the farmhouse.

"It's my second job. I did Lily's, too. Do you know Lily?" She looked around the room as if searching for her.

"I met her on the day I opened. She's quite a spirit." I paused to be sure she got my next point. "Like you."

Megan grinned, as if pleased to be described that way. We

were quickly distracted by people huddled around the table, who were shifting to make room for a couple of women in search of food. I soon found myself between Beverly Winters, Georgia's sister, and Liz Pearson, Marianna's best friend and the wife of Jack Pearson. More of the many intersecting lives of people on the Square. Marianna's step-daughter, Rachel, was at the sink washing dishes. I recognized her from one of my mornings at Biscuits and Brew.

The sound of metal hitting metal suspended the buzz of conversation. Georgia was standing at the table tapping the lid of a kettle with a spoon. It worked, because everyone turned to look at her, including me.

"Elliot?" Georgia called out. "Where's Elliot?"

Appearing in the doorway, Elliot grinned at her. "Right here, Peaches. What do you need?"

A soft blush traveled up her neck to her cheeks. "It's time for the toast. I'm appointing you to make it."

Peaches? How funny. I had a feeling that nickname had started back when they were kids.

"Sure thing. Everyone grab a glass." In a louder voice he added, "Turn the TV down, boys."

Apparently, someone in the next room obliged because football commentators' voices vanished.

Elliot stood next to Georgia, one arm casually draped around her shoulders, the other holding a glass high. "Georgia and I want to thank all of our friends and family for joining us to celebrate our first Thanksgiving as husband and wife. We, all of us," he moved the hand holding the glass in a large arc around the room, "have much to be grateful for, so let's raise our glasses high to another successful holiday season. But most of all, a toast to friendship."

"Salute," echoed through the house.

I hung back a little and observed the crowd of guests form a buffet-style line that wove around the kitchen. That made it easy for everyone to fill their plates with a little of this and a little of that, from turkey and ham to three kinds of potato dishes, to dressing and gravy. And what would a Midwest Thanksgiving be without the French style green bean and onion casserole? Candied yams and other squash dishes added bright colors to our plates along with broccoli and cauliflower.

"Save room for desserts," Georgia reminded us.

Plural. *Desserts.*

Along with a couple of young women I recognized from the yarn shop on the Square, I stood with my back to a hutch at the far end of the kitchen, not really separate, but not yet part of the buffet line either. With their plates filled, people found places to sit in the living room and at the end of the table in the dining room. A few perched on stools in the corner of the kitchen. It wasn't long before the periodic groans and cheers came from the living room. The game was once again the focal point. I looked at the line, expecting to see Eli, but he wasn't there.

As I moved to slip into line, I wondered where he had taken his plate. But then, almost as if I'd called out to him, there he was.

"Time to get some dinner," Eli said, rubbing his palms together. "Not that we're in any danger of running out of food around here."

"Watching the game?" I asked.

"Oh, sure. One game after another if we feel like it." He leaned in closer and added, "You probably think it's a waste of time."

"I never said that. Why...?" I didn't even know how to respond.

Eli took a plate off the top of the pile and handed it to me. "I know. But sometimes I wonder why I bother with football, especially on Thanksgiving. All the hype for nothing. So, I could guess that you might feel the same way. But with a houseful like we have today, I kind of hang out like we've always done."

"What would you do instead?" I asked, lifting a slice of ham off a platter with an over-sized fork.

Eli grinned. "I don't know. Hadn't thought that far ahead."

"My family used to have Scrabble tournaments on Thanksgiving," I said. "I think my parents wanted to keep us quiet and maybe focused on each other. Then we turned on football late in the day."

"Sounds nice," Eli said.

"It was." I spooned some green beans on my plate. "Funny, I hadn't thought of it in a long time."

"A nice memory, though, huh?"

He knows that's what I was thinking.

His plate full, Eli chuckled. "Well, I guess I'll go back and waste some more time with Elliot and a couple of our cousins."

With that, he was off, leaving me with my plate piled high. But that was okay. Somehow, when he'd come to my side to go through the buffet line, my uncomfortable moments were over.

I found an empty chair in a corner of the sun porch where Marianna and Art had staked out some space. I was drawn to them, as individuals, but as a pair, too. I sensed they understood themselves and equally important, each other. As we made small talk, mostly about Black Friday on the Square, I noted Doris' absence. Megan and others had all emphasized that Georgia invited everyone, and that meant no one was excluded. So where was Doris?

Those questions and many more roamed around in my mind as I finished my meal and sipped my wine. I joined Marianna and Art when they took the initiative to start clearing away the serving dishes and platters, replacing them with several types of pies and bowls of whipped cream. Georgia brought out plates of different kinds of cookies and wrapped chocolates.

Many of us traded in our wine and beer for mugs of coffee and tea served from banquet size urns. It seemed as if the house, bursting with people and conversation, had finally taken a breath and fallen into relative silence.

When I went to the urn to refill my coffee cup, Georgia came to join me. "Enjoy your coffee now, because I have a feeling Eli will want to leave soon," she said. "He's opening the store in the morning and is supervising the crew getting ready for what we know will be a crazy day."

"Well, I'm ready whenever he is," I said, "but I've had a lovely time. I've met so many people, too. I really appreciate the invitation…Peaches."

Georgia laughed and flashed a lopsided grin. "I guess I'm stuck with that. Elliot started calling me that when we were still in grade school. He's the only person who gets away with it."

"Anyone can see there's a lot of love behind that moniker," I teased.

She nodded. "True enough, so I don't complain. And thanks so much for joining us today—and for bringing the wine. This has been the best day. A first Thanksgiving for Elliot and me."

The air shifted. Eli. He'd moved into the space behind me.

6

Dark and quiet outside, stars hung in the black sky. Only a sliver of the new moon pierced the peaceful darkness of nighttime in the country. Inside the truck with Eli, though, the silence was nerve-racking, the opposite of the serene night. *Unacceptable*. That had to change, and I'd have to be the one to attempt to shift the atmosphere.

"So, aside from enjoying the amazing array of food, did your team win or lose?" I asked.

Barely a second elapsed before Eli responded. "Ha! Elliot lost the bet. Again."

That wasn't a direct answer, but his smile told me he and his twin brother had been challenging each other to bets on the game since about the time they'd started talking.

"Again, huh? You must be a better judge of football than he is."

"I am."

That was it? No elaboration?

"Well, it's a shame for you to drive me all the way to the Square only to have to drive back to the farmhouse." I glanced his way.

"Oh, I don't live there anymore," he said, apparently surprised.

"Really? I don't know why, but I thought you did."

"You haven't heard about the house shuffle?" He chuckled at his choice of words.

"No. Tell me about it." At least that would get him talking.

"It all started when Georgia's uncle died. She moved into his house. Then she got Lily to come back to Wolf Creek, which is another whole story. At the same time that situation was developing, Nathan left his father's law firm in Green Bay, and he and Jack opened Country Law."

When he stopped talking to check for traffic before turning onto the road into town, I said, "I'm waiting, but not patiently. You've got my curiosity up now."

Eli chuckled. "Just trying to be careful. Lots of bad drivers out on a holiday night. So, when Nathan and Lily got married, Georgia gave them the family home, and since the wedding was less than a month away, Georgia moved out to the farm."

He stopped abruptly. I sensed why. He was about to become part of the story.

"So, you had to figure out where the shuffle would leave you?" I kept my voice low because in my heart I knew the truth. In the game of house-switching, Eli felt like an extra person, and not in a good way.

"Yeah. I didn't feel comfortable staying out there anymore. They're newlyweds, you know."

"Where do you live now?"

"In the apartment above Country Law. That's where Nathan and Toby used to live."

His voice had softened. A feeling came over me, like small stabs, just short of painful. But like the children's game of musical chairs, someone was always left standing alone. For a time, that was Eli, a player out of the game.

"Well, now I know we're neighbors on the Square. And what a great location!" I hoped my positive twist would lighten the mood. If I hadn't been looking at him I'd have missed his subtle nod. Maybe he'd also been trying to convince himself about all the advantages of being in town.

He drove his truck down the alleyway to my back door and turned off the ignition. He twisted his upper body as if preparing to get out of the car. Odd. I hadn't planned to invite him in. Another time, maybe, but not after the slightly awkward ride to the farm and back.

"Don't bother getting out. I'll be fine." I reached across the console to touch his arm. "Thanks for driving. I enjoyed being out at the farm with everyone."

"I'm glad," he said. "I'll wait here until you're inside and have locked your door."

Ah, it was a safety thing with him. Amusing, given the well-lit drive and the nature of Wolf Creek, but kind of sweet, too. "Okay, then, good night."

He nodded.

I let myself in through the back and flipped the lock. A few seconds later I heard the sound of the truck pulling away.

My body was tired, but I was much too keyed up to sleep. I poured myself a glass of red wine and sat in the chair at the window that looked out to the Square. My mind continued rehashing all the snippets of conversation I'd heard at the farmhouse, from news about the museum to Megan's engagement. Her guy, Clayton, and his mother, Sadie, were getting a ready-made community along with Megan.

I sipped my wine and smiled at the thought I'd found the same thing the minute I bought the building and started planning the shop. The more I mulled it over, the more I decided I'd made the right decision about moving to Wolf Creek and becoming part of this community. Warm and cool air swirled around me. Apparently, the girls agreed.

***

Julia knocked hard on the front door, having arrived in plenty of time to have a cup of freshly brewed hazelnut coffee before we launched Black Friday. The coffee was my special treat, my reward for having such a successful opening. When I unlocked the shop at exactly 9:00, I was once again surprised by the number of people, mostly women, who were crisscrossing the Square or clustering in front of various shops at such an early hour.

Seeing the group through my shop window, I opened the door wide and gestured for the women to come inside. My eye was drawn to one solo shopper who planted herself in a corner of Square Spirits and removed a folded sheet of paper from her purse. Systematically, she moved her hand down what looked like a very long list. Wow, having never been much of a holiday shopper fanatic myself, I was being introduced to a world I'd known little about—at least until now. The woman brought to mind the term "power shopper."

Julia meandered over to her, offering assistance, and within seconds was showing her various choices of amethyst stones, followed by laying out the three different lavender-hued note cards, lavender candles, and finally, blank journals in various designs. I didn't have to be an intuitive to know she was buying girl gifts, identical and in bulk. Within minutes, Julia was wrapping each stone, card packet, and journal in lavender tissue paper, and loading them into a large Square Spirits shopping bag. And it was only 9:30!

Even better, my first shopper of the day was smiling when she left and walked briskly across the Square, swinging that bag with my logo. Others would notice her, and the bag. What a great start.

The shop soon filled with groups of two or three women out for a day of bargain hunting and fun with friends. They didn't all buy something, of course. Many said they'd be back after they'd made the rounds. I stayed busy at the register, while Julia answered questions and was an all-around sales maven.

What about lunch? Julia couldn't exist on sips of water from the chilled bottle I stored under the counter for her. I no sooner thought about food than I laughed out loud at the sight of Sarah coming in with a plate. Underneath the plastic wrap, we found cheese, crackers, apple wedges and chocolate squares.

"Sarah's the mayor," I explained to Julia who looked astonished at the gift of lunch.

"All in a day's work," Sarah said. "Well, at least on Black Friday." With that she waved and took off.

"What a life saver," Julia remarked. "I'll put the plate on the table in the back. We can take turns munching."

"That's some mayor," one of the shoppers said with a grin.

"I know," I said, "and this is some town."

We had a few lulls, which I took advantage of to head

to the basement for replacement stock, especially more polished stones and candles. The inspirational quote packages were selling well, too. I had a sturdy carton with hand grips reserved to carry bottles of wine. Julia must have replenished the gleaming wooden wine racks twice by early afternoon.

Finally, as the sun set and dusk approached, I stood back and admired the empty shelves, bins, and wine racks, pressing my palms together in silent thanks. I had plenty of what I needed to fill the empty spots from stock stored downstairs for the next day and the day after that. My body tingled with energy and happiness.

Then Eli walked in the front door. The energy shifted, and his scowl wasn't exactly subtle.

After noting that Julia was with a group of late shoppers at the wine racks, I stepped forward to greet him.

"Well, hello. What brings you by, Eli? Is there something wrong?"

"Sarah asked if I'd help you bring boxes of wine up from the basement."

I stiffened my shoulders. "Uh, I didn't ask her to do that. I don't know why she would have suggested such a thing." Somehow, I had to make the situation clear to him. I was *not* some weak little lady who had to be watched going into her own house or who couldn't lug a few bottles of wine up the stairs. At nearly six feet tall, I was rarely mistaken for a damsel in distress.

On the other hand, there *were* a few holes on those wine shelves. With Eli carrying one crate, I could handle another. The work would go fast.

The energy around Eli shifted, not dramatically, but I noticed it. Had Sarah really sent him, or had he suggested a quick trip to my shop himself? Maybe he wasn't disgusted at all. The situation was cloudy. More than likely, he wanted to help me, for whatever reason, but was puzzled by his own impulse and didn't want me to know it.

He stood silent, frowning, but in a thoughtful way. All signs of the earlier disgust had faded.

Not wanting to play games, I asked if he wanted to help

in some way. "Or do you feel obligated because Sarah asked you to help me—if I needed it, that is?"

I'd noted the respect Sarah received from people associated with the Square. Not surface salutations, but deep-seated admiration.

"No, no problem," Eli said, his face lightening up a bit. "I'm here now. Elliot's at the store getting ready to close." He nodded at the wine racks. "Seems you could use a little replenishing."

He'd engineered this all on his own. That settled it.

"Okay. If you don't mind, this shouldn't take long." I waved for him to follow me.

I tried to take a direct route to the door leading to the basement, but Julia had moved to the shelves of stones and had stopped me to ask a quick question about a collection of various colors of calcite pieces. I answered her, and made quick introductions, noting curiosity on Julia's face. She might have at least tried to hide it, but no, not Julia. Fortunately, a customer asked a relatively easy question about a crystal shaft, and that pulled Julia away.

I led him down to the bottom of the stairs, where we navigated around a pile of still unpacked boxes of New Age books. I pointed to a wine crate I'd already arranged with bottles of mixed red wines. "Let's start with these."

"Whatever suits you," Eli said, his voice surprisingly cheerful. He lifted the large carton so easily it might as well have been filled with pillow down. Watching Eli's strength in action took my mind in a different direction. And then I saw his arm muscles flex.

What? Stop it, Zoe!

As if I'd never seen a man with strong arms before…how ridiculous.

With Eli making quick work of moving the wine, I decided to replenish the bookshelves, especially because Julia was still around to help me arrange them.

Eli took the second box upstairs, and when he came back he hoisted the full box of books from my hands and rested it on his shoulder. I might have known he'd do that.

Before we went back upstairs, I remarked that I'd never

expected to sell so much wine so fast. "I need to call home tonight and get more delivered."

He glanced at the wine. Briefly. Then he said, "Julia probably needs your help."

That was the Eli I knew. No extra words, just the slightly grumpy tone.

Still, something ruffled my thoughts when he was around, to say nothing of the tingling in my body.

Once upstairs, he raised his hand, which passed for a wave goodbye, and out the door he went before I could shout my thanks.

"Wow. Quite the hunk," Julia said, coming alongside me at the bookshelves.

I forced a completely phony eye roll. "Not my type."

"*Liar.* Look me in the eye and say that again."

A giggle escaped. I turned away and she gave out a hoot that reverberated through the shop.

Me? Giggling? *Never.*

Finally, it was a little after 7:00, and the last shopper left. I locked the door and switched off the inside lights. The glow from the antique lamp posts filled the room, enough for us to see the stairs to the apartment, but not so bright as to intrude on the mellow mood.

I sighed in contentment. "I love the shop when it's lit by the outside lights on the Square."

"Don't you love a good tired?" Julia asked. "I'm worn to the bone and it feels great."

I chuckled and nodded. "Even better, we can get a super Crossroads lasagna for dinner. Apparently, it's a Black Friday special. I've not had it, but everything I've tried is excellent."

"Hey, a jelly sandwich would taste good right now." She grabbed the last chocolate square on the plate Sarah had brought over and popped it into her mouth.

The two remaining apple wedges had turned brown, but all the cheese slices and crackers were gone. I'd tell Sarah how I appreciated her way of looking after us. But it felt odd, too. I didn't need another mother, after all. I had a mother I loved with all my heart, but at times she insinuated herself into my life in unwelcome ways. Sarah was a colleague. Yet, I imagined Sarah took care of all the shop owners that way on these special days. A plate of food was one thing, but sending Eli in to help was something else. Of course, I was pretty sure Eli had engineered his trip to my shop on his own. I couldn't be sure what role Sarah had played. No wonder the situation was confusing. Still, no matter how it happened, Eli had shown up unbidden once again.

Wanting to refocus, I said, "Let's go eat and when we come back we can putter around down here and restock the shelves and displays. If I let myself relax too much, I'll never haul myself out of the chair and get moving again."

She started up the stairs first. "I'm famished, but I need a quick shower and fresh clothes. I reek of lavender."

"Reek? What's that supposed to mean?"

She drew her arm up and took a whiff. "It's not a bad smell…"

"But?"

She grinned. "Let's just say it's like eating too much of a very good chocolate cake. Too much of a good thing and it loses what makes it special."

"Nice recovery, cousin," I said, laughing. "But I know what you mean. You handled the merchandise more than I did."

"The customers seemed to really like your shop," Julia said. "Congratulations on what you've created here." She wrapped her arms around me and squeezed hard. "I really enjoyed myself today. Thanks so much for letting me help."

"Having you here is my good luck charm," I said, stepping out of her hug. "Anyway, take your time getting ready. It's probably a rush over there now anyway. I'll call home and order wine while you're showering. I need them to deliver a dozen cases in the morning—as early as possible."

Her shower and my call took all of fifteen minutes and then we left for our quick dinner. As we sat over our lasagna, Julia gave me her observations of the day and what had attracted attention and why. I jotted her thoughts on a notepad I carried in my handbag, and that let us put together an immediate plan of action.

For one thing, I needed to stop erratic reorders and instead do it all in one day. We both noted that only the pendants and pendulums were slow to sell, but we weren't sure why. I needed a more varied book selection to satisfy the kinds of curious customers that had wandered in. That meant more titles, and fuller shelves might give them the little kick they needed to attract more attention. On the other hand, the journals seemed to be jumping out of their bins!

After dinner, we walked to the shop, but before entering, we stood back a few feet to look at the window display. The tiffany lamp on a table with a couple of large amethyst pieces and a low stack of books drew my eye. Smaller groups of candles sitting in holders and arrangements of note cards sat on shelves of varying height. The small wine rack set at an angle in the corner appealed, too.

The best part of the window display were the two woven rugs on the floor, one with a rising sun design and one with moonlight shining on water. I'd had them for a long time. They were among the few items I claimed from the house Tyler and I had lived in. I'd taken almost nothing, but I wouldn't have parted with the rugs. Now, like me, they'd found a perfect home.

Once inside, Julia started reorganizing the wine, adding a few flourishes to the way I'd initially displayed them. She created a trio of each type on the top of the racks, explaining how they would draw the eye and invite a shopper to come closer.

I saw some of Mom's ideas in her arrangements, and I trusted Julia enough to set her loose. "My mother taught you well, I see. She has a light, but effective touch when it comes to displays."

"I hope I'll be back at the winery fulltime," Julia said. "It's actually not the sales end that interest me the most. I really enjoy helping Devin with winemaking, along with the labeling and bottling process, of course. And I've always liked working with your mom on special events."

The wistful way she said Devin's name surprised me. On the other hand, Devin had lost Hannah to cancer a few years back. Maybe Julia sensed he was ready to move on.

I didn't know one way or the other. Devin and I weren't communicating well on any subject. He and Hannah hadn't started a family, and I wondered if Devin regretted that he might have missed his chance. Of course, I'd not had kids either, but since my parents never warmed to Tyler anyway, even Mom only tactfully probed that area a couple of times. The tensions in the family had kept me distant from them for many years, and Mom had probably been afraid that if she'd asked me outright about that choice, she'd drive a wedge between us. And it's true that I wouldn't have welcomed her questions.

"You might want to talk to Mom again," I told Julia, avoiding the topic of Devin.

With that, we worked quickly and in rare silence. But when Julia picked up her earlier train of thought, I wasn't surprised.

"Do you think Devin is ready to remarry?"

My earlier passing thoughts were one thing, but I didn't want to move into this territory with Julia. I kept my answer brief. "I've never discussed it with him."

"No gut feeling?" she asked.

"I can't say I have any about that area of Devin's life," I replied truthfully, "but I don't think you'll find out unless you ask him."

"Do you think he'd tell me?"

I shrugged. Devin was an enigma that way. Neither of us had handled the loss of our partners well. A death in his case, abandonment and divorce in mine, we'd been brought to our knees in grief. We functioned, we looked normal on the outside, but that didn't match what was going on inside.

Talking to Julia about Devin made me conscious of my peculiar and confusing reactions to Eli. Every time I encountered him, questions flooded my mind. It all came down to: What was going on beneath his taciturn exterior? What had really prompted him to show up to lend a hand? Why had he appeared at my side in the buffet line on Thanksgiving at the exact moment I'd begun to feel overwhelmed by the mix of energies in the crowd?

I had no time to contemplate the answers to questions

about Eli, and I was certainly in no position to second guess my brother or what he wanted. When it came to figuring out Devin, Julia was on her own.

***

Small Business Saturday dawned bright and crisp. We were at least as busy as we'd been on Black Friday. Having become more familiar with the stock and already a semi-expert on wine, Julia exuded even greater confidence. But as the day passed, our level of fatigue morphed into a giddy state, or as Dad would have said, we were "punch drunk."

We pulled out sheet after sheet of lavender tissue to wrap stones and candles. The supply of small shopping bags diminished by Saturday afternoon, and I brought out some plain white bags to use for books and cards. After closing, we ate deli takeout from Farmer Foods, washed down with the local apple cider they sold. Then we crashed, asleep by 9:30.

I was up at dawn on Sunday and at the computer placing orders for stock and supplies, knowing that every dime of the extra money I'd spend on shipping was worth it. The coming week might bring fewer people to the Square, but I wasn't taking any chances. *Over-stocked* was my new watchword.

On Sunday, traffic on the Square was steady, but not frenzied. That gave me a chance to put on my starry night poncho and make my way around the Square to visit some shops while Julia was still available to cover for me. I first visited The Fiber Barn, where the owners were flushed and rushed. I wandered through their shop, soaking up pleasant energy, but only waved hello. I visited Marianna and marveled at the quilts hanging on the walls and the bolts of fabric filling the store. Clayton's gallery was busy, with SOLD signs on quite a few framed watercolors. Megan reintroduced me to Nora while they wrapped plant pots and garden art. I waved and went back to my shop, where Julia was sending a customer out to the Square. Julia wasted no time boasting that the woman had left with one shopping bag filled with candles, scarves, sachets, stones, and lavender essential oil, and another loaded with books.

Shortly after that, the shop and the Square emptied, and we drifted to closing time. After such a busy couple of days, I was sorry to walk Julia to her car and say goodbye. Once back inside, I turned the shop lights off and sat at the table in the back room massaging my temples to ward off a mild headache. I got those sometimes when I was tired and my thoughts and gut feelings were driving hard. I worked on inventory lists, pleased to see the results on paper.

Later that evening I sat with a glass of wine by the front window overlooking the Square. Fairy lights, woven within the branches of the trees and around the evergreens created the Square's magical look. Almost all the upstairs windows in the other buildings were lit, bringing the image of cocoons to mind. Cozy, warm cocoons that enveloped so many of us at the end of the day.

I had yet to meet the owner of the Inn, and there were a handful of other people on the Square I had only a passing familiarity with. A few buildings were still vacant. My gaze kept returning to the corner building at the far end, Country Law.

Eli lived there. And the lights were on.

Huh? Stop it. Was I looking for hidden messages in a lit up apartment? What was going on with me?

I shook my head to clear it, as if I could dislodge this nonsense. Then, as I crawled into bed and closed my eyes, Eli's face appeared. Not the grumpy Eli, or the guy with the scowl. No, it was Eli's special smile that kept returning to my thoughts.

***

The next morning, I woke up with Grace and Rose on my mind. Thankfully, they'd made themselves scarce during Julia's stay. I was surprised, and yet not. They were a little shy, those two. But after coming back from morning coffee at B and B on Monday morning, they greeted me with warm and cool breezes. They kept that up through the morning.

Were they clearing the air, lifting any heavy energies left behind from the crowds? I didn't know, but every now and then the alternating cool and warm air covered me like a cloak.

I told the girls all about Julia and our wonderful weekend, speaking to them as if they hadn't been there and watched each day unfold. My first holiday season on the Square was a story worth telling, and it filled me with joy to recite the details out loud. I also mentioned my day at the farmhouse with the Reynolds' family and all their guests. I thanked them—profusely—for not scaring Julia. Intuitively, I thought it best *not* to mention Eli. If I started bringing him into the stories of my days, I feared they might send their warm and cool air his way and make him uneasy.

The day traffic the rest of the week was steady with my evenings each mini-Christmases. Every time I opened a shipment box I smiled until my cheeks hurt.

Oh, what a good hurt that was, right up to the last box. Maybe my smiles also had something to do with my growing belief that my hunch about moving to Wolf Creek had been right. The Square was feeling more like home every day.

DECEMBER
7

When I turned the calendar to December, it seemed almost impossible that the busy days in November had been only a lead up to the weeks before Christmas. I noted the many empty boxes, which meant I could focus my attention—my energies—on what was still an ongoing launch of Square Spirits. Most mornings, I headed to B and B, wanting to strengthen my ties with others on the Square. At times I braced myself and struggled to keep my emotions in check, for no other reason than the camaraderie I'd gradually become a part of made me ache with regret.

For years, I'd lived in my own small world, managing the clinic, catering more than I should have to what Tyler wanted. Old friends from high school and college had drifted away, my social life revolving around what was good for my husband's personal and professional image. What was good for the clinic was good for him and vice versa. Actually enjoying the company of particular men and women was irrelevant. For Tyler, it had been all about getting ahead. Until it wasn't.

I still reeled at my own complicity with Tyler's plans for our life. I'd remained steeped in the fantasy world of our partnership, even speaking with pride about us as a couple who knew how to be in business together. When it all crashed around me, I'd had to look squarely at how becoming preoccupied with a busy life led me farther and farther away from the reality developing under my nose.

Most of the time, I pushed those regrets aside and replaced

them with celebrating the recent decisions I'd made which had strengthened me at my core. As I sat sipping hazelnut coffee with Marianna, Doris, Georgia, Sadie, and Sarah, and on many mornings, other women, too, I knew the Square provided the energy center that continued to fuel my growing sense of wellbeing.

So far, it had been fun to be one of the new shops, along with The Fiber Barn and Clayton's. For the established shops, they served as proof of the ongoing trend toward more traffic and more buyers, more coffee and muffins sold at B and B, and a crowded dining room at Crossroads.

One morning early in December, I heard trucks on the Square before opening time. This was unusual, of course, in the pedestrian only space, but entertaining all the same. I watched the trucks pull up around the walkway with the crew picking up bales of straw and all the plants and decorations associated with autumn. Another couple of trucks came and the workers transformed the area. They placed large boxes wrapped like presents and wooden statues of Santa and his elves in designated places around on the Square. A crèche appeared in the empty space between the flagpoles, and candy canes and wreaths embellished the lampposts. Only the white lights already woven in the branches of the trees stayed.

In the afternoon, I had another pleasant surprise when Melanie, the manager of Crossroads, came in to see me about featuring a variety of DmZ wines in the restaurant in January.

"Sorry for not getting here sooner, but this time of year I'm like everyone else. I simply don't have enough hours in the day to do everything." She moved to one of the wine displays. "Your mother and I are choosing the wines to feature at Crossroads."

"That's great. My family is happy with your plan."

"Would you mind if I asked you how the wine got the name *DmZ* Winery? It sounds like an odd play on words."

"Ah, you're not the first to ask. It's simple really." And so it was. "D for Devin, Z for Zoe, M for Miller, but a small m, because we kids are the most important part of the name."

"Now, you'd think I could have figured that out," Melanie said, laughing.

"Well, if you'd asked my dad, he'd go into a long story about the thought process before finally settling on the whimsical name he wanted," I said.

"So, do you have a preference for the wines we should feature?" Melanie asked. "You'll need to have plenty in stock yourself."

"I'll defer to my mother on that," I said. "She's the expert on pairing wine, and often will recommend certain varieties to go with roast pork or lamb or even vegetarian stews. She'll study your menu and make recommendations."

"Sounds good to me," Melanie said. "This is going to be fun." She scanned the shop, but checked her watch and headed for the door. "Next time, I'm going to take a look. I think your shop speaks my language, if you know what I mean."

"I like the sound of that," I replied.

The door closed with a jingle. I liked that sound, too. I hadn't been aware of it all weekend, probably because the door opened and closed so often it was lost in the buzz of conversation and activity. But in the quiet of the empty shop, it sent its happy message. And my spirit did a little dance.

***

The night of the business association meeting, large fluffy snowflakes rapidly blanketed the Square, making me especially glad I could walk to the meeting. One of the pleasures of living in Wolf Creek was that I so seldom needed to drive. Only mere steps away, I could find almost everything I needed. That evening, I was one among many who simultaneously converged at the entrance to the private dining room of Crossroads, and right on time. I'd quickly observed Sarah was a stickler for punctuality at these meetings, and she showed her appreciation by greeting each of us and pointing the way to the snack and beverage table.

When she greeted me, she nodded to the glass she held. "DmZ."

I glanced at it. "Hmm…let's see. Rich, deep, and very dark. I'm guessing it's a blackberry merlot. How do you like it?"

"Very nice. And compliments of Melanie. She thought we should taste it since she's featuring this variety in January. She's put others on the back table." She gestured around her. "Your family is already here somewhere."

At the sound of her name, Sarah moved away to greet someone else, leaving me to wonder if Devin had actually come along or if he'd decided to leave the public relations to Mom and Dad. The room was rapidly filling up with the people who had become so important to me. As I went off to find my parents, I waved to Marianna and Art, and Megan and Clayton, who were coming through the door.

It didn't take long to locate my parents. My mother's distinctive laugh guided me in her direction. No need for introductions. My family had already made themselves part of the group, and surprisingly, that included Devin. He and Eli had their heads together, nodding at each other's words. I wondered what they found so interesting in their conversation. I was about to move closer to find out when Sarah tapped the microphone.

"Welcome everyone," she said. "We're having refreshments at the beginning of the meeting tonight. That's because Melanie is giving us a mini wine-tasting this evening. She's featuring DmZ wines at Crossroads in January and adding a few varieties to her wine list. She also invited the owners of DmZ Winery, Judith and Russ Miller, and their son Devin, to join us this evening. As you know, Zoe sells her family's wine at Square Spirits. So, help yourself."

That's all she needed to say to send the group back to the table to try the different wines. It wasn't long before conversations comparing one wine to another traveled around the room.

Sarah rapped the podium to get the attention of the room and conversation immediately fell off. "I have one more surprise. No agenda for tonight. I've officially declared this a wine-tasting party. We're all working nonstop every day, so for now, just enjoy yourselves."

The noise level went up a notch or two, and I made a beeline for my parents. Dad looked well, standing taller than I'd seen him in a while. Mom was her usual animated self. I nodded to Devin and waved to Eli, still curious about what they'd found to chat about. Rather than interrupting, I left my family alone to mingle, something they were very good at. Meanwhile, I slipped in next to Sadie Winston, Clayton Sommers' mother. I had chatted with her once or twice at the morning gatherings.

"Are you a history buff?" she asked, her many bracelets sparkling in the bright lights of the room.

"Well, I'm certainly curious about Wolf Creek," I said. "I would like to learn more about the building I'm in. Things like who built it, what kinds of businesses have occupied the space. That sort of thing. Conversation starters to share with the customers." Not that I'd breathe a word about Grace or Rose.

"You know, I work for Matt Alexander. A branch of the Alexander Foundation is helping the town renovate the museum. I stay busy cataloguing the items people have donated through the years. Most are common items, but we've come across some unusual pieces that could be worth something. The most valuable items are the boxes stacked shoulder high and filled with letters and diaries. And the print copies of old newspapers have been fairly well preserved. The papers were microfilmed years ago, but now they're digitized, available with a keystroke at the newspaper's website. Still, some people like to look at the real thing."

Hmm...letters and diaries. Maybe some would explain the circumstances of the fire in the building on the Square. As I listened to Sadie, my mind jumped ahead.

"As for the buildings," Sadie said with a shrug, "we're working with the town clerk to compile a more complete record of the buildings on the Square, and other structures in town, as well. I'm quite sure we can help you get the information you need."

My stomach flipped over, but I wasn't sure why. Just

talking about the building had aroused a sense of excitement. "Really? That's wonderful."

"Why sure. It's a big part of my job. This little town is proud of its history—and its living history, the continuing story of Wolf Creek. Sarah and Charlie Crawford are direct descendants of the founding families. And there are many others in town, or in nearby communities who can trace their family's roots to Wolf Creek."

I was about to ask about the condition of these boxes of diaries and letters when Clayton and Megan joined us, and the conversation shifted back to the holiday crowds and present day Wolf Creek. I receded from the group, not physically so much as mentally, becoming an observer. I mostly watched my family interact with the shopkeepers. I smiled inside, watching Mom and Melanie deep in conversation as if they'd known each other for years, not days. As for Devin, now circulating around the room, I was relieved I could avoid him by heading in a different direction. I regretted feeling that way, but I sensed the resentment between us wouldn't heal simply by arguing about it. We always ended up in the same place. He'd expected me to adjust to the end of my marriage to Tyler by throwing myself into the winery, apparently forever. I had never expressed that desire, let alone the intention to do any such thing. Mom understood, Dad tried to, but Devin was stuck in his own mindset.

When I saw Mom pat Melanie's arm and turn away, I knew she'd said goodbye and would soon be on her way back home with Dad and Devin. I went to her so she didn't have to look around for me.

"Good time?" I asked.

"The best. Your dad enjoyed himself, too. And there's Devin with one of the twin brothers. I can't remember which one. They've been talking away all night."

"That's Eli," I explained. "I told you about him. He drove me out to the Reynolds' family farm for Thanksgiving."

Mom's eyebrows lifted in interest. "I see."

Going for a quick change of subject, I asked if she was getting ready to collect Devin and Dad so they could head home.

"I sure am. Your dad feels good now, but long days tire him out."

"Let's go find him. I'm sure Devin will wrap up his socializing." I could see Devin chatting with Marianna and Art, with Doris standing close by. Devin's stiff demeanor communicated good manners, but nothing like the intense interest I'd observed when he and Eli were deep in conversation.

Mom hesitated, but only for a second. Then she gave me a quick hug. "You go mingle. I'll say your goodbyes to your dad. We'll stop by the store again soon."

I didn't argue. From the firm set of her mouth, no further words were needed. She wanted to leave well enough alone with Devin and me. "Well enough" defined as no interaction at all.

Mom patted my arm and left my side.

As I took a few steps toward the snack table to do some serious mingling, an idea popped into my head. I'd host an open house, and schedule it to coincide with the winter solstice, which would add something unique to the holiday gatherings. I'd hire Melanie to put together a few hors d'oeurve trays, and I'd serve wine. Not the varieties Crossroads would carry, but others from DmZ Winery.

I'd ask Eli to pour the wine. Wouldn't that keep him interested? A little voice in my head qualified my idea... *If Eli came at all.* Well, if I invited Eli, then surely he would show up. I'd get a case of sparkling water from Farmer Foods, too, and the flowers would come from Rainbow Gardens. The whole Reynolds family would be involved. *Whoa!* I was getting way ahead of myself. Besides, in this gossipy little community I had to be careful about linking Eli with me. Only *I* needed to know that the more I thought about Eli, the more I considered him a kindred spirit.

I brought my attention back to the room. Watching Melanie clear the tables of wadded up napkins and empty glasses, it occurred to me she either wanted to close or had to set up for another event. I smiled to myself when Sarah took charge and answered my question.

"Time to bring this party to a close," Sarah said. "Melanie

needs to set up this room for an event tomorrow morning."

We'd arrived in groups and that's the way we left. I grabbed my poncho off the back of a chair and joined the crowd of those heading to their homes on the Square. A biting wind greeted us as we left the Inn. Trying to quickly pull my black gloves on for the short trip home, I accidently dropped one. Out of nowhere, a hand—Eli's hand— retrieved it, before I could bend down to pick it up. Then he held it open for me to slide my hand inside. I laughed at the funny, sweet gesture. And so did he.

He held my hand a tad longer than necessary. That was okay. A sense of strength and warmth coming from him traveled through the glove to my tingling palm.

Wow. Naturally, I noticed. There it was again, that quality in his energy that had a strange effect on mine.

Without saying anything, he walked alongside me the short distance to Square Spirits and waited for me to go inside and relock the front door. I lifted my hand in a quick wave, then stood in the shadows by the wine display to watch Eli walk down the Square. His pace was slow, as if he didn't have a care in the world. Or, maybe he was in no hurry to get home. He stopped to look in the windows of Rainbow Gardens and Clayton's before opening the door to Country Law. As he had at other times, he looked rather lost. With himself? With his circumstances? Some situation he had no control over? I didn't have the answers, at least not yet.

Climbing the stairs to my apartment, I told Grace and Rose all about my evening, but before I got to the top of the stairs my lights came on. "Okay, you two," I said, "I'll tell you more. I talked to a woman named Sadie, and she offered to help me learn about the history of Wolf Creek."

I paused. Should I or shouldn't I continue? I knew I was taking a chance, so I added, "Sadie also said she'd help me find out about this building and the fire."

The air currents swirled around me, strong and unmistakable. The edges of pages on the table ruffled under a rose quartz paperweight. "I understand," I said. "Whatever happened that caused your deaths was traumatic, I know.

But learning about the building and the fire will help me get to know you better."

I closed my eyes as soft, alternating waves of cool and warm air buffeted my face. That was all well and good, but these girls had limits—boundaries. If I was to ease their trauma, I needed to respect them. "Better now. See? You're safe with me."

8

The next morning, it was still dark outside when I brewed a small pot of hazelnut coffee and sat at my antique desk. I had everything I needed to place orders and track inventory downstairs in the shop, but the desk upstairs was where I liked to write down ideas and plans. Maybe because I had invested so much time into it. I'd never refinished a piece of furniture before, but I'd been drawn to buy this desk and bring back the richly grained walnut, an outcome accomplished over a period of many weeks. Then I'd replaced the old plain drawer pulls with brass ones from the same era as the desk. Rather than moving it to my office at the clinic, as I'd originally planned, the desk became the centerpiece of our home office.

All these years later, I'd created a corner in my apartment next to the front windows, where the desk was again the focal point of the room and a special place for me to work. That morning I made a list of shops on the Square, and then wrote invitations to my winter solstice open house, which I'd scheduled for the following Monday, the date of the actual solstice. It would start right after closing time. If for some reason Crossroads' catering was booked, I could put together light finger food trays from whatever Eli and Elliot could supply.

As I wrote the invitations, the more excited I became about hosting my first event. I doubted that my shopkeeper friends thought much about December 21, other than as four shopping days before Christmas. But to me it was an important day, and this year, it would be a kind of coming out party for my presence on the Square.

Before opening time, I quickly made my way around the Square. I slipped the invitations through the old-fashioned mail slots in the front door of the shops, or in a few cases where those were gone, under the door. I made it back just in time to unlock my shop. I was breathless, which reminded me that as hard as I was working, I'd let my fitness routine slip. But I had too much at stake to let my lax attitude continue.

I'd always been in good health. Even after Tyler left me and I temporarily lost my ability to sleep or concentrate, I had managed to stay fit. Now it was especially important to feel energetic and strong. I put in long days, doing everything in the shop, from inventory to selling to the decorating I'd need to finish up before the open house. And in my mind's eye, I saw the years stretching out in front of me, where I'd celebrate many anniversaries as the owner of Square Spirits.

By closing time, I'd received text and email RSVPs from almost everyone invited, and most said they'd be delighted to come to my open house. I went to bed happy that my hunch to throw a party seemed to be right on track.

***

Having a long history of being an organized holiday shopper, the number of last minute shoppers on the Square amazed me. As it turned out, Square Spirits was an appealing place to find a perfect last-minute gift for someone special. Most evenings, I found myself puttering around in the shop, replenishing the wine racks, neatening up the bookshelves, reorganizing the hanging scarves, and adding stones to the bowls.

Until I had the idea for the open house, I hadn't thought much about decorations inside. The Square was festive, and my shop had candles and crystal jewelry and wine, but it occurred to me I had better put out luminaries and weave strings of white fairy lights in strategically chosen locations, like on the floor near the window and around the wine racks, the darker area of the shop.

I found myself talking to myself, or that's the way it would look to an observer. But whether downstairs in the shop, upstairs fixing dinner, or relaxing with a book or a movie, I noted my observations and spoke about my plans with Grace and Rose. They'd become like friends, those two, and I shared my day—and my ideas—with them.

One night, I finished reorganizing my displays, but didn't feel like heating up soup or leftovers. A quiet dinner at Crossroads sounded so much better.

When I ran upstairs to get my wallet, I noticed the light coming from Eli's apartment above Country Law. Eli was home. On an impulse I grabbed my phone and punched in his number.

"Eli here."

"And Zoe here," I said, keeping my voice light. "I've decided I'm too tired to fix supper. I think a plate of Crossroads' stew or pasta sounds much better. Care to join me?"

"Um, oh, ah, well…"

Keeping my voice low, I said, "Eli, I'm not asking you out on a date. I'm hungry, and thought maybe you are too. So, we'll enjoy a late evening meal."

"When you put it that way, sure."

"Good. I'll meet you there."

He ended the call. I frowned at my phone. "No, Eli, it's not a date. You can exhale now."

Was that sarcasm I heard in my voice? Maybe just a little. I took the amethyst stone out of my pocket and rolled it in my palm. I didn't unlock the mystery of Eli by doing that, but I stopped myself from becoming frustrated with him.

I grabbed my coat and checked my hair and lipstick. By the time I locked my shop door behind me, Eli was almost at my front door. I had expected him to meet me at the restaurant, but no matter.

He said hello and after that, nothing. I groaned inside as we started across the Square in silence. I immediately questioned my haste in inviting him to be my dinner partner.

"Hectic days," I said, "but I suppose it's busy at Farmer

Foods, too."

A nod. Then silence. *Oh, brother.*

When we approached the entrance to the restaurant, I spotted Marianna Spencer and Art Carlson approaching from the other side of the Square. Eli waved to them. He looked relieved to see familiar faces.

We exchanged greetings and when Art opened the door we filed in, and he asked us if we cared to join them.

That sounded good to me, and I looked to Eli for agreement. A foursome might ease the awkwardness and unfamiliarity between us.

Eli nodded. "Sure."

I smiled, and so did Marianna. Maybe she was used to Eli's one-word responses. With plenty of tables available, the hostess led the way to a table for four by the window. Art and Eli were across from each other, as were Marianna and I. But then, before the waitress arrived, Art said something to Marianna and they switched seats, which put the men next to each other and me next to Marianna. Seemed odd to me, but I didn't say anything.

Once again, I saw relief in Eli's expression. Being next to his friend rather than between two women had calmed him. If he was that afraid, then why did he agree to have dinner with me at all? If he'd said no, or if I'd not asked, I'd be enjoying a companionable dinner with Marianna and Art.

But I wanted to be with Eli. I wanted to get to know him better, silent or not.

"Hey, by the way," Marianna said, "thanks for the invitation to your open house. Rachel immediately looked up the winter solstice on the internet." She chuckled, apparently amused by her step-daughter. "I guess the day gets lost in the holiday rush. But I always notice it. It's the shortest day of the year, a marker of sorts."

"Well, it's a pretty significant day in some ways, mostly symbolically," I said. "It turns up in mythology around the world. I'd be happy to talk with Rachel about it at the open house."

"She'd like that, especially because she's like a sponge for knowledge. She thinks she missed out on a lot of information because she wasn't such a great student as a kid." Marianna laughed. "But she's one competitive person."

"She loves outdoing Alan, my son," Art added. "If she knows something he doesn't, her confidence gets a boost."

"Seems like I was introduced to Rachel at the coffee shop the other morning," I said. "She and her little boy live with you, don't they?"

Marianna nodded. "And she works with me in the quilt shop. She's close to earning her GED, and she's raising Thomas."

"Quite a load."

"She's quite a girl," Art said, grinning.

"I'm very proud of her," Marianna said.

Marianna and I looked at the insert in the menu that listed the specials for the day, but Art and Eli began their own conversation about all the traffic on the Square. Farmer Foods had taken on another temporary employee, a student from the community college on holiday break. I was about to ask Marianna about her shop when the waitress stepped up to the table and we all ordered some type of DmZ wine. "Look at this, Melanie has already added my family's wine to the list," I said to Marianna.

"How did your family come up with the name DmZ for the winery?" Art asked.

I repeated my dad's Devin and Zoe configuration, going on to explain that since Dad had served in Viet Nam, he juggled the initials around, claiming our sibling fights were like the war. "He settled on DmZ, thinking it would lead to peace."

"Really?" Eli stared, seemingly amazed at my story. "Your brother never mentioned that the other night at the meeting."

So, they'd talked about the winery? I tucked information away. "I suppose my dad's thought processes weren't unique as far as the way companies choose their names." At least I hadn't thought about it that way. Many families named their businesses after their children.

"I was just thinking that during our long conversation about wine," Eli said, frowning, "the name of the winery never came up."

"It's an interesting name," Marianna said, shaking out her napkin and putting it across her lap, "but not as interesting as Square Spirits. Now that's *intriguing.*"

"Like Quilts Galore and Art&Son and Farmer Foods." I tipped my glass to each of them and then took a sip. "Ooh, this is good. And relaxing after a busy day."

"I usually drink beer, but this..." Eli looked at his glass "...this red has spirit."

A buzz rushed through my upper chest and down my arms. *Deliberate choice of words. He's sending me a message.*

The waitress brought a basket of hot bread and took our orders. Hadn't I resolved to keep my hands off the pre-dinner bread? Maybe, but these rolls were too good to pass up. Art offered the basket to Marianna, then to me and Eli. In silence, we each buttered a crusty roll and drizzled honey over it. Suddenly, we laughed simultaneously. We'd fallen into silence momentarily and were all but lost in enjoying the aroma of the bread and watching the butter melt and blend with the honey. I saw the pleasure in their faces and knew my own expression was probably the same.

"No wonder you all flock here," I said. "Who can resist this incredible bread—and every item on the menu?"

"Shh," Marianna said. "Keep that to yourself. We like knowing we can always get a table."

"Right you are," I whispered, as if entering into a conspiracy.

"By the way, Eli, do you have time to make a fruit basket for me?" Marianna asked. "I want to offer one as a door prize this weekend."

Eli settled back in his chair, keeping his fingers circled around the stem of the wine glass. "I can make one up for you anytime."

"Door prize?" I asked.

Art patted Marianna's hand. "Meet the Queen of Marketing."

Marianna laughed. "He calls me that because I'll do anything *within reason* to get customers to come in and buy."

"Can you tell me the kinds of things you do?" If Marianna had found ways to increase sales, then I wanted to hear them. Maybe some of her promotion methods would work for me.

"Well, the gift baskets are always a draw. A purchase of any amount qualifies to get a ticket. The box with the slips sits next to the register and the customers give me names and email addresses and phone numbers. So I build my mailing list, too."

"So you indicate on the ticket when you'll draw a winner?"

Marianna took a sip of her wine and nodded. "My current promotion won't end until Sunday night. That way, weekend shoppers can enter."

I filed that information away. Then the waitress came to the table balancing a tray with the pasta dishes for Marianna and me, and pork roast platters for Eli and Art. Dinner went by quickly as almost all our conversations revolved around the holidays. As for me, I had a hard time not exclaiming over the pasta and sauce with every bite, it was so delicious. Then we finished off our meal with various kinds of pie, already one of my favorite Wolf Creek traditions.

Finally, it was time to go, and Eli insisted on paying for my dinner, even when I pointed out that I invited him.

"You pay another time," he said with a shrug.

I didn't argue, but it had been my intention to make it my treat. Still, I liked the idea of another time. When the four of us stood outside Crossroads to say goodnight, Marianna gave me a quick hug and Art did the same. I took that gesture as more than a simple social nicety. No, I viewed it as a sign of acceptance into the Wolf Creek Square community. This was the first time I'd spent an extended period of time with Marianna and Art. I was grateful to them, too, because Eli seemed more relaxed in their company.

Marianna gave Eli a quick one-arm hug. In the light of the antique lamp posts I saw a red tinge on his neck. But, I also noticed he put his arms around her in return.

Art and Marianna headed west to the far end of the Square. We turned in the direction of Square Spirits. I commented on the paper covering the windows of the museum as we passed it. That triggered a loud laugh from Eli.

"You should have seen Megan's windows last spring. She'd drawn flowers on hers. Since she was always exact about changing her window displays, the paper over the windows got a lot of attention. We all razzed her about it." He grinned slyly. "Especially me."

"I'll just bet," I said. "Megan is lovely. Do you know she brought a bouquet to me when I first opened the shop?"

"I'm not surprised," Eli said. "She cares about people. She grew up when the Square was struggling, and some people wanted it all torn down. She values the whole town, but especially the shops on the Square and all the people who own them and keep the place going."

"And you? Do you feel this way, too?"

"This is my home. I've got no plans to leave."

He'd shortened his steps, slowed his gait and looked into my shop when we arrived. "Different."

"Does that mean you don't like it, or you do?"

"Don't know, really. But I see a lot of people coming in and out. What's in there besides a bunch of stones and candles and books? Well, and the wine."

I let out a loud, but mocking groan. "Someday, Eli, let's talk more about what it is I do and why I sell these items." I turned to unlock the front door.

Eli came up the two steps to the door. He placed his hand over mine.

Warmth, strength, energy. Want.

I turned and looked at him, nearly eye to eye. Shadows highlighted the planes of his face and my heart beat faster. I reached up and touched his upper arm. He leaned toward me, before he quickly backed away.

He wanted to be closer.

The intensity of the buzzing energy racing through me stopped me cold.

From the start, Eli had intrigued me. Too much. I needed to escape. I turned the key in the lock and opened the door. "Good night, Eli."

He nodded. "Zoe."

As I'd done the other evening I locked the door behind

me and watched Eli walk across the center of the Square to his home. *And once again, I felt his loneliness.*

Tears pooled in my eyes, an unexpected reaction. *Whose loneliness brought on the tears? His or mine?*

9

The searing questions from the previous night left me with raw nerves and heightened emotional reactions. Was I confused about my feelings for Eli? You bet I was. And I had no time for introspective questions about loneliness over the next few days. I had my shop to run, and every day was new. What spare time I had was directed to practical jobs like ordering inventory for the days following Christmas. From what I'd heard, the end of the year sales would be a repeat of Thanksgiving. Besides, I liked my freedom, the sense of independence that my life was mine to do with as I chose. Even thinking about a man threatened the boundary I'd drawn around myself.

One morning before opening, I gathered my notes for my solstice party and started out for the Inn. I was sidetracked, though, by the smallest detail. One corner of the paper covering the museum window had fallen, leaving it looking messy. Taking advantage of my height, I peered inside and saw Sadie carefully wrapping small pieces of glassware and tucking them into a box.

On impulse, I rapped on the window to get her attention. Her face lit up, and she invited me inside.

"What brings you by so early on this cold morning?"

"If you have time, I want to take you up on your offer to help me learn more about the background of my building."

"Why sure," Sadie said. "How and when shall we start?"

"I'm thinking I'll have some time during the week between Christmas and New Year's Eve. Would you be available to help me one evening?"

"Evenings are fine for me," Sadie said, brushing dust off the back of her hand, as if she'd just noticed it was there. She grinned when she added, "I set my own hours at this point, but there's no need to wait. I'll start gathering some of the documents and we'll go from there."

"Sounds good to me," I said, reaching out to shake Sadie's hand and enjoying the sound of the jingling bracelets she wore. "Well, I'm off to see Melanie about the treats for my open house. I hope you'll come."

I started for the door, but turned back. "By the way, I love your bracelets."

Her quick laugh let me know she enjoyed hearing the compliment.

I went on to find Melanie in her office in a state of deep concentration at the computer. I knocked on the door molding to get her attention.

"Come in, come in." She gestured to a chair next to her cluttered desk. "I was just on the phone with your mom. I need more DmZ wine in stock to cover New Year's Eve."

"Big party?"

"I'll say. Since most of the guests are staying at the Inn, it will last all night and move right along to an early buffet breakfast the next morning. Lots of work, but, oh, so much fun."

I grinned. "Then I guess the order for my open house will be easy for you."

Melanie grabbed a legal pad off the top of one of her piles of paper. "So, what did you have in mind?"

"Porridge and dried fruit," I deadpanned, enjoying the surprised look on her face.

"Ha ha…just kidding."

"That's a relief," Melanie said, send me an amused smile. "We're running low on oats this week."

Quick retort. I liked that. I handed her my list of suggestions. "I want simple, but elegant food, one and two bite wraps or crackers and spreads, vegetable and fruit platters, and then, of course, holiday cookies and special chocolates—maybe truffles."

She went down the list, checking off some items, but

questioning others, offering price ranges and recommending certain Crossroads' specialties.

"I leave it to your judgment," I said, standing.

"I'll email a final list and confirm a few days before."

"Uh, the party is Monday…" My chest tightened. "I hope I didn't wait too long." Would my small request get lost in the shuffle? She had bigger parties looming.

"Right, right." She frowned, as if slightly distracted. "I'll get the final details to you tomorrow. I'll bring the trays around myself, just before your closing time when guests should start arriving."

We left her office together, and after closing the door behind us, she hurried off through the back of the dining room and into the kitchen.

On the way back to Square Spirits I ran into Megan and Clayton on their way to the Inn.

As usual, they looked happy. I envied them their perpetual aura of contentment.

"I was just thinking about you earlier this morning," I said, directing my attention to Clayton. "Can I talk to you a minute?"

"Why sure, Zoe. What's up?"

"I'd like to give my parents one of your paintings for Christmas. You know, something special."

He winked at Megan and then in that smooth, crisp voice of his said, "Aren't all my paintings special?"

Megan laughed and playfully slapped his arm.

The air around them vibrated from the joy they were finding in their new love.

"Oh, of course. I wasn't implying they weren't," I said dryly. "I just meant I want something unique, particularly suited to them."

"You're off the hook," Clayton said, grinning. "Stop by tomorrow. I can think of two or three that might be a good fit."

"Great, thanks." I waved and went on my way and let myself into my shop.

But when I got inside… Oh, boy. What a mess. A colossal mess.

Two upset spirits had done this, I was certain of it. Papers were scattered about the checkout counter; a wine bottle lay shattered on the floor in a pool of red liquid. Books had been toppled off the shelves and baskets of cards were overturned. Most surprising of all were the candle jars. Every one of them had been turned upside down.

"All right, ladies," I said, my voice rising with each word, "what's this all about?"

I needn't have asked. The answer appeared immediately, but it still left me shaken.

Strong currents swirled around the room ruffling my notes for the open house. I held the paper in my hand.

"The party?"

Hot air whipped close, again moving my papers.

"The guests?"

I'd crossed into new territory. For most of my life I'd known that spirits live among us and many can be contacted, called in. But I'd never been in close proximity to spirits who regularly made their presence known. I'd relied on trial and error to learn to communicate effectively with these girls. I thought I'd succeeded, especially in earning their trust. But now, with the evidence that the two could be destructive, I needed to immediately understand what they were trying to tell me.

"Okay, girls, the guests I invited to my party are people who work on the Square. Many live here. They're our *friends*. You know who they are. You've seen most of them in the shop already."

Cool and warm currents set the air spinning in mini-tornados.

"Okay, there's something more?"

The tornadoes continued.

"Is it because you don't know them or you think someone is going to hurt me?"

The flurry calmed a bit, the spinning air transformed into soft swirls. It seemed my position relative to the others on the Square had begun to calm them. They didn't believe any of my new friends and colleagues meant me or them harm.

"You were okay with Julia being here overnight. The

party will last a few hours and then everyone will go home. I'll be here by myself again—with you."

Suddenly, the tornado wind started again, first whirling around me, but soon moving away. Out of the corner of my eye, I saw books traveling in the air from the floor back to the shelves and arranged in an orderly row. I laughed out loud, knowing very well that I'd need to go behind them and regroup the books by subject matter and then alphabetically by the author's last name. These spirits were good, but not that good. They were able to flip the candles over one by one. The papers were once again stacked in a pile on my counter.

"Well, thanks," I said. "You're good at cleaning up after yourselves. So what about the wine bottle and the spilled wine?"

Tiny air currents swirled around me, but the glass remained. "Oh, okay, I'll do it."

Within minutes, I'd wiped up the wine and swept the glass away. Everything was once again in order. I shook my head, more amused than upset by this episode. True, they had chosen a drastic way to grab my attention. And it worked. But at the same time, I wondered what would come next? And what if someone at my solstice party triggered the girls' fears?

"I need a cup of tea," I said aloud. "I trust that meets with your approval?"

Warm and cool air currents caressed my cheeks as I climbed the stairs. I had so much on my mind, but I also had a strong feeling my tea break was going to be my last moment of quiet before the weekend.

***

On Monday morning I was prepared to turn my attention to the party that evening, but I was diverted by a hectic shopping day. Fortunately, I'd done most of the work. The shop sparkled with the white lights I'd arranged around the displays for the rest of the holidays. Later, I'd added more white luminaries in the darker corners the shop. The food would arrive just after closing, and I had the white wine chilling in the fridge upstairs.

When it was almost closing time, I dismantled a display rack to clear some space, and then arranged a few chairs near the table in the front window and at the table in the back. I hoped some of the guests would stay long enough to sit and chat. My excitement had grown as the late afternoon passed.

Disappointment lingered, too, though, and I found it impossible to shake it off. For days I'd been waiting for Eli to RSVP, but he hadn't sent a note or email, and he hadn't called. Nothing. He was the only invited guest who had not responded. Had the girls been trying to tell me something else? Maybe they were afraid my feelings would be hurt.

But why? Eli's gesture, coming closer to me at my door the other night, was only one small moment in time. Nothing more. But that's what I found difficult to accept. Was his warmth toward me only a glass or two of wine talking? Was that possible? Not knowing the truth, I was obviously trying to turn the moment into something more meaningful than it had been.

Determined not to let anything interfere with the fun of what I hoped would be my first *annual* Square Spirits winter solstice open house, I suppressed my lingering sadness as closing time approached. Then, right on time, Melanie and one of her associates carried in the party trays.

We put the largest circular platter on the front table and the smaller trays on the glass display counters. Melanie said she'd be back, but could only stay a short time. I was glad she could come at all, given how busy Crossroads always was. The bell jingled its happy sound when she left.

I dashed upstairs to reassure Grace and Rose that everything would be fine tonight. I needed to forget about Eli, while admitting to myself that one reason I'd wanted him to come was to be with others who recognized and appreciated the essence of the shop, and therefore, saw my essence, too.

As I changed into fresh clothes for the party, I repeated to myself what I knew to be true. Eli had to take care of his own emotions and inner conflicts. I couldn't—*wouldn't*—take them on. Hadn't I declared my life my own? Wasn't independence my deepest desire? I'd made the mistake of pampering Tyler, indulging him and making it my job to take care of him and supply whatever his happiness required. Two years ago, I'd vowed not to ever be in that position again. *If* I considered sharing my life with another man, and that was a big *if*, I'd do it only as equals.

Before going back downstairs I gave my clothes a final check in the full-length mirror on the back of the bedroom door. I'd chosen an all-white look, from my white silk blouse and wool slacks to the crystal necklace, bracelet, and earrings. I even wore white leather flats and cinched the blouse with a white woven belt. I'd fixed my hair in a French braid, with a small white band to secure it.

"Okay, girls. I'll say goodbye for now. I trust you to behave and remember that only the people I've invited to be our guests will be coming in and out."

With that, I closed my eyes and enjoyed the feeling of wellbeing that went along with the gentle swirling of cool and warm air.

Rachel and a young man I assumed was Art's son, Alan, arrived as soon as I was downstairs. I'd met Rachel, who looked festive in a bright red cape and white gloves. I quickly introduced myself to Alan, then led them toward the makeshift coat room I'd set up in my reading room.

"Let me know if you need any help," Alan said, his voice cheerful. "I can carry the coats back here and leave you free to be with your guests, Z."

"You will forever be known as 'Z'," Rachel explained. "Alan calls everyone by their initials."

"So I've heard," I teased. "Marianna told me a little about you two. She's very proud of you both."

Alan's cheeks turned pink, which brought a giggle from Rachel.

"Beautiful pin," I said, recognizing the sapphire stones in the eyes of the teddy bear pin that Rachel wore. "Great workmanship."

"Alan made it for me for my eighteenth birthday. The "T"

107

is for my son, Thomas."

The bell jingled again. "Looks like your party is underway, Z," Alan said.

Reed, Nolan, and another man came in. Based on resemblance, it seemed a third Crawford man had joined the party. With three more coats in my arms, Nolan followed me to my reading room and grabbed hangers to help.

"I'm glad you could come," I said.

"I hope it won't matter that Reed and I brought Charlie along. He's our cousin."

"The more the merrier," I said, keeping remarks about their resemblance to myself. They probably tired of hearing them. "I'd like to meet him."

"Looks like you'll have a crowd. We saw lots of people from the Square locking their shops and heading this way."

Everyone but Eli.

"Invite and they will come," I quipped.

"So, put me to work," Nolan said. "How can I help?"

I thought a minute to how best use his offer. I wasn't happy about it but reality intervened so I asked Nolan to help with the job I thought would be Eli's. "If you don't mind, will you uncork a couple bottles of wine and pour a few glasses. Then enjoy yourself."

I made a mental note to mention to others that Nolan had painted the sunburst on the ceiling. Customers had commented on it, along with the whole look of the shop.

By the time Nolan and I returned to the front of the shop, the people of the Square had arrived and were in full party mode. The Irish melody I'd put on filtered through the shop and blended with the laughter and snippets of conversation that filled the room. I stood back, taking a minute to enjoy watching Nolan pour wine and Alan and Rachel pointing out the food platters to new people coming in.

"Great idea, Zoe. Thanks for the invite," Elliot said, approaching with Georgia. He casually put his arm around Georgia's shoulders, as I'd seen him do at the farmhouse. I wondered if he knew how sweet that gesture looked to the rest of us.

"Eat, drink, and enjoy the solstice," I said, laughing.

I spotted Doris, Sarah, and Sadie coming in the door, apparently sharing a laugh over something funny that had occurred that day. I was too late to follow the conversation, but their laughter added to the lively mood.

I turned to see Nolan uncorking more wine bottles and filling glasses. He'd found the sparkling water I had in a cooler and looked completely at ease. Yet Eli slipped back into my mind. I quickly shook my head as if the action itself could break up a line of thought that led to Eli. It alarmed me to realize I was at risk of sinking into the muck of disappointment.

Doris touched my hand, distracting me. "This is a beautiful shop, Zoe. Everything is so bright and shiny. And the fairy lights for the holidays are a lovely touch."

Then Doris wrapped her fingers around my arm.

Why? To steady herself? I didn't know, but I got a flash of an image. A hollow form that looked like her.

A whistle pierced the air, pulling me away from that wispy image of Doris' energy. The room quieted, and Clayton raised his glass.

"Let's have a toast," Clayton said. "To Zoe. The newest owner on the Square and our hostess for this evening."

"To Zoe," rippled around the room.

Clayton bent forward in a subtle bow. "Tell us what made you pick the winter solstice for a party."

I cleared my throat and, while holding my glass in both hands, I said, "I suppose I like to observe holidays linked with nature. And tomorrow, we start another countdown to June and the longest day of the year."

"Not that we'll notice," Georgia said, "since we'll get a few seconds more daylight tomorrow."

"It's a start," I said, "and absent natural light, we bring in more in the form of lights that decorate the Square. It's not called the season of light by accident."

I lifted my glass. "There's plenty of food and sparkling water and wine. And thanks so much for making me feel welcome on the Square."

When I finished, the chatter resumed and the laughter began again.

After an hour or so, the youngest people of the group, Nathan and Lily and Alan and Rachel, were the first to approach and tell me it was time to leave. They had kids to pick up at Sally Johnson's day care.

"Doris tells me you first suggested pairing toys and books in her shop," I said to Lily as she put on her coat.

"I have to give credit to Toby for that idea. He was playing with a toy while he had the book in his lap."

"Well, in any case, it's great marketing. Like Marianna and her special drawings."

More departures soon followed, including Marianna and Art. But before they left, Art reached into his coat pocket and pulled out one of his signature blue boxes.

"Here's a little gift to welcome you to the Square," he said, "but wait until your guests are gone to open it."

"Oh, my. I don't know what to say."

"No words are needed," Marianna said, smiling fondly at Art.

As they walked away, I slipped the box into my pocket where I kept my amethyst stone. I could almost feel the energy coming from the box. But I couldn't stop to open it. I still had guests getting ready to leave.

As I said goodbye to the people leaving, Nolan carried trash out the back door and packaged the used wine glasses to be returned to the Inn while Reed stacked empty trays next to the glasses.

"Thank you, guys," I said. "I couldn't have done it without your help."

Nolan grinned. "Hey, no thanks needed. Glad to have been invited."

I nodded to Charlie Crawford, happy to have had the chance to meet him. I'd already heard about his company— C4—over morning coffee at B and B. He'd built an incredible reputation with his remodeling and renovation projects for several owners on the Square.

"So, Charlie, I have you to thank for sending Reed and Nolan my way. They can work for me anytime."

"They're talented young guys, all right," Charlie said, his voice casual. "The Square is growing quickly, so we stay busy keeping up."

"I guess I've officially crashed your party," Melanie said, joining my conversation with Charlie. "But I have to get back to work. I'll send someone over in the morning to get the glasses and trays."

"I'll walk out with you, Mel," Charlie said.

Along with Nolan and Reed, Mel and Charlie left and with the Square nearly empty, I stood outside my front door to watch as upstairs lights came on in a few buildings on the Square. My guests had arrived home. A wave of fatigue crested, and even though I'd planned to put the shop back in order before going upstairs, I changed my mind. Rather than heading to B and B for coffee in the morning, I'd use the time to tidy up the place.

Unable to wait another minute, I locked my door and went upstairs. I sat by the front window and opened the blue box. What I saw made me gasp. Art had fashioned a pin that would serve as my version of a smock or an apron. He'd taken a flat piece of metal and hammered stars and crescent moons in a random pattern as a background. He'd forged one S next to another S to represent Square Spirits. And in keeping with the name, he'd added a small silver wine bottle with DmZ stamped on it. Next to it, Art had hung a small amethyst stone dangling in a wire cage. My energy soared, and my heart hummed a melody. Art, a gifted jewelry artist, had captured the essence of my shop in the pin.

A small note in the box explained that I could wear it as a pin or I could attach a chain to the clasp and create a necklace.

Art had no idea what the gift, not only the beauty of it, but the gesture itself, meant to me. He had affirmed my deepest hope that I'd found my home.

With my eyes watering, I held the pin to my heart and breathed in deeply. As I looked out the window, it was inevitable that I noticed that the windows above Country Law were dark.

Oh, Eli. You should have been here.

10

After a restless night, I dressed quickly and went downstairs to have my coffee and straighten up. I hurried to immerse myself in Square Spirits business because it was the best way to keep my spirits high. I focused on my successful open house and the rush of holiday sales. Directing my attention to what mattered at that moment would prevent me from backsliding into my vague concerns about Eli.

With Christmas only two days away, shoppers were already milling about the Square, and it was still an hour to official opening time. Small groups huddled together, their gloved hands wrapped around to-go cups from B and B. I smiled, thinking how busy Steph would be trying to keep up with the breakfast and lunch crowd and the constant demand for hot coffee and tea.

By the time I unlocked the front door, any evidence of the previous night's open house was gone, and I stepped outside to invite shoppers inside. Katie from The Fiber Barn waved and laughed. She, too, was outside gesturing to the shoppers to come in.

That morning, books, calendars, scarves, and wine were attracting the most attention. Last minute gifts. At one point, a young woman approached me carrying one of my new shopping baskets. "I've hired Megan Reynolds from Rainbow Gardens to be my wedding planner," she said. "We've been talking about jewelry. I told her how much I like your pendants and earrings."

"Thanks. Seems that most women like to wear gemstone pieces."

"Exactly. That's why I want my bridesmaids and miniature bride to wear matching sets."

I nodded to the basket. "Let's see what you've picked out."

She lifted a pendant of cut crystals on a fine silver chain from the basket, with crystal point earrings. Both pieces were among my favorites.

"Wonderful choice! How many sets do you need?"

"Three more for the attendants and one necklace for the little girl."

Another woman sidled up to the customer. "Did I hear you say Megan is your wedding planner? I thought she just handled flowers."

She'd effectively inserted herself into the conversation, because my customer was only too happy to talk about Megan. She explained that the wedding planning end of her business had started with Georgia's wedding. "A friend of mine and I happened to be on the Square the day of the wedding. The groom was Megan's brother. Everyone was invited to join the festivities. It was quite the party. That's what made me decide to talk to her about my wedding."

"I have to talk to her right now," the curious customer said. She nodded to me. "I'll be back later."

The first customer laughed. "Isn't this exciting? The Square is becoming the one-stop destination for brides."

I hadn't heard that before, but I made a note to talk to Megan right away. Somehow, my jewelry had become notable enough that she'd mentioned it to one of her clients. Excitement bubbled up. If it happened once, it could happen again. I jumped ahead with my imagination to putting together gifts for wedding shower guests and the wedding party. I could offer something appropriate for many wedding-related events. I took in a breath to refocus and led the woman to the display of hanging pendants and earrings.

I left the customer to browse and hurried away to the register where a woman stood with a fairly full basket of items. I'd taken to calling those collections as "a little of this and a little of that." It sounded better than calling it a hodgepodge of things.

When I returned to the customer-bride, she had found a crystal earring design she liked better and I had three necklaces in stock that matched. The choice for the ten-year-old had slightly smaller stones.

I happily gift-boxed each piece, along with a circular amethyst pin she'd picked out as a Christmas gift for her mother. I put all the little boxes in one of my signature bags. And as a gift for the buyer, I put in a selection of four polished stones in an organza bag. I was excited to see her face light up. Everyone left with a complimentary gift, whether it was a tiny crystal or a candle, but for a large sale, I'd taken to packaging stones.

The morning passed quickly and led into a lull around noon when apparently, some shoppers were done and left the Square, while others headed to Crossroads or B and B for lunch.

I decided it was a perfect time to call Mom to see if she needed me to pick up anything on my way to her house on Christmas Eve. I would close when most other shops on the Square would, around 3:00. "I'll bring the empty wine crates back," I said.

"Isn't it *exciting* that the wine is selling?"

I laughed. "Melanie adding it to the wine list at Crossroads has led to a big jump in sales. Just wait until January when it's the featured label."

"I know. It's wonderful." She paused. "Zoe? Is everything okay?"

I might have known Mom would ask. She always knew when my emotions were unsettled. I was excited about my earlier wedding jewelry sale and I'd wrapped up so many "some of this and some of that" collections of items. But it made no sense to even try to hide my unsettled feelings rippling beneath the fun of the day. Mom had well-developed intuition. She often joked she'd kept all of us safe for years because of it. I told her about the sales, but didn't mention Eli's absence from the party.

"By the way, how's Dad?" Did I think Mom wouldn't notice I was evading her question? No, but I hoped my tactics would buy me some time.

"We'll talk when you get here," she said.

It worked. Just then, the bell in the shop jingled as a fairly large group entered.

"I heard that sound," Mom said. "You take care of business—and travel safe."

With that, I turned my attention to a group of six, who were beginning their quest for perfect gifts. More harried than the typical customer, they ended up gathering up lots of candles, and, I noted, they didn't blink at the price of glass paperweights. Shaped like angels, snowflakes, or stars, they were one-of-a-kind pieces produced by a Wisconsin company. That added to their appeal.

I moved from that group to assembling two gift boxes for a woman buying items for her twin granddaughters. She'd picked out journals, books, paperweights, calendars, note cards, and a small luminary for each box. "Pens?" she asked.

"Sorry, I don't carry them." But I wouldn't let that happen again. It didn't make sense to carry note cards and journals, but not also have a special selection of pens to purchase—I could pair them as a two-for-one special sale.

She waved her hand dismissing my apology and settled on a bracelet for each girl. "I only found out yesterday that they were coming for a visit, and even when they were little girls, they loved to get a box filled with a lot of different items."

"They'll have great fun with these," I said, finishing the gift wrapping of the second box. I handed her two small cards in miniature envelopes. "And here are two gift cards you can fill out later."

A bag in each hand, and her complimentary bag of stones, she grinned as she walked through the front door I held open. The little bell never failed to jingle. It was the last I'd hear it that day, though, as I turned the lock and let out a sigh of satisfaction over a successful day.

The minute I was alone, Eli popped into my mind. Where would he spend Christmas? And was he looking forward to it? Or maybe he was like me and harbored a jumble of mixed feelings about his family gathering. At B and B one morning, I'd heard Georgia describe her decorations at the farmhouse. She was so excited about her first Christmas with Elliot. Megan had shared with me that she and Clayton were headed to New York to be with his artist friends for Christmas Day. Where did that leave Eli? I wished I hadn't asked the question.

I replenished my stock for what I'd been led to believe would be moderate sales on Christmas Eve day. But Friday and Saturday would bring shoppers looking for post-holiday sales and end-of-the-year bargains. And there were the inevitable returns and exchanges.

The busy day had energized me, but once upstairs, I became preoccupied with anticipating Mom's questions about my internal state. I also didn't like where my intuition was leading me when it came to Dad's health. Most of all, I hoped we could get through a family dinner without fireworks between Devin and me.

Perhaps by now I could say I'd successfully waited out or worked around Devin's complaints about leaving the winery and striking out on my own. But I knew in my heart that as cordial as he'd been to the people on the Square, he held fast to his belief that I'd abandoned the family—and especially DmZ—when they needed me the most. I didn't want to spoil the holiday with a repeat of an old battle. The iciness between us wasn't good for Dad, and that alone made it hard for Mom.

When I unlocked the shop door the next morning, I was trying to make the anxious butterflies in my gut quiet down. My trip to see my parents was still several hours away, but I was already nervous about it. Shoppers came in bursts, just as Megan and Marianna and others had said they would. I ended up taking small breaks when others on the Square came in to wish me well over the holiday. Sarah and Sadie made those rounds together, and their friendly mood alone kept me from dwelling on my problems for long.

Problems? Why would I use that word? Mine were so small it was almost laughable to call them problems. My dad wasn't a problem, he was a concern. Devin wasn't a problem, not on a day-to-day basis. My parents accepted my decision to pursue my dream, and if Devin resented me for it, then whose problem was it? Not mine. But those realities didn't stop my mixed feelings about our supposed quiet family dinner.

"We'll have to get a start on your building research, huh?" Sadie said, fingering a bracelet and adding it to the three on her arm. When Sarah and I both nodded in approval, she said, "I believe I'll wear this home."

"No reason not to," I said, grinning as I reached out and pulled off the adhesive price tag. "You're all set."

While Sadie paid for the bracelet, Sarah checked out the bowls of polished stones. "You know, I've already written a section for my book about this building," she said. "Would you like to read it?"

"Are you *kidding*?" I said. "Absolutely. Your work can probably lead me to all kinds of information—and shortcuts in my research."

"Are you going to your folks for Christmas?" she asked.

"I'm leaving right after I close up, but I'll be back late tomorrow."

"Okay, then, I'll drop it off on Friday." Sarah turned to Sadie. "You'll help me remember. Right?"

Sadie nodded, as if given a solemn responsibility. "I will. I want that book ready to sell next summer when we reopen the museum."

With that, we exchanged hugs and they were on their way out, just as a couple of people came in. Once again, the bell made its happy sound. But I looked down the Square, harboring thoughts of Eli, again asking: Where would he be tomorrow?

The rest of the day flew by, and with barely a break to breathe. I wedged Clayton's wrapped painting on the passenger's seat, securing it with my purse. The trunk and back seat were filled with wine crates and my overnight bag was balanced on top of the pile. As I drove out of town, I found my mood had become at least a little lighter.

Long ago, I'd noted that gratitude weighs far less than regret and grief. I would never forget that as an adult with a broken heart, I'd gone "home" to heal. I'd never, *ever* imagined making such a drive. But with my will to recover intact, I slowly, over time and with emotional support from Mom and Dad, found my center again. And from the day I made an offer on my building on the Square, I knew I'd keep that center and grow from it.

As I drove down the highway, I let my mind drift to the past and the years of coping with a sour atmosphere between Tyler and my folks. Devin didn't think much of Tyler either, so every Christmas was a chore. One year, I'd booked a trip to the Virgin Islands over Christmas, using Tyler's need to get away as an excuse to skip the whole thing. The end of my marriage had brought the end of that tension, though, or so I thought. It seemed all I'd done was exchange one conflict with another. Tyler was gone, but Devin remained. Yet, despite that, I was looking forward to spending time with Mom and Dad.

Light flurries started when I merged from Highway 29 East onto Highway 41 South on the north end of Green Bay. In half an hour I'd be back in my parents' familiar home. I hummed along with the Christmas songs on the radio.

Even as I drove toward my family, I also looked forward to making the drive back to the tight-knit community that had taken me in as one of their own and supported my shop. No wonder I traveled with a lighter heart. I couldn't have even hoped that my sense of belonging would solidify so quickly. It somehow made my family problems less important.

And how would I repay my new community of friends? I hadn't figured that out yet.

By the time I parked the car in the driveway of my parents' house, the flurries had gathered into large fluffy snowflake balls that the windshield wipers pushed away but let pile up to create a snow frame over the glass.

I grabbed the painting and my bags and walked to the back door, the entrance most everyone used, family and friends alike. When I had returned to this house, I'd always known it wasn't *my* true home anymore. On the other hand, Devin had returned to the family home after Hannah's death and immediately found solace by devoting his free time to the workings of the winery. The years since Hannah's death had passed quickly, and Devin had stayed on. The winery, and working in partnership with Mom and Dad was Devin's way to find *his* home.

I walked into the kitchen filled with mixed aromas of gingersnap cookies and yeasty dinner rolls. Mom wiped her hands on her apron, greeting me with a hug. "Were the roads bad?"

"Wet, but not slippery." I set my bag on the floor and stood the picture next to the stool by the door. I hung my coat on the empty hook that had always been mine. "How's Dad?"

"Resting. The new medicine makes him sleepy."

I snatched a cookie from the cooling rack. "Maybe rest is what he needs most now."

She slipped another pan into the oven, and then with her forehead wrinkled in thought, she asked me to take a tray of sandwiches out of the fridge. "I think that's all for now. We'll eat when Devin gets home."

My stomach churned. "Let me ask you this straight out. Has he changed his attitude toward my moving?"

"I'm afraid not."

"So, I guess I can expect his little barbs all evening," I said, my tone not exactly matching the season of good will. What had happened to my brighter mood?

Mom nodded as she poured a cup of tea for each of us and motioned for me to take a seat at the table.

My body stiffened in reaction to the strong energy vibrating in the air. Something major was off.

"Devin has resigned from the bank," Mom said. "He's fulltime with the winery now. I know he felt obligated to give up the bank, but that isn't the problem. He wasn't happy there. It's that your dad is no longer well enough to do the physical work, and Devin had to act quickly. I want to spend as much time with Russ as…as we have." She brushed her face with her hand and took a sip of her tea. "But the winery is my life, too. No matter what happens with…with your dad, I want to keep it going and build on what we've created together."

Without fanfare of details, the reality of Dad's congestive

heart failure had been placed in my lap. But I could see the emotional complexity of the situation way beyond Dad's health. The winery had been of much greater interest to Devin than the bank job he'd had for years. Hannah was devoted to the winery, too, and before she got sick, she and Devin both worked what amounted to second jobs there. Hannah's death had affected the family business every bit as much as Dad's failing health was now. Regardless of how boring Devin had found the job at the bank, it had become comfortable, like an old shoe, and going fulltime at the winery meant acknowledging how profoundly life was changing for our family. It also, in some subtle way, meant he'd be taking on the wine-making business without Hannah. That wasn't the way they'd planned it. I wasn't surprised that part of his transition felt wrong.

Before I had a chance to fully sort through all the feelings spinning inside me, the back door opened and Devin came into the kitchen. He nodded to acknowledge my presence. No greeting, of course. That would have involved using words.

Just like Eli. No wonder they were comfortable side by side at the business association meeting. But those two quiet men had found plenty to talk about.

As Devin closed the door behind him, Dad came in and squeezed my shoulder. "Glad you're home safe."

"It was an easy drive." I stood and gave him a hug. When he'd sat in the rocker in the corner of the kitchen, I arranged the afghan over his legs. I pulled the footstool closer and sat next to him, where I could take hold of his hand. It was so cold I held it between my two palms.

"It's getting slippery now," Devin said, taking the cup of coffee Mom offered him, but slapping his hand when he tried to reach around her and snatch a cookie off the rack.

"Everyone wants dessert first tonight," she teased. She reached for one of her holiday cookie tins, layering the treats in with parchment paper.

An image of helping Mom make cut-out cookies surfaced. I was so young I could hardly reach the table top, but I recalled her lifting me onto a chair where I could "help."

Devin was able to kneel on a chair and do his part to create the messes. Mom never scolded us about the flour dust that turned her kitchen white.

As he got older, Devin lost interest, but I never did. I always wanted to bake with Mom, eating my own creations. Mom and Dad ate whatever I baked. Only Devin wasn't shy about groaning and making obnoxious boy noises to let me know the ones I'd made were the worst cookies he'd ever eaten in his life, and not only that, even the birds in the yard wouldn't eat the crumbs we tossed out.

I shook off the mix of sweet and sour memories and forced my attention back to Mom. "As long as it's just the four of us, let's go ahead and eat in the kitchen," she said. "It's nice and warm in here. Then we can do our gifts later."

I nodded, but the vibrations were still present. Something was wrong.

I rose from my spot next to Dad and got busy putting placemats out and then set the table.

Mom brought out the potato salad and the vegetable and fruit platter to go with the sandwiches. The Miller traditional Christmas Eve dinner.

Devin pulled out a bottle of DmZ wine and opened it. "It's our newest," he said, "semi-sweet and a little spicy, too."

The light red color added a holiday touch to our dinner.

As usual, Dad said grace, always a message of gratitude for family and a hope for peace. I felt a little lighter after hearing Dad's voice. We ticked off one more holiday tradition when Mom read letters from her side of the family, mostly my aunts who'd moved with their families to Colorado.

"It's been an incredible time on the Square," I said, going on to describe the crowds, making Dad laugh at my descriptions of people carrying heavy shopping bags all over the Square. "And my open house was a success. After the shops were closed, I had the party, and then by early the next morning, everything was back to normal. The place was cleaned up and ready to open."

My light banter took us right up to dessert. I refilled all

our wine glasses, while Mom arranged the tray of frosted cookies, all cut in the shape of a wine bottle. Devin was quiet, not unusual, but the air vibrated, and not in a good way. This wasn't happiness or excitement. It was pure resentment. And it was directed at me, no matter how hard he tried to hide it.

We munched cookies and I kept up about the light patter about the Square, and eventually, even the heavy energy around Devin lightened up.

Devin might resent me, but he loved our dad. He took over settling him in a corner of the couch closest to the fireplace in the living room. I was saddened to see Dad succumb to Devin's attempts to make him comfortable. It seemed Dad had lost ground since the association meeting. It was still early in the evening, yet he looked worn out. I caught Mom's eye, and instantly saw that she'd easily read my expression.

I picked up the painting and got my gift for Devin out of my bag before joining them in the living room. The short evergreen tree in the corner took me by surprise, although it shouldn't have. In all the years I'd lived in this house, as a child or a woman, we'd had trees glowing with strings of multi-colored fairy lights that created a glow around the tree. I recognized many of the ornaments Devin and I had made in school over the years. On first look, the tree appeared too heavy, overdone, each branch almost burdened with ornaments. But when I looked closer, I saw the tree was, as always, the history of a family. My family.

As a CD of Christmas carols played, I was happy to see that Dad looked comfortable on the couch next to Mom, but there was still something off about Devin, who claimed the recliner. As near as I could tell, he wasn't actually in the room with us. Maybe a fresh wave of pain from losing Hannah had come over him. I closed my eyes and acknowledged my gratitude that thoughts of Tyler no longer made me sad. At least that energy wasn't being added to this mix of emotions permeating the house.

I added a couple of logs to the fire and hoped for the best.

Then I sat on the floor near the tree and claimed the

privilege of passing out the first gifts. "I'm excited about this one," I said, handing the painting to Mom and Dad. "I picked it out—and believe me there were plenty of choices."

Mom grinned as she pulled off the paper, exposing the picture. "Wow…"

"Double wow," Dad said, taking hold of one side while Mom held up the other.

I'd chosen one of Clayton's still lifes, grapes in a ceramic bowl with part of the vine on a table.

"Clayton Sommers is the resident painter on the Square," I explained. "That particular piece was done with a new watercolor technique he developed."

"So," Dad said, "we can say we own a Clayton Sommers original."

"Absolutely." I handed a package to Devin.

He righted the chair and hesitantly unwrapped the box. "Art&Son Jewelry. Isn't that one of the shops?"

I nodded. "One of the best. Art is the resident jewelry artist on the Square—and his son is coming right along with him." He opened the box, and then quickly closed it. "Thanks."

I'd asked Art to make a stick pin for Devin's ties using garnet stones crafted with silver wire to look like a wine bottle. I'd used my hands to describe my idea and Art understood what I wanted. Of course, I'd had no way of knowing that Devin would no longer be wearing ties every day to the bank. Instead, he'd be wearing jeans and T-shirts at the winery.

Embarrassed, I babbled something about the gorgeous pin Art had made for me that would serve as a name-tag of sorts. But I soon ran out of words and retreated deep into myself and avoided Devin's eyes. Mom quickly opened an envelope addressed to her and Dad from Devin. It was a new fermenter that Devin had bought primarily because he'd been telling them that to remain competitive, they needed to up production, produce more volume.

Their gift to me was a long belted sweater coat in deep purple wool. It wasn't quite warm enough for our cold winters, but it would be perfect for spring and fall. I smoothed my fingers across the soft wool. "It's perfect," I said with a happy sigh.

"Perfect for a woman as tall as you," Mom said with a laugh.

That lighter moment was extended when Devin disappeared into the garage and a few minutes later, carried in a new high-definition television with all the bells and whistles.

"I love it," Mom said, smiling at Dad.

"It's a whole lot more TV than we need," Dad, always practical, pointed out. But that didn't keep him from smiling broadly.

"I knew that's what you'd say," Devin said dryly, deigning to glance my way.

"So, for once in your life, you can have more than you need," I said, intentionally matching Devin's tone. "Get used to it."

They suddenly grinned, even Devin.

"We've been keeping a secret," Dad said, pointing with his chin to a box under the tree. "It's time, Devin. Pull it out."

"Have at it," Devin said, handing the box to me. Then, as if he'd left the room, he picked up the instruction booklet for the TV and began to study it intensely.

Ignore him, enjoy the moment...the return of his bad attitude isn't about you.

Hmm...a wooden box, the kind that held wine. I lifted the lid and immediately understood why a bottle of wine was nestled in the box. The label read: *Zodiac*. I laughed out loud. It was *mine*.

Devin already had a few varieties of wine named after him, but this was my first.

I found only simple words. "Thank you...thank you so much."

"We wanted to make it unique to you, honey." Dad said. "Thanks to Devin's help, I think we got it right."

"I don't know what to say." I directed my comment to Devin in hopes of getting his attention, but he kept his head buried in the TV installation instructions. I wanted to make my feelings known. "Thanks for your part in this, Devin."

"You don't have to say anything," Mom said, when Devin stayed quiet. "We know what this means. And it was time you got your label, just like the rest of us." Mom knew well that I needed to hear that even though I was gone, I still belonged.

I rubbed my fingertips across the label again and again.

"We'll serve it with dinner tomorrow," Mom said.

"And we have a box ready for you to take home with you," Dad added.

"*This* is her home." Devin stalked out of the room. We all heard his door close. Slam was more like it.

I flinched, the energy in the air painful.

"Don't worry, Zoe. He'll adjust," Mom said, kneading her temples, as if warding off a headache. "I think he's concerned about leaving the bank and being responsible for the winery. But he's a natural winemaker. He'll do fine."

I bit my tongue to keep from lashing out about his rude behavior. As wrong as it might be for her to keep trying to soothe feelings, she was acting from habit. She only wanted to ease the tension. Sadly, she'd taken on the "mom-in-the-middle" role far too often, somehow thinking it was her job to take care of everyone's feelings. But at least the real issue behind all the tension was out in the open.

***

Knowing I wouldn't fall asleep easily, I stayed up to enjoy the peaceful glow of the fire and the tree lights. I couldn't completely ward off the little twinges of guilt that intruded on my otherwise peaceful mood. Had I impulsively bought the building in Wolf Creek without considering how leaving the winery would affect my family as a whole? Not really. Only Devin hadn't accepted that the winery was never going to be a major part of my future.

"Penny for your thoughts?"

Preoccupied, I'd not heard Mom come to the doorway of the living room. She stepped in to twirl around in what I recognized as a new bright red robe and fuzzy matching slippers. "From Julia," she said.

"Beautiful," I said. "She was such a big help in the shop on Thanksgiving weekend. Couldn't have managed without her."

"As soon as she got home, we figured out how she could work for us fulltime."

"I suggested she call," I said, "but at that time, I didn't know Devin had plans to leave the bank."

Mom shrugged. "They kept increasing the workload, but not the compensation. And he was putting in long hours at DmZ. It finally became apparent he couldn't do both."

I nodded to indicate I understood. I was happy to see him leave the bank, a bad fit from the start.

"I need to be at the wine shop, and Julia can divide her time between production and sales. But we'll also pay her to help us here at home. I don't want to call it glorified housekeeping, but that's what it is."

"Well, that's a big step, but she's perfect for all those jobs."

"It seemed to come out of long discussions about bringing her into the business, at least to an extent," Mom said, sitting on the footstool in front of my chair.

"So, what does Devin think about that idea."

"I can't say I know one way or the other." She shrugged. "You know Devin. He's been clear that he and I can't keep the winery going by ourselves."

What was left unspoken, I suppose, was the reality that Dad wouldn't ever be back at the winery fulltime.

"Then maybe you can make the arrangement work." I looked away and stared into the fire. But I didn't fool Mom.

"What is it?" she asked. "What are you *not* saying?"

I chewed over my information, unsure how to proceed. But I thought it best to broach the subject. "Uh, when Julia was in Wolf Creek with me, she asked if I thought Devin was ready for a new relationship."

Mom frowned. "Nothing like that came up when we talked."

I rolled my eyes. "No surprise there. She certainly wasn't going to ask you about Devin's love life."

"Fair enough," Mom said with a shrug. "But my, oh, my. And what did you tell her?"

"Oh, I took the easy way and told her to ask him." I laughed, but then I couldn't resist teasing her. "You really did miss that vibration coming from Julia?"

I could also see the wheels turning in her head, wondering how she could have missed sensing Julia's feelings. She had a hard time admitting it, but when it came to Devin and me and our personal lives, she was the proverbial snoop. Antennae always working, trying to pick up subtle hints of something. We'd learned we had to guard our privacy like trained dogs keeping away intruders.

She got to her feet and put another log on the fire. It made me uneasy in a way, because I knew she wasn't ready to end our conversation.

"Still not ready to go to bed?" I asked.

Sure enough, keeping her eyes on the fire, she said, "From the moment you came in the house I could see—and feel— that you're happy, Zoe."

"I am happy. I'm excited about what opening a business and buying the building has brought to my life. I'm finally standing on my own."

Why had I said that? Mom equated happiness with love and marriage. Even though she knew better, she'd never been able to break out of that old mold.

"Are you saying, you'll never want to meet a man again?"

"No, Mom, I'm not saying that, but it's not a goal, something I believe is necessary for my happiness. I really like being independent."

"I know. But…"

"I mean it," I said, keeping my voice low. "I'm wrapped up in Square Spirits. The excitement I feel every day when I turn on the shop lights and open the door. Wow. There's nothing like it."

Mom grinned. I'd won a small victory.

"Okay, message received." She stood, and bent over to give me a hug. Whispering her good night, she left me to my thoughts. But I knew I hadn't heard the last of her gentle probing.

127

I had to laugh at myself. I talked a good game, but I couldn't deny that intrusive thoughts of Eli had become a feature in my life. I couldn't have told Mom that, or she'd make too much of it. Besides, there was no thread to follow. All I knew was that I'd had a strong reaction to Eli. I was certain he'd been hurt, badly hurt, and had suffered losses and experienced lonely times. I saw in him what I saw in me.

Being honest with myself, I admitted the emotions surrounding him were wispy, not connected to anything concrete. I knew nothing of Eli's dreams, joys, fears, or failures.

I sat alone long into the night and watched the fire burn down. Finally, I made my way to the kitchen to turn out the lights in the quiet house. As I climbed the stairs to my old room, thoughts of Eli lingered. Maybe it was time to find out what had caused my reaction to him. Learn more about him, or just quit thinking about Eli altogether.

11

Even with only the four of us, Christmas Day had its rituals and we stuck to them. With all the changes in our lives, it was comforting to fix dinner with Mom, as we'd always done. As usual, though, she prepared most everything ahead of time, which she claimed was easy because we didn't deviate much from the old favorites, starting with both ham and roast chicken. She always left the mashed potatoes for last, to be fixed on Christmas Day. As far back as I can remember, Mom claimed the repetitive motion of peeling potatoes helped her let go of any lingering holiday tension.

No matter how hard we tried to pretend it was just another holiday, Dad seemed pale and tired. My spirits lifted when he went outside to replenish the bird feeders and insisted on helping Devin carry in wood for the stove and the fireplace. But then he sat in his rocker and watched Mom and me as we fixed the meal, occasionally dozing off.

Devin turned his attention to installing the new TV in the other room. Judging from the periodic outbursts, the process was not glitch-free.

"I don't know if I've heard Devin laugh out loud once since I arrived yesterday," I remarked to Mom.

"According to him, there's not much to laugh about lately." Mom sighed, sad but apparently resigned.

"That's not good."

"Leave it alone, Zoe," Dad said.

Given Mom's look of surprise, she hadn't thought Dad could hear us.

"I'm on to you," I joked. "You were only pretending to

be asleep."

Dad grinned to acknowledge my teasing, but had more to say. "I just don't like to hear you talk about Devin, you know, not only behind his back, but like you don't understand him."

I thought I understood Devin very well. "And what am I missing about him, Dad?"

"Well, he doesn't have many men friends around him, not like women do. Devin has always kept his feelings locked up inside. It's one reason it's taking so long for him to get over losing Hannah."

"You're right," I conceded.

"Speaking of friends," Mom said, "from what I could see at that last business association meeting, the Square is filled with women who seem close."

A not so subtle change of subject. Off of Devin, back to me. "I'm getting to know some of those women, but I opened the shop at the start of one of the busiest times on the Square. Not much time to socialize, but I hear people get together more during the slow time in the winter."

That answer seemed to satisfy Mom, and she soon sent me off to set the dining room table, reminding me to use the *good* wine glasses.

She needn't have worried. I wouldn't have forgotten. As a tribute to Mom's grandmother, each time we served a new wine we used her nineteenth century crystal glasses. This Christmas dinner was such an occasion, because we'd taste Zodiac for the first time as a family. Of course, Mom, Dad, and Devin had all tasted it in its early formulations and a wine was considered finished only when all three were satisfied with the result.

Devin made quick work of carrying in the various serving dishes while I lit the candles on the table. We barely acknowledged each other's presence—which was fine—until we had to sit down together.

With our traditional Miller Christmas dinner awaiting, each of us said a few words about what we were grateful for, which was our way to bring Dad's grace to an end. I mentioned being grateful I could sell my family's wine in my very own store. That might have irked Devin, but it was true.

Hearing Dad's voice, a little shaky these days, left me struggling to hold back tears. Out of the corner of my eye, I saw Mom brushing her fingertips across her cheeks. Devin looked downcast, his edginess gone, at least for the moment.

Before we could begin eating, we had one more ritual left. Devin started it when he opened the bottle of Zodiac, a light transparent sparkling wine, a blend of grapes with a hint of strawberries. While not overly sweet, it certainly wasn't the driest of the DmZ label. I liked that mine sparkled.

After Devin filled our glasses, he said, "Okay, Zoe, I'll make the toast. May Zodiac be as successful as every other wine with our DmZ label. Now you get the first sip."

We clinked glasses.

Filled with gratitude for Devin's graciousness, I took my first sip of Zodiac. I held the blush wine in my mouth a few seconds before swallowing it. "Perfection!" I took another sip, a bigger one than the last. "I love it. Thank you so much."

I raised my glass high again and we all touched our glasses for a second toast.

Devin managed a pleasant demeanor throughout dinner, until finally, as if on cue, the four of us fell back in our chairs in an exaggerated show of satisfaction. That had always made us laugh and despite the tensions, we stayed true to the tradition. Only a knock on the back door interrupted our antics.

"Hello—anyone here?"

I immediately recognized Julia's voice and pushed back my chair to greet her, but Mom motioned for me to stay where I was, while she went off to the kitchen. I stole a glance at Devin, but I couldn't read anything in his neutral expression.

"Santa left a bag filled with packages with a note telling me to bring them here," Julia said, coming into the room behind Mom. "And I had instructions to arrive in time for the best part—dessert."

We all laughed because Julia was familiar with Mom's

apple-cranberry pie, always served warm with spiced whipped cream. We had it every year, no deviations, and I never heard anyone turn down a piece.

Mom waved Julia to come closer. "Let's have pie before the presents."

"Fine with me," Julia said, slipping into the chair next to Devin.

Devin passed her the first piece, followed by the bowl of topping cream.

"You have to taste Zodiac, *my* new wine." I went to the china hutch and got another crystal glass and poured what was left in the bottle into it.

With all of us watching, she took a quick taste. "Well, as of today, this is my new favorite." She ran her tongue over her lower lip. "Smooth and light, but full-flavored. Wow."

Julia didn't bother with the technical language of wine making. We laughed at her description, because anyone could understand them.

"That's what we like to hear, Julia," Dad said, grinning.

Julia's arrival had lifted my lingering sadness over Dad's condition. But as much as I'd enjoyed being with my family, I was happily anticipating getting back to Wolf Creek and my own life.

With full stomachs and empty plates, Devin took Dad into the living room for the trial run of the new TV, or as Dad called it, "his new toy."

Mom went into the kitchen and filled containers for me to take home, including a huge wedge of pie. From the living room, the volume coming from the television grew louder and louder before it suddenly went soft. In his deep, strong voice Devin went through a list of instructions for using all the features with the remote.

When Mom came back into the dining room she rolled her eyes and shook her head. "I'm going to need a lesson, too."

"Maybe we can learn together," Julia suggested. "It can't be rocket science. It's only a TV remote and a mere 400 channels."

I laughed along, glad to leave the teaching to Julia. By

the time I came back for another visit, the new TV would be an old hat. Mom and Dad would have no trouble using the remote and he'd tell me about the small black and white TVs of his youth.

Glad I hadn't specified when I needed to be on the road, I decided it was time to leave.

"I'd like to be back in Wolf Creek before dark," I explained when I gathered up my things and set my overnight bag in front of the door. The only really difficult moment came when I gave Dad his goodbye hug. I could tell he sensed how difficult it was for me to pull away when he said, "We'll come to see you soon. We'll have dinner at Crossroads."

"Anytime, Dad. I'm already looking forward to it."

Out in the driveway, I looked through the front window at the scene I was leaving behind. Devin and Dad fiddling with the remote, Julia and Mom watching them from a few feet away. I noted Clayton's painting propped up against the coffee table. The television had become the focal point. I couldn't deny feeling a little let down that Mom hadn't asked for my opinion about a good place to hang their new painting.

Not surprisingly, Devin had made himself scarce when it came time for a farewell hug. He'd managed to be pleasant at dinner, and that would have to be enough.

I chased away rising painful feelings. Although Mom had managed to make the day memorable, the stress of Dad and keeping the winery going were taking a toll. My move hadn't made her life easier, either. She definitely appeared more tired than she had in years past when the holiday was winding down.

I took a final look at the house, and with the aroma of the wood fire lingering in my nostrils, I drove down the circular drive and out to the road. I let my tears gather and fall. Such a mix of emotions. I was eager to get back to Wolf Creek, to my own peaceful place, but guilt tugged at my heart simultaneously.

As I put the miles behind me, I reminded myself that I wasn't like most people. I was different, and in my family only Mom understood. But unlike me, she had not been overwhelmed by unbidden information coming in, stirring up her energy and complicating her life. Within the family, no one, not even Mom, was aware of how Devin's nastiness toward me stung, made worse because I not only saw his unresolved grief, I felt it as well. It was a relief knowing that I could retreat to my private space.

My energy shifted as I drove closer to Wolf Creek. The vitality of the town and the Square strengthened me, a lovely familiar feeling.

Finally there, I parked behind the shop. My arms full, I unlocked the door with my free hand and inhaled the scent of lavender. With my eyes closed, I felt the shifting air currents around my face as the girls welcomed me home. I felt lighter, my mood lifting. Those two girls, with all their tragedy and ability to strike fear in so many hearts, had healing powers that worked their magic on me.

"Hello, girls," I whispered, "I'm home."

Rather than going upstairs, I put the rising energy I got from simply being home to good use. Humming Christmas carols to myself, I put my shop in order, making a couple of trips to the basement for candles and note cards to fill out empty spaces in the displays.

From my overnight bag, I pulled out a bottle of Zodiac and placed it prominently on top of a case of wine. Julia had arranged a selection of wine glasses and cork screws on that wooden case, and now, sitting on its own small silver tray, Zodiac became part of my store.

After only a couple of hours, Square Spirits sparkled. I was ready for the day-after-Christmas sales.

I went upstairs and put Mom's leftovers to good use and made a half a ham sandwich, with a layer of cranberries replacing the mayo. I poured a glass of eggnog and took my meal to the front window. I'd left the case of Zodiac wine in my car thinking I'd wait until morning to bring it in, but after eating my snack I changed my mind. The temperature was falling, but if I hurried I could manage without a jacket.

I grabbed my car keys and once downstairs, I used the chair from the back table to prop the door open. I hurried to my car, parked only a few yards away across the alleyway opposite the back door. For the two years I'd helped at the winery, I had easily handled 12-bottle cases, but when Devin began using the larger, 16-bottle crates, I struggled to lift and move them. Staring at the large crate, I had to either take multiple trips, carrying only three or four bottles at a time, or I could challenge myself to haul the sixteen bottles in one herculean effort.

Laughing at myself, I felt like a superwoman when I lifted the box out and rested it on the edge of the trunk. My body strained, but I wasn't going to retreat. This was important to me. If I was going to sell wine then I needed to be able to carry more than a few bottles up from the basement with each trip. Manhandling this case of Zodiac was a beginning. It was my wine, after all.

I took a deep breath and carried the crate inside the back door and lowered it to the floor. I ran to the car, closed the trunk and hurried inside. I had just locked the back door when a knock on the front door startled me.

I turned to see Eli through the glass.

I waved and walked the length of the shop, noticing that his silhouette created by the antique lamp light accentuated his tall, muscular frame.

Appealing, so appealing. He was a force, and I had to be careful. Or maybe afraid? I shook off that thought because I was so pleased to see him. I unlocked the bolt and swung the door open wide and waved him inside.

"Merry Christmas, Eli. What brings you by at this time of night?"

"This came after you left yesterday," he said, his tone typically matter-of-fact. "The driver didn't want to leave it by your door so he left it with us." He turned and gestured toward Farmer Foods with his free hand.

I closed the door after he'd stepped inside, and reveled in the bell making its happy sound.

Eli handed me the package.

I gasped. Never had I expected this.

"Something wrong?" He leaned over my shoulder to read the return address. "Who's Tyler Goodman?"

"My ex-husband."

"Your ex sends you Christmas presents?"

"I haven't seen or heard from him in more than two years," I replied. "So, to answer your question, no. He's not in the habit of sending gifts."

"Better open it. Might be something awful." A smile tugging at the corners of his mouth, he leaned forward again and smelled the box. "Nope. Nothing rotten."

I laughed. "You would have smelled it before now."

Eli shifted his weight from one foot to the other. "Aren't you going to open it?"

"Um, sure." An idea came to me, and I acted on it before I could second guess myself. "Let's go upstairs. We'll celebrate the holiday with a new wine—*my* wine." I grabbed the bottle of Zodiac I'd put on the silver tray. As an afterthought, I took the tray, too, and handed both to Eli.

He held the bottle up to the soft light from outside. "Zodiac. Sounds like it belongs in here."

"My gift from my family. It's a sparkling semi-sweet wine. It looks like light strawberry soda, but it tastes so much better. It's a blend of strawberries and grapes."

"That's unique."

And impressive, based on the inflection in his voice.

"Follow me." I started up the stairs, both curious about Tyler's gift, and also wanting to get the act of opening it in front of Eli over.

"The corkscrew's on the counter, glasses in the cupboard."

I paid attention to the sound of Eli's foot steps behind me. Other than my family and Julia, no one had been in my apartment. Well, besides, Nolan and Reed. And the girls, but they hadn't made an appearance since Eli arrived. I hoped they would stay quiet for now.

Since my apartment resembled a studio, with only the bedroom, bathroom, and a huge walk-in closet walled off, most of the space like a cavern with little more than a kitchen table with a couple of chairs, a couch, a soft, sunken reading chair, a lamp, and an area rug covering it. And the desk, of course. No end tables or coffee table or bookshelves, although one needing assembly was packed in a carton and pushed to the far wall. All that was yet to come.

Eli noticed the sparseness of my living space. "This looks like a bachelor's place." Then he pointed across the room to my desk, my gleaming pride and joy. "Except for the desk. Now that's a piece worth keeping."

"I brought it back from the dead," I quipped. "It was a lot of work, but well worth it."

He nodded. "I'll say. Good for you."

It pleased me that he'd noticed the one piece of furniture that meant something to me.

"What kind of flowers are these?" he asked, lifting the Clayton Sommers original off the floor where I'd left it leaning against the wall.

"Lavender. The scent is added to all sorts of products. I've got sachets and candles and a few other things in the shop. That's what you smell when you enter the shop."

Eli raised the painting higher. "Want help hanging it?"

My stomach did a little back flip at the pleasure of his offer. "Hmm…I'd say yes, but I don't know where I want it yet. I was thinking I might bring it downstairs. A perfect fit for the shop."

"Let me know if want me to bring my ladder over. No need to call Nolan or Reed for a little job like this."

He replaced the picture against the wall and started opening the wine as I got out two glasses. He poured us each a generous portion. The pinkish-red shimmered in the intense light from the ceiling. When he handed a glass to me, our fingers touched and his eyes grew large. *He felt the energy.*

"A toast to Christmas." I raised my glass to him. The clink from our salute echoed off the empty walls.

"I like the holiday, at least most of it, but I'm glad it's over." Eli nudged the package I'd set on the table. "Going to open that?"

Why so curious?

"Sure, why not." I searched a drawer for a sharp knife and struggled to cut through the layers of packaging tape, finally succeeding. Inside, I found a gauzy purple and white cotton woven shawl. And a note. I'd never forget his handwriting, if you could call his doctor's script that. It was mostly scribbles of abbreviations and phrases. He'd signed the card with humps and bumps for his name. But it was Tyler's handwriting. No one else had written it for him. Of that I was certain.

"What'd he say?"

A bold question. At least for Eli, the proverbial man of few words. And did I want Eli to know anything about Tyler? I wasn't sure, but the note was about as impersonal as Tyler could possibly make it. "It says, *'Made by a local woman in a crafts collective. Thought of you when I saw this one'.*"

"Must have been the purple," Eli said.

Another stomach flip. My penchant for various shades of purple hadn't been lost on him.

He gestured to the box. "I noticed the box came from Haiti. Is he there?"

Eli's interest in Tyler's whereabouts threw me.

I nodded to answer his question. "It really is pretty." I draped it over my shoulders and went to the front window to see my reflection.

Eli hung back by the kitchen counter. I saw his blank expression reflected in the window, but couldn't read his underlying emotions. I took the shawl off and hung it on the back of the soft chair by the window. Outside, the lights of the Square twinkled in the misty air. "You bring the wine over and I'll get another chair."

"We can sit at the table," he said.

Instantly, I got it. Eli didn't want anyone strolling on the Square to see him in my home. Why was that? Boy, the man was confusing.

"Sure. Although looking out over the Square is one of my favorite things to do to unwind when I come upstairs."

"That, and figuring your profits, I'm guessing."

I chuckled at that. It sounded like much too personal a remark for Eli to make.

"Don't laugh," he said. "You think I don't notice the women coming in and out? For a brand new shop you're doing great. Better than great."

"It's been gratifying, all right," I said.

We sat across from each other at the table and our conversation came to a halt. Our words might as well have circled a drain and disappeared. The silence lingered. Why didn't Eli bolt and run? I would have understood.

"So tell me, Eli, what did Santa bring you today?" Maybe some levity would help.

He grinned, his entire face lighting up. "As a matter of fact, Elliot and Georgia gave me something original *and* fun. It's a drone with a camera. I'm going to fly it over the Square on New Year's Day when there aren't any shoppers around. I'll get an aerial view, and maybe Sarah can use it. As for Megan, she stuck to the script and gave me shirts and socks. That girl is always trying to spruce me up."

I laughed out loud. Not a polite one either, but strong, filled with humor. "That sure sounds like Megan."

Eli blushed, but tried to cover it by topping off our glasses. Neither of us had been shy about sipping while we chatted.

"Why would shirts be on the 'script', as you call it?"

With his eyes softening, Eli said, "When our mom died Megan did it as a kind of remembrance. Mom always gave Elliot and me shirts, so Megan carried on the tradition. Now I expect them." In a quiet voice, he added, "My little sister really is a great kid, but I have to stop calling her that. She's a grown woman now, engaged and everything."

"Between the drone and some new clothes," I said, "seems like your new year is off to a good start."

I stared into the room at nothing in particular. "Devin and I don't have a close relationship. I mean, we don't have our shared traditions. Even when his wife, Hannah, was alive, we didn't get together much, except for awkward Christmas dinners. Devin and Tyler didn't think much of each other, and my parents never took to him either. It led to a poisoned atmosphere."

Oops, I said more than I'd meant to.

Eli's brows lifted in surprise. "I took to Devin pretty well at the association party. I've got an idea to try winemaking, you see, and he didn't seem to mind me picking his brain."

So that was why they spent time together. Wine was certainly Devin's favorite subject. I hadn't realized Eli was that interested.

Eli finished the last drop in his glass and slid his chair back from the table. "Time for me to go. Another busy day tomorrow. The Square will be filled with shoppers looking for bargains—and takeout lunches and dinners, too. The deli business is great this time of year."

"I'm looking forward to opening my door tomorrow and welcoming another big day on the Square," I said.

That brought a smile to Eli's face. "Somehow, we've managed to keep people coming back year after year."

Wow. I enjoyed the note of pride in his voice. Eli was passionate about his hometown and the businesses on the Square. Yes, there was much more to Mr. Eli Reynolds than he let people see.

I led the way downstairs and to the front door, but Eli had another idea.

"I'll go out the back."

Of course. Eli loved his community, but he hoped to avoid becoming the subject of its gossip.

When I was back upstairs, I ran my hand across the shawl as I went to the front window. I looked out just in time to see Eli turn and wave before disappearing in the darkness.

12

When I unlocked the door a few minutes early it was purely to send Eli and Tyler on a trip out of my thoughts. I'd had a restless night because of those two. Receiving the beautiful shawl had brought back memories of other times. How odd to think that the gift that most reflected something I'd really like came more than two years after he'd left. Other gifts had been the showy jewelry I didn't care to wear and cocktail dresses that suited *his* taste. And then there was Eli talking about his kid sister buying him socks and shirts every year, based on a tradition that went back to childhood.

I needed distraction.

Unfortunately, shoppers were sparse during the morning, many less than I'd been led to believe would show up. Maybe it was the weather. The steady icy rain had the salt trucks on the streets behind the Square and the town's maintenance crews had been out early to salt the Square. I stayed busy rearranging the candles and battery luminaries and adding a few necklaces to displays that were already full. When I checked the books on the shelf I was surprised by how many had sold during the days before Christmas.

The books reminded me of Doris and our last conversation. We'd sat next to each other a few days before Christmas and, while the others at morning coffee were discussing holiday plans, we'd chatted about books and authors.

When she'd mentioned a New Age author, Jacob Wright, I paid closer attention. I'd mistakenly thought she'd seemed dismissive of New Age philosophy, mainly because of the scanty number of New Age books in her store. Then she mentioned her husband had read extensively in many areas and had a knack for helping shoppers choose the perfect book for themselves or as gifts. She looked away, but not in time to hide her damp eyes. She'd fought back the tears, but couldn't hide her grief. Unfortunately, it struck me that her chronic sadness was an underlying theme that influenced everything else in her life.

"I loved Ralph," Doris had explained. "Owning the bookstore was his dream. And the customers loved him. And why not? He was so good with people."

Her sentences were short, but they told an elaborate story. It was as if only Ralph could be good with people. Yet, she had a stake in the bookstore, too. "Don't you like the shop?" I asked.

She opened her mouth as if to speak, but no words came out.

Why had I asked such a tricky question?

A couple of seconds later Doris found her voice. "Does yes and no sound wishy-washy? As you've quickly learned, owning a retail store involves hard work that never ends. You finish one festival and have to get ready for the next one. And special events? So many of them. We couldn't leave for a real vacation. Ralph said he did all his traveling through books."

Others on the Square had spoken about Ralph as if he were a special guy. Maybe so, but didn't anyone read between the lines? Couldn't they see that maybe Doris' desires were brushed off? I felt like asking her why she didn't take a vacation on her own? But I held back. I was painfully familiar with how hard it was to ask that question of myself.

In a tone I fashioned to be curious rather than demanding, I asked, "Why did you decide to stay in Wolf Creek after he was gone?"

"Where would I go?" she'd responded without hesitation. "I know everyone here. I couldn't imagine starting over somewhere else. Not at my age."

She was hardly an old woman. Only her demeanor

sometimes made her seem that way. But I understood why she hadn't left town. As a woman a few years younger than Doris, it was easy to say I'd made a decision that gave me a chance to do exactly what she hadn't allowed herself. From the ashes left behind, I plucked out the chance to create and follow a dream. Doris believed deep inside that it was too late for her to start over.

Her situation left me saddened, and when Sarah's watch had beeped, we gathered cups and plates and wiped the table with our napkins. But I knew I wouldn't easily forget that conversation.

With traffic on the Square slow, I considered paying Doris a visit at Pages and Toys later that day. I wouldn't miss making sales if there were no shoppers.

That idea went flying out the door when the rain eased, the sun came out, and the ice melted away. The bargain shoppers that came were serious. I had a few inevitable returns, although not too many. A few noted Zodiac, and when I described the color and taste, I sold a few bottles. I thought the light red color would make it a great pairing for a Christmas or Valentine's Day affair, but when I mentioned it was a sparkling wine, shoppers' thoughts jumped to New Year's Eve celebrations. I took a minute to send Mom an email about delivering two cases of Zodiac to me when the truck came out our way with the Crossroads' order.

In the midst of the activity Sarah dropped in, but she stayed only long enough to put the envelope she carried next to the credit card machine. No explanation. Just a quick wave on her way out.

Unfortunately, when I locked the door and turned the sign to Closed, I noticed the windows in the bookstore were dark, but the upstairs was lit up. Too late for a visit tonight.

Before I turned away I saw Nora Alexander running across the corner from Rainbow Gardens. She waved her arms as if trying to get my attention. She succeeded. I opened the door and waited for her to arrive. "Hi, Nora. Busy day for you?"

"Can't understand it myself, but it's exciting, huh? This is my first year on the Square so everything is new." She took a few deep breaths. "Can't run very well on my leg yet."

At morning coffee she hadn't been shy talking about the death of her husband years ago and the more recent car accident. When she'd talked about her July wedding to the most eligible bachelor in Northeast Wisconsin she'd flashed her signature radiant smile.

"Come in and sit down." I motioned to the chairs in the back.

"I won't be staying that long. This is very last minute, but Matt and I are hosting a party at the Sorenson house on New Year's Eve. The renovation has done wonders for the house and Matt—and especially Gus, Matt's grandfather—want to show it off. We've invited everyone on the Square, but you can bring a guest, too, if you want."

I considered her happy expression, her excited voice. But that didn't lure me away from what I knew was the right answer—for me. "That sounds like fun, Nora, but I'm going to have to decline. I already have plans for the evening."

"Oh, darn," she said, exaggerating a disappointed tone. "I told Matt we waited too long to make a decision about hosting a party."

"I hope I can see the house another time."

"Yes, *anytime*." She pivoted to leave, but then turned back. "I want to schedule a reading in early January. You do them privately, don't you? Not as part of a festival or fair? I want a glimpse…well, what I mean is, I have a feeling about some things in the coming year." She shrugged. "I'd like to ask you about them."

"As you can imagine, I haven't had time for readings in the midst of opening the shop at the start of the holiday rush. According to Sarah, and everybody else, things slow down in January, so I'm sure we can arrange a time. If need be, I can do a reading for you one evening."

"Great. Terrific." She flashed her mega-watt smile and started to leave, but then came back again. The little bell jingled through it all. "I almost forgot to ask. Are you looking for help in your shop?"

"It's hard to say. It's possible I'll need someone part-time in the summer and to help with the festivals. Why?"

"My sister, JoAnn Clark, and her husband have moved

here to be part of Gus and Matt's foundation work. David is busy with his office in Green Bay, too, which leaves her with some free time. She's looking for a part-time job."

A part of me wanted to jump at the chance to secure some help, but I didn't know JoAnn—I barely knew Nora. Staying on the safe side, I said, "I'll need to think about it as we get into the year, but thanks for the suggestion."

"Okay, now I really *am* leaving," Nora said, opening the door. "And it's snowing!"

I stepped outside to enjoy the soft, silent snow. The Square was empty. No shoppers milling about, no holiday music coming from the mayor's building, just a surreal quiet. The kind of night for reflection.

About Eli?

I was no longer surprised when his name came to mind. Why did I react so intensely to this man? I still knew so little, yet felt so much.

Back inside, I locked the door and turned off the shop lights. At that moment, warm and cool air gently surrounded me. "Been an interesting day, ladies. And starting tonight I hope to learn more about you." The air shifted. Were they excited or upset? The air movement, though strong, was nothing compared to the way they'd reacted to the candles I'd lit when I'd first arrived. Wow. I wouldn't make that mistake again.

Only time would tell how they'd react when I began learning more about them. I'd peeked in the envelope Sarah had dropped off, so I knew she'd pulled together her research about my building. For me, that meant shedding light on Grace and Rose. I was eager to get started.

I'd begun to fancy Farmer Foods' meatloaf, so that's what I used to make a sandwich. Paired with a pre-cut salad, also a Farmer Foods' creation, I had a no-fuss dinner. When I sat at my kitchen table to eat, I looked into my apartment and tried to see it through Eli's eyes. I'd been hit hard by his comment that the place looked like a bachelor's home. I wondered if his new home looked like mine. I doubted it. Except for the desk, did my living space have the energy I wanted Eli—or any of my new friends—to experience when they were inside my home?

I added that question to my ever growing list I would reflect on during my private New Year's Eve. As much as I didn't want to wish time to pass any more quickly than it already was, I was looking forward to having an evening and New Year's Day to clear my mind of daily sales numbers. It was time to think about and plan the coming year.

And what better way to start than to spend a few minutes reading Sarah's history of my building. I cleared away the few supper dishes, poured myself a glass of Zodiac, and opened the envelope.

***

Tragedy in Wolf Creek

By Sarah Hutchinson

As the calendar days passed and spring pushed winter aside, the farmers living near Wolf Creek gathered at the Wolf Creek Seed Company. Their discussions and debates, which often would continue for hours, were mostly about the weather or decisions about whether to plant more oats than hay. Each farmer needed to decide soon. When the rains thawed the ground and the planting began the time for talking would be over.

As the owner of the seed store, Cyrus Hart and his wife, Adelaide, worked equally long hours in the spring. The seeds needed to be hauled from Green Bay, and Cyrus made the trips himself. He would sell only the best seeds and in order to guarantee their quality, he sampled every bag before loading them onto his wagon. With Adelaide's skill at record keeping and numbers, the farmers could go back years and review their purchases. No one ever questioned Adelaide's accounts.

Spring started slowly. A few days of light rain and warm temperatures were followed by cold winds from the north. That weather pattern continued for weeks. Soon everyone became edgy that the ground wouldn't be warm in enough time for the seeds to germinate and mature.

When the warm temperatures of summer came, the rains continued. The fields became wet, sodden acres. Then the rains moved east, and warm sunshine dried the land. The farmers rejoiced. Horses and plows were seen in every field. The atmosphere in town was again hopeful.

But, Mother Nature was not kind to the farmers that year. After the fields turned green from the new growth, the rain never returned. As the summer days passed, the hot, dusty winds blew for days, scorching the land and killing the crops.

Again, the farmers gathered at the seed store. There would be no harvest this year, no profit from the crops. Many of the farmers wouldn't be able to pay for their seeds. The whole town would feel the rippling effect of the drought.

***

Cyrus and Adelaide were blessed with two daughters, Madeline and Hazel, ages 11 and 9 respectively. The girls were well aware that their parents worried about the money they would need to pay their bills. But the girls were comforted by their parents' love.

One evening, Adelaide settled her daughters for the night and put a lit candle on the table between the beds. She tied the curtain aside to keep it away from the flame. [Author's insert: It is only speculation that the winds during the night loosened the knot and let the curtain fall into the flame.]

No one in the town noticed the fire that consumed the upstairs living area of the building until Cyrus began coughing from the smoke. He made Adelaide go downstairs while he went to awaken his daughters.

Hot, raging flames and dense black smoke forced Cyrus to retreat. He was fortunate to make it out of the building safely.

Townspeople gathered to form a bucket brigade of water to save the building. They failed. Cyrus found his wife screaming and fighting to go to her daughters. Only he was able to prevent her from entering the burning building.

By morning, all that remained of the Hart building was a smoldering pile of burned lumber. A few sacks of seeds were scorched and then ruined from the water. Cyrus stood nearby, surrounded by neighbors who had been with him all night. They had been watchful for sparks or ash falling on nearby structures and starting another fire.

When the pile of timber was cool enough to handle, the townspeople helped Cyrus find his daughters' remains, and they were buried in the Wolf Creek Cemetery.

Adelaide never recovered from their loss. Cyrus returned with her to Ohio, where Adelaide's family would help care for her.

[Author's note: Weather and time has eroded the writing and crumbled their stones. The exact location of the girls' graves is unknown.]

13

The night I read the account of the fire, my sleep was scattered with images of a frantic mother and townspeople desperately trying to save the children—and the entire town, as well. When my alarm buzzed I didn't want to forget those dreams, disturbing as they were. To imprint the images in my memory, I kept my eyes closed and stayed in bed a while longer. I'd jot the details of the dream in my journal later, and give myself time to decipher what they were telling me.

What would I have done if those girls had been my daughters?

I'd gone to sleep with that question and I'd awakened with it. As the minutes passed, I considered the possibility that I'd been given the responsibility of seeing Grace and Rose on a peaceful journey to the beyond. I understood their names were Madeline and Hazel, but for me, they would always be Grace and Rose.

Thus far in my life as an intuitive, I'd had no experience with coaxing spirits across to the other side. I had never witnessed an exorcism, either. As I understood it, these spirits were stuck between worlds, traumatized by the event that caused their death, yet unable to let go of this realm.

I chuckled to myself at the thought of casually talking about my resident spirits over morning coffee at B and B. "So, Zoe," someone would say, maybe even Eli, "how are the girls? Did they sleep well last night?"

No, I couldn't tell anyone about what was happening with the girls. Even if there were believers among my new friends on the Square, it was too risky. I had to handle Grace and Rose on my own. Once out of bed, I grabbed my pen and journal, and scribbled notes about the dream. I also wrote notes in the margins of Sarah's pages. It dawned on me that there was one person I could talk to about this. Mom.

As I was considering this new information, I also considered that inevitably, my world would become much bigger if I committed to researching the building and the girls, while also trying to fulfill what I now called my responsibility. My privacy was critical, too. I didn't want to find myself any less welcome in my new hometown.

While my coffee brewed, I glanced out the front window where the flurries from the night before had covered the ground and walkways. The beauty of it was being disturbed by a street-cleaning truck clearing the walkway and the paths that cut across the center of the Square. I smiled. The shops didn't open for another couple of hours, but Mayor Sarah left nothing to chance.

I turned away, and dressed in black wool slacks and my Christmas gift from Julia, a cable knit sweater. I added a crystal quartz pendant and matching earrings to brighten the deep plum color of the cotton sweater. Lately, I'd been gathering my hair to the nape of my neck, sometimes using a barrette to hold it in place, but that morning, I chose a hand-dyed mini-scarf in mauve and white to hold it back in a low ponytail.

Still bothered with a sleep hangover, or rather the mental dullness that comes from lack of sleep, I filled my largest thermal cup with coffee and went downstairs to greet the day. With any luck, lots of shoppers would keep me alert and focused.

There were none. Periodically, I peered into the Square and noted foot traffic, but my morning passed without a single person coming through my door. I missed the bell's jingle, which had been such a steady companion through the days leading up to Christmas. To pass the time I began the tedious job of year-end inventory, no matter that the shop had been open for such a short time. That meant counting every stone, candle, and bottle of wine. The bigger crystals and chunks of amethyst and rose quartz, along with the jewelry were easy to count, as were the journals and books and note cards.

I'd avoided this job as long as I could, although there was something oddly soothing about the repetition of inventory. It was also a way to confirm that the computerized inventory system worked. What good was it to have if it didn't work efficiently?

Unfortunately, I couldn't shake Tyler out of my thoughts. The shawl was gorgeous, and I'd enjoy throwing it around my shoulders on a cool summer night or a fall day. But my thoughts kept returning to the question: Why was Tyler sending me a gift?

I was in the process of trying to banish that question, when the sound of the bell caught my attention. Not shoppers, but Sadie and Sarah. Sadie held three brown folding boxes with the B and B logo on the sides.

"Want to join us for lunch?" Sarah asked. She stopped to finger a blank journal with a paisley cover, saying only. "Hmm...pretty."

Sadie walked right on past me to the table at the back of the shop. "Don't say no. I'm hungry and I'd rather eat here than anywhere else. The atmosphere in your shop is so inviting."

"I'd be happy to join you," I said. "I'm counting stock to check my inventory control system. It's admittedly mind-numbing work."

"Sarah and I are holidayed out, even though there's one big one to go," Sadie said in mock relief. "But I'm not a fan of all these night parties. Never was."

Sarah pulled out a chair to join us. She opened her box and unwrapped the croissant sandwich. "They're all chicken salad. Made it easier that way. Hope you like it."

"Thanks. I need to pay you." I started to stand, but Sadie swished her hand in the air, a motion which made all her jingling bracelets slide down her arm.

"No worries, we had Steph charge your lunch to your account."

"But how did you know...?" I mimicked her motion with

151

my own hand swishing the air. That brought a grin to her face.

"Just a guess," Sarah said before biting into her sandwich. She chewed and swallowed.

An image of an old lady in a rocking chair traveled across my mind. She held the hand of a man in the chair next to her. They rocked in matching rhythm.

Well, well, Sarah. Who was that man?

Sadie shivered and pulled her jacket up over her shoulders. "Just had a wave of cool air pass by. Don't you have the heat on?"

I took a quick bite of a carrot stick to keep from having to answer immediately. I noticed Sarah looked down into her lunch box and picked up a celery stick. She also began eating it with a degree of enthusiasm unusual for celery. I'd find out soon enough how much she understood about the building.

Sadie probably didn't know about the girls, but she was going to learn about them very soon. After reading Sarah's history of the fire, many people in town could put two and two together and come up with the reason for the mystery surrounding the building. At the very least, they'd have a story to go with their haunted building.

Would Eli think I was crazy?

As much as I wanted to tell Sarah I found her writing interesting and informative, with Sadie present I held back.

"Whew! The furnace must have started." Sadie threw off her jacket. "Did you have a good Christmas with your family? Fortunately, Sarah invited me to join her family since Clayton and Megan went to New York."

"We had a nice time. Did some traditional family things, but I was glad to be back in Wolf Creek before dark." Now was not the time to talk too much about my concerns about my dad or the strain between Devin and me.

We stuck to small talk, and by the time the bell jingled again, we were each polishing off one of Steph's famous chocolate chip cookies. Sadie and Sarah gathered the empty boxes and slipped out the back door, while I talked to my first customers of the day.

From the look of it, I guessed two mothers were shopping with their two grown daughters, but they stood by the door and hadn't ventured deep inside.

I stepped toward them. "Welcome to Square Spirits. May I help you?"

Dressed in high boots and leggings, the first young woman said, "A friend was here a couple of days before Christmas. She gushed about your shop and just about every item in it. And the wine!" She swept her arm toward the displays. "She wants me to bring two bottles of each of these." She opened her giant handbag and pulled out a list and handed it to me. "If you're sold out of some of them, then I can substitute. But I'm not to return empty-handed. Not with New Year's Eve around the corner."

I glanced at the list of wine. "Luckily, I do have these in stock. You look around, and I'll start packing a box."

For this large a sale, I went to the corner of the reading room and retrieved a couple of rope-handled wooden crates, each holding eight bottles. A sale this size definitely called for special packaging, and these customers alone were going to make up for a zero-sale morning.

On my way back to the wine rack, I changed the CD to one with upbeat instrumental renditions of songs from the 70's. I thought a livelier rhythm was better for shoppers than the heavy symphony I'd been listening to before Sadie and Sarah arrived. Even Sadie had commented on its sad sound.

By the time I packed the first crate, another pair of women had entered, lifting my spirits even higher.

Spirits? That thought brought my two resident spirits to mind. Cool and warm air immediately surrounded me. Another first. Grace and Rose hadn't made their presence known in the shop when customers were around. Or at least I hadn't been aware of them. Were they becoming comfortable with strangers in their building? Oops, *my* building?

It appeared that the two new customers were acquainted with the other four, so the shop became alive with the energy of happy greetings and holiday cheer. The two younger women hastily set in motion a mid-afternoon meeting for the six of them at Crossroads for wine and pie.

Wouldn't Melanie love to hear that? Truthfully, I envied these women and their camaraderie. It had taken all of a minute to make their plans to share an afternoon treat. Anyone could see how delighted they were to have run into each other.

No denying it or explaining it away. Devoting myself to launching Tyler's dream clinic and then running it smoothly had taken a toll. To be fair, my own graduate program in psychology and advanced classes online in quantum realms also ate up time and energy. I'd never carved out time for myself to enjoy friendships with other women.

As I carried the two filled crates to the counter, I kept my eyes and ears open to the pleasant sights and sounds of the two generations interacting. The retailer in me kept a tally of the items that drew interest. Was there a pattern? If there was, I couldn't find it. All six were drawn to the scarves and journals, and to what I considered my go-to items, the candles and stones. As I wrapped and packaged their buys, I mentioned that my family made the wine and hosted wine-tasting events throughout the year.

"What about a couples' wedding shower?" the youngest of the women asked.

I gave her one of the brochures Mom had designed for the coming year. "Best to call and talk with my mother, Judith. She's the scheduler and customizes the events. I'm quite sure she'd be happy to arrange a wedding shower." It was possible that Julia would take over the special events. I simply didn't know and I wanted to stay out of that part of the business.

"Most people think the shower and bachelor party should be separate events," the young woman said, "but we're a little different. That's why a party organized around a wine-tasting sounds like so much fun."

The bell on the door jingled and Megan stepped in, but she quickly nodded when she saw the customers clustering at the counter and left.

"So, why don't you pull your car around to the back," I said to the woman buying the wine, "and I'll carry the crates to your trunk."

Her face brightened. "That's a relief. I was wondering how I was going to lug two crates of wine across the Square to my car." She turned to the others. "Go and grab a table. I'll join you soon." She waved an added, "And Mom, order a piece of chocolate mousse pie for me."

I led her to the back door, which was closer to the lot where she was parked and gave her directions to come into the alleyway.

By the time I returned to the front, the others were filing out, each carrying a bag with my logo on it. Nothing in the morning, but big sales in the afternoon. My earlier doubts disappeared.

Within minutes, the buzzer on the back door rang, and the customer and I wedged the two crates in her trunk, which was already half-filled with bags from other shops on the Square. My store hadn't been the first stop on the foursome's shopping circuit. Judging from the number of boxes and bags, they'd enjoyed their day on Wolf Creek Square.

Megan was waiting for me when I locked the back door.

"Hey, the traveler returns. Was New York exciting?" I myself had always found it a great place to visit, but as the saying goes, I wouldn't want to live there.

"Very exciting, especially spending time in Clayton's world, his former world, that is. I came by to see you because I said yes to an opportunity, but to make it happen, I need everyone's help. Including yours."

"Sounds intriguing, Megan. I admit I'm usually up for a challenge."

Like Eli. Oh, please, leave it alone, Zoe.

"Come, sit down and tell me how I can help." With one hand, I picked up my notebook on the way back to the table, and slipped the other hand into my pocket to touch the amethyst stone. I wasn't sure why, but Megan's excitement had heightened my emotions, making me extra-sensitive to her energy.

She sat and pulled off her gloves and hat, and unbuttoned her coat. She was settling in, which made me even more curious. I had a feeling her opportunity had something to do with her budding wedding planning business, and I was right. She filled in the history I had heard in bits and pieces before.

"I've heard some of the stories about your skills over morning coffee," I said, grinning. "Seems Georgia and Lily both say they couldn't have had their special day without you. Well, they're quick to give a little credit to everyone else on the Square."

She laughed, but continued fidgeting with the double strand of red beads she wore with her white sweater. "Thanks, but now I may have taken too big a chance."

I waited...and waited. Finally, I leaned toward her. "Well, are you ever going to tell me?"

"I just reserved a vendor spot at The Wedding Extravaganza, a wedding show in Green Bay at the end of January."

"That does sound exciting. And how lucky you were able to get a spot this late in the game."

"I know. They had a cancellation...two, actually, so they were happy to have me call."

She's glowing. She's in love, but there's more. She stood in a circle alone, but just outside of it a couple of women were clapping. Cheering her on?

"So, here's my idea. I'm planning my booth to feature the Square as the place for couples to come when planning their wedding. 'Look no further, folks...find everything you need on the Square.' We're kind of a one stop shopping wedding supplier—the whole Square." She began to tick off each shop as she talked. "There's Art&Son for rings, Pages and Toys for the wedding planning books, Styles for dresses, Steph's sister, Cindy, for the cakes and desserts, the Inn if the wedding is small or the Community Center for a large one, like Lily's, flowers from Rainbow Gardens." She raised one finger high in the air and took a breath. "Country Law for any legal needs, like contracts and stuff."

No wonder my earlier vision included women clapping. It was a fabulous idea. Unique and creative. "Wow, Megan, that's brilliant."

"As you've probably guessed, I want to include you, too."

"Well, thanks. Wow, again. I'd love to be a part of it."

Megan narrowed her eyes in thought. I wondered if something was wrong, but I waited it out.

"I'm glad to hear you react this way, because I came here to get an honest answer."

"From me? And not half a dozen other places?"

She shook her head. "Everyone else carries around years of baggage about me and the Square. They know my history and my family, and they know how close Wolf Creek came to razing all these buildings and going modern. I figured you have a fresh opinion of us. Of me, frankly. That's why your opinion counts."

I grinned when she stopped to take another breath and shake out her hands, but before I could respond thoughtfully, she continued right on. "See what I mean about the Square as a destination place for brides and grooms?"

The idea of putting together Square Spirits' bridal boxes as gifts for attendants or hostess gifts came immediately to mind. Like the matching crystal necklaces I'd sold to a bride. I could see Megan's idea and wanted to be part of it from the ground floor. "Like I said, I think it's brilliant. Where do I sign up?"

Megan's eyes sparkled. I knew she'd been sincere in asking for my opinion, unencumbered with history, but I also understood she wanted the answer I gave her.

"So, fill me in. What comes next in your tight timeframe?"

"The show is held on a Friday and a Saturday and I think all the shops who want to offer services should have a presence, but I know that isn't feasible. Are you sure you want to close up for at least part of those days?"

"Leave that to me." I sounded more confident than I felt, but Nora had mentioned her sister's interest in a part-time job. I'd simply act sooner rather than later.

I noticed Megan's expression change from ecstatic to thoughtful again. Details, I thought. I could almost see Megan's mind running down her to-do list. "Do you want me to keep quiet about this until you talk to others? Maybe Sarah?"

After being on the Square for only two months it was evident to me that Sarah had her finger on the pulse of the Square at all times.

"Thanks for that offer," Megan said knowingly, "but I'm heading next door now. I think she's going to jump on the idea." She stood and hoisted the straps of her overstuffed attaché over her shoulder.

"Love that bag," I said, "very smart."

The pretty eyes sparkled again. "A gift from Georgia. She said I needed to upgrade now that I was going to be in front of the public more often. 'Red leather makes a statement,' she said. And I love it." She patted its side. "I'm already overstuffing it."

We walked to the front together and I opened the door for her. She glanced up at the bell as it jingled. "Thanks for your support, Zoe. Sometimes I jump into things before thinking them through. But I just *knew* this would be great for the Square."

"Do let me know how it goes with Sarah."

She nodded and left, waving as she headed next door.

What a turn of events. And I could be in the middle of it if I planned carefully.

The shop empty, I picked up the phone and called Mom. Not to tell her about Megan's idea, although it was tempting, but to order more wine and to give her a heads-up about the bride-to-be who might call about the couples' shower.

When Mom answered the phone, she didn't waste a minute saying, "The woman, Paula, already called."

I had to laugh. Nothing like caller ID to eliminate the need for a formal greeting.

"And, she and Keith, the groom, are coming out Sunday afternoon to look around. I'm sure we can do something special for them."

"Good. I'm glad to hear she jumped on the idea." I hesitated, but I wanted to know. "How's Dad?"

"About the same. Frustrated he can't do more, but Julia has been a big help already."

"I imagine so. She can help out in so many ways." A rush of *something* went through me. A second later, I realized that it had been a wave of relief that the day-to-day work of the winery was being skillfully handled. Besides, I didn't want to be involved, not when every day seemed to bring me a new experience on the Square.

I gave her my wine order, and then ended the call without mentioning the shawl from Tyler. It would have brought up questions and concerns. Mom always had been skeptical that he was really gone for good. I didn't want to fuel her skepticism.

My next customer distracted me from that thought. She carried a large garment bag with the Styles by Knight and Day logo prominent on the front. Must have been quite a sale.

"Mimi thought you might have an idea," the customer said, opening the bag to reveal a deep forest green sheath dress with a matching loose jacket with rounded edges. And beaded with tiny crystals.

"Wow. Must be a special occasion," I said.

And so it was. The woman's daughter was the first in the family to graduate from college. They planned to throw a big party after the ceremony in January. "I wanted something special to wear, which is why I came to Wolf Creek Square. My friends talk about the beautiful clothes at Styles all the time. And since Mimi doesn't carry much in the way of jewelry, she sent me here."

"Hmm…it's a gorgeous dress. Mimi knows I have some crystal jewelry. If you want one-of-a-kind handcrafted gemstone and metal pieces, Art&Son is your best bet. But for this dress, something that lets the beading speak for itself might be nice. And these are moderately priced items."

We experimented with polished malachite and green aventurine pieces, but when I laid them on the dress their color faded into the matching dress. "Nope," I said, "we need contrast."

I chose other necklaces I thought might work, realizing this was a new experience for me. If she was pleased, maybe she'd tell her friends that like Mimi and Jessica, I was willing to spend time searching for the perfect piece.

Then I saw it, a necklace made up of multiple strands of

crystal, alternating with silver rings. When I laid the piece on the fabric, the necklace—and the beading on the dress— sparkled. "And I have earrings to match."

"Oh, they're beautiful. But buying both might be out of my price range."

I quickly totaled the cost for the two pieces. "Not too expensive for jewelry you can wear anytime."

"You're sure?" she said, her eyes wide. "I thought the total would be much more."

I laughed. "My post-holiday sale is your friend today. Maybe you'd like to add a scarf?"

"No, no. I'd better not."

I could feel in the energy around us that this woman was a proud mother. And she'd feel like a million dollars, as my mom used to say, in her new clothes and jewelry. I boxed the jewelry and was ready to process the sale when she brought over a light raspberry colored scarf with wispy clouds painted on the silk.

"A little something for my younger daughter," she said, grinning. "She loves this sort of artsy look."

I brought out another gift box, taking pride in my choice of dark lavender tissue paper. It made a perfect nest for the scarf in the box.

I put her boxes in one of my shopping bags as she closed up the garment bag. What fun it was to hold the door open for her and see her leave happy with her purchases. I thanked her, and she assured me she'd send her friends. I was relaxed after she left—such a contrast from my early days in the shop. During the busy holiday shopping days I'd often been so focused on getting the job done I missed the pleasure of chatting as I packed up the items. Some days the shop had been so full, it was all I could do to keep the line flowing. That was great—better than I'd anticipated or even dreamed of, but I had to keep my natural inclination to read energy at bay. No time for that.

An image of Marianna Spencer and her persistent belief that soft marketing helped every shop on the Square came to mind. I decided to bring Clayton's painting of lavender downstairs and hang it in a prominent place. Maybe Jessica and Mimi would loan me a dress form and one of their special party dresses or business suits to accessorize for a window display. And Georgia had mentioned Country Law's contract with Rainbow Gardens for counter bouquets and decorations throughout the year. I needed to do that, too.

Yes, it was time to become more involved with the other shops on the Square. I'd add that to my goal list for the coming year. Along with contacting Nora's sister and setting up the systems for having an employee.

Doubts floated in. Perhaps I should play it safe, maybe wait to see if my shop was sustainable, able to attract more than the occasional impulse purchase. To say nothing of being part of Megan's vision of Wolf Creek Square as a couple's one-stop destination for wedding needs.

While I was deep in thought Eli walked in.

Funny, he was going to go to the top of my goal list, although I couldn't explain why.

After a quick greeting, I asked what prompted his visit.

"Nora's invite for New Year's Eve. You going?"

"No. By the time she told me about it, I'd already made other plans." I didn't want to tell him, or anyone else, I'd be spending New Year's Eve alone in my apartment. I needed the time to re-gather my energy and inner peace after the hectic start of my new life. Even when married to Tyler, I'd been grateful for a quiet start to a new year. That hadn't happened often, because he liked to throw a big open house on either the 31st or the 1st.

"Oh. Um. Okay."

"Are you going? I bet it will fun to see the house. Nora was telling me about the progress Nolan and Reed have made already."

Eli rolled his eyes. "It's about time, too. That house has been an eye-sore in this town for years. Glad someone finally bought it."

That circled back to the Alexanders and to Nora. "It sounds like the Alexander family has brought a lot to Wolf Creek recently."

Eli nodded, and then grinned. "So, Madame Zoe, are you

going to be around New Year's Day? I'm flying the drone over the Square at noon."

That was a quick change of subject. Choosing to ignore his teasing nickname, I said, "I wouldn't miss that. I expect the video will be amazing to see." I'd put in an appearance, mainly because everyone else on the Square planned to be there. And I was curious about the way Eli would handle being in the spotlight.

"Hope it doesn't crash." He laughed. "I'd be in for a lot of kidding if that happens."

As he spoke, Eli had wandered over to the wine racks where the latest sales had left behind conspicuous empty spaces. "I'll bring some bottles up for you," he said, striding to the basement door. "You'll need to come and tell me which ones you need."

I froze. Alone in the basement with Eli? I was nervous, but that was silly. I wasn't afraid of him, after all. My reliable inner voice said, *No, you're afraid of yourself!*

I repressed that thought by making a quick note of the wines I needed, including a few bottles of Zodiac that I'd take upstairs for myself. When I displayed Zodiac on the silver tray sales had increased immediately. I'd noticed most customers didn't take the time to look through all the varieties in the racks. More often they bought the ones they could readily see.

Eli was waiting for me downstairs. He'd already put three bottles of Zodiac into the box. How did he know I wanted them? As I named the varieties I needed he filled the box. I found another empty box and we filled it, too.

While he carried one box upstairs I grabbed a few candles to fill the empty shelf by the window. My arms full, I stood at the bottom of the steps waiting for him to return.

But as he clomped down the stairs, I sensed a change in him. His eyes danced and the smirk he wore gave me pause. Without asking, the usually reserved Eli Reynolds wrapped his arms around me, candles and all, and kissed me. "Happy New Year, Zoe."

I stood there surprised, stunned and shameless. It had been a long time since I'd been in the arms of a man and my body responded by molding to his muscular frame. Almost. With my hands full I couldn't return the embrace, but maybe that was okay. We stood there a few moments before awkwardly moving apart.

"Same to you, Eli." The words tumbled out.

He quickly grabbed the other box and went up the stairs ahead of me. He busied himself filling the racks with the wine. I stole glances at him, but didn't catch him looking at me. Finally, I stopped waiting for him to say something or look at me. I priced the candles and placed them in the empty places around the shop.

I laughed to myself. He was filling all the empty spaces, but I didn't have the heart to tell Eli that I needed to put price labels on each bottle. I didn't care. I'd simply make the rounds and do it later. I'm sure he didn't even think about it, not with all the items at Farmer Foods being scanned at the checkout.

He carried the empty boxes to the back door. "Need anything else before I go?"

Maybe another kiss? *Maybe?* Oh, yes.

"No, but thanks so much for helping me. You sure saved me lots of trips up and down those stairs."

He walked to the front door and made the bell jingle extra loud. He laughed and batted the bell again to keep it going. "Elliot's idea years ago. Nice, huh?"

Out the door and not a word about the kiss. Or about seeing me soon, or how about another dinner at Crossroads. No teasing goodbye to Madame Zoe. No *"Where have you been all my life?"*

Now it was time to laugh at myself. It was just a kiss. Or was it? I never believed in the concept of a simple, uncomplicated kiss. Was this the way of the Square? I seriously doubted it.

With Eli gone, I went to the window and stared at the walkers on the Square. Another layer of snow was building on the walkway, with each snowflake shimmering in the fairy lights on the trees. As frustrating as my thoughts were about him, I couldn't erase the nice feeling of Eli's body against mine.

I stayed away from B and B New Year's Eve morning. Since I'd declined Nora's invitation, I didn't welcome questions about my plans, and I could see the renovations everyone was talking about soon enough. Her grandfather-in-law, Gus Alexander, had bought the eyesore of a mansion, the Sorenson house, for Nora and Matthew to live in with him. I didn't know Gus other than by sight, but he seemed the kind of man who always had a surprise up his sleeve.

Like Sadie, I was more interested in the history of the mansion. Sarah had told us that an early settler in the town had made his fortune buying wheat from the local farmers and selling it to the grinding mill in Green Bay. He'd built the house for his young bride, who died in childbirth, leaving a son who died within hours of his mother. Shortly after burying them both, Sorenson left Wolf Creek and the house was sold. Far too big and expensive to maintain for the average family, it had a checkered past and had been vacant for a couple of decades. Sarah in particular was happy for a revival—but she was even happier with the Alexander family's interest in Wolf Creek itself.

Like the rest of the shops I'd only be open until noon. I was happy to turn the Closed sign, but I swatted the bell for the fun of it.

As I headed upstairs, I couldn't put into words the excitement about the coming year. My biggest worry was going to be when the town's people learned about Grace and Rose, and the presence of a real psychic on the Square. Me. Not fortuneteller, Madam Zoe. Except for a little teasing from Eli, Madame Zoe was gone, and I'd moved in. My worries weren't necessarily justified. Nora and many others had come for readings at the fall festival. They understood that I wasn't a carnival attraction, regardless of calling myself Madame Zoe for the event.

I went upstairs and poured myself a large glass of Zodiac to sip during the afternoon and evening. I'd already bought my lasagna dinner from Crossroads. The full dinner came with a salad and crusty bread. No cooking for me. I'd planned an afternoon and evening of relaxation and contemplation.

The afternoon passed quickly, because I dispensed with

JANUARY
14

I slept peacefully in my warm bed and awakened to bright sunshine and frosted windows. The predicted cold front out of Canada had passed during the early morning hours and plunged Northeast Wisconsin into mid-teen temperatures. Eli was right. I needed to dress in warm clothes for his flying-of-the-drone demonstration.

But first things first. Breakfast. With Farmer Foods next door I'd fallen into the habit of relying on their deli for most of my meals, hot and cold. Even on days I skipped coffee at Biscuits and Brew I gave little thought to food, cooking or eating it. Bagels and yogurt had served me well in the mornings.

It was time for a change, though. I'd added it to my list of New Year's resolutions: *Mix it up for breakfast.* Laughing at my choice of words, I searched the refrigerator for the makings of an omelet. In addition to half a dozen eggs, I had a bag of Farmer Foods cut up vegetables and a chunk of Crossroads' crusty bread left over from my lasagna dinner. I brewed a full carafe of coffee, so I could take some outside in a thermal cup.

As I whipped the eggs and waited for the vegetables to steam, my mind traveled into Tyler territory. Yes, the shawl was handmade, so perfect it was as if someone had me in mind when they'd made it. But my mind stalled on the morning he left. And not only me and his partners and all the employees, but his patients, people who had relied on him to manage their health. Were they hurt that he was suddenly replaced by a stranger? Or was he made to sound like a hero going off to save people who needed him more? I could imagine that exact scenario emerging. In that version of the story, Tyler wasn't escaping, he was sacrificing. Right... Tyler the hero.

My thoughts drifted to Eli, who now had a tiny slice of knowledge about Tyler. I was under no obligation to tell him more about my relationship and marriage, but at the same time, I was willing to drop my shield of privacy just a little in order not to keep secrets from Eli.

Oh, really? Okay, I was keeping the girls hidden. But for how long?

Why was I even thinking about Tyler? He was out of my life. Forever. And Eli wasn't fully in it. He didn't need to know the details about my past just yet, if at all. Besides, he had a past, too. I could feel that in the energy surrounding him. As curious as I was, no other information had left an impression with me. So, I would wait for him to tell me about his life in his own time, assuming he would be inclined to confide in me. I sometimes wondered if the loneliness that came from Eli was linked to a lack of one special confidant.

The eggs and vegetables were done quickly. By the time I buttered the heated bread I had a tasty breakfast to eat on the first day of the new year. And I'd make more meals like this for myself in the coming year. Right?

I laughed out loud at the absurdity of that idea. Why would I bother to cram cooking into my already hectic days? And end up with too many leftovers. I could eat healthy food without having to cook it myself.

I put the dishes in the sink about the time the phone rang with Megan's name appearing on the ID.

"I'm rallying the troops this morning," she said with a happy lilt in her voice. "Steph's opened B and B. She's made soup for later. You know, after Eli's flying exhibition. Come join us."

Megan had strung a bunch of short phrases together in similar fashion to Eli. Maybe it was a Reynolds' family trait. They always got their point across.

"Sounds fun. I'll get dressed and meet you over there.

And thanks for letting me know."

How nice that the first call of my new year came from someone in my new community. The warmth of that thought filled me up and made me smile.

"See ya." Then she was gone. Call ended.

Think warm. Starting with leggings under my jeans and a cotton turtleneck under my bulky, but warm Irish fisherman's knit sweater, I must have looked like an overstuffed cartoon character in my coat. I pulled on a snug wool hat and tied a scarf around my neck for good measure. What was I thinking? In less than three minutes I'd be at the coffee shop and would undo the layers.

Why had I stayed in the frozen upper Midwest? Why hadn't I opened my shop in a beach town, a place where the water was warm and the breezes balmy? I could have done that. But now that was a remote thought. Eli had wedged himself into my life…kissed his way into it.

Before I went inside, I could see through the windows that Biscuits and Brew was filled to capacity with many more people than usual. The rich aroma of strong coffee greeted me when I opened the door. I took my place in line behind the two women I'd met only once before, Beverly Winters and Virgie Saunders. I recalled that Beverly was Georgia's sister, Virgie an old friend. Jessica was ahead of them and joined our conversation by reminding me that these were the two ladies who designed and made the one-of-a-kind vests Styles exclusively sold.

"I'll have to stop in and see if you have anything in lavender or plum. Those are my signature colors in the shop."

"We'll stop by your shop soon now that things have quieted down around here. We were rushed with our holiday orders and not out and about much," Virgie said.

"We can make a custom one for you," Beverly offered, "but we'd still sell it through Styles. They handle all of our special orders."

Steph handed us each a large takeaway cup filled to the top with a blended brew. "Only one flavor today. I'm not working that hard." She laughed. "And the coffee's on me this morning. And the soup, too. Once Eli has brought us his air show." She waved her hand in the air as if waving to an airplane.

Grinning, we moved away from the counter and found a corner to stand in and sip our coffee. All of the chairs at the tables were already filled. I didn't mind, and the others didn't seem to either.

With her free hand, Beverly pulled a business card out of her pocket and handed it to me. "Here's one of our cards."

"I didn't think to pick up a few of mine." I knocked my knuckles on my temple. "I'm not as on the ball as so many of you."

"Georgia reminds me to give one to every person we meet. They did that at Country Law when they first opened. They were handing them out to people on the bus tours, and sure enough, some clients have come back to the Square and sought out their firm."

"Well, please stop in when you get a chance," I said. "I think you'll like some of my lovely hand-dyed scarves and gemstone jewelry."

The crowd shuffled when someone near the window saw Eli enter the Square carrying his spidery-looking drone. The entire group shifted and moving in herd-like fashion, we headed to the exit.

Descending on Eli, who was standing in the center of the walkway near Farmer Foods, we all wanted a closer look at his "electronic toy of the year." It seemed like every big box store had a drone to sell. Even Lily mentioned she'd ordered a few less expensive ones for kids.

Eli's was most definitely an adult version. With my first look, I thought it resembled a spider on steroids. Kind of ungainly, but functional. Since I'd never seen one before, I didn't know if there was such a thing as a good-looking drone.

In fairly long sentences, at least for Eli, he described the drone's design and pointed out the camera mounted at the center junction of the arms. He laughed. "Those aren't my words, folks. That's what it says in the instruction manual."

With the drone sitting on the ground in front of him, he

pushed a button on the remote control box he held in his hand, and the motor started. The device rocked back and forth as the engine speed increased. Another hand motion and the drone lifted off the ground into the air. Both Eli's hands were busy executing a series of moves that caused the machine to go up and down, forward and back.

When it went as high as the tops of the trees in the center of the Square, spontaneous cheers broke out.

We all looked up, but I quickly became just as fascinated by Eli's expressions and his total focus on the machine. Perhaps sensing I was watching him, he glanced my way, and his concentration broke. The drone quickly dipped toward the ground. I'm sure the loud gasp from the crowd brought his attention back to the controls.

A few fast hand movements later, the drone again reached flying level. More cheers and applause.

"So, everybody, I'm going to engage the camera now and walk around the Square. But I don't want anyone walking under it. I'm not ready to take it on tour yet."

Low laughter from the crowd. All eyes on Eli.

He'd claimed he didn't like being in the spotlight, but he does.

He started at Farmer Foods, moving the drone up and down the front of the building. Instead of going down the row of buildings on that side of the Square, as I thought he would, he brought the drone directly in front of Square Spirits. It hovered in front of my big window upstairs for a few minutes.

"All you'll see is dirty dishes in the sink," I called out, showing my lighthearted mood. Again a ripple of laughter went through the crowd.

Next the drone paid a visit to the mayor's building, where Sarah's drapes were drawn closed. "No snooping in my house, Eli," she said.

"Hiding secrets, Sarah?" Elliot said. As usual, he stood with his arm casually across Georgia's shoulders.

"As tight as Fort Knox," Sarah quipped.

We followed Eli and the drone on its journey around the Square. As we approached Pages and Toys, Doris stepped out and waved to the crowd. I doubted she knew her picture was being taken. I wondered, too, why she hadn't joined us at B and B for coffee.

No one could have been more pleased by the demonstration than Megan, who stood to my right. She looked especially pretty in a bright blue fuzzy hat and matching muff.

She applauded when, as a finale Eli flew the drone over the center of the Square. It had taken only a few minutes to get an aerial view of the Square. Then, he hovered the craft in front of Square Spirits a second time.

"I wonder if he can land it," Clayton said to Megan.

"Never doubt Eli. It seems my brother can do anything he puts his mind to," she responded.

At touchdown, the muffled applause that had started slowly grew louder as we clapped our gloved hands. Eli, appearing a little self-conscious, took a couple of little bows to acknowledge the appreciative crowd.

Alan Carlson, Art's son, stepped forward to join Eli. "Let's look at the video. I brought my laptop. We can crowd around a table at B and B. Okay, Steph?"

"Works for me. Soup's on." She headed off to reopen the café.

I didn't rush ahead, but held back with some of the others. We couldn't all huddle around the small screen at once and the video was only a few minutes long. I could wait until the crowd thinned.

Once inside, Alan and Eli set up the computer at a far table. It didn't take long to begin playing the short video. I followed Sarah and Sadie to a table at the far end of the room. In the short time I'd been standing outside my feet had become very cold. The rest of my body was toasty warm under my layers, but even with wool socks the cold had penetrated my light weight boots. I had some fleece-lined boots in one of the many yet-to-be-unpacked moving boxes stacked in my apartment. I made a mental note to go rummaging for them.

Sadie rubbed her hands together. "Brrr…I need something warm to drink."

"Ask and ye shall be given." Rachel, who waitressed

part-time at B and B, offered cups of hot chocolate from a large tray. "Soup's coming next."

Sadie grabbed three cups before Rachel moved to the next table.

All of a sudden there was a burst of laughter from those watching the video. Everyone was talking over each other with more laughter punctuating their comments.

"Seems like Eli is a big hit today." Sarah sipped from her cup. "I know it's not been easy for him. You know, being alone after having a brother and sister close by for so many years."

I didn't want to drop into that kind of speculative conversation, so I changed the subject. "Do either of you know much about crystal glassware? Quality stuff."

"There are a few pieces in the museum, family pieces, but nothing recent. Something on your mind?" I'd seen Sarah answer a question with a question before, and understood her method of getting more information before giving her real answer.

Sadie also had a casual way of not saying much, but still staying in the conversation. "I have friends," she added.

"Yesterday I came up with the idea of maybe selling some crystal glass pieces in Square Spirits. Expand my inventory."

"What brought on that idea?" Sadie asked.

"Customers keep asking me if the crystal bowls I use for the stone displays are for sale. I thought it might be a good idea to meet the demand."

"Would it also be part of Megan's idea about the Square being a go-to place for wedding couples?" Sarah didn't push, but instead let her comment fill the air.

"Maybe." I really hadn't thought about it that way, but why not? A crystal bowl could be an exquisite gift for women in the bridal party. "What do you think of her plan?"

"I think she's stumbled into a terrific idea," Sarah said. "Something we all can support."

"And it can evolve," Sadie added. "Megan is enormously creative. She'll find a way to involve everybody on the Square."

Sarah nodded along when Sadie said, "I'll make a few calls to my friends in the crystal business and then stop by."

"Thanks," I said, talking over a burst of laughter exploding across the room.

Alan's deep voice broke through the conversations of the small groups in the room. "Okay, folks, we're about to start the movie again."

Sarah grabbed her cup and was the first to leave. "I want to see this before Eli and Alan get tired of showing it."

We stood to follow her and navigated around chairs and tables to the opposite end of the café, where I took an empty seat in front of the screen.

The air moved. Eli was behind me.

"Okay, Alan, roll 'em," he said.

The video fulfilled its promise. Eli had focused on each building, filming close-ups of the window displays and the sentimental image of Doris waving generated a few ohs and ahs.

I stiffened when the last picture of Square Spirits came on the screen, although I managed to stifle a gasp. Most people wouldn't have differentiated the images in the window from the sun's reflections, but I did. *Grace and Rose.*

No one seemed eager to bring the gathering to a close and Stephanie's chicken vegetable soup and free-flowing coffee, hot chocolate, and tea took us through lunch into the late afternoon. The darkening sky brought flurries with it. I couldn't decide if that was an omen or not.

When I stepped outside to return home, Sarah and Sadie joined me, and surprisingly, Eli. Sadie left us at the museum, and Sarah gave us both a hug before unlocking her door.

Eli wasted no time. "Do you want to tell me about it?"

I'd rather have put it off, but on the other hand, Eli was asking now.

I didn't answer him directly, but said, "Come upstairs with me. I'll pour us a glass of wine." I silently asked the girls not to make their presence known. Maybe one day, but not now.

Back in silent mode, Eli waited for me to unlock the door. After relocking it, we walked around the displays and

I stopped as we passed the wine racks.

"These racks will be gone at some point," I said, "sooner rather than later, I hope. I'm going back to my original idea of shelves. Customers don't seem willing to pull the bottles out to look at the labels and make decisions. I had a feeling that would happen. But they do pick up the bottles I've got on top of the racks."

"Sure, it's an easy impulse buy." He studied the area around him, the stones and candles on the glass shelves. But he said nothing more, and waited for me to start up the stairs before he followed. He took off his jacket and hung it on the back of the chair. I hadn't put in a coat tree, so I ended up stashing my coat and hat and all the rest in the bedroom. I replaced my boots with a pair of clogs.

Eli stood by the table.

"Sit, Eli, please." The only wine I had on the counter was Zodiac, so I started uncorking it, but my hands trembled. Instead of sitting, Eli moved closer and stood behind me.

He reached around and put his hand over mine. Eli's hands were large, working hands with long fingers. "Let me. You get the glasses."

I took two of my favorite wine glasses out of the cabinet and put them near him. My mind scrambled with what to tell him, *how* to tell him. And *why*.

As jittery as I was, I no longer thought of Eli as a visitor. He'd been upstairs with me before. This quiet, taciturn man had learned more about me during that single visit than I'd revealed to anyone in a long time.

"Zoe?"

"Hmm?"

"You can trust me." He handed me a glass, and then pulled a chair from the table, taking it to the front window.

So, he no longer cares if someone sees him in my house. Interesting.

"I don't know where to start." Why was my voice so weak? I slipped my hand in my pocket and touched the amethyst stone, more out of habit than need. I didn't need the reassurance or the centering.

"Why'd you come to live here?" He pointed out the

window. "Here in...Wolf Creek."

I sat on the edge of the seat in the sunken-in chair. My hands hugged the glass. I mustered the courage to look Eli in the eye, but when he reached out to hold my hand I pulled back. His touch stirred something deep inside me. I needed a clear head to talk about the path that led me to this town, this building. And even to Grace and Rose.

I started with my family: Mom's support, Dad's health, and Devin's attitude toward my decision to leave the winery, when Devin thought they needed me more than ever.

I jumped back in time to Tyler and his decision to end our marriage. But even as I spoke, I saw the purple and white shawl hung on the back of my chair. Eli noticed it, too, and his slight frown revealed his misunderstanding, or at least confusion. I liked the shawl and hadn't hidden it out of sight. But as a gift, it had no secret meaning, at least as far as I was concerned.

Eli had barely moved since I'd started talking, except for maybe a quick glance out the window or a look around my bare living room.

He wants to understand me.

"I need you to know that I am a psychic, Eli. Not a fortune teller, not an astrologist, and definitely not a mind reader."

"So, that's why you bristle when I call you 'Madame Zoe'?" He grinned slyly. "You know I'm just razzing you."

"I know that now, but I didn't at first. But that was my fault. I took that name on for the festival here, never imagining I'd come back to stay."

I thought his light remark would make him more open to what I said about being a psychic, but instead he sat back in the chair, folded his arms across his chest, and extended his legs out in front of him. When he crossed his ankles, he'd put the final brick in the unmoving wall. I wondered if he would listen to anything more I had to say. But I plunged in.

"I know you understand a little bit about sensory skills, Eli." I paused and took a breath. "Maybe more than you let on. I sense feelings and sometimes even events that happened or are going to happen to people. Sometimes images form internally, and sometimes, I see things externally."

I stopped to take a sip of Zodiac and gather my thoughts.

"When people learn about my abilities, some jump on board and want to book a reading and see what I have to say about their future. Others back away, fearful that their private thoughts aren't private any longer. So I've learned to keep my intuitive impressions to myself, unless I'm asked. And I get the positive reactions right along with the negative."

I kicked off my clogs and pulled my legs up under me in the roomy chair.

"Last September when I came to Wolf Creek to be part of your festival, it never occurred to me that this would be where I'd find a place of energy and peace. *For me*. A place where I can be myself—or so I believed, anyway." With a scoff I added, "Tyler will never know that him leaving turned out be such a good thing for me."

My mouth had gone dry from talking, and probably nerves. I stopped for another sip. Eli rose and fetched the bottle from the counter. When he came back, he topped off our glasses.

"But what about *this* building?" Eli asked.

"At the festival, I looked at the empty building on the corner and in the upper windows I saw two young girls screaming for help while the building was engulfed in flames. That was one of the external images I saw, rather than coming from within. I saw their faces in the windows. Their mother stood in front of the building watching the horrible nightmare unfold while the townspeople worked frantically to put the fire out."

My hands shook as I relived that first vision. I tightened my grip on the wine glass, but Eli reached across the distance between us and took my glass from my hands. He was careful not to make contact.

"That vision left me with an overwhelming need to help these girls find peace by crossing into another dimension. I made an offer on the building that day, even after Sarah warned me about all the businesses that had failed here. Sarah has done a little research on the history of this building and the tragedy that surrounds it. I think she knows something is different about it." I took a breath. "But there's likely more to learn."

I almost basked in the gathering inner calm moving through me. It was time for the next step. First, I reached out to take my glass from Eli's hand. "Grace? Rose? Come meet Eli."

Surprised by my invitation to meet two spirits, Eli jumped out of his chair and sent it crashing to the floor on its side.

I chuckled. "Don't worry. They're not going to hurt you or whisk you away."

He picked up the chair, his face pink from the lingering embarrassment. "You sure about that?"

At that moment, tall, strong Eli Reynolds wasn't so confident. He wasn't the man on the Square flying his drone and cracking jokes.

Cool air swirled around me. "Eli, this is Grace. She's the eldest sister. Calm, but very protective of Rose. From reading Sarah's history of the building, I learned their real names are Madeline and Hazel, but they'll always be Grace and Rose to me."

Just then a warm flash butted up to my side. "And Rose has arrived now. She's the more intense spirit of the two."

Eli suddenly swatted the air. Hmm…did he feel them or was he only warding them off?

"Girls, girls. Be nice. Eli won't hurt me. Or you." I nodded to Eli to get his support of my comment.

"Hurt? How can you hurt a spirit?"

"Speaking unkindly to them hurts them, just as sure as if they had flesh and bones. Not listening when they tell you something, or dismissing them hurts, too. That part is the same as it is with the rest of us."

I waited for the tense energy to ease, a sign the girls were becoming comfortable around Eli. "You're smart. You'll know when you've upset them."

Eli grabbed the bottle from the floor and emptied the remaining wine into our glasses.

It's not every day you meet a spirit or two. Huh, big man?

The intensity of his expression made me realize he was far more intuitive than most people. I needed to remember that.

"They're gone." He scanned the room as if searching for them.

"Yes, they're at ease everywhere in the building. They sometimes come into the shop when customers are there." I grinned. "The hot and cold air circulates around and some people think my furnace is acting up. But I know better."

"They let themselves be in the video."

So, Eli finally jumped to the reason he'd come to my apartment.

I considered my words carefully before I spoke. "Most people will believe they are reflections of the sun on the windows. Maybe you should simply delete that part of the video. You showed Square Spirits early in the video, so you have no need to repeat it and test fate."

His frown told me he'd missed my meaning. More than anything, I wanted to avoid questions or upset skeptics on the Square who couldn't handle someone like me nearby. After all, how do you really explain that you've come to know two lively spirits? On the other hand, Eli had caught on…fast.

"So now you know all about me, Eli, and why I came to Wolf Creek." I stood up. My legs had tightened under my weight, but even more, in telling my story, I'd drained all my energy away. I had never wanted anyone to know my full history, mostly because I didn't want to admit how devastating Tyler's actions had been for me. And how facing that led me to question my own complicity with the way we'd arranged our lives almost completely around his needs.

I caught on to Eli's ability to sense my energy when he stood and gathered the empty bottle and our two glasses, putting them on the counter. He grabbed his jacket off the chair. "Get some sleep, Zoe." He grinned, pleased with himself. I saw it in his face.

"You, too. You were a real star today on the Square. And your drone is great fun."

And you saw the girls as sure as I did. And that was Grace's and Rose's decision, not mine.

15

Over the next few days, I debated with myself about attending the January business association meeting. I hadn't seen or talked to Eli since I'd told him about Grace and Rose. Maybe he had decided to avoid me. True, I'd had fewer chances to run into him because I hadn't been to B and B for morning coffee but once since New Year's Day where, with or without his presence, Eli's drone video was the favorite topic of conversation.

In the end I decided to go to the meeting. I had eagerly become part of the community and was grateful for the warmth of the welcome I'd received. No one had been anything but generous to me. And if Eli didn't want to talk about Grace and Rose ever again, then I'd adjust to that. Even if he was avoiding me, and I had no proof of that, I wouldn't avoid him.

I walked into the meeting room, greeted by Sarah and her calm smile.

She has good news. A strong, positive energetic field surrounded her.

I chose the open seat next to Megan. Clayton sat on her other side. They were holding hands. Something about them and the freshness of their love made me smile.

Megan leaned toward me and whispered, "It's crunch time. Sarah's announcing my idea tonight, so if you want to back out, you have the next five minutes to say so."

What a hoot she was. "No way. I want to be in the booth with you. You're the best entertainment around. By the way, I need to talk to Nora. Now." I stood up and pivoted around until I spotted her talking with Georgia. "I'll be right back, Megan. Save my chair."

I hurried across the room and waited for Nora to finish her conversation before telling her I'd realized I'd need some part-time help after all. "I'm wising up, and there's no way I can handle my shop alone, even during these slow times."

"Good. I've been spreading the word about her, so don't wait to call." Nora pulled her phone out, scrolling, and then I entered JoAnn's number into mine.

"Thanks," I said. "If I get back early enough, I'll call her tonight."

"I think she'll enjoy working in your shop."

I found my seat next to Megan right before Sarah tapped the microphone to begin the meeting. She waited for the room to settle and the buzz of conversation to die down, then she welcomed us to the beginning of another year on Wolf Creek Square. She lifted her arms in celebration, and the clapping began. It didn't last long, because Sarah raised her voice and quickly ran down a list of improvements and developments that occurred over the last year. "We're all aware that the new shops are bringing more people to the Square, and we've seen great success from our advertising campaign."

The agenda itself had all of two items: Snowman Saturday and The Wedding Extravaganza.

"I'm going to let Art and Clayton discuss their ideas about ways we can do even more to promote the Square as a year-around shopping destination. They tell me they're open to any and all ideas." She stepped aside to make room for the two men to stand behind the podium.

With a sweep of his hand, Clayton deferred to Art to start.

"This is one of those ideas that comes without intention and is forged on a napkin," Art said.

Laughter rippled through the room, which is no doubt exactly what Art wanted. I always read a level of contentment with Art…never too high, never very low. But happy.

Art explained that the idea was born when Clayton asked him if he should close his shop during the winter months. Other than the occasional shopper looking for a gift, Clayton couldn't foresee many sales.

I'd been wondering about the same issue. Megan's wedding idea was the only reason I was concerned about needing help. If I was expected to be in The Wedding Extravaganza booth then I couldn't also be in the shop. I couldn't bi-locate. I snickered to myself. If I could be in two places at once, the people on the Square really *would* try to avoid me.

"I told Clayton that we probably all needed a rest after the summer rush and holiday frenzy," Art said. "But I wondered if we could attract people for special events, like a Saturday where the kids could all make snowmen on the Square. We could all have special sale items chosen around a snowman or winter theme, if possible."

"Great idea…if we have snow," Elliot called out.

"When *doesn't* Wisconsin have snow in January?" Jessica added.

"I think it is a great idea, but do we have time to get the PR ready so people know what we're offering?" Marianna asked. She held her grandson, Thomas, on her lap. He was turning the pages of a small book.

"Focus, honey," Art said. "You have two weeks."

As low-key as Art was, everyone knew he and Marianna had found something special. They had their own shops and separate lives, and weren't particularly showy about their love. Yet, hardly a day went by when they weren't together, usually at Crossroads for dinner or sometimes just dessert.

"Okay, then, I guess we won't have time for pie and coffee at Crossroads," Marianna teased.

"No problem, I'll order takeout and bring it to you myself," he countered.

Steph raised her hand and stood. "I think we can set aside some space to make hand-cranked ice cream with the kids. We can serve hot chocolate and a cookie for a snack. Maybe simple sandwiches. I'll revamp the menu, and if it's not too cold everything can be taken outside."

Steph was obviously into the idea, and Clayton's face brightened. He and Art had won an ally.

"What if there's a blizzard?" Someone in the back called

out.

"That's always a risk," Elliot said. "We have to take our chances."

That was one point everyone could agree on. Over the next few minutes, the group batted ideas back and forth, addressing possible objections, but it didn't take long to reach consensus. Snowman Saturday was a go, with the only major investment being the advertising.

"Any more comments?" Clayton asked.

Sarah walked to the front and resumed her role as chair. She quickly wrapped up the conversation by asking for advertising ideas and reassuring everyone that she'd get the ad buys underway. "Okay, Megan, you're up next," she said.

Megan, who seemed at ease and friendly most of the time, looked oddly nervous when she went to the podium with her small notebook. She covered her nervousness with her beautiful smile. She was petite and pretty, where her brothers were tall and muscular, but the family resemblance was strong, especially in their facial expressions and the way they spoke.

"You all know I jump in with new ideas and opportunities before I consider the long-term benefits and consequences," she said, tilting her head to indicate she was joking...sort of.

But I heard the self-deprecating tone and wished she could snatch the words out of the air and start again.

Her confidence came back when she talked about helping Lily and Georgia plan their weddings. "I became a wedding planner almost by accident. But now I've got Nora helping out at Rainbow Gardens and I'm focused on brides and their special day.

"So, when I reserved a vendor booth at The Wedding Extravaganza in Green Bay, I realized that my really big dream is to promote Wolf Creek Square as the go-to place for couples planning their wedding."

Low murmurs traveled around the room. Good. Megan had focused and now she had command of the room. She began listing the shops and how they could be involved. Everyone had a role to play. Tracie and Katie raised their hands. They wanted in. Clayton and Art. Jessica and Mimi.

Doris and Marianna.

"What about you, Zoe? Are you in?" Megan asked.

Until I heard my name I'd been fascinated by watching the various people step up. "Yes. For sure. I'll help with whatever needs to be done."

Sarah again stepped in to make sure everyone was on board. Without any dissenting comments, she announced that the Square would now be promoted as a one-stop-opportunity for weddings. "But don't head to the snack table yet," she said. "I actually do have a third item."

Someone groaned in the back.

"Oh, stop," she said. "This is very good news. The deal was finalized just this afternoon. Nolan and Reed Crawford have purchased the empty building between Quilts Galore and Pages and Toys."

This news brought cheers and a round of applause, led by Elliot. Eli had told me that his brother's dream was to have every building on the Square transformed into a bustling shop.

"They're going to renovate and bring it up to code." She motioned for the two men to get to their feet. "Come on, stand up and tell us more."

Nolan, the more outgoing cousin, spoke, "Nothing complicated. We'll do the same thing as Charlie did with Clayton's building. Remodel, renovate, get it ready for a new retail shop to open."

"We're going to live upstairs for now, so expect to see lights at night," Reed added. "That's when we'll be doing most of the work."

"Well, only one empty building left to fill," Sarah said, pointing to Elliot, who responded with a double thumbs-up.

With that, the meeting ended, but no one seemed in a rush to leave. I stayed close to Megan, who was fielding questions from the women who had stepped up to be part of her wedding vision. The men gravitated to the Crawfords and their project.

Out of the corner of my eye, I saw Doris slip out of the room without speaking to anyone. I was certain Megan had included her in the vision. Wedding planning how-to books for starters, but also the wedding guest books and photo albums. They'd be a cinch to carry. But maybe Doris couldn't see that she had a part to play.

"Zoe told me earlier that she wanted to be in the booth with me," Megan was saying, her voice authoritative, "so on this first venture, she and I will be working closely together. If you have ideas, stop in and tell them to her. She's going to be my go-to person. We'll need some brochures and your display samples."

I'd never agreed to be her go-to person, but I didn't mind. I took her comment as a sign of another 'jump-right-in' decision.

Standing behind Megan, Liz Pearson said, "I think we need a group brochure that promotes each shop on the Square and details what they specifically offer for the bride and groom."

"Terrific idea." Megan reached out to bring Liz closer. "Have you met Zoe Miller from Square Spirits?"

"We met briefly at morning coffee," I said.

"Liz wears many hats," Megan said, "and has helped all of us at different times."

Liz and I shook hands. I felt exactly what I expected. *Busy, colorful energy, a spirit lifter, like her clothes.*

Mimi mentioned the gift certificate Liz had designed for Styles. "She's done them for most shops, so let's get her started on a brochure."

I mentally filed away that point, but Megan took a minute to jot the idea in her open notebook.

Seeing Liz reminded me that the gift certificates I'd used were right out of a standard stationary store. I definitely needed a new design that reflected Square Spirits.

The talk turned to a handbook to give out at the show, a brochure, with Liz handling the designs. Liz's and Megan's pens were flying as they threw out ideas.

My attention gradually waned as our talk of the upcoming wedding show wound down, and when I looked away and out into the room, I saw Eli standing off to the side. Alone. Again. The lonely energy pulsed from him.

Sarah soon shooed us away, reminding us that Melanie

needed to let her crew in to set up a private brunch in the morning. We soon filed out of the room, with a few staying behind to get a table in the dining room to have coffee or a drink. The rest of us left through the hotel lobby, where remnants of Christmas remained, from wrapped up packages to Santa and his elves.

Outside, some odd-looking and small hand-made snowmen still stood. Some kids had built them from the light snow we'd had on New Year's Day. A fresh layer of light snow covered the Square, with the tree lights providing bright spots against the dark sky.

I joined Sarah, Megan, and Clayton heading to our corner of the Square. Megan stopped talking only long enough to take a breath. Ideas were still flowing from her, the good, the bad, and the very ugly. Clayton freely gave his opinion of each one.

When I stepped inside Square Spirits and turned to relock the door, I saw the lights above Country Law shining.

Why, Eli? Why didn't you wait for me and walk me home?

***

The next morning I ignored my recent resolution to add variety to my breakfast. Instead, I opted for my usual and quickly toasted a bagel. Along with my last carton of yogurt, I took my food and coffee and went downstairs to start the day. I chewed a bite of the bagel and flipped my day planner open. Whoa! By the time half the bagel was gone, I'd jotted notes and filled in dates; January was no longer a lazy winter month to while away in hibernation. Snowman Saturday and The Wedding Extravaganza loomed.

Shortly after eight I called JoAnn. After a quick greeting she simply said, "Nora called last night, and the answer is yes. I'd love to work with you."

"Wow. That was easy," I said with a laugh, "but I'll need to get you up to speed on the inventory and such in a hurry. January is shaping up to be a hectic month."

"I know working in a specialty shop isn't the same as the department store jobs I've held over the years, but I love a challenge," JoAnn said. "I can start tomorrow if you want."

I agreed, and made a note to get her employee paperwork started. Next to JoAnn's name I wrote *Grace and Rose*. They'd been respectful of Julia, receding into the background so as not to frighten her. Would they be as kind to JoAnn?

"I'm counting on you, Grace and Rose," I said aloud. "I need JoAnn to help make running this shop a little easier for me."

Faint shifts in the air followed. I needed a stronger response. Hmm…I'd have to talk to them again.

Looking around the display area I decided to keep my white holiday decorations of hanging stars and crescent moons and snowflakes. They'd be fine for January. I hadn't given much thought to changing decorations each holiday, or every month the way some owners did. I'd heard Megan and Marianna groan a little about the challenge of coming up with fresh ideas for these ever-changing displays. Smiling smugly, Doris had said, "That's Lily's job." On the other hand, Nora seemed to revel in the challenge that Megan had dropped in her lap.

When I unlocked the door, only a handful of people were milling around the Square, but within minutes the bell jingled and Liz came in. Arms loaded with her laptop case, file folders, and her well-stuffed bag hung from her shoulder.

I led her to the back table where I offered her a cup of tea and she readily accepted.

"That cold wind this morning is bone chilling," she said.

"I've been focused on the month ahead and barely noticed," I said. "Would you like to look around while I make our tea?"

Liz bobbed her head back and forth. "Maybe later. I don't want to distract myself from the real reason I barged in without calling first."

"You'll always be welcome here," I said, grinning. "And I'm in need of your skills."

I went into the reading room to heat the water in my electric kettle, while she spread out her files on the table.

"I couldn't sleep last night thinking about the brochure

for The Wedding Extravaganza," she said, excitement in her voice. From what I could tell, that was fairly typical for Liz.

I went back to the table while I waited for the water to heat. She had turned her computer screen so I could see it. "I already mocked up a couple of sample brochures."

Not wanting to overstep my say-so, I suggested we call Megan to have her join us.

Liz narrowed her eyes in thought for a few seconds. "Let's put three samples together first. If she doesn't like any of them she can tell us her ideas. And she trusts your judgment."

"I know you two have worked together before," I said, "so let's just say I trust *your* opinions on how to proceed."

I went back to the reading room and, using what I had on hand, I brewed a pot of peppermint tea.

By the time I came back with the teapot and mugs, I could almost see the wheels turning in her brain. I probably could have added water to yesterday's coffee grounds and it wouldn't have fazed her. I filled the mugs and then pulled the empty chair around to sit side-by-side rather than across from her. But in what I hoped was a subtle move, I shifted the chair to create more distance between us. I had to keep her energy from bombarding me.

Liz was great fun, and a wonderful generous heart. Although her currents—her vibes—were strong, focused, and positive, her joy was easily transmitted to those around her. She also could be overpowering at times, at least to me. I knew that just from being near her on occasion at B and B.

Her exuberant energy spilled over into her samples. Each one, though different in color, layout style, and emphasis, focused on the charm of Wolf Creek Square and what each shop offered.

She looked around the shop, but she soon caught a glimpse of the large amethyst piece on the shelf above the bowls of stones. "I wasn't sure what to add for Square Spirits, other than wine, but obviously there's much more here." She pointed to the high shelf. "The amethyst is incredible."

"Ah, it's the rich purple that draws me. And as you probably guessed, my signature fragrance is lavender." I explained that over the holiday month, I'd sold hundreds of candles and small polished stones, along with many dozens of journals and books and pieces of jewelry.

"The lunar calendars and note cards with pen and ink drawings of the constellations were big sellers, too," I added. "But for the bridal end of things, Megan and I thought I could put together gift boxes—she's named them Bride Boxes—with lavender hand cream, polished amethyst and rose quartz stones, a journal, maybe a sprig of dried lavender. The crystal jewelry could be added for the more elaborate boxes. Each bride can personalize them to suit her attendants or special people in the ceremony."

Liz was jotting notes as I talked, underlining what I assumed were buzz words—power words—to use in the brochure. "I like that. I can highlight that this is different from any other shop. And like Doris' guest books, they'll make standout display items in the booth."

"So the plan is to get the brochures ready by the end of the month?"

Liz gave the table a light slap and then swallowed a big gulp of her tea. "You bet. Print shops are often slow in January, so we can get a rush job if need be. No one wants the extra cost, though."

Each of us would need to pay a fee to seed the project, which made sense. All of us understood the risk involved.

I pointed to the version of the brochure with a bride on the cover. Liz had included a small map of the Square with instructions for getting to Wolf Creek from all four directions. After a few lines to explain the one-stop concept, the shops and their themes were featured alphabetically. "I like this one the best."

Liz nodded. "It's even-handed. No one shop is weighted as more important than another." She pulled another printed version out of her briefcase. "In this sample, the order follows the location of each shop and I take the viewer/reader on a trip around the Square to feature each shop."

"I like that one, too," I said, "very much. It's a logical way to guide people around the Square."

She had printed another sample and put that one in front

191

of me. "I tried a different approach with this one, which was to list the shops in the logical order of use." She chuckled. "But trust Jack to point out that my logic might not match the way brides and grooms think. My husband-the-lawyer would think of that, so I put it aside."

The pride in her husband was evident in her smile and the tone of her voice. Such affection, too.

Would I ever hear anyone talk about me that way?

Tyler used to heap praise on me in front of other people, but I eventually realized that had been just for show.

When the bell jingled and a customer came in, Liz quickly gathered her files. Before she had a chance to hurry away, I gave her one of my shopping bags with my logo and asked her to design a gift certificate and a new business card. "You have a great eye, Liz. I trust your ideas."

Liz nodded, but stayed by the table when I went to greet the customer, a young woman.

"Megan Reynolds is my wedding planner and she sent me over," the woman said. "I need gifts for my attendants."

"Of course," I said. "Let's see what we can do."

Liz flashed a quick smile and waved goodbye.

Since I hadn't yet prepared a full complement of ideas for the boxes, I had to improvise. I'd put an express delivery order for the actual white boxes and wrapping as soon as the customer gave me an idea of what she wanted. As the bride and I spoke, I gradually surmised that she preferred a dominant white design for the box, with the lavender accents. I offered to put a few samples together for her to look at in a week or so.

"I want real keepsakes," she said, jotting notes in her pocket-sized notepad, "including the box itself. And what you offer is different—fun, especially the stones."

Since she wanted Scott, the groom, to see what she chose, that meant stopping by the shop on the weekend. She handed me her business card with all her contact information… including Facebook, twitter, and through her blog.

"I can reach you about six different ways," I teased.

"That's the idea," she said, nonplussed by what was meant to be a light comment.

After she left, I went to the computer and searched for the kind of boxes that would work, not just for this customer, but also for others. They came in every style from sturdy fiberboard to velvet-lined, printed or plain, folded or latched. A couple of months ago I'd have never jumped ahead and thought this kind of item would be important to the future of Square Spirits. Of course, I hadn't even known Megan, let alone about her new concept. The fluttering in my gut was partly from excitement, but also from nervousness. A lot was riding on my decisions, and I was determined not to disappoint Megan—or myself.

Suddenly, cool and warm currents enveloped me. "So, you approve of my new direction." In that moment, I realized how much I counted on communicating with these spirits. My heart sank a little. The time would come when Grace and Rose would be willing to complete their journey away from this realm and on to another. As right and expected as that was, I'd miss them.

I perked up again quickly. With the shop empty and box samples and packaging ordered, I elaborated on my arrangement with JoAnn to Grace and Rose. Even after telling them they'd be alone with her in the shop, neither seemed upset. They just kept sending the warm and cool air in gentle swirls around me. I sighed, knowing those air currents would be gone one day.

Right before closing time, Sadie stopped by. Dressed in a tailored wool coat, she wore a multicolored hat and matching scarf. Nothing covered her hands. I shook my head. "Sadie, this is Wisconsin. People get frostbite here. You need gloves or mittens."

"Couldn't find them." She flicked her hand to dismiss the subject. She unwound the scarf and unbuttoned her coat, but she left her hat on.

"What brings you by?" I asked.

"Information."

I found her deliberate vagueness intriguing, so I played along.

"About?" I didn't know if she was referring to the history of the building or something else.

"Crystal."

My whole body relaxed. Why had I assumed she might want to discuss Grace and Rose? With her job in the museum, if she didn't already know about them, she soon would.

"With Megan putting the Square as a destination for wedding couples, it's perfect for you. The couple could even list Square Spirits as part of their registry."

"There's an idea," I said.

She reached into her coat pocket and brought out a brochure and a sheet of handwritten notes. "I called a couple of friends who own a crystal shop in Manhattan. I told them about your shop and they would like to talk to you. They can answer all your questions."

Somehow, the day was crowding in on me. Too much, too fast? I wasn't sure, but I needed to catch my breath. "Oh, but Sadie, since I mentioned the bowls the other day, I haven't given the idea much thought. Megan's idea for the Square has grabbed my focus. I could be spreading my resources in the wrong direction."

"For what it's worth," Sadie said, "I don't agree. First, you don't have to sell the most expensive line of crystal. In fact, that would make shoppers who come to the Square feel priced out. That's not to say they don't appreciate quality, because they do. Look at the business Mimi and Jessica do at Styles. Nothing ordinary about what they carry, but it's all within a price range that suits *this* region. Your choice of crystal pieces could be the same."

I understood. I'd lived in Tyler's artificial world and never wanted to spend money we could barely afford just to look good on his arm at some so-called important event. But what was wrong with offering my customers a little bling? One could argue that crystals and jewelry and wine were all about *adding* a touch of bling.

I set my jaw in an obvious way and squared my shoulders. "You are so right. I'll give them a call soon." I didn't want to commit to actually doing business with them before I learned more.

"'Night, Zoe," Sadie said heading to the door. "Glad

you'll give it some serious thought."

"Find your gloves," I called out. Too late. The bell was already jingling.

I locked the door and looked over the Square. The daylight hours were getting longer, if only by minutes, but that didn't mean the harshest part of winter was over. It was just beginning.

As I was turning away, I noticed Eli leaving Farmer Foods and heading toward Country Law. Feeling bold, I unlocked the door and stepped out. "Eli? Want to grab supper at Crossroads tonight?"

He immediately reversed his direction and came toward me. "Oh, hi, Zoe."

The way he said my name brought my attraction to him to the surface. No wonder my cells came alive.

He came closer, just to the edge of the outer circle of my comfort zone.

Out of habit, I had the urge to step back, but I didn't. I stood my ground. I trusted Eli wasn't invading my space, so to speak, to gain some psychological advantage. This was Eli, not Tyler.

"So? Dinner?" I asked again.

"Sure," he said, his voice cheerful. "I was going to meet Megan and Clayton anyway. Now you can join us."

"Well, I don't want—"

"You're not intruding. Grab your coat."

I ran upstairs and fixed my makeup and thought about loosening my braid and letting my hair hang loose. But that would take too long. I grabbed my starry night poncho and purse.

I found Eli looking at the wine racks again. "Have you asked Nolan or Reed about the shelving?"

"Not yet," I said, "and after buying that building, I doubt they'll have time."

"I can build them for you."

"You?" I hadn't heard anyone mention Eli knowing anything about wood working or even having an interest in it.

"Shelves aren't hard," he said with a grin. "I've made

many for the store throughout the years. Actually, I always wanted to be a carpenter."

Not waiting for me to react, he went to the door and walked out, then waited for me to lock up.

"Can you do it soon?" I asked. "I'd like them installed before the Square gets busy again."

"I'll stop by tomorrow and get measurements, and then I can give you an estimate."

Lucky me. I'd learned another facet of Mr. Eli Reynolds.

We were a fun foursome at dinner, starting with our shared bottle of DmZ wine. Our conversation was all about Megan's one-stop-wedding-destination-plan, and Eli and I couldn't help but laugh at Clayton's attempt to keep her ideas on track.

We were winding down our evening over coffee, when Eli said, "I've decided to convert the upstairs of Farmer Foods into an apartment—my apartment."

"Really?" Megan asked. "I hadn't heard you talk about that before."

"I've been thinking about it. And, what's more, I'm going to do the work myself. Well, almost all of it. I'll ask the Crawford guys for help here and there if I need it."

Megan almost jumped out of her chair. "We'll be neighbors. Isn't that exciting?"

My heart beat fast, my head felt light. I grabbed the edge of the table. *Eli would be closer, almost within arm's reach.*

"Zoe? Are you okay?" Eli touched my arm, and his energy shot from his hand into me.

"Oh, yes, it's just been quite a day. A lot for me to absorb." The warmth in my face intensified when I saw Megan and Clayton exchange a pointed look.

I became conscious that I'd gripped the table edge so tightly my knuckles turned white. I let go and rested my hands in my lap. "That's quite a project for you isn't it, Eli?"

For all of our talking I still knew so little about Eli's past or future dreams or plans or what was on his to-do list for tomorrow.

"We've got a long winter ahead," he said, his hand still

on my arm.

I wasn't used to that kind of concern directed toward me. I didn't want Megan and Clayton to think Eli and I were more than friends. But I didn't want to pull away.

Clayton removed a small pad of paper and a pen from his coat pocket and handed it to Eli. "Show us a sketch of your plans, Eli. You going to leave it open concept or make it a multi-room design?"

Eli made a few lines on the paper. "Nothing elaborate. I'll put up a false wall here to separate the store's office from the apartment. Bedroom, bath, kitchen, fireplace…"

"Fireplace?" Megan was incredulous. "You were so adamant that I not have one in my place, but now *you'll* have one?"

"I'm enjoying the one in Nathan's place," Eli said. "I admit I thought it was an unnecessary expense. I was mistaken."

"I believe you called it 'frivolous', Eli," Megan said, chastising him, but not in an angry way.

"Oh, by the way, I like that Charlie put the washing machine in the bathroom," Eli said. "Good idea. Convenient."

Hearing Eli describe Nathan's place made me feel like a poor relative. "I don't have either of those features in mine."

Eli laughed. "You don't have anything in your place. Well, except for that antique desk. Now that's a piece." Just to emphasize his knowledge of my place, he looked at Megan and Clayton. "I know what I'm talking about. I've been up there. It's as empty as a warehouse."

I laughed along with him, but I'd have preferred to disappear, or at least, crawl under the table. But it was one of those times when silence was the best response. That's not the route I took. "I'll get myself unpacked and settled in eventually. I poured every bit of my energy into the shop."

"I'll bet," Megan said, "and it shows."

A soft rose color appeared on Eli's face and neck. "I'm sorry. I didn't mean to imply that it wasn't a nice place."

"It's okay," I said with a light laugh. "I know you were only teasing."

When Clayton put his napkin on the table, we all took it

as a sign to bring the evening to a close. "I wish Melanie ran accounts for us like Steph does at B and B," Clayton said.

Megan burst out laughing. "Oh sure, it would be even easier to skip fixing dinner. We'd end up coming here every night, honey."

We all seemed to get past Eli's awkward remark, except Eli. He'd gone quiet, and his discomfort made me want to become invisible.

As we walked to the front of the restaurant, someone dining with other people stopped Eli, asking him a question about Farmer Foods. Megan and Clayton waved goodbye and went on ahead, but I hung back and waited.

After we'd left the restaurant and started home, Eli continued his silent mode. As we approached Square Spirits he cleared his throat. "I'm sorry, Zoe. I didn't think my words would come out like I was mocking you. And they did. I shouldn't have said anything about being up in your place anyway. You've been so well accepted here in the Square and I know you don't want anyone to get the wrong idea about us."

"So, there's an 'us'?" I said, showing no expression on my face.

"Is that what you want?"

"Eli, I don't know, really I don't. I mean, I have feelings for you, but..." It had taken all this time to get my independence back. I didn't know what "us" meant to Eli. I couldn't define it for myself. I was only certain my next relationship couldn't ever be like it was with Tyler. Besides, I didn't know Eli well enough to explain. "I mean, my past has been complicated."

"Right." He backed away.

"Wait! Eli, let me explain…"

Eli didn't wait for me to elaborate or stumble around finding something to say. He took the words at face value and kept walking. But out of the corner of my eye I saw him watching me from a distance until I'd locked my door. Then he continued on to Country Law.

Why didn't I call out, stop him and make him listen to me? Simple answer. I didn't know what to say. He'd taken a risk, asked me what I wanted and I'd failed him—and myself—by offering nothing back.

As I closed the door the bell jingled, the sound a lonely echo in the shop. It sounded hollow, mournful. The bell hadn't changed. I had.

16

JoAnn arrived in an upbeat mood, which I needed. My energy had been sad and unsettled all night. For sure, Eli would avoid me. I'd most likely driven him away. So much for my wine shelves.

Fortunately, JoAnn's cheerful smile lifted my spirits. Or, at least made it easy to pretend all was fine with me. She arrived dressed to fit into the atmosphere in the shop, black slacks and a pink sweater. Her small diamond necklace and matching earrings sparkled in the bright lights.

"Like I said on the phone, I'm not a complete retail novice," she said, "but I haven't worked for a while. I left my last job when Nora needed help to recover from her accident, and David and I relocated to Green Bay to be with her. So, I'll need to learn your system from the bottom up."

"Did Nora tell you about Megan's wedding destination idea?"

"Ha! Are you kidding? She hasn't talked about anything else. I wish I were as creative as Megan."

"Be careful what you wish for," I joked. "Besides, you don't know that you aren't as creative as anyone on the Square."

She smiled—a very skeptical smile. But from what I could tell, she had active creative energy.

My energy lightened up because of the feelings I'd gathered from JoAnn, and without her realizing it, Grace and Rose had been by my side. They helped, too.

By the end of the week JoAnn had spent enough afternoons in the shop that I was confident she could help customers on her own. And that cold week brought very few. My sample gift boxes had arrived, so I spent time playing around with various content combinations, trying to settle on a basic menu of options that was flexible enough to allow each order to be customized. JoAnn was eager to offer suggestions, but not in a forceful way.

We found a good rhythm when we were in the shop together. And she was willing to take her work hours as they came, more for some weeks, fewer for others. For the next two or three weeks I'd not need her fulltime except when I was away for the whole day, and after that, we'd have to see how the spring and summer business developed.

I asked JoAnn for her ideas about the upcoming Snowman Saturday. I was stumped. Nothing in the shop was connected to snowmen, and by the end of the week I was beginning to accept that Square Spirits wasn't the type of store that would feature snow creatures.

In the midst of pondering the problem, I glanced out the window and saw that the decorations on the Square had been changed from the holidays to snowmen, some traditional and some more like the new style action figures. Some had real hats and scarves, others were decorated with only painted cutouts.

Then an idea hit me. I could have cutout snowmen, or snowwomen, in my case, wearing necklaces and pendants, maybe a few with scarves.

But where would I get the cutout figures?

Before I stopped to consider, maybe over think what had passed between us the last time I saw him, I punched the speed dial for Eli's cell.

When he answered with a flat hello, I asked, "Could you possibly make some snowmen for me?"

"Out of snow?"

Of course, that's what he'd think.

"No. Let me rephrase the question," I said with a laugh. "I got excited and forgot to explain myself. I need wooden ones, like the kind in the Square."

"That big?"

"Oh, no, no, something smaller for the shop." Had I

expected him to read my mind and immediately understand what I wanted?

Yes…that's exactly what I expected.

"Hmm…"

"I'm thinking of using them as displays for pendants or scarves."

"How many you need?" he asked.

"A dozen."

"Big job."

"Okay, six." *Please…*

"Sure."

"Uh, I need them for the weekend." *Please…*

"Okay…want to help?"

That threw me. "Uh, I don't know anything about working with wood."

"We'll go to the farm after work. I'll cut, you paint."

Call ended.

Silence.

Smiling to myself, I mentally shuffled through my closet to figure out what I could wear to paint. And have fun.

***

Three evenings later we carried six snowmen into the shop. They varied in size from 12 to 18 inches, and Eli had given them whimsical faces after I'd done the basic painting. One had an exaggerated wink, and another had her mouth open as if she'd thrown her head back in laughter. Another had big, rounded teeth showing her friendly smile. I put her near the register as a symbol of a happy customer. Another sat on the table in the front window.

I'd learned a whole lot more about Eli Reynolds, the man, out at the farm. In contrast to me, he'd never married, and had spent most of his time alone. He'd had a few girlfriends, but the relationships hadn't lasted long. He loved his family, Wolf Creek, and his work. That's what kept him going.

"No love-of-your-life story to tell me?" For some reason, probably self-consciousness, I'd let out a burst of laughter, regretting it instantly because, of course, he turned away.

I might as well have poured salt in the wound.

The most revealing part of the conversation wasn't strictly about Eli at all, though. His parents had a strong commitment to Wolf Creek and keeping it a viable small town. They had been determined to make a go of Eli's grandfather's small grocery store, the first full-sized market in town. By the time their father had groomed Eli and Elliot to take over the business, Eli's desire to become a carpenter had been put aside for the future of the family business.

Intuitively, I knew there was more to his life's story. All along I'd sensed that one major event had paralyzed Eli and kept him from having a serious relationship with a woman. Just in the course of casual conversation I'd learned something major had driven a wedge between Georgia and Elliot and kept them apart for most of their adult lives. No wonder those two were so happy now.

While we worked at the farm, they had come to the workshop to see what we were up to and watch us make progress, but most of the time they had left us alone to work. Knowing a little about Georgia and Elliot's story was all well and good, but it didn't offer much insight into Eli.

Eli talked easily as we worked in the workshop next to the barn. It was as if keeping his hands busy loosened him up, and all my awkward questions and tactless remarks seemed not to irk him.

Back in Square Spirits with the six snowmen unloaded, Eli went to the wine racks and ran his hand across the top. "I'll stop by to measure for the shelves tomorrow. I'm going to want one of these for my apartment. And you should take the other one upstairs."

"So you think I need more furniture, do you?" I smiled all the way through the comment, hoping to be clear I was teasing, not holding any ill feelings about his remarks about my empty apartment.

But he didn't comment.

Eli soon left, quickly and with no lingering at the door to say goodnight. That was okay. At least we were back to acting like friends, which created easier, uncomplicated energy between us. What a relief.

Early the next morning, I filled my over-sized thermal cup with my favorite hazelnut coffee and trekked downstairs to get to work on my snowmen display. Before I'd draped the hand-beaded scarf around the fat neck of the last snow-woman cut-out, Eli knocked on the back door.

I let him in, and immediately his warm energy enveloped me. Then the girls surrounded him—and me, too.

"Grace and Rose are here," Eli spoke calmly, as if their presence was an everyday occurrence. No dramatics, no resistance.

"They're comfortable around you." He had no idea how happy that made me.

One thing I knew for sure about Eli was that he wasted no time in idle talk. So, with Grace and Rose acknowledged, he got to work, simply handing me one end of the tape measure. Like carpenters and contractors and builders of all kinds everywhere, he took a tiny spiral notebook out of his shirt pocket, along with a stub of a pencil and made his notes.

"Good to know," he said, once the measurements were done.

"What's good to know?" I asked.

"Oh, well, just that Grace and Rose are okay with me being around." Eli's voice was steady as if he'd been around young spirits every day of his life. Then, as if that subject was done with, he drew a sketch of the shelves and turned to me. "I think you should have glass on the top of one set of the shelves. That will let the light through."

He'd startled me. His idea was exactly the solution to a problem that had bothered me from the beginning. "You're right. This side of the shop has always felt heavy. Even dark. Now that I'm mixing it up a bit, I'm inclined to put some of the wine bottles over there, too." I pointed to the areas where my New Age items were displayed.

"Better marketing that way. Wouldn't work well in every shop," Eli said. "We couldn't mix up the apples with the cookies, but we do put displays of crackers and cheese or bags of soup vegetables and ready-made salad greens together. It's eye-catching. It could work in here, too."

"Eli, do you remember Clayton's painting upstairs? The lavender?"

He nodded and looked toward the wall in the alcove by the small table. "There. I'd put it there." But then he backed off, turned a little pink around the collar, as if he'd over-stepped. "You might want it somewhere else, or not even down here at all."

"But I do, and I'll post a sign indicating that it's a Clayton Sommers original. I'm going to pick up the pace with the soft marketing Marianna talks about." I was still thinking about asking Jessica and Mimi to loan me a body form and a great looking outfit to put in the window. I'd accessorize it and let shoppers know that the clothing came from Styles.

Lost in thought, I didn't notice JoAnn at the door until the bell jingled. From her expression, I could tell she couldn't place Eli, so I explained to her that he was Megan's brother. "One of them, anyway. Elliot is his twin."

"Welcome to the Square, JoAnn," Eli said, gathering his measuring tape and notes. "Time for me to get to work at Farmer Foods."

He nodded as he said, "Zoe."

His familiar tone sent a ripple through me.

Oh, Eli. What are you doing to me?

JoAnn put her coat and purse in the back room, which had turned into a bit too much of a "catch-all" space. Half unpacked boxes of newly arrived scarves and loose stones needed to be logged into the inventory system.

Even though I'd already given JoAnn a rundown on the systems of the store and some of the items I carried explained themselves, I needed to talk to her more about the New Age theme. It could puzzle her, or like a few customers, be a bit much. A few shoppers had taken one look at the crystals and pendulums and headed for the exit.

I'd barely begun the conversation when the first customer of the day arrived. I nodded to JoAnn to help her and quickly learned the woman was looking for a hostess gift.

"It's all adults, a few friends having dinner and a quiet evening together. That sort of thing. Not all women, though, like a book club. Some couples and a few single people."

JoAnn pointed to the wine. "But, you might also want to look at some of the newly marked down calendars. It's still early enough in January to give one as a gift." JoAnn picked up the end of an unusual midnight blue beaded scarf. "This is a personal kind of gift…any woman would love it. Or, you could keep it casual with one of these blank journals." JoAnn picked up two, one with the yin-yang circle in the center in gold and white against a black cover, the other a soft lavender shade.

The woman sighed, and lifted the scarf off the rack. Grinning, she said, "I'll take a scarf for myself, thank you very much. And for my hosts, I'll take a journal for Gwen and a bottle of wine for Troy."

I laughed to myself at how easily JoAnn had made a substantial sale. So far, I'd sold at least a dozen of the beaded scarves.

"If you're interested, I have a new wine, as of Christmas," I said, figuring it was time for me to interact with the customer. "My family owns DmZ Winery and Zodiac is the newest variety. It's a semi-sweet, strawberry and grape sparkling wine."

"No," she said, "as tempting as that sounds, I'll go with a dry red."

"Of course, I'll get a couple to show you." Odd how a stranger rejecting my wine, my Zodiac, made me feel a little rejected. *Get a grip, Zoe.*

While JoAnn wrapped the scarf and the journal, I went off to get two bottles of wine. By the time I came back, the customer had noticed another scarf, one that I draped around the neck of a snowman. Heavier than the blue beaded one, this style was made from light gray wool with a bright sunburst design that stood out against the background.

"Is this one for sale?"

"You bet," I said. "I love that one." What a morning. The quick sale JoAnn had managed left me upbeat and happy, no longer nursing my little hurt over her rejection of Zodiac.

JoAnn took the scarf off the snowman and held it out for the customer to see.

After putting it on and tucking the tails into her coat, she said, "I'll take this one, too, and I want to wear it."

"Good for you," JoAnn said. "If you come closer I'll cut the tag and you won't have to take it off."

I stepped aside and let JoAnn finish up. Then I put both bottles on the counter, and explained the merlot versus the cabernet. I almost laughed out loud when the woman instructed JoAnn to add both to her sale, explaining that she had another party coming up, so why not buy both.

While I rang up the sale, JoAnn finished packing one of the large shopping bags with the wrapped items.

"Now that's one satisfied customer," JoAnn said after the woman had left. "She actually wore one of her purchases out of here. Are people always so easy to please?"

"I wish," I said, wondering about the fast sale myself. "You did a great job with her. I think holding that wool scarf out for her to see made an enormous difference. And seeing it on the snowman also helped."

I went to the scarf rack and brought out another with the sunburst pattern. "Let's not let one of these little snow-people curiosities go unadorned. When one scarf walks out the door, then have her don another."

JoAnn laughed at my humorous phrasing. "May all these scarves simply walk out the door."

By closing time I knew JoAnn would be ready for The Wedding Extravaganza weekend.

After locking up, it suddenly hit me that after three nights of painting and several days training JoAnn, I was beat. I went upstairs and changed into my jeans and put a warm flannel shirt over a turtleneck, and sat in the chair by the front window. I breathed deeply and enjoyed the sensation of my body unwinding. Dinner could wait, a cup of tea could wait. I was ready to sit for a while.

My conversation with myself ended when Eli called.

"So, how was your day, Madame Zoe?"

"In a word, *interesting*. I think JoAnn is a good fit for the shop. But honestly, I don't know how you and Elliot work seven days a week and still have energy for fun."

"We don't work nonstop. Years ago, Elliot and I started covering alternate weekends. We slip in other time off, too.

We have a bunch of good people working for us."

His voice was low, soft, like he was communicating more than the words he spoke. But wasn't it always that way with Eli.

Eli's thoughtfulness about my day and his willingness to make shelves for the shop, to say nothing of the fun we'd had making the snowmen, made me wonder why a generous guy like Eli had chosen to be single. He was outgoing and always willing to step in and support activities on the Square. As far as I could tell, he was not only respected, but well-liked. His clipped way of speaking was just Eli. Or, maybe he was more like me and had been badly hurt and gun shy, to say the least. He'd built his life the way I'd forged my new independence. Maybe he was afraid to change.

My hedging, the need to cling to my deep need for independence, had probably confused Eli, made him wary of me. Mostly to protect myself from my mother's annoying nosiness, I continued to insist I was happy on my own and uninterested in having a man in my life. But was that true? When I thought about my new friends on the Square, I counted any number of happy couples among them.

"Oh, I know you have a great staff," I said. "I've met many of them."

"Well, I just wanted to call and be sure you enjoyed your day."

"Thanks, Eli. That was sweet of you."

Eli's call stayed with me, prompting important questions. Could Eli and I be together? Could we have our own lives and be a couple, too?

And why was I asking?

***

The few days leading up to Snowman Saturday became a blur. JoAnn continued to pick up knowledge about my stock and why I sold particular items. I'd given her a copy of a book I sold in the shop about the lore around crystals and other gemstones, and she studied it like she was still in school.

Early on Friday morning Eli called to ask if he could come and install the shelves.

That came as a shock. I'd been prepared to wait weeks. "Already? Aren't you working today?"

"I'm off today." His voice carried a hint of happiness I'd rarely heard in his voice before.

"Well, then by all means, bring them over and we'll help you."

"Unlock the back door. I'll be right there."

As soon as Eli arrived, I left JoAnn to handle the customers so I could look on while Eli installed the shelves with the same kind of efficient speed he'd used to build them. By noon, the new shelves were installed and cleaned, and he had helped me give Square Spirits a new look. He freely offered his opinions about the way I placed wine bottles among the stones and candles. He nodded in approval when JoAnn draped one of the scarves around a bottle. Eli put a bottle of wine next to one of the snowmen and I added two glasses. The three of us laughed at the effect we created.

I stood back and scanned the shop. I liked what I saw, especially the way the glass top shelf allowed light into what had been the darkest corner of the shop. Nodding, I said, "Well done."

With that, Eli flashed a smile and left before I could offer him so much as a cup of tea at the back table. But, somehow, that didn't surprise me.

***

The next morning we got up to bright sunshine and another layer of snow. Wolf Creek Square couldn't have asked for a more perfect day to launch a new event. I opened the front door to the sounds of children laughing. As they ran by, their coats and hats and boots created a kaleidoscope of colors. When a man dressed like a huge snowman held up a basket of candy, I understood why the kids were in such a hurry.

Steph had a large table set up, every corner of it filled with urns of coffee and hot tea and trays of bite-size pieces of muffins, sweet rolls, and bagels. Warming lights sat at each end. Rented, I suspected, and most likely Sarah's doing. If the Square was to make a habit of outdoor winter events, Sarah would probably add these kinds of lights to the town's budget. I grinned in surprise, when I realized Steph's assistants were none other than Nolan, Reed, and Alan. Always reliable, those three, and helpful, too.

Eli approached me balancing a tray of cups, each sporting a snowman on a stick. He wore a bright red stocking hat, along with his usual heavy jacket and lined boots. "Don't you dare laugh at my silly hat," he warned.

"I wouldn't dream of it," I said, making a great show of suppressing a laugh. "You match the occasion."

"Steph called for some extra hands, and she gave me the job of delivering hot chocolate to the shopkeepers." He bowed slightly.

"Thank you, kind sir," I said, bowing back. "I'll take two, if you don't mind, so my helper has one. She's coming this way now."

JoAnn approached, giving us a smile that reminded me of Nora. Her smile quickly transformed into a burst of laughter at the sight of Eli in his stocking hat.

Eli held out the tray so she could take one off the tray.

"You have an important job, Eli, but so do I. I'll keep an eye on the shop. That way, Zoe can stay outside." She lifted the cup. "Fortified by hot chocolate, I'll be on my way."

That left Eli and me standing together. But out of the corner of my eye, I saw a couple walk into the shop. "Oops, first customers of the day. I have to go, but thanks for the hot cocoa."

"You hired JoAnn to cover for you. She'll do fine. Walk with me."

I glanced at the couple walking into Square Spirits. Eli was right. I could be gone a few minutes. "Okay, where do you want to go?"

"We'll pass on Farmer Foods and go visit Katie and Tracie."

"I haven't spent much time in their shop yet."

"Enterprising ladies. Good addition to the Square." Eli lifted the tray high when he saw three boys running down the walkway and realized—just in time—he was directly in their path.

I also saw the kids and tugged on his arm as he stepped to the side when the boys whizzed by.

Eli laughed. "Whew! That could have been a mess."

With the steady stream of women entering and leaving The Fiber Barn, Eli stopped. "Kind of crowded in there. Might not be a good idea to bring in a tray of hot chocolate."

"Maybe you should wait here." I took two cups off the tray. "I'll deliver them. Those people coming out will hold the door open for me."

And that's exactly what happened. But Katie and Tracie were too busy to chat. Tracie took the cups from my hands and told me to pass on their thanks to Steph. With that, I headed back out, but Tracie's voice stopped me.

"I almost forgot," she said, extending her arm to hand me a flyer. "We're starting a knitting night. Maybe you'd like to come."

Before she could tell me more I overheard a young woman, "My kids are playing outside. Could I have some help?"

"Be right there." Tracie rolled her eyes and hurried off.

Back outside, I saw Eli deep in conversation with three men. I waved and strolled over to my shop. Based on the crowd and the number of people gathered in The Fiber Barn, Snowman Saturday was a success. When I went inside, I saw my new employee smiling broadly.

"Oh, Zoe, you didn't have to come back so quickly," JoAnn said. "This is a good test for me."

I glanced around the shop. A couple of women were browsing the bookshelves, another woman had a half-filled basket, and a man was browsing through a selection of wine. JoAnn would be just fine. "All right. If you are sure, then I'm going to Styles. I want to find something new to wear at the wedding shindig. But you call me if you get busy. I can be back in a couple of minutes."

I ran upstairs for my purse and slid my phone into my pocket. When I went into the Square I noticed that the presence of excited children making snowmen, supervised by a couple of volunteer parents, had brought a new level of energy to the air around me. I stood still for a few seconds to absorb all I could, to fill up the well. I was on a mission. Instead of making my way around the Square on the walkway in front of the shops, I cut through the Square on the walkway that connected the corner buildings. The children's voices faded when the door of Styles closed behind me. Soft classical music filled the room.

As I walked past racks of clothes, I spotted three outfits that intrigued me. Even if I didn't find anything else, I was going home with the apple red pantsuit. A change from my lavenders and purples, and exactly the look I wanted for The Wedding Extravaganza. I took it back to the fitting room and the minute I put it on, I knew for sure the collarless jacket would look great with one of my favorite scarves. The straight-leg pants were perfect for someone my height. And the pants had a pocket, too, where my amethyst stone would always be handy. My amethyst point went with me everywhere. No options, no excuses.

With that purchase certain, I went back to the clothing racks, spotting a forest green long wool skirt. I could easily see myself wearing it often in the shop, with one of my lighter shade of lavender sweaters. I'd started wearing some of the jewelry I stocked, and the skirt would be a perfect complement to many of the gemstone pieces.

Then the rack of Virgie's Vests caught my eye. How could I have missed them when I'd wandered into Styles last fall? Each one was a creative masterpiece, although I was disappointed that none on display showed much in the way of purples or lavenders.

"Glad you stopped in," Jessica said, coming alongside me. She glanced out the window for a minute. "Not much business for us today, but it's good for the Square."

"I had some browsers, but I was fine with leaving the shop to JoAnn, my new employee," I said. "But a day for the kids is okay, too. They'll be shopping adults one day and have memories of the Square."

"Halloween is a little like this. I used to complain until some of the mothers came back by themselves to shop here."

"That's one of the ripple effects of all these events, I guess." But how would I know? I was simply making social conversation.

"Have you decided to have Beverly and Virgie make a vest for you?" Jessica asked. "I can have them come to Square Spirits, if that's more convenient for you."

"First things first. I'll take this red pantsuit, and the skirt, and…" I debated buying a bright blue long sweater… "that's it for today."

Jessica took the clothes to the register and I trailed behind her, still holding the sweater. I laughed. "I changed my mind. I'll take this, too."

"Great match for jeans." She gently folded the sweater and put it in a bag. The suit and skirt were left on hangers and bagged in a long zippered front clothing carrier. I think everyone on the Square had learned something about elegant packaging from Jessica and Mimi. I know I had.

"By the way, I've heard Marianna talking about soft marketing, and how it helps everyone," I said, "and I thought about you. Would you like to loan me a mannequin and an outfit? I could accessorize it with jewelry and scarves, maybe even one of the shoulder bags I've ordered. I'd put a sign indicating that the clothing came from Styles. I do that with Megan's flowers." I pointed to the bouquet of red roses on the corner of the counter. Megan's card was visible in front of it. I'd soon do the same for Clayton's painting.

"Why that would be lovely of you," Jessica said, her eyes lighting up. "I'm sure we have an extra "lady" somewhere in the back. And we have clothes that would blend in with the artsy atmosphere you create in your shop. Marianna's ideas have brought a lot of shops together. Even her customer drawings have added buzz on the Square."

"I can pick up one of your ladies, as you call them, whenever it's convenient for you." I nearly laughed out loud, knowing for sure JoAnn and I would give the mannequin a name. If I named spirits without knowing who they were, wouldn't I do the same for a display lady?

Jessica frowned in thought. "I've got a better idea. Let me bring her over. That way I'll get to see your shop. Mimi gave me one of your deep space photo calendars as a gift for the New Year, but I haven't really looked closely at what else you carry."

I opened my purse to pay for my new clothes and saw the flyer from The Fiber Barn I'd folded and stuck inside. "Did you and Mimi get an invite from Katie and Tracie for knitting school?" I had to admit I wasn't eager to take up knitting—or any other craft, for that matter.

"Ah, yes, and we're so excited. The winter Marianna taught basic quilting we weren't able to go, but all we heard about was the fun the women had."

Her enthusiasm convinced me I needed to go. While I'd met the women on the Square, I really didn't know them, like girlfriends. And I wanted that to change.

I left Styles with an eye-stopping outfit for The Wedding Extravaganza, along with a small twinge of self-consciousness knowing one reason I'd bought it was so Eli would see me wearing something entirely different from the clothes I wore in the shop.

Naughty me? But why not? A girl's gotta have fun.

I hurried back to Square Spirits and found JoAnn walking through the empty shop, stopping to adjust a pendulum on the metal rack. "Been slow?"

She shrugged. "One guy came in to get a gift certificate for his wife, but he couldn't leave fast enough. However, he did stop to look at the wines. Didn't buy a bottle, though."

"I'm sorry. I was hopeful when a few people came in earlier. I suppose you feel like you wasted your day."

But she echoed my thoughts. "How could anyone know? It was a first time event."

I saw an open book on the back table. "Have you been studying?"

"I sure wish I'd known about stones and the beliefs around them years ago. It's fascinating."

"I'm glad you feel that way. Some people are a little put off by them, but if nothing else, they're beautiful to have around."

When the bell jingled, I turned around to see Megan come in and hold the door open with her body so she could pick up a banker's box off the ground and carry it inside, with her red handbag sitting on top. This was not the hesitant Megan she'd been when I first opened the shop. This new Megan had many layers of vibrating energy surrounding her.

She held up the box and said, "Wedding Extravaganza stuff. Gotta minute?" Then she put it down in front of her.

"It's almost overflowing," JoAnn said.

"Why don't we go upstairs? We can spread out, and we're not being rushed by shoppers today."

"I'm slow at Rainbow Gardens, too," Megan said, "but like Sarah says, 'it's planting the seed,' or something like that."

"Well, considering how many seeds she's planted that have grown and blossomed, I guess I'll take her at her word," I said.

I took her bag and led the way up the stairs. Had I left a mess? Too late to worry about that now.

Megan let out one of her characteristic hoots. "Oh, my, Eli was right. It's a big time warehouse up here."

"Such teasers you Reynolds are." I stretched my arm out toward the row of boxes along the wall. "I haven't had time to unpack. Besides, I spend most of my time in the shop."

Megan waved me off. "You'll get to it...some day. But first we need to focus on the show."

I quickly cleared the table, putting a stack of my papers on the floor by my desk.

In Megan's energetic style she emptied the box, dividing the contents into separate piles. "I'm trying to be organized, but whenever I mention that Clayton bursts out laughing."

"Men." I shook my head. "But being a wedding planner means juggling all sorts of information for different brides. It must force you to be organized."

"Each woman has her own notebook and folder in the computer," she said, moving the files around on the table. "I got a system underway when I was planning for both Lily and Georgia."

I watched her work. By now she'd rearranged the piles twice. "Would you like a glass of wine?" I asked.

"Perfect," she said in her enthusiastic Megan way.

Without going through all the choices, I poured us each a glass of Zodiac.

"Ahh. Wine," Megan said, "the elixir of the Gods."

We touched glasses in a toast and that launched us into our afternoon of brainstorming, decision-making, and debating the best way to promote Wolf Creek Square as a wedding planning destination.

"Zoe?" JoAnn called up the stairs. "It's time to close. I'll lock up when I leave."

"Wow, Megan, where did the time go?" I ran down the stairs.

"I'm glad you were here. Megan and I accomplished a lot. The hours really flew by, but we got the booth layout designed, so the setup will be quick."

JoAnn and I agreed I'd call her to finalize a schedule that worked for both of us.

She left through the front door and when I locked the door behind her, I saw the lights on above Farmer Foods. So, Eli must have started his remodeling.

By the time I was back upstairs, Megan had gathered her notes and drawings, leaving me a sketch of the booth and a list of details that needed to be done. She gathered her things, looking pensive.

"I know some of the shopkeepers are skeptical of my latest scheme, but when you agreed it was a good idea, I knew you and I could do a terrific job selling the Square."

"Why thanks, Megan," I said. Her words touched me, and I could see ahead to a close friendship forming between us. "What did Sarah say when you explained what you wanted to do? You never told me."

"She gave me her pat answer when she won't commit. 'Planting the seed.'"

She put her coat and hat on and before we started down the stairs, Megan engulfed me in a warm hug. I didn't pull away, but returned it.

Megan was one of the younger women on the Square but that didn't mean we couldn't be good friends. And, for that matter, what did age have to do with friendship, anyway?

Later, as I got ready for bed, I realized that agreeing to

work with Megan had me involved in a new happening on the Square, and during our short time together I'd absorbed much of Megan's energy into mine. Each step I'd made into being part of this community reinforced my happiness. It occurred to me that I'd invited Megan upstairs and hadn't told the girls about her or asked them not to scare her off. They'd accepted JoAnn, too.

"Thank you, for that," I said out loud.

Cool and warm energies swirled around me and came with me as I climbed into bed.

***

I quickly learned that helping Megan also meant meetings, lots of them, with Liz, who was making progress pulling together the booklet that would be the hallmark of the Square at the wedding show. Over morning coffee at B and B, Liz, Megan, and I fielded a steady stream of questions about the event, and how the idea could develop over the long term.

The event seemed to invite wedding energy into the air at B and B. Everyone had some kind of wedding story, including Doris who found it amusing that younger people needed to consult a book to do everything, even get married. That didn't prevent her from carrying how-to wedding planning books and provide samples of the guest books she'd carry as part of the one-stop concept.

Lily and Georgia, being the newest brides on the Square, enjoyed reliving their special days and were staunch in their support of Megan. They also urged her to continue to stay positive and ignore the few negative voices among approaching day.

Megan's checklist became shorter and shorter as each item was completed, but her anxiety level kept increasing, her mind constantly busy worrying that those skeptical about the venture. On the other hand, excitement kept building and was fueled by the rapidly she might have forgotten something. She assured me she'd calm down once the event actually started. I wasn't so sure, but I tried to match her positive attitude.

At the end of the busy day, I laughed to myself. The reality of my day had exceeded my vision for the store and my life on the Square.

17

On Friday morning, everything went as planned, with JoAnn coming in early to open and all set to close up at the end of the day. With weather forecasters waffling about a storm building to the south of Green Bay, I had no way of knowing if Megan and I would be back that evening.

Dressed in my new outfit and mentally prepared to be the best sales person I'd ever been, I put on my coat and gloves. I'd spent extra time with my hair, putting it in a complicated French style braid, weaving in a strand of tiny crystal beads.

"Break a leg," JoAnn called out as I left the shop.

Encouraged by bright sunshine and only a dusting of fresh snow, I walked the short distance from Square Spirits to the back door of Rainbow Gardens. Megan's van was parked by the door, presumably packed and waiting for the last minute items.

I reached for the door only to be surprised when Eli opened it.

"Hey, Zoe." He motioned me inside.

I scrambled to understand why Eli was standing there in a charcoal black suit and white shirt. His apple red tie matched my pants suit as if we'd planned it. "Eli?"

"Change of plans. Megan's sick." He raised his hand toward her upstairs apartment. "Nothing serious, but maybe the flu. Clayton's staying with her."

"But…but…"

"I'll be with you today and tomorrow."

"You're not working?" *Well, obviously not…get a grip.*

"Elliot's weekend. Besides, in emergencies, we change

219

the schedule if we have to."

"Any last minute instructions from Megan?" I asked not once, but twice, just to be sure and to stave off rising panic. Eli and I would be sharing a small space, 12 x 12, for *two* days.

"Zoe…Megan says you know *everything*. She is completely confident you—we—can do this, so let's get this van moving." He grinned as he spoke.

I reached into my pantsuit pocket and grabbed the amethyst point. If I ever needed to be focused and calm, today was the day. The town of Wolf Creek and the owners of the shops on the Square depended on me—us. "Okay, we'll see if Megan's right."

Eli put his hand on my back and guided me to the passenger's door. He surprised me when he handed the seatbelt to me and closed the door. We pulled out of the Square and headed to Green Bay in Eli style—silence.

I wanted to keep the atmosphere between us light. It was going to be a very long day if we didn't talk. "News flash, Eli. Megan agrees with your assessment of my apartment. She's been teasing me about 'my warehouse'."

He laughed. "Well, you can't deny the truth."

"I'll get to filling it up soon enough."

"Sure, sure."

He might be silent, but the man knew how to tease. Probably from having a twin brother and a kid sister.

We exited the highway and followed signs promoting The Wedding Extravaganza. When I spotted a sign that said "Vendors Only" we followed it to the unloading bay at the back of the exhibition hall. We were fifth in line to unload, but within minutes, a second receiving area opened up and we were told to pull in there. Eli put his experience at Farmer Foods to work and backed the van as close as possible. Then pulled the flat cart over. Together, we unloaded our wares and were ready to be on our way.

"What's our vendor number?"

I opened the envelope Megan had given him. "Number 83."

Within minutes, one of the facility's workers escorted us

down the aisles to our booth. The artificial tree, pre-strung with fairy lights, and the body form were our biggest items. The rest of our supplies were in labeled boxes, thanks to Megan's attention to detail. With our escort willing to help, the three of us unloaded the cart in only a few minutes, and the worker rolled it away.

"So," I said, "let's create a booth that will promote Wolf Creek and make the Square shine."

Eli hung his overcoat on the body form and when he took mine from me, he let out a low whistle.

I rolled my eyes and made him grin, but inside I said, *Thank you, Styles.*

"Let's hang the banner first, then you can dress the lady," he said.

I surmised Megan had told him our plans for the booth and that we'd be using a wedding dress from the museum.

"Oops, sorry," he said with a sheepish grin. "Didn't mean to be giving orders. Happens at the store all the time."

I laughed. "We don't have time to worry about stepping on toes, Eli. Let's just have fun today and sell the Square."

We worked quickly, with Eli and I both using our sense of design to take the raw materials and create a showpiece. Minutes before the show opened, we'd stashed our empty boxes and extra supplies under the table and took a few minutes to introduce ourselves to a DJ from Milwaukee on our right and an invitation designer from a graphic arts firm on our left. We left our brochures and took theirs.

The show's promoter stopped by to welcome us. "Never had a town promoting itself before." He nodded his approval and moved on.

Eli stood a little behind me and to my right. His energy zipped through me and into the overload zone every time his body casually touched mine as we moved around.

A hush fell over the hall when the overhead lights came on full strength.

Showtime.

It could have been awkward. I might have even predicted that Eli and I would have a hard time figuring out how to present the concept without Megan's passion. But it wasn't long before Eli and I fell into a rhythm, having fun with the brides-and-grooms-to-be and whole families who stopped at the booth.

How funny it was when some of the would-be clients thought we were a couple ourselves. When necessary, Eli blushed and stumbled over a few words of explanation, but most of the time we let the comments hang in the air.

Thanks to Liz and everyone who contributed, our booklet was a great sales tool and allowed the Square to sell itself. I listened attentively when I heard Eli's pride as he talked about Wolf Creek and all the Square had to offer. He played the role of town ambassador with panache.

Mid-afternoon, I pulled a couple of wilted flowers from the bouquet Megan had sent along with us. It had been difficult to protect them from the cold weather when we unloaded.

With our attention on the supply boxes, we both turned to the sound of a familiar voice.

"This is beautiful...nicely done."

Sarah. I might have known she'd come around. "Well, it's nice to see a familiar face," I said.

"Any interest in the Square?" she asked.

"A lot," Eli said, joining me by the table. "Seems like we haven't stopped talking since the show opened."

Naturally, Eli would think that. He usually avoided lengthy conversations. But I decided to skip a teasing remark.

"I heard about Megan," Sarah said, glancing around, "but I see you and Eli are doing fine. Anything I can get you?"

Eli had left us to talk to a young couple. Sarah only nodded to me. I understood, though. She knew Eli was well out of his comfort zone.

"Water, coffee, and something to munch on," I said, grinning. "Since you asked. We forgot about packing food, and it's been too busy to leave the booth."

Sarah opened her large bag and brought out two granola bars. "I don't have water with me, but I'll get some—and two coffees." She backed away when a foursome approached the table.

A few minutes later Sarah put two cups of coffee on the corner of the table and set a bag down next to them. She waved and left.

"I think we passed muster." Eli peered into the bag and pulled out a cheese plate and two bottles of water. He opened them both.

"You mean Sarah?"

He nodded. "As you may have noticed, she's very protective of the Square and the image we promote. I'm not surprised she came by."

Our day ended on a positive note when a couple we'd talked to earlier in the day returned for more information. "We both work crazy hours and don't have time to run around and handle all the details." She referred to the booklet to make sure she had the right name. "Do you know Megan Reynolds, the wedding planner?"

I reached over and put my hand on Eli's arm to bring him closer. "Meet Eli Reynolds, Megan's brother."

"Guess you can recommend her," the man said, extending his hand to Eli.

"She'll work very hard for you," Eli said, his voice serious. "We all will. Megan is coordinating our one-stop concept, but almost every shop is involved."

"I think we'll call her now," the woman said, pointing to a refreshment area with tables and chairs. "Let's go where it's quiet and get this show going. It's time to delegate." She laughed at her own remark.

After they left I turned to Eli. "Why didn't you tell them she was sick?"

"They'll reach her answering machine, and leave a message. I doubt they necessarily expected to talk to her today. We don't want them to go elsewhere, do we?"

"Maybe they'll be our first wedding couple." I pointed to our banner: *Weddings at Wolf Creek.* "Wouldn't that be something? Congratulations are in order." I leaned over and gave Eli a kiss on the cheek. His aftershave had long since lost its enticing smell, but his day's beard growth pricked my lips. Did I mind? Not on my life. A new surge of energy went through me.

The lights blinked, signaling the end of the day. We packed away the items on the table in the boxes and I poured the last of my water into the flower vase.

We didn't wait around, but made our way to the van and headed home. The sun spread its last rays into the darkening sky as we headed west. Eli turned on the radio and found some easy listening music.

He looked my way. "Let's think about dinner."

"Do you think there'd be anything left in the deli at the store?" I shook my head. "I keep resolving to keep more food around, but I end up with your deli takeout nearly every day."

"I'm glad you like it, because I'm thinking we'll raid the cooler, and then bring it upstairs. I'd like you to see my apartment plans."

"A picnic? I'd like that. I'm tired, but then again, I'm not. It was exciting. I haven't talked all day since the holiday sales were on."

Eli reached across the console and took my hand. We traveled in silence, but easily, comfortably, unlike the awkward silences of our previous rides.

He'd driven out of Green Bay on a back road, avoiding the highway. Thinking he was simply choosing the scenic route, I enjoyed the change. But suddenly, Eli pulled onto the gravel shoulder of the road as we approached a junction. He brought the van to a stop and shifted into park. That's when I came to full alert, conscious of both light and heavy energy inside the van. I reached into my pocket to touch my amethyst point.

In slow motion, Eli released his seat belt and twisted in his seat toward me. He swallowed, then set his jaw.

Knowing something significant was about to happen, I waited.

"When I was in high school…" He swallowed again. "When I was in high school, there was a special girl in my life. I'd planned to marry her. My parents liked her, and her parents liked me. I was happy and ready to take on the world."

He reached up and grabbed the steering wheel. "It was a

night, almost like tonight, except there was a layer of snow on the road. There were stop signs for the other direction on the corner then, but none going this direction." He motioned to the signs in the arc of light from the headlights.

"Candy was driving alone when a drunk driver barreled through the stop signs and plowed into her car...on the driver's side."

I reached for the hand he'd pulled away. He let me hold it. "Candy?"

"They said she didn't suffer."

And you've been lonely ever since that day.

The energy grew even heavier, bringing me to the edge of tears. "I'm sorry, Eli. We never forget losses like that. And we shouldn't."

"I usually don't come this way, but I wanted you to know."

"Thank you. Thank you for trusting me."

No more words were needed. He rebuckled his seatbelt and we were on our way. I understood his silent message when he pulled up to the back door of Square Spirits. We'd have our picnic another time.

"See you in the morning, Eli."

I went upstairs, changed into comfy sweats and poured myself a large glass of wine. Sometimes health resolutions needed to be broken. I sat in my chair overlooking the Square, and tried to absorb all Eli had shared with me. He had lost a love and never recovered. I claimed to be recovered, but was that true? Maybe, like him, it was time for me to open my heart again.

18

I woke to gray skies and a gray spirit, with no idea how Eli and I could be together all day and promote the Square with smiles and joy.

Megan opened her back door when I knocked. Her bright red nose looked like a clown's. I broke into laughter, which seemed to chase some of the darkness away.

"Morning, Zoe." Eli's tone of voice reverberated through me.

"Megan, Eli. How are you feeling?" I'd directed my question to Megan, but when Eli shifted I knew he'd tuned into my spirit.

"Better." They answered in unison.

I laughed. "I'd expect that synchrony from Elliot and Eli, but not you two."

"Time to go." Eli fist-bumped with his little sister. "Get well."

"Stop by when you get home. I'm feeling sorry for myself after Sarah told me she'd seen you—and with only good things to say about you and the booth."

I turned back to ask, "Did a couple call you yesterday afternoon?"

"Yes…" She stopped to clear a cough. She waved us away when the cough continued. "Later."

"Drink some wine," I yelled to her when Eli opened the door for me.

We headed east on the highway, repeating our route from yesterday. Eli commented on the fewer number of cars on the road.

Meaningless small talk. I groaned inside.

"Most people don't know about Candy," Eli said. "Well, Elliot does, and Georgia, and maybe Sarah, because we were all kids together. But I've never told Megan the story."

"I'd never talk about it to anyone," I said. I wondered if I should continue with what was on my mind, and finally decided to open up. "Whether you understand this or even care, you give off strong energy that I pick up on. It doesn't happen with everyone, but it happens with you. And for a long while now, I've been getting impressions of your... your loneliness, for lack of a better word."

"Is it like your loneliness?"

My stomach rolled over. "Mine?"

Eli didn't need words. His sidelong, "give me a break" look said it all.

I was at a loss for words. That was the last thing I expected him to say.

After we parked the van and headed inside the building, we were greeted by a television crew. They stepped in front of us, blocking our way forward, but then the reporter quickly introduced herself. I recognized her as Bridget Sims from one of the local TV stations in Green Bay.

"Mr. Reynolds, Ms. Miller. Would you agree to have us shoot a segment at your booth for the evening's news? We're covering the show as part of the weekend review segment."

Eli didn't consult me, but took the lead in responding. "I...we...will want to see the segment before it airs."

Bridget turned to someone I assumed was her producer and shrugged. I knew from experience that reporters didn't like making those commitments.

The producer nodded and said, "No problem. We can send it directly to your tablet or phone before we leave."

"Okay, then, stop by," Eli said.

When the lights blinked to announce that the front doors were opening, Eli and I hurried to our booth to put out the displays we'd taken down last evening.

The surge of the morning rush began. While we were talking to an exceptionally beautiful young woman and her handsome man I was blinded by the intense lights of the camera crew when they arrived.

Bridget quickly wedged her way into our conversation with the couple and, with a microphone in her hand, proceeded to ask about Wolf Creek Square and our wedding planning destination. As the microphone came my way, Eli stepped forward and became the spokesperson for our town and the shops on the Square. That was okay, because it freed me to sell the concept to the customer. Besides, he looked great in his suit, navy blue that day.

As I spoke to the couple, I knew it was no accident that these stylish, attractive people had caught the reporter's eye. The camera operator panned the booth, spending quite a bit of time filming the antique wedding dress on the body form, an eye-catching element of our booth. In a subtle way, it reminded people of our special town.

When I finished talking with the couple, the producer moved toward them, confirming my impression that he wanted to put them on camera. Meanwhile, the lights had drawn an amazing number of people to our booth. Eli and I handed a booklet to anyone who reached out. I grabbed another couple of dozen from the box under the table, but if we ran out, we still had individual business cards from every shop as a backup.

When the lights blinked late in the afternoon, Eli and I did a high five. We had done the best we could to let the public know about our town. "Good job, Eli. Now what do you think of your sister's idea?"

"Nice exposure for the Square." He hadn't answered my question, but his smile told the whole relationship story. He loved his sister unconditionally.

I stopped for a moment. Why didn't Devin and I have that kind of relationship?

"Something wrong, Zoe?"

"No, no. Let's get out of here."

While Eli went off to get a cart, I hurried to put the antique wedding dress in its special box and gathered our supplies and business cards. I dumped the limp flowers into the nearest trash bin.

When Eli came back with the cart, he was flanked by the

TV crew. "They want to show us the video before they head back to the studio."

My heart surged. "You bet. I want to tell Megan all about it."

Eli was behind me as I looked over the shoulder of the cameraman. This opportunity would let me see Eli as others saw him. I was learning about Eli from many angles, and each time, I felt him move deeper into my heart. Who was I kidding? He'd already taken up residence there.

My body tightened when I saw the pain behind his eyes, a pain so deep I hadn't felt it before. Was he that good at hiding it, or had it been there so long it was part of him?

Eli put his hands on my shoulders and pulled me back toward him. With all eyes on the clip, I doubted anyone saw us touch.

I wanted to stay next to him, to be with him, so I laid my hand over his.

When the clip ended, I moved away from Eli. "Can you email me a copy of it as a gif file?" I asked. To assure Bridget I meant it, I handed her my business card.

"Sure. No problem." She slipped my card into her pocket. "Everyone loves their fifteen minutes of fame."

I could have hit her. After covering the region, did she really have no idea how special that video would be to Wolf Creek? If she even knew where it was. I turned away, too tired to engage her.

We finished loading the cart and left. Home sounded wonderful.

The weatherman missed with the forecast of measurable amounts of snow. Only flurries bombarded the windshield as we pulled out of the parking deck.

"Hungry?" Eli was the first to engage.

"Starved. And thirsty."

"You eat hamburgers and fries?"

"Love 'em."

Eli pulled over into an empty parking space on the street, put the van in park, and dug his phone out. "We'll have our picnic tonight." In the language of carry-out he ordered two hamburger platters maxed.

Gini Athey

"Sounds like fun."

We picked up the food at the Creekside Pub, an old tavern that Eli assured me served the best burgers and fries in the area. He'd grabbed a six pack of beer and told the cashier to add it to our bill. "Gotta have beer with these burgers," he said.

And it was fun. He took me upstairs to his future apartment above Farmer Foods and put an old flannel shirt on the floor for me to sit on. I had worn my new wool skirt and tall boots. A soft cream-colored cashmere sweater had kept me warm during the day. He offered a second shirt for me to put over my sweater. "Ketchup would do a lot of damage to your sweater."

Well, that did it. He was thoughtful, a rare quality, I'd discovered. That one thing reinforced my decision to bring Eli into my life. Win or lose, I'd see where the relationship went.

We kept our conversation light. He asked about the girls and I told him that they'd accepted everybody I brought in, but he was the only person who had sensed their presence.

I asked him to draw a floor plan for his new home. He grabbed a pencil from the work belt hanging on a sawhorse and drew a simple sketch, similar to the one he'd drawn at Crossroads.

"Only one bedroom?" I pointed to the room next to the bathroom.

"Why would I need more?"

"I thought the same thing until Julia stayed overnight. Maybe an office or a workroom of some kind?" I looked around the open space, then pointed to the corner by the front windows. "Fireplace there, kitchen there, a nice soft couch by the front window." I could see Eli's apartment in my mind.

He chuckled in that soft tone that made me want to be closer to him.

I looked into his eyes, to feel his wants and needs only to observe that the wall he'd built around himself years ago was gone.

"Want more?" he asked.

230

For a moment I held my breath. When I saw he was referring to his home, I shook my head to dispel my thought.

"Yes, a laundry room." I looked again at the large expanse he had available, not the limited space like mine. "Maybe a separate room for that—or, expand your bathroom and include it. And…" I stood up and walked around the empty area. "Another room, like a walk-in closet. You know, to store stuff, seasonal clothing, holiday decorations. No house has enough storage space."

"I agree." Eli began to gather our picnic throwaways. "Time to go see Megan. I texted her that we were eating dinner, but I didn't tell her where. She'll want to know how the show went, minute by minute."

Megan was under a blanket on her couch when we arrived. Clayton didn't look particularly chipper, either, when he met us at the door. "It's been a long two days for her, but the coughing is getting a little better. She needs sleep, but I can't keep her off the phone."

"I just wanted to tell her that she put Wolf Creek into the minds of a whole bunch of potential couples." I peeked into the apartment hoping to see her.

"Zoe? Eli?" A raspy voice called from the living area.

"Stay where you are, Megan. I'm not interested in getting your bug." Eli's light tone brought good energy into the room.

"Me neither," I added, making light of the situation.

"You rest, Megan," Eli said, still standing just inside the door. "Zoe can tell you all about the weekend later. I'm tired and I need to get out of these clothes. I haven't worn fancy duds all day for a long time." He frowned. "Matter of fact, I don't remember when I've had a suit on for longer than it took Georgia to marry Elliot."

Megan laughed. "Oh, Eli…" That was as far as she got, because a bout of coughing took over. She waved goodbye, giving in.

"Don't forget to watch the local news tomorrow," I said. "You're in for a great surprise."

"Really?" Megan managed.

"Really," I said, tugging on Eli's arm so we could leave.

"Call if you need help, Clayton," Eli said. "I know my sister can be a handful when she's not feeling good."

"Only then?" A soft blush crossed Clayton's face, like he'd revealed a family secret.

***

The light snow crunched as we walked down the alleyway behind Farmer Foods and turned onto the Square at my shop. The lights in the front windows blinked.

"Guess the girls are welcoming you home," Eli said.

I'd have barely noticed if he hadn't pointed it out. I was distracted by Eli, who was being extra careful that our hands didn't touch as we walked. Mixed messages from him everywhere. Or was I the one sending them?

You won't figure it out tonight, Zoe. You're too tired for heavy analysis.

We exchanged quick goodnights and then I locked the door after going inside.

In the glow from the lamppost, I could see that JoAnn had the shop stocked and ready to open the next day. She'd left a few notes on the counter, and I took them with me upstairs. My big decision was wine or tea? My New Year's resolution about more often ending my day with tea crossed my mind, but I poured a glass of wine. I took it to the window, where I let the Square's nighttime peacefulness influence me. How comforting to see that nothing had changed in the two days I'd been away.

Warm air swirled near me, but not as close as usual, which surprised me. Giving it more thought, I concluded that I'd brought many new scents into the house on my clothes, from the exhibition hall, from upstairs at Farmer Foods, our picnic dinner, and by way of Megan's apartment, which was filled with the mix of fragrances of Rainbow Gardens. It was no wonder the girls were cautious.

"A shower, then bed," I said to my resident spirits.

The shower relieved most of the tension in my muscles, but didn't wash Eli from my mind. Just the opposite. I was thinking about Eli as I fell asleep, which probably caused him to be at the center of the dreams that added to a restless night. Some dreams contained romantic images of the two of us, but other dreams were disturbing and disjointed, and in wispy sequence, Eli morphed into Tyler. Exactly what I feared about being involved with another man.

Like most dreams, none of them made logical sense. I hadn't heard from Tyler in more than two years, except for receiving the shawl, still draped over the chair. Why hadn't I hidden it in the back of the closet, or given it away? And Tyler and Eli were nothing alike. But that didn't stop my fear of becoming trapped.

With such a busy night of contrasting dreams, it was no wonder I'd opened my eyes in the morning more tired and confused than when I'd gone to sleep. Not the frame of mind I needed for a day in the shop.

Before I unlocked the door, I walked through the shop, front to back, touching the gemstones, picking up candles, rearranging some books on one of the shelves. Nothing needed my attention, but it was my way of reconnecting. The afternoon brought only a few people venturing into the Square, which freed time to check in with JoAnn and answer a couple of her questions. It had been a slow two days, but she'd still managed respectable sales. She laughed when describing the woman who came in and used the gift certificate her husband had bought earlier. I remembered JoAnn telling me about him. The woman was surprised her husband hadn't bought a bottle or two of our wine, but she didn't use her certificate for wine, either. Apparently, the spirit of books and jewelry attracted her more than wine spirits.

I smiled to myself when I got a text from Bridget telling me the feature on The Wedding Extravaganza would run that night. I forwarded the text to Sarah and she took it from there, sending it on to everyone in the association. I eagerly watched the evening news, waiting through sports and weather until the weekend roundup came.

Sure enough, there we were, Eli in his suit, me in a cream sweater and my new long wool skirt. The exquisite antique gown was in the background, but it stood out and added to the overall impression of our booth. Eli had done a nice job promoting the Square.

I went to B and B on Monday morning, and soon after I stepped in, a few people at our tables of regulars stood up and applauded. I laughed, knowing that Eli and I would both be grilled about the atmosphere and responses. After my Sunday of regrouping and renewing my energy, I was ready for whatever came next. Although not completely recovered, Megan was already talking about the email inquiries she'd had after the TV news segment, and a couple of calls that had come in. It seemed that all the shop owners on the Square left B and B in high spirits that morning.

Throughout the next couple of days, I had to laugh when Megan texted updates, practically every time a call or an email inquiry came in. Having become her informal sounding board, I either supported her newly brainstormed ideas or suggested modifications as they came to me. One by one, Megan addressed items on her checklist. Georgia had written a letter of intent to be signed by the bride and groom or third parties who were paying specified expenses. Georgia had mentioned misunderstandings and corrosive issues with her first wedding planner, which had led her to asking Megan for help.

Since Mom and I had arranged my wedding with Tyler, I was a novice when it came to hiring a wedding planner. But as I was quickly discovering, some weddings were more like extravaganzas with so many moving parts an organizer was practically a necessity. The great feature about the one-stop concept was that engaged couples could pick and choose among our various offerings, with or without an organizer.

Late one evening, Eli called to ask me about one of Megan's ideas. I liked that he sought my opinion, but once that part of the conversation was over, the energy shifted to the TV clip.

"Your hair was pretty hanging down, Zoe. Made me want to keep looking at you all day. No wonder that video clip of the booth turned out so well."

"Well, thank you for the compliment. I got a kick out of dressing up for those two days."

Silence. But I knew he had more to say.

"Eli? Was there something else?"

"Well, yes. I'm going out to see Devin at the winery on Friday. I was wondering if you'd like to go along with me. Uh, your Mom invited me to stay for lunch."

"The winery? Really?"

"I'm taking Devin up on his offer to coach me on wine-making, you know, just an overview for now."

This all came as a surprise, but a pleasant one. "Sure. I'd love to go along with you. Let me check with JoAnn, but I think she can cover the shop that day."

"Good, then. It's settled. Friday, it is."

With that, he said good night and ended the call.

I was beginning to recognize the different inflections in Eli's voice. I noted a hint of joy when he had said good night.

February
19

If past was indeed prologue, then it made sense that everyone expected February to be a slow month on the Square. On the other hand, when I picked up the agenda for the month at the business association meeting I wouldn't have described the month as slow. Based on comments around me, the full calendar surprised others as well.

I took a seat next to Marianna and Art. Georgia waved as she went by to join Elliot. As always, Sarah tapped the microphone to get the meeting underway. It occurred to me that if anyone wanted to learn from her methods, Sarah's control of the room would have been a study in management, communication, and even diplomacy. When she spoke, people listened.

"We all want to hear about the wedding show," she said, "but let's leave that for the end of the meeting. First, some breaking news."

Everyone laughed. She was famous for making surprise announcements, and this one was about Tom Harris bringing his first winter tour bus to Wolf Creek the coming weekend. Marianna had mentioned that tour company at coffee one morning, and Sarah gave credit to Megan for getting to know him well enough to keep up his interest in the Square.

"Tom says the group coming include some repeat customers, who really like the Square and all we offer. Only weather will cause him to cancel. So be ready."

Sarah's news brought smiles to many faces. Others

jotted notes, and I wrote one myself about trying out a door prize idea.

"On to the next item," Sarah said. "We have another first to report this year. With Valentine's Day in the middle of the week it appears people are celebrating either the weekend before or the weekend after. The Inn will be full both weekends."

Sarah gestured to Melanie, who was standing along the wall.

"I'm not used to turning business away, but as it stands, we have reservations to cover both Saturday nights and only a few left on those Fridays. So, don't come in expecting to be seated right away."

A round of applause filled the room, along with a few groans.

I laughed at the mixed reaction.

Megan was next, and without any hint of shyness or reluctance she thanked Eli for stepping in to help me in the booth. He waved from the back of the room.

"I know most of you are probably tired of hearing me talk about The Wedding Extravaganza," Megan said, "but as a result of Eli and Megan's efforts at the show, four couples have signed contracts with me—us—to use all the shops on the Square for their needs. The segment about us on the news was terrific promotion." Megan looked my way and then smiled at her brother. "Once again, we can thank Zoe and Eli for doing such a great job."

That brought a happy buzz rippling through the room.

"I've referred one couple to Liz Pearson for personalized invitations. She's stepped forward to be available for this kind of design work, as well as for wedding websites."

No one could miss Liz sitting between Jack and Lily. Her jacket was a splash of reds and blues in the crowd.

"So, now we need to make sure we're all keeping the promo material in our shops, and handing it out to customers talking about weddings or engagements. That includes the parents of the brides and grooms, of course. If you can, jot down names and numbers and I'll follow up."

"When are you going to have time for me, sweetheart?"

Clayton called out in a pouty little boy voice.

With the room erupting in laughter, Megan covered her face and left the podium.

The people on the Square, including the romantic pairs, teased each other all the time, but their light-hearted bantering surprised me again and again. Megan and Clayton were fairly new at it, but I'd seen Art and Marianna playfully spar. Elliot and Georgia added their share, too.

Why did I have trouble seeing myself enjoying that kind of relationship? Unfamiliarity perhaps?

With meeting over, Sarah turned off the microphone and joined the crowd. When the air shifted behind me I turned to see Eli holding my coat. I slipped my arms into the sleeves. *Message sent, Eli.*

It seemed everyone saw him, and a hush fell across the room. It lasted all but a second or two, and Eli noticed. He didn't react, though, but put his hand on my back and guided me out of the building.

The cold night air greeted us when we left the Inn. Eli took my hand in his and we walked the short distance to Square Spirits in Eli mode. Silence. I'd come to understand that Eli didn't need a lot of conversation to be content. For that matter, neither did I.

I stopped at the front door, but Eli pulled me a little farther toward Farmer Foods. He pointed upstairs. "My new home. You'll see lights up there now, not above Country Law."

"Really? But there's nothing up there." I didn't try to keep the surprise from my voice.

"Enough for now. You'll see."

I thought Eli was inviting me upstairs, but he turned around and we headed back to my shop.

"So, we're all set for Friday," he said. "I talked to Devin, and he's letting your Mom know you're coming with me."

"I'll be happy to see her. And JoAnn is fine with minding the shop. She'll come back Saturday, too, to help out with Tom Harris' tour bus stop."

Eli frowned slightly. "You know, your brother and I started talking about the winery back at the association meeting when he visited with your parents. I told him I was interested in the process of making wine. We've been emailing back and forth ever since."

I looked into his eyes as he spoke and found the man that matched my core. And then I froze.

I wanted my independence, and that more or less cancelled out having a partner. *Didn't it?* My mind quickly jumped to the other couples on the Square and found independent women, strong women, willing to open their hearts to love.

"Zoe? I thought you knew Devin and I have become friends."

It was so painful to admit that I knew nothing about him communicating with Devin. But why did I think Eli couldn't talk to my family? He could. It immediately came to me that maybe Eli could be the bridge that brought Devin and me together.

"Devin and I haven't communicated much in the last few months." I paused. "It will be nice to see him on Friday." I hoped I sounded neutral, casual.

"So, we leave mid-morning. I'm bringing the video of the Square to play for your mom and dad. They might want something similar for the winery."

Suddenly, Eli smiled broadly. It was an expression of such happiness I knew it would be forever imprinted in my mind.

He leaned in, not even looking around to see who was watching. His arms brought me to him and encircled me. The kiss started softly, and then built with need.

Eli backed away when Megan and Clayton walked past.

"He's a goner," Clayton said.

Clayton's teasing words broke the moment.

"Just showing you how it's done, Clay." Eli's quick reply sent a new charge of energy into the air. He stood silent and waited for them to move further away before whispering, "Grace, open the door."

Nothing.

"Grace, please open the door."

The bolt clicked.

"I've been waiting to try that for a while now," Eli said with a faint smile, "just to see if they trusted me with you."

"Guess you got your answer," I said, still shocked by his kiss. "But you have to mind your manners and say please."

I adopted a teasing tone, but never, ever, would I have believed either of my spirits would follow a command, no, a request, from anyone but me. The girls, like Eli, were full of surprises.

He gave me a light kiss and held the door for me. Another quick kiss and with a little bow he said, "Zoe."

He knew. He knew his tone of voice aligned our energies. Yes, Eli Reynolds was a kindred spirit.

***

I worked in short spurts of concentration to prepare for the weekend, but waves of a fantasy life with Eli would periodically appear and send me off course. JoAnn was happy to be working both days, because she'd begun looking forward to the atmosphere in the shop, but also being on the Square.

"The Saturday tour bus should be fun," I said, "especially if some of the people coming aren't familiar with Square Spirits."

I reminded Grace and Rose that JoAnn would be in the shop and that I would be out with Eli. Now that I'd seen they trusted him, I was firm in telling them not to unlock the door for anyone else. "No one."

When I climbed into Eli's truck on Friday morning, I asked him two questions: "How is the remodeling coming?" and "What are you most interested in seeing at DmZ?"

I never got another word into the conversation all the way to Mom and Dad's. With his spirit light, almost buoyant, Eli bounced between the two topics.

He had some things on his mind, too, namely layout ideas for his apartment that he'd received from Charlie, Nolan, and Reed. He wanted me to see the three different plans before he "put the first nail in."

Did he know his words sent a thrilling, little shiver through me? His energy bounced and ricocheted around the cab of the truck. Since it was happy, buoyant energy, I absorbed as much as I could.

Eli parked in the driveway and Mom, tall like me, with her shoulder-length graying hair fixed in a stylish twist, came out the back door when we walked up the sidewalk. She wrapped her snowflake sweater closer to her body as she waited for us to reach the stairs. She drew me into a mother-daughter hug that made me feel safe.

Eli waited for us to separate and then handed Mom a paper shopping bag decorated with hearts. "For you, Judith. Some of the homemade jams and pickles we carry at the store."

She peeked in the bag and then welcomed him with a one armed hug. "Thank you, Eli. Come in, come in. This kind of day is such a great change for Russ. He can't wait to go to the fields with you and Devin."

"I hope he'll get a kick out of the video I'll produce with the drone camera," Eli said. "It will give you a whole new perspective on your land."

The kitchen was warm and filled with the aromas of made-from-scratch cooking. I saw a pie cooling on a rack and would have bet a month's sales it was apple-cranberry.

No sooner had Eli and Dad begun talking, Devin and Julia came in. Devin nodded, and Julia grabbed onto my arm. Her smile went from ear to ear.

"What's first for you, Eli? Winery or vineyard?" Devin asked.

Well, well, I hadn't seen Devin this happy in years. Between the six of us, the room almost glowed from our happy energy.

"As long as the sun is shining, let's do the vineyard first," Eli said. "Forecast is for clouds this afternoon."

"You guys go and I'll stay here with Mom," I said. "I can help her get lunch ready."

Devin shrugged. "Your choice."

Julia went with the men, dressed for the cold, but she grabbed an extra scarf off the hook and wrapped it around my dad's neck. Within a minute or two all of the noise of their leaving became silence.

I moved closer to the stove. "So, what's for lunch, Mom?"

"Scalloped potatoes with ham, Jello salad, coleslaw, corn bread with honey, and pie for dessert. Wine, off course. Nothing last minute. We might not see them for hours."

Uh, oh. Mom and me alone for hours. Poor planning on my part, but it was good to see her more relaxed than she'd been at Christmas.

"How's Julia working out?" I asked.

"Very well. You wouldn't believe the change in Devin since she's back, and doing so many different jobs at the winery—and here at the house. She's always smiling these days."

And I bet always talking.

"Do you think Devin likes her?"

"You just watch them," Mom said. "They're in love with each other, but it's too soon for them to understand it."

Me, too, Mom, but I'll guard my independence—and my privacy—for now. Making a fast switch, I told Mom about being part of Megan's wedding services for the Square. I gave general answers to her questions until she said, "We saw the video clip of you and Eli in the booth. That was a beautiful suit you wore."

I'd been had.

Mom only smiled when I sheepishly looked her way. It was clear I no longer had any reason to avoid the subject of Eli Reynolds, so I told her about him making new shelves to replace the wine racks and the way he volunteered to make the cutout snowmen. "He's moving closer." I turned away. "Literally. He's building his own apartment in the large empty space above the food store."

"I see," Mom said.

And I knew she did.

Before she could probe for information, as I knew she would, Julia and Dad came in through the back door. I was surprised to see them, since they'd only been gone an hour.

"The guys have moved inside and Devin is describing each process and piece of equipment in detail to Eli," Julia said.

"I don't know when they'll come in," Dad said with a grin, shrugging out of his coat.

Julia settled Dad into the rocker in the kitchen and stayed close by in case he needed help removing his boots. Always watchful, Mom put her hands over his feet to make sure they warm. He waved her off, but slid his feet into the slippers she'd brought him.

And, even with all the fussing over him, Dad never stopped talking about Eli's drone and how eager he was to see the video. I told him about Eli using the drone to take a movie of the Square. I still hadn't told Mom about the girls visible in the window. At some point, I'd tell her about Eli and his awareness of them.

The pounding of feet outside the door announced Devin and Eli's arrival and their efforts to get as much snow off their boots as possible.

Once inside, Eli said, "The drone is back in the truck, but we'll have show time in three minutes."

"I'll hook up the TV," Devin said. "We can all see it better on the TV than on the computer screen."

Dad settled into his corner of the couch, which I noted had the remote on the table next to him, a throw across the back cushion, and a TV tray nearby. It hurt to see the evidence of how limited Dad's life had become, but I was sure Devin's Christmas gift had made the long days easier for him.

"Might make the image a little fuzzy, but we'll try." Devin connected the cord between the television and his computer. When he pushed the start button a bird's eye view of the house came on the screen, soon moving on to the plowed roads through the fields and around the winery buildings.

Sitting in the living room reminded me of the nights Mom and Dad had shown us the old home movies of us when we were kids. The slide shows of our vacations were also family pleasers. In both movies and slides, we waved a lot and wore huge smiles. Those days seemed carefree in their way, and a long time ago. We'd taken those trips before Dad started the winery and our vacations became wine growing projects or visiting established wineries in the state.

Mom and Dad sat next to each other on one end of the couch. The love seat had been moved away from the side windows and was closer to the television. Devin and Julia claimed that spot and sat side by side, their bodies touching. I sat in the lone soft chair off to the side. Eli perched on the arm of the chair, refusing Mom's offer to sit next to her and Dad on the couch.

One family. Three couples.

I lost focus on the video until Eli touched my arm and nodded to the screen. "Not much to see with the snow covering the ground, but come spring when the leaves are on the vines, we'll make another movie."

"Maybe we can use it on the website." Julia had turned around and placed her hand on Devin's shoulder.

Devin and Julia? Mom was right. Well, good for him—them.

When the video ended Devin reran it to make a copy. He handed Eli the chip. "Thanks. We can use this view in our marketing. And now we have one more piece of information than we had yesterday. It will help with our long-term planning."

He talked like a banker, a businessman, the owner of an enterprising company. Which he was. I had no doubt that he'd be a successful head of DmZ Winery, building on what Dad and Mom had already done. From what I could see, Julia would likely be right alongside Devin.

Over Mom's casserole and cornbread lunch, the conversation around the kitchen table never wavered far from the workings of the winery or from the scheduled events to the test batches of new varieties.

I sat back in my chair and realized I no longer had a role in the conversation. On the other hand, Eli was asking questions and referring to his next visit. My family obviously accepted him. Meanwhile, I'd keep selling the wine, which I knew was an important part of marketing the winery itself.

Not long after Eli polished off his second piece of pie, I touched his arm and suggested we be on our way. "The tour bus is coming tomorrow," I said, "and I still have a few things to do to get ready."

Eli stood, adding that he and Elliot were opening early and they'd both be in Farmer Foods all day.

"A tour bus in the winter?" Mom's face showed her

surprise at my announcement.

"It's part of Sarah's campaign to make the Square a year round destination," Eli said. "This is the first time a tour bus will come our way in the winter."

"Well, then, let's hope for lots of shoppers," she said.

I grinned. "Needless to say, I'm with you."

Mom packed up containers of leftovers for us. Eli asked for a piece of pie, but I preferred a bag of cookies.

On our trip home Eli was chatty and happy. He repeated everything Devin had told him, and then said he wished he'd met Devin years ago. With Eli's shyness gone, I saw a different man.

"I'm sure you can go back anytime you want," I said. "Devin's already invited you."

He drove down the alleyway behind Square Spirits and got out of the truck. Good. I wanted Eli close. He didn't disappoint me.

The first kiss was soft, light and teasing.

"Such a great day," he said. "I'm glad I got to see the winery with you along."

He didn't wait for a response, but pulled me close and kissed me until I needed to breathe. "'Night, sweetheart."

"That's Clayton's word," I teased him.

"Okay, 'night, beautiful." He drew his fingertips along my jaw line. Then he gave me another quick kiss before stepping back and climbing into the truck. I unlocked the door and let myself inside, still lightheaded from the kisses.

Before I headed upstairs I spotted the note JoAnn had left on the counter: *Great day. See you tomorrow!*

I went upstairs, relaxed and happier than I'd been after my visit home to my family at Christmas. And minutes later, I let the soft swirls from the girls lull me into a gentle sleep, still thinking about Eli Reynolds.

20

With the mid-morning arrival of Tom Harris' tour bus, the number of shoppers on the Square significantly increased. Most on the shopping tour wanted to pay a visit to Square Spirits, primarily because they hadn't been to the Square since I'd first opened. JoAnn was good at making customers feel special, and for the occasion, each shopper received a gift of a small tube of lavender hand cream.

Following a slow week, I hadn't expected much business on the weekends that bracketed Valentine's Day, but as a steady stream of shoppers came in each day, my heart soared. Mid-week Nora stopped in just before opening time. She carried a container with flowers covered by tissue paper and had a box tucked under her arm.

"You are a lucky lady, Zoe," Nora said as she uncovered three deep-red roses vased with baby's breath and greenery. She handed over the card and gave me one of her radiant smiles. I smiled to myself. It was clear she wasn't about to rush away until I opened the card.

To make the suspense linger, I opened the box first and gave Nora one of my own happy smiles. Nestled in white paper cups were six of the largest chocolate dipped strawberries I'd ever seen, a specialty of Cindy's Confectionaries.

Then I opened the card. *To three beauties. L, Eli.*

"Eli sent me flowers."

Nora let out a happy chuckle. "Under threat of death to Megan and me if we tell anyone."

"Really?"

"Oh, it's so romantic," Nora said. "Who would have

thought Eli had it in him."

I would. And only I know who the three beauties are.

Nora waved and hurried out the door.

I wasn't going to be the only one to enjoy the flowers, so I put them on the counter next to the register. I bent over and inhaled deeply, letting their heady scent work its magic on my heart before taking the card and strawberries upstairs.

When I called Eli, I got his voicemail. He was probably busy with customers or working in the walk-in cooler or stock room. I hoped my tone in the message I left conveyed my surprise.

I had occasion to call him again later that day after I got the text from Katie reminding me that the knitting group was meeting. My first thought was to call Eli so he would know my lights would be off and I'd be next door to him at The Fiber Barn.

I didn't need to do that, of course, but after our trip to see Devin and my parents, we'd started talking regularly on the phone, almost nightly. Every now and then I'd hear hammers pounding in the background, and it was usually one of the other guys helping with the apartment.

I hadn't forgotten that he'd said I should see his floor plan before the work started, but my approval didn't really matter. I wasn't going to be living there, after all.

On the evening of the knitting group, I wasn't surprised to see most of the women on the Square in The Fiber Barn, along with some new faces from town. Tracie handed me a ball of yarn and two straight needles. "You'll be in my group tonight."

I was a true novice, only attending because I wanted to spend some non-work-related time with the women I'd come to know. As a teenager, I'd knitted now and again with my maternal grandmother, who would have liked me to become passionate about it. But with college, and then marrying Tyler, I never bothered with it again.

Katie and I had been told about Marianna's baby quilt project, and she and Tracie decided to focus their knitting night on scarves for veterans. Since both Katie and Tracie had lost their husbands in the war in Afghanistan, they were close to many veterans in the area and active in making sure these men and women got what they needed. Katie and Tracie had a strong effect on me, stirring up my heart energy, especially because they'd forged a path through their grief.

"So they don't have to be perfect," Tracie assured us, "but they'll be warm."

I gave myself over to the process, determined to put aside my reluctance and enjoy myself. By the time the evening ended, I fell into a rhythm of sorts, relying on old memories of learning Gram's stitches to guide my hands. I was surprised at how comfortable looping the dove gray yarn around the needle to make a stitch was for me. But I wasn't perfect, and more than once Tracie came to my rescue to pick up a dropped stitch.

Later that night, I sipped a mug of hot herbal tea and in the quiet of my dark apartment I told Eli about the evening, and the scarves we were making.

"Makes you feel good, doesn't it?" he asked. "I mean, making something for someone else as a gift. Especially a vet."

"It does. And the women really seem to enjoy these winter get-togethers." I hesitated before I confided that I'd also had a few inquiries about doing psychic readings. "I'm glad people are asking me about them. I've missed doing readings, and these slower months are a good time to start."

"What exactly is a reading?" Eli asked.

"Hmm…let's see. You probably do them without even knowing it. Anyone who sees spirits and gets them to open doors is already working with energies." It probably wasn't a good idea to offer, but I plunged in anyway. "I could give you a reading, if you'd like, although with your ability I couldn't tell you much more about yourself than you already know. On the other hand, I can't read my impressions of myself at all."

"Well, we'll see. About the reading, I mean."

His reluctance was clear. Maybe he was okay with Grace and Rose, but he could have been ambivalent about the idea that I could read his energy at will.

It was late by the time we said good night, but I slept

well, feeling good about growing closer to Eli, reading or not.

***

Going to B and B to begin most days had become one of my joys, so there was almost always an empty chair waiting for me when I arrived. One morning, the subject for the day was the arrival of cold weather and a major snowstorm predicted to follow in a day or two.

"Won't be any shoppers then. Can't make any money that way." Doris' voice was flat. I'd noted she was unhappy the last few times I'd seen her. I couldn't help but wonder if something more serious created her fluctuating emotions. That thought, or impression, fueled my nagging uneasiness. When I reached across the table and touched her arm a cold chill went through me as she transformed into a hollow figure wandering in the darkness. I'd dismissed these feelings before, but even if I decided to act on my impressions, who would I tell and what would I say? Doris hadn't opened up to me about what was happening in her life.

Marianna was describing a quilt pattern known as a Double Wedding Ring, and the family of a summer bride who wanted to give a quilt with that pattern to the couple. And they wanted Marianna to make it.

Georgia brought up the question of time…like when would Marianna have any?

"I can get a lot of it done the next two months. I have good help in the shop, and besides, it feels good to be making a quilt for someone again. Like the scarves we're knitting."

I nodded in agreement. "I'm with you."

It was in these brief exchanges that I'd realized I no longer felt like the newest kid on the block. Slowly, these women were becoming friends, girl friends. What had once been an empty part of my life was filling in nicely.

I left B and B with a pleasant feeling of familiarity and the pleasure of the rhythm of the life I'd created. Although

I wasn't expecting any early morning shoppers on such a cold, overcast day, the jingling of the bell drew me away from the computer.

Lily had come in carrying two bags.

I immediately moved toward her. "Here, let me help you." I grabbed one of the bags and peeked inside. Books, and lots of them.

Lily took a deep breath. "It's a long way across the Square with heavy bags. Guess I should have made two trips." She stopped to take another breath. "I'm hoping you can use these."

I lifted the top layer of books out of the bags and recognized a variety of New Age authors and titles. "Cleaning out the store?"

"Well, not really. You see, Doris doesn't remember ordering them."

I waited for her to say more. When she didn't respond, I extended my hand, palm up, as an invitation to say something.

Lily sighed and thrummed her fingers on the counter. "She's been forgetful lately. The last couple of months we've received duplicate orders or she's forgotten to place an order."

I touched her arm, just lightly, to give her comfort.

And felt two heartbeats.

I released her arm and refocused on the books. "I wouldn't have ordered some of these titles, but I'll put them out and see what happens. We can go from there. Glad to help, Lily."

"Please don't say anything about the books to Doris. She gets upset, sometimes really angry if I mention a mistake."

"I promise. Not a word." I brushed her hand when she passed me a book and the heartbeats were stronger this time. I suppressed a smile. I'd heard about Lily's return to Wolf Creek and her love story with Nathan and Toby. She'd worked hard to repair a once damaged life. She deserved another gift.

Lily left at the same time Sadie entered.

"I will be so glad when we don't have to wear heavy

coats and hats, and wrap ourselves in scarves." Sadie spoke as she gathered a few books and looked at their spines. "Haven't read much New Age material, at least not lately. I've been stuck in history."

"Take a look at the new inventory," I said, pointing to the stacks on the counter. "Those titles just came in." I would keep my promise to Lily even if it meant not being completely honest with Sadie. "Something I can help you with today?"

"Yup. Two things. Crystal and Sarah's history."

My stomach clenched. I hadn't made a decision on the crystal, nor had I finished reading Sarah's history of my building. With all that had been going on, I'd put aside Sarah's pages and had all but forgotten about the small amount I had left to read.

"I've been so busy I haven't made a decision about adding another line to my inventory, although I can see it being a nice compliment to everything here." I swung my arm in an arc toward the front of the shop.

"Give it a try. If it doesn't sell, I'm sure my friends will take it. Or I will."

"You?" I hadn't heard Sadie mention anything about wanting a business of her own. She seemed happy working at the museum.

"I would partner with Clayton for a small corner of his gallery." She shrugged. "I may do that anyway with some kind of product that will be a match with Megan's wedding destination business. I'm betting on that idea."

"If you're that sure, then I'm in. Guess I needed a little push."

Her smile suggested she'd gotten her way.

"So, I did read the first part of Sarah's writings, but I've been too busy with everything lately. Something else always takes priority."

Right… Something like Eli.

Sadie bit her lower lip, as if trying to solve a problem. "I'm only asking because part of the new displays will be open to the public this summer. My hope is to have a book of the town's history available to sell. That's doubtful, though, because there are still many sections to add. Sarah was in last week looking for material on Doris' building to start writing that portion."

"Have you thought about small pamphlets on the buildings she's done? Perhaps a way to entice the visitors to collect each one?"

"Then we could put them together in a book." Sadie had picked up my thought and ran with it. "Then, when we have the grand re-opening for the museum Sarah could do a book signing."

"Great idea—that would add to the special occasion." In my mind's eye, I could see Sarah happy to sit at a table selling books to curious customers, some Wolf Creek residents, some not.

Sadie gathered her coat together and pulled the sash belt into a knot. "I need to talk to Matt about this idea, but please read the rest of the section soon. And let me know when the crystal arrives." She was out the door so fast the bell barely jingled.

During the time I'd spent with Lily and Sadie not one customer had stopped in, which wasn't a true worry, but it did make me wonder if adding crystal to my inventory was a sign of business savvy or just overdoing it.

Before I talked myself out of my decision I went to the Atwell Crystal website and chose twelve items for my first order. Establishing an account with them was accomplished with a simple five-minute phone call. In a week to ten days the twelve pieces would be in my shop.

I ran upstairs to grab a small green salad from the deli to go with a cheese and cracker plate I'd put on a tray. I searched for the manila envelope in a pile of files on my desk. Finding it, I took lunch and Sarah's pages downstairs. Now that I was focused on it, I was curious what Sarah had written in the next section of her story. From what I could tell, Sadie didn't know about spirits living in the building. So far, only Eli and I were privy to that information.

I cleaned off the back table and heated water for tea. Good food and a good story, perfect for a winter day.

Rebuilding

By Sarah Hutchinson

The charred building remained an eyesore in the community for over a year. No one knew if Cyrus would return to Wolf Creek, or if the building was for sale.

Two years later, Cyrus deeded the building back to the community. In a letter, he explained that Adelaide had died from grief and he would not be returning himself. He hoped the town would find it in their hearts to care for the graves of Madeline and Hazel.

Although the tragedy lingered in Wolf Creek, opportunities were growing in the new farming community. A young man, Leland Shaw, became fully aware of the need for a seed store, having spent one spring hauling seeds for the Crawford Freight Line. Sam and Keith Crawford surprised the young man when they agreed to invest in the store if Leland did the work. Leland began to sort the burned timbers, hauling unusable materials to the town dump, and sorting and stacking any lumber still strong enough for building.

With the help of townsmen and friends, Leland rebuilt the structure. Everyone referred to it as the Hart building and it continues, to the present day, to be known as such.

Leland told stories of lamps going out at unexpected times or horrible crying sounds coming from the attic area of the building. Through the years, the building was thought to be haunted, although no reliable evidence has ever existed that proves the claim.

The rumors didn't deter Leland from running a successful seed business, but some of his customers would no longer enter the store after hearing about the unusual goings-on. Leland only smiled and charged them extra for delivery.

Years later, Leland was financially able to buy out his partners and continue the Wolf Creek Seed Company on his own as a cornerstone of the community. Eventually, Leland's health deteriorated, brought on from years of breathing the fine dust escaping from the bags of seeds. He sold the business and returned to Illinois to be closer to his family.

The Hart building suffered numerous business failures in the years following Leland's departure.

The author, in conjunction with the town clerk, has recorded an as accurate as possible list of when the building was bought, sold, or abandoned in the years and decades that followed.

When asked why they left the building, many business owners cited strange happenings or sounds within the structure that couldn't be logically explained.

***

Sarah's story got me thinking about the building and how much Grace and Rose had been a part of the town long after their deaths. They were part of it now, although they were trapped, almost as if afraid to leave the familiar.

I stood and stretched, not realizing how much time had passed. I'd had no interruptions, because I'd not had even one customer all day. Disappointing, even alarming, I locked the door and turned off the lights. Balancing the tray in one hand I went upstairs.

Once up in my apartment, I realized I hadn't felt Grace's and Rose's presence since early morning. "Hello, ladies. Were you afraid Sarah was going to tell everyone about you?"

The currents swirled around the room.

"Well, she didn't. If she knows you're here she didn't make you part of the story. But she did mention the various owners who bought the building and then sold it when their businesses failed. You wouldn't have had anything to do about that, would you?"

The girls came to rest on either side of me.

"I thought so."

I found peace sitting in my chair watching the activity on the Square as another day came to a close. The people who were part of my life now drifted through my mind, especially Eli. When I was with him, I felt safe and protected in a way that was new for me. And I felt wanted, too, in a way that was different from my early years with Tyler.

Eli hadn't used words to convince me. We communicated in a different language. His touch, his glances, his voice. And his kisses. Each time I saw him now I released a little more of my heart and gave it to him. Tonight, I would tell him how much.

When the phone rang my heart soared. Ever since the night we'd come home from the visit to the winery he'd been calling me "beautiful" or "sweetheart," insisting that Clayton didn't own that term of endearment. The change in the way he spoke to me had surprised me at first, but then, Eli was a man of many surprises. He'd used the same tone of voice as when he called me "Zoe," making me forget about my troubles and think only of him.

Tonight I was going to reverse his pattern, so, without checking the caller ID, I answered with, "Hello, sweetheart."

"Now that's what I wanted to hear." A sinister laugh followed.

Tyler!

"Why…why are you calling?"

"To hear your voice," he said, his own tone chipper and light in a crazed, haunting kind of way. "I've missed you… so much."

Panic rose from my gut up my chest, my throat closing fast. "What do you want?" I forced the words out in a low croak.

"Like I said. I want *you*. And it won't be long before I hold

255

you in my arms again." He spoke seductively, enunciating each word. And typical of Tyler, he expected me to respond.

"*No* Tyler. Our life is *over*."

"Oh, Zoe, I made a mistake. But I'm coming back for you—for us." When he returned to the sinister tone that chilled me, he added, "And I'll be there soon."

The high-pitched laughter that followed convinced me he was either strung out on drugs, not something he'd ever done, or he was crazy. And that's what almost made me unable to speak.

"No, no, no." I said the words with as much force as I could manage. "I want *nothing* to do with you." I ended the call and put the phone down, as if touching it was a dangerous act.

My young spirits swirled close, then moved away, then came close again. The air currents bounced off the walls sending papers to the floor. In front of my eyes, the purple shawl lifted off the chair and both ends twisted into a knot. That shocked me, even with my sense of how powerful the girls were.

I dropped to the floor in front of the window, rocking back and forth to calm myself. Tyler was coming to Wisconsin, to Wolf Creek. *To me.* I looked out the window, searching the area I could see of the Square. *Maybe he was already here. On the Square, waiting.*

Rage took over my body. If blood could boil, mine would be rolling. I'd spent two years gaining insight into his shallowness, his lack of understanding me. I went after my dream and I had it in my hand. And he thought he could come here and take it away?

I heard pounding on the door downstairs. It was Tyler. I was sure of it. I got to my feet and turned off the lights. Then I went to hide in my bedroom. The pounding continued, the voice yelling, "Open the door."

I covered my ears and huddled on the floor next to the bed. My rage had transformed into terror.

Two strong arms pulled me close to his body, but I fought him off, all the while repeating, "Let me go, Tyler, get out of here… Let me go!"

"Zoe, sweetheart. It's Eli. I'm here, Zoe." His soft steady voice calmed me, brought me out of the haze of panic.

He pushed my hair off my face and when I saw him, saw who it really was, the tears began falling.

"He called, Eli. He said he's coming here to get me. I think he may already be here, but I couldn't see him on the Square."

"Who? What happened?"

"Tyler called," I said, shifting in Eli's arms so I could talk to him and wipe away tears at the same time. "When the phone rang, I thought it was you, so I said, 'Hi, sweetheart.'"

"Then?"

"He didn't sound like himself at all. He had this crazed laugh and scary voice. He said he's coming here to be with me."

Eli's body stiffened and that shifted the energy. I tried to stand, and he held out his hand to help me to my feet.

"Wait, Eli. Why did you come up?" My body was still shaking, but I managed to get words out. "How did you get in?"

He held up his hand and went to the kitchen. I followed, but by the time I slid into a chair at the table, my knees were weak. Eli put a glass of water in front of me. Using my foot, I pushed out a chair for him, but he shook his head.

"Eli. Don't go into silent mode on me. Not now. How did you happen to come here—and how did you get in?"

"You called out for me. I mean, that's what I heard. You screamed that you needed help."

I knew I hadn't called for him in words, and that he couldn't have heard me anyway, but some part of me had reached out. He'd come because I needed him.

"Grace unlocked the door," he said.

"What? Grace?" I thought about what I'd said to Grace. "I told her not to do that anymore." Well, that wasn't strictly true. I'd told her not to let anyone else in but me.

"She wanted to help." Exasperation filled his voice. "So did I, obviously. I only knew you needed me because I *felt* it."

It hadn't been my intention, but the incident had left Eli

super-sensitive, and to his ears, I'd pounced on his effort to help me. He moved toward the doorway leading downstairs.

"Stay, Eli. I want you to stay. Please." I went to him on legs no longer weak from fear. I put my arms around his waist and rested my head on his chest. "I was going to call you 'sweetheart' tonight when you called."

"You said that already." A soft chuckle rumbled in his chest. Right next to his heartbeat. Easing back and away from me, he said, "What are you going to do about Tyler?"

"At the moment I'm not thinking of Tyler." I moved my hands to his neck and stretched my body full length against his. "Any objections?"

I didn't give him time to say no, but drew his lips to mine. The kiss only made me want more of him. I pulled him to the couch.

Eli and I sat until the early hours of the morning. We held hands, we kissed, we talked of the future, about our dreams. We, of course, talked about Tyler and my concerns that he hadn't sounded like himself at all. But I was determined to make him understand that I wanted nothing to do with my ex. *Nothing.* I had a sense that if Tyler ever called again, I'd not respond with fear. Yet, I had a lingering thought that his mental state would keep him from *hearing* my words.

Eli finally left as the sun brightened the sky over Wolf Creek.

***

Nora called early. "Got your calendar open?"

"Hold on. It's here somewhere." I smiled to myself. What would she think if I told her that a couple of girl-spirits had made a total mess of my house? And all because of a phone call from my ex-husband. I felt a cool shaft of air lead me to the spot where my book had ended up under a magazine. "Ah, here it is." I found the page for the month of February. There were only two days left in the month.

"Can you do a reading tonight, maybe tomorrow?"

After Tyler's call and the late night with Eli, my energy was as scattered as the items in my living room. I needed a few days to gather and realign the currents and energy for myself.

"Sorry, Nora. I'm busy those days." I turned the calendar page. "But I could see you the evening after the association meeting ends."

"Terrific. I've inked it in."

When I disconnected the call, I realized I was anticipating a pleasant evening with her. I'd heard about her working for Megan at Rainbow Gardens and how her husband, Matt, and his father had launched a foundation to support small historical projects. The renovation of the museum in Wolf Creek was their first project.

It had been a while since I'd done a one-on-one reading. I'd have to talk to the girls to make sure they'd stay quiet, but also not see Nora as a threat. She had radiant energy, though a kind of calm that made other people around her centered. But within her energy, I saw the grief and a physical struggle. Her first husband's death perhaps, along with a long recovery from her accident. I'd seen those signs before.

I started my day looking forward to my first scheduled reading—a new phase of my life on the Square.

March
21

When I walked into the business association meeting on Eli's arm, Sarah, in her usual spot at the door, greeted each of us with a hug. Somehow, I knew that with Sarah aware of us, Eli and I had more or less gone public with our still budding relationship.

With the room filling quickly, we grabbed chairs next to Megan and Clayton. I thought Eli might visit with some of the men before the meeting started, but no, he'd stayed with me. Eli took Tyler's declaration that he was coming back for me as an actual threat. Yet, realistically, we both realized Eli couldn't be with me every minute. We had businesses to run and lives to lead. I also wanted to keep information about Tyler private—I wasn't about to tell the whole dreary story to everyone on the Square. But the fear Tyler had planted in me was real and never left for very long.

As Sarah moved from the doorway, she stopped to talk with Lily for a few minutes. Then she continued to the front of the room.

She tapped the microphone. "Time to start. Short agenda tonight."

A few murmurs of approval came from the crowd.

Sarah told us how appreciative Tom Harris was for the welcome we gave his passengers and we could expect to see him later in the spring.

"I also want to welcome Richard Connor, who as most of you know is Nathan's father." Sarah waved to Richard. "Please stand up, Richard, so everyone can see you."

Delight came through Sarah's tone as she explained that Richard was moving from Green Bay to Wolf Creek, at least part time. "Richard will be living in the apartment above Country Law."

"We've already got clients for him," Nathan said from his seat a few rows in front of Richard.

I knew I was witnessing another father-son duo who would successfully work together, just as Dad and Devin were finding their way.

"Okay, since we have new shopkeepers on the Square it makes sense to quickly review our winter weather policy," she said.

"You're a little late with that one, Sarah."

I laughed at Sadie's remark. Only she could talk to Sarah that way and not have one of Sarah's notorious pointed looks cast her way.

"You're from New York," Sarah said, "and around here we don't declare the end of winter until we get thirty days without snow."

Sadie grinned. "Touché."

"Okay. If schools are closed, so is the Square." She held up one finger. "The Square is plowed only after the streets in town are done." Finger number two joined the first. "We check on each other, and help each other shovel. This is our Square and we watch out for each other."

By now she'd used four fingers, and then her thumb appeared. "Finally, let's hope we finish the season with mild weather."

That sounded good to me.

"We're just about done here," Sarah said, "but I've got an item that's not on the agenda."

"And why not?" Elliot kept his voice light, which brought a few laughs from around the room.

"It's a secret." She flicked her hand to dismiss his question. "Come forward you two." She motioned for Nathan and Lily to come to the front of the room.

Many pairs of eyes watched them join Sarah.

Nathan took Lily's hand and kissed it. "Richard Connor is going to be a Granddad again."

"Yes!" Richard jumped up and ran to the front of the room. He hugged Nathan first, then Lily. He turned to the group with a smile filled with love. "Lucky me. A grandfather again."

The rest of us clapped and watched the threesome. I could sense the gracious hearts and feel the energy in the room. Wolf Creek Square would be welcoming a new member to our tight-knit community. The meeting was over when most everyone in the room left their seats and moved forward to congratulate Nathan and Lily. Richard stayed close to Lily's side.

I hung back a little, not knowing Lily as well as many of the others. But when I gave Lily a hug she whispered, "You already knew."

I acknowledged that with a slight nod. It wasn't the right time or place to say more.

Eli and I left a few minutes later. We went up to my apartment for a glass of wine. At the moment, our pattern had evolved to Eli hovering. He was either with me or we were in regular phone touch: texting or talking. I needed time alone, and we hadn't yet had a chance to talk about my need for independence and solitude, although he knew I had those needs, just as he did. Would Eli understand if I told him I felt safe even without him being nearby?

Really? Was that true? Would I ever feel safe not knowing if or when Tyler was coming? Just because he spouted off and said he was coming didn't mean he'd actually show up. I'd learned too late that Tyler wouldn't always do as he said he would. Yet, the threat of him just showing up one day was never far from my mind.

As we sipped our wine, we talked about Nathan and Lily and how their lives would soon be changed. Neither Eli nor I had children, but we agreed that young families brought energy to the Square that would always be needed to continue and improve upon Wolf Creek and steer it into the future.

Before Eli left, I mentioned that I had a reading scheduled for the next night. I'd mute my cell and turn off the ringer on the landline phone. I didn't mention who the reading was for, and Eli didn't ask. I'd need to keep my zone of privacy with my clients. I was happy Eli understood that.

***

Nora was relaxed and happy when she settled into one of the two padded folding chair in the reading room.

"At some point, I'll add a comfier chair," I said, sitting across from her, "but you're more or less launching my foray back into readings. I'm delighted, too."

Nora laughed. "I'm only too happy to help you launch this part of your business." She reached into her handbag and pulled out an envelope with her check in it, saving me from having to remind her at the end of the reading when we'd both be spaced out. Or, maybe a better term would be super-relaxed.

With all my senses engaged, I focused on the quiet surroundings of my reading room—the dim light coming from a salt lamp sitting on a small table in the corner, and two luminaries on the table. I had put a pitcher of water and two glasses on the corner of my computer table. I had a tendency to become parched during a reading, and so did my client. I liked being prepared.

"So, did you bring an object of yours for me to hold?" I asked. I didn't necessarily need to hold something touched by the person I was reading for, but it sometimes helped. And it often eased the person into the process, helped them relax.

Nora handed me a silver and lapis earring. "One of my favorites."

"A little nervous, are you?" I asked. Maybe more excited than nervous, but I thought I'd mention it. I had a feeling about what she wanted to know, but I wasn't sure I would be able to answer.

"Yes, yes, yes. I admit it."

I closed my eyes and held the earring in my palm. "This is old—your grandmother's?"

"Yes. We were close. She outlived our mother, actually."

"She's hovering around you. I don't always sense other

beings, but I do sense the spirit of a very loving woman." I let out a quick laugh. "Wow, she sure loves you. Even from the other side."

I opened my eyes. Nora was staunching tears.

"These are happy tears," she said, reaching for a tissue from the box.

"I know," I said. Oh, how reassuring it could be to realize a beloved relative is watching from the other side. "Most people are touched at some point in a reading."

I went on. "I also see a very lively older man, very much on this earth plane...what a character." I closed my eyes again. His spirit was strong, but he seemed weak in body.

"Must be Gus. Lively is how most everyone describes him, and he's a character all right. Is he okay? Is he well?"

"Yes, I don't mean to alarm you, but he's fighting something. I think his back hurts a lot and takes something out of him." The image of a bent over man with a cane moved into a space in my mind's eye. "Nothing you can do but listen to him and try to understand."

"I get it," Nora said, nodding.

Nora's radiant spirit stayed bright and her aura was strong, even with her concern for Matt's grandfather. "Tell Matt there's not much he can do, but if you can persuade Gus to get therapeutic massages it might help him a lot." I smiled to myself at the pair of hands that had sprung up in my mind. Nothing esoteric there. "His doctor might have mentioned it. Why don't you ask him?"

"I will. I suggested it once or twice, but he said he was too busy."

It was time to be honest with Nora. I couldn't answer her question. "When I saw you at the festival last year, you had bright lights in front of you, with the darkness behind you growing dimmer as it receded into the past. From what I can see, you still have an aura, almost like a sign of happiness. I see flowers growing...that could be Rainbow Gardens, but it's also your happiness blooming, growing."

"Could it mean, maybe, that I could have a baby?"

"From the last reading, I knew that's what you wanted, what you still want. But I don't read an element in your energy that leads me one way or another. But the thing is, Nora, happiness isn't usually dependent on one thing."

I opened my eyes, the earring still in my palm.

Nora looked defeated, her shoulders slumped.

"You don't believe me," I said. "Not fully."

"That's what Matt says." Nora shook her head. "He says we started out our marriage knowing it would most likely always be the two of us. If a baby comes, fine, but we wouldn't make it a focal point of our marriage."

"Your energy sings happiness, Nora. Just like before. You're like the girl in the fairy tale that got her prince. And you don't care if there was some kind of protest about your marriage." And there had been. I saw an image of a wall—a family objection. "You're a natural at happiness. I'd focus on that. Whether you have a baby or not, your life is full right now, this day, this hour. I don't know where the bumps will come in the future, but I'd cherish what you have."

Wow. I was lecturing her, but I saw what I saw and felt what I felt. The flowers were blooming all over her energy field—and Matt's. There were times in a reading when I wished my client would simply live in the moment and leave well enough alone. This was one of those times.

"I knew you were going to say that," Nora said with a laugh. "I've never been this happy, even with Dan, my first husband. We were good together, but we were young and didn't have time to learn how to be good partners over a lifetime."

"Don't sell yourself short. You took away a lot from your first marriage." I rolled the earring around. "But the funeral is long over, and your new story brought you a wedding."

I poured us each a glass of water. A hush fell over the room, but the spell was fading, as it always did at some point. We were done. I almost apologized for not being able to answer her unspoken question about a baby, but then I held back. I was honest with her, no apologies necessary. I'd had to remind myself often that it wasn't my job to make a person's dreams come true.

"It's remarkable, really, that you've moved past the objections to your wedding," I said. "Matt, too. I think that's because of Gus. And by the way, this is simply 'conscious Zoe' talking now, friend to friend. This isn't about reading anything. He just seems like such a champion of you and Matt."

Nora nodded. "He's my grandpa-in-law, and I love him dearly. We'll take care of him as long as he needs it. It's part of our commitment to each other. I don't at this point actually have other in-laws. Maybe that will change, maybe not."

"One of your strengths is some kind of innate wisdom that you can't control other people." I laughed. "What a concept! It takes most of us a lifetime to learn that."

"I think losing Dan so young taught me that." Nora gulped down her water and stood. "I'm going to sleep on everything you said."

"Good idea. And watch your dreams. You might see some images, interesting symbols."

"Thanks, I will. Oh, and by the way, Zoe, Matt knows where I am. I'll mention it to JoAnn, but I'd just as soon not have everyone on the Square know about this reading."

I raised both hands to reassure her. "Say no more. This is strictly confidential. You are free to disclose what I say if you wish, but I never disclose what I've seen or felt on my end, and I never reveal a client's name. Only the client can do that."

Nora nodded and began walking toward the back door, closer to her car. "I thought that was the case. I'm not big on gossip."

"Me, either." I doubted very much that Nora was speculating about Eli and me.

I stood in the doorway and watched her cross the alleyway and go into the parking lot. She turned and waved when she reached her car, and as she backed out of the space and into the street, I closed and locked the door.

I turned off the luminaries, but kept the salt lamp on as I did every night. I made my way upstairs, a little drained, a little tired, but still eager to go over my day with Eli, minus my reading with Nora.

***

In the middle of the following week, we had occasion to activate the Square's winter weather policies. The local TV news meteorologists had repeatedly used the adage for March: "In like a lion, out like a lamb," or they reversed the order if that best suited them. Measurable snow was predicted, common for March in our part of the world. However, a raging blizzard brought more than a foot of snow to Wolf Creek and the surrounding areas. Oops, the weather forecasters quickly regrouped and covered their mistake…as best as they could.

When I looked out over the Square only the black hats of the snowmen peeked through the drifts. The sunshine glancing off the new snow produced a glare that made it almost too difficult to keep looking. But to me, the beauty that came after a storm was as luminous as a rainbow following a summer thunderstorm.

I wrapped my sweater tighter around my body as I stood there. The coffee in the mug warmed my hands. At least we had electricity. I was more or less waiting for Eli to call. He had a funny way of checking on me to make sure I was okay. Not that the snow would bother me as long as we had power. I'd noticed that the men sometimes checked on the women whether we needed it or not. No doubt someone was making sure Doris had what she needed.

My musings were interrupted when the phone rang. I didn't like it, but as a precaution I'd taken to checking the screen each time there was an incoming call. Tyler could call me, but no law said I had to answer. No worries there. Eli's name appeared.

"Hello, sweetheart. Glad to hear from you. Are you all right?"

"Why wouldn't I be?" He chuckled.

He didn't wait for me to answer, and admittedly, it was a meaningless question. "Get dressed and come out. We'll shovel the entryways. The truck and crew won't get here anytime soon."

"Well… I don't know. I'm kind of enjoying my coffee."

"Come on, we're strong, you and I. We can help remove the snow. Besides, it will be fun. We can have coffee later."

Enthusiastic about spending time with Eli, I dressed in wool slacks and a heavy sweater. I sighed when I looked at my unsuitable boots, more designer than rugged. My fleece-lined boots were still packed away in one of the boxes stacked in the living room. No time to search for them.

Eli was waiting for me when I opened my front door. He had two shovels, one in each hand. "For your health." His smile warmed my heart when he handed me the smaller one.

"Right on, Mr. Reynolds." I bent my arms like I was a strong body builder. "Where do I begin?"

"Shovel your steps and a little more out into the walkway. Throw the snow that way, too." He pointed toward the middle of the Square.

"Good to know." I filled the shovel and pretended that it was too heavy and tossed it toward him.

"Women," he growled, but sent a shovelful onto my steps and headed off to Sarah's next door.

A few minutes later, I looked around and saw many others doing their share to clear the entryways. I waved, but everyone was focused on the job to be done.

After a few hours we heard trucks approaching. "They're clearing the alleyways for emergencies."

No matter how long I'd worked and moved, my feet still grew colder and colder. Finally, I gave Eli his shovel and headed inside Square Spirits. "I need to warm up my feet."

His eyes danced. "I'll help."

"Be my guest."

As we went inside the shop the air felt cool, but not a Grace cool.

"Saving fuel?" Eli took off his glove and touched the cold glass countertop.

"No, not really. The shop should be warmer than this."

"Was it cool this morning?"

"I didn't notice, but then I wasn't thinking about heat. I was enjoying the beautiful scene from my window."

"I'll go down and check the furnace."

A minute or two later, I heard Eli's voice coming from

the basement. "Right." Pause. "No." Pause. "Tomorrow. No, that's good. She'll be okay."

From the noise that drifted up he must have put a metal door back on the furnace. I waited for him at the top of the stairs.

"I talked to Nolan. Your furnace blower motor isn't working. He can't get one today, and the repair guys won't be able to get out here."

I shrugged. *No problem.* "I have extra sweaters and quilts. I'll be okay. Soup and hot chocolate will keep me warm. It won't matter in the shop since we'll be closed anyway."

"Uh, uh. You grab your toothbrush and whatever else you need. You'll stay at my place."

With my back stiffening, I stepped away. *Whoa. Was he giving me orders?* I was done with that. I was no damsel in distress. "I *said* I'll be fine." My sharp voice and hard words took me aback. I hadn't known just how threatened I felt until I spoke.

Immediately air currents rippled through the room. The girls had been comfortable with Eli being with me, but his words and tone had triggered their protective nature. My vibrating energy only added to the intense situation.

He raised his hands in surrender. "Have it your way, then. But you can't say I didn't offer." He turned to leave.

"You didn't offer, Eli. You issued a *command.* I'm not one of your employees."

I pivoted on my heel and started up my stairs, unconcerned that I was leaving an unlocked door behind. Before I even reached the top step I heard the bell jingle.

I filled a kettle of water to make hot chocolate, trying to ignore my cold hands and feet. My hair was wet from the snow, and probably had developed a few tangles. Like my thoughts and feelings.

I kept to myself the rest of the day, in my heaviest sweater and wrapped in a blanket, not wanting to venture out, even to Crossroads, where I'd no doubt run into other people. I wasn't up for a social afternoon. I whiled away the time sitting in my chair by the window and watching the few people that ventured out to crisscross the Square.

By late in the day, trucks with plows and front end buckets arrived to clear the walkway. Tomorrow was another business day on the Square.

Fearing that Eli and I would never work out a rhythm between us, I couldn't keep the tears at bay. I felt so alone. What was next for us? Was there even still an "us"?

22

Everything returned to normal, sort of, depending on how I defined that. The furnace was fixed, the shop opened, and Eli weighed on my heart. But then, when I headed to The Fiber Barn to spend time with women I admired, I, at last, had an evening that wouldn't be consumed thinking about me, me, me.

After settling the group into a circle of chairs, Katie and Tracie gave us the pattern for the scarves we'd be knitting, the last session having been only a chance to practice for the stitches we'd be using. I sat next to Georgia, also a novice knitter and one who could laugh at her mistakes. I'm certain we laughed more over our mistakes than we accomplished. Georgia had much on her mind, too. She and Elliot were on the brink of breaking ground for their new home, so being excited was her natural state. She joked about seeing floor and fixture samples in her dreams.

"We have so many to choose from, and I haven't even decided if I want vintage or contemporary," Georgia said, smiling wryly. "And Elliot's no help. He says yes to every picture I show him."

I nodded as if I understood her dilemma, while also trying to concentrate on my knitting.

Katie and Tracie were a study in patience. Now and again, Marianna, who was on the other side of me, added a story or two about teaching this same group quilting. "The evening isn't about getting a scarf done, so much as it is a chance for the women on the Square to get to know each other outside of our shops and B and B and association meetings." She grinned, adding, "Not that all those things don't bring us together for some fun."

My furnace problem never came up. And my dilemma, my off mood, wasn't about the furnace anyway. I couldn't talk about the way I'd treated Eli and his so-called invitation. I was right, but then so was he. I wasn't ready to talk about it with anyone.

The time flew. I'd barely started finding my rhythm when Katie told us to attach our names to our project and put them in the tote she had placed in the middle of the circle. Hugs all around ended the evening.

As Sarah and I walked home, I noticed lights on above Farmer Foods. Sarah didn't miss them, either. "Eli's been quiet lately. Isn't at coffee, either, like you. Problems?"

Well, nothing like being frank. I was a little taken aback by her question, and I wasn't one to be an open book about my personal life, anyway. I shook my head. "No. Nothing I care to talk about." I thought that would put an end to the inappropriate inquiry.

"He's a good man, Zoe. You're a good match for him. He needs a strong woman."

I stiffened against her presumptuousness, but then she gave me a hug when we stopped in front of Square Spirits and I dropped my irritation. "Matchmaking, are you?"

Sarah waved me off. "Not my place to be involved, but if you want to talk I'm always available."

Funny how she said that after voicing her opinion.

Amused by Sarah, who I was certain meant well, I went inside and locked the door. Grace and Rose greeted me with soft swirls at the bottom of the stairs. We went up the steps together and I started water for tea, but changed my mind and poured a glass of Zodiac. When I sat in the chair by the window I could see the glow of lights above Farmer Foods, but not into Eli's apartment. Tears fell when I realized I didn't want to be alone sitting in my chair. I wanted to be with Eli.

I was at loose ends, with my plans for the next day uncertain. Eli and I had made plans to go to the winery again the next morning. I'd arranged for JoAnn to come in.

But I had to assume those plans were off. Why? Because I was being stubborn and unwilling to reach out to him?

I took a deep breath and picked up the phone and punched the number two button. Number one was reserved for Mom and Dad.

"Eli, here."

"Hello, Eli. I'm…I'm sorry."

"Stop, Zoe. I don't want to have this conversation—"

I talked over his voice. "I'm sorry, Eli. I've been acting like a high school girl, not a woman halfway through her life."

"*Zoe, listen to me…* I don't want this space between us when we talk. I want to look into your eyes, feel your energy."

"Oh, I see." Feeling sheepish, I waited, like I should have done in the first place.

"Open the front door. I'll be right over." He chuckled. "Or have the maid do it."

"Watch it. I don't think Grace thinks of herself as a maid. Besides, I've told her repeatedly not to let anyone in."

"Even me?"

"I'll make an exception tonight."

Before Eli disconnected the call I heard the bolt click on the front door.

I had been undoing an intricate braid in my hair when the bell signaled Eli's arrival. I also heard him relock the door.

By the time he'd made it up the stairs I had two glasses of wine poured and reached out to give him one. "Nothing but the best—Zodiac."

"No wine can compare to you, sweetheart."

I didn't know what to say so I back-stepped and held up my hand to keep him from approaching. "Here goes. I'm sorry for dismissing your attempts to keep me safe, not to mention warm."

Eli had taken one of the kitchen chairs to the front window and waited for me to sit in the comfy chair. I was sure he noticed the shawl from Tyler. Unknotted now, it was draped over another chair. He swung his chair around and sat, resting his arms across the back of the chair. "It's more than the furnace, Zoe. You kiss me, then you push me away and hide up here. People notice that and ask questions."

"Everyone's aware of us?" Sarah had basically said the same thing.

"In this gossipy, little town? How could you miss that?"

"Too many other things to think about, I guess. The business, Dad, Devin. Now Tyler."

"Well, I owe you an apology for acting like you'd immediately go along with my idea. You're right. I didn't ask if you wanted to hang out at my place. I meant well." He paused. "But what else is wrong here, Zoe? I thought you wanted to be together."

I took a sip of wine to give myself a minute to think of the right words. "I'm afraid, Eli. Afraid of losing my independence again, like I won't be strong enough to hang on to it. That's why I bristled earlier. I let Tyler make too many decisions for us and made what I wanted less important than *his* goals. Then, when he left I was a mess."

I swished the wine around in my glass, surprised I'd said the words out loud and without emotion over Tyler. The emotion was over the journey I'd been on. "I ran home like a frightened child, and had to work hard for two straight years to believe in myself again. I needed to learn to make a decision and stick with it, good or bad, right or wrong. I'm not sure I'm strong enough to do it again."

"No one, especially me, is asking you to give up anything."

He reached across the space between us and offered his hand.

Yes. No. Yes. I put my hand in his.

"I'm kind of independent myself, you know," Eli said. "Been that way for my whole life. Maybe if we stick together we can find our way to make this work."

"So, where do we start?" I asked, squeezing his warm fingers. "Tell me."

He frowned, as if gathering his thoughts. "It wasn't easy to tell you about Candy. I don't talk about her with anyone, but I finally told you. You rarely voluntarily say anything about Tyler to me, let alone to other people."

"But…" I didn't know what words should come next.

He squeezed my hand. "Open up, quit hiding all your secrets. Tell me more about Tyler and how he hurt you and why you're so afraid of him coming back. Then, at some point, confide in Sarah or Megan, somebody besides me. We're good people here on the Square, Zoe, but we're not perfect. We've all made mistakes." Grinning, he let my hand go and stood. "We don't just let anyone buy one of our buildings, you know."

He came to me and drew me up and out of the chair. "You're not an island here. You're not alone."

I knew what he was saying was true, and I was aware, more than he realized, that he'd had a rough time with these issues. He'd spent too many years on the periphery of other people's lives.

"I'll tell you a secret if you promise not to tell anyone," he said.

He was so close to me I could almost feel his heart beat. "Cross my heart," I said, making an X over my heart.

"I fell in love with you last September. It was Labor Day weekend. Your dark eyes, your endless long hair." He inhaled, closing his eyes, opening them again when he let all the air out of his lungs with a deep sigh. "I wanted to get lost in you. I was also afraid of you. I wasn't ready to have my wall broken through...no, not me. I'd been walled off for years. But with your energy being what it is, I didn't know how I could stop it."

I met his gaze. "For years, you say. What about others... in all this time, have you loved others?"

He shook his head. "Only Candy. And that was a long time ago."

I nodded, understanding.

Stepping back, he held me at arm's length. "Let's take a chance, Zoe. You and I. I have my life, you have yours, but we can still take care of each other." He drew me against him. "The energy is so powerful when I'm with you. Seems like we can do anything."

When he kissed me, it was as if I had everything I could want and need. I returned the kiss with a passion I'd not felt in a long time. Eli played with my hair, running his hands through the long length until he encountered a snag.

I drew my head back. "Darn braid. I love the look, but it's the only time I get these tangles."

He ran his hand through my hair again. "Get your brush," he said with a laugh. "I'll work those snags out for you."

I tilted my head, smiling like a flirtatious ingénue in the movies. "You have some experience brushing a girl's hair?"

His eyes danced. "Megan wore her hair long when she was younger."

Oops. I'd just learned another facet to Mr. Eli Reynolds.

I hurried to get my brush, and with his slow, gentle strokes he lulled me into a fantasy of Eli caring for me with the same tenderness he was using on my hair. So romantic.

He gathered me close and gave me a kiss that circled my heart. We'd left the subject of my independence and he'd brought me into his image of a world filled with love and beauty. There were so many layers to Eli. What a joy to know that in order to be myself I didn't need to be alone.

In that moment of the kiss, I knew I could be an equal partner with him. I inched back. "Eli, I thought I knew what love was when I married Tyler, but I didn't, and that's why his leaving brought me to my knees. People who love, they care for and support each other. They build a future together and withstand the defeats and troubles that come along. They don't run away." I paused and met his gaze. "I didn't get it that I can love my independence and love you, too."

I stepped away from him, pulled my arm free when he playfully hung on. "Wine." I held up my empty glass. "For a toast. No. For a joining of the spirits."

Grace and Rose had swirled between us since Eli's arrival, but in a calm sort of way, as if listening to us being honest with each other. But then again, the girls liked Eli, always had.

So did I.

No, that wasn't the whole truth. I loved Eli. Luckily, I liked him, too.

Now, what was I going to do about it?

I poured a small amount into each of our glasses, and in a mock dramatic toast I raised my glass high. "To Eli Reynolds and Zoe Miller. May their love and energy entwine."

Eli kept his arm raised. "To Zoe. The most beautiful woman I know."

He took my glass and set both of them on the counter. Eli drew me into his arms, for a second time, and we stood there as one. "I don't want to, but it's time for me to go."

"I know."

I walked down the stairs with him, our progress slowed when we kept holding on each other and sharing our energy.

When Eli opened the front door, he recognized Doris walking past the shop.

I shivered. *Something was very wrong.*

Eli stepped into the glow of the lamppost. "Hi, Doris. Are you out for an evening stroll?"

"Hello, Eli." She looked my way, her expression lost, confused.

He tried again. "Out for a stroll?" He had put her hand into the crook of his arm and rubbed it like it was cold.

She peered into my face again and frowned. "I'm looking for Ralph. He went for a walk, but hasn't come home." In the light I saw her moist eyes glistening.

Eli pulled out his phone and, in a voice too soft for me to hear, called for help. Then he slipped his phone into his pocket. "Sarah's coming. She'll help us find him."

"He couldn't have gone far," Doris said in a plaintive voice. "He always walks around the Square twice at the end of the day."

I took Doris' other arm and guided her into the shop. "Step inside, Doris. It's a tad cold tonight to be waiting outside."

"I don't think I've ever been here before. All those crystals and stones. Is this a magic store?"

Oh, dear. This was bad. "Something like that," I said.

The bell jingled when Sarah and Sadie stepped in followed by Eli. Sarah nodded a greeting before turning to Doris. "Good evening, Doris. Has Ralph come home?"

"No. No." Her voice was barely a whisper. She looked about the room as if she was standing in a foreign country.

"Well, don't worry," Sarah said. "Sadie is going to take you home and stay with you tonight."

"Who's Sadie?" Doris asked.

"Sadie's your friend. Some mornings, you have coffee with her at B and B." Sarah switched Doris' hand to Sadie's arm.

Sadie patted her hand. I knew she hoped to send a message of comfort and security. "Come on, now, let's go home and wait for Ralph."

"All right." Doris looked around before heading out. Eli held the door for them, then bent down and gave Doris a kiss on the cheek.

"Ralph won't like you doing that." She reached up to pat Eli's cheek.

"Don't worry," Eli said, "I'll tell Ralph all about it."

"I'll call Doris' sister in the morning," Sarah said, swiping away her tears. "Sadie said she'll stay with Doris until other arrangements can be made."

Eli and I watched them lead Doris away. Then he gave me one more kiss and left.

I stood in the quiet of my shop and remembered what Eli had said. "We can take care of each other." That was true—it was the way it would work between us.

***

It was inevitable. The next morning, Doris' situation was the topic of the day at B and B. Word had spread quickly, and no one knew the final outcome and what it would mean for Doris and for the Square. Sadly, it appeared that Doris would no longer be able to manage Pages and Toys. That meant Lily had to consider what to do, and the baby coming complicated Lily and Nathan's decisions.

Before too much time had passed Eli stood and I followed his lead. He was ready to get underway.

"We're heading to DmZ this morning. Don't wait up," he said.

So public… Heat rose up my neck and into my face.

Sarah playfully swatted my hand. "Have fun."

I ignored a couple of adolescent comments coming from the men's table as we left.

Our trip to the winery was a repeat of our first trip, only this time Eli fired questions at me, mostly about how I felt about Square Spirits and since I'd started doing readings again, did I mind that I'd be known as a psychic. I admitted my mistake about billing myself as Madame Zoe, but he laughed that off.

"It was kind of fun to call you that, I admit." He frowned. "At the time, I don't think I understood my own abilities, like the girls, or sensing energy. Or, maybe I thought everybody was able to do that." He sighed. "It explains why I've had what seemed like odd reactions to certain people. Maybe that's why I've been so grouchy all my life."

"Could be." I grinned. "In a way, though, you're right. Almost everybody reads energies whether they're conscious of it or not. So, we're all psychic to a degree."

"Why didn't I see the girls before?" he asked.

"Hmm…good question. Probably because they hadn't known you before. You weren't in their space. They trust me, and I talk to them regularly and assure them no one will cause them distress. Whatever that would be for them. Once they showed themselves to you, it was clear that they'd come to trust you."

Eli laughed. "Sometimes I can't believe I'm having these conversations."

"I get it," I said, amused. "Fortunately, my mother is like me, so it isn't such a leap, even though I wasn't accustomed to talking with spirits, either."

Devin was waiting outside for Eli's arrival and was surprised when I stepped out of the truck.

"I hope you have a lot of energy today," I said. "Eli hasn't stopped talking since we left Wolf Creek."

"Nice to see him willing to put in the time it will take to become a wine maker." He paused, and kept his distance, too. "Good to see you, Zoe."

Eli had come around the truck and put his arm across my shoulders, just the way Elliot casually draped his arm around Georgia. I wondered if they'd grown up watching their dad do that with their mom. Twins or not, I was very happy to be on the receiving end of Eli's feelings.

Eli and Devin headed off to the winery building, where Julia and Dad were waiting for them. I could hear the two men already speaking the language of wine making.

What had I expected? Eli made it clear that he was overwhelmed with the process of winemaking and all the equipment he would need.

I hadn't enjoyed a true non-work day in a long time, and once inside I found Mom in the kitchen stirring white bean soup.

"Smells good," I said.

"Lunch." Mom took a bowl of apples off the counter and put it in front of me, and followed up with a paring knife and the cutting board. She didn't have to say anything else. I began quartering them and went to retrieve a casserole dish to bake them.

"It's all falling into place, isn't it?" she asked. "I mean, with you and Eli."

"Yes." I kept it at that, but smiled. No need to put up my defensive posture against Mom's inquiries.

She let out a quick laugh. "Well, if that's all I get, it will have to do."

"For now, that's all I'm going to say. It's new between us, but going well." True, my growing bond with Eli was fresh and shiny new. But on a deeper level, it felt as if we'd known each other a long time. It's as if we'd been waiting for each other. I felt a jolt in my gut. No maybes about it. That's exactly what we'd been doing, *waiting for each other.*

"I feel peaceful energy coming from you," Mom said, "but also jolts of passion and sadness."

"Uh, try some anger, too, and fear. Tyler called."

Mom stopped stirring and spun around to face me. "I'm about to ask if you were kidding, you know, in that rhetorical way, but I know you're not."

I told Mom about the shawl, the call, the threat to come to see me. "He thinks he can just show up and somehow I'm going to drop everything and run off with him."

Looking at the grimace on my mother's face, I could see the very thought of Tyler upset her.

"Speaking of falling into place," I said, "are things

coming along with Devin and Julia?"

"Seems so," Mom said, a dreamy look passing over her face. "Your dad is happy for Devin. He's been sleepwalking through his life ever since Hannah died, but he's more alive now. Happy. And being away from the bank seems to have injected some new energy in his life."

"That's good," I said, deciding against asking too much about Dad. The news was probably not good, that was likely to be the case for as long as Dad was still alive.

As if reading my mind, my mother said, "Your dad is holding his own."

So, that was that. Just as well not to probe.

We passed the time talking about upcoming events at the winery, and I filled her in about the new clients from The Wedding Extravaganza and JoAnn. I mentioned Doris' problems, but didn't dwell on them. "It's the first time anyone has left the Square in quite a few years now," I said. "Eli was saying that in these last years, they've become used to new people filling up the vacant buildings, not the other way around."

I had a hard time shaking off the reality that the Square would lose Doris. It made me wonder if I'd made enough of an effort to get to know her. Now I wouldn't have that chance.

When Eli came back with the others, he had an exuberance about him that I'd seen only a few times. He was talkative and lively as we ate Mom's soup and rolls and finished off the meal with baked apples and vanilla ice cream.

By the time hugs were exchanged all around and we climbed into the truck, Eli had become a little mellower and pensive. We rode in comfortable silence until Eli pulled off the highway at the exit before the one we'd normally take to go directly to the Square.

"Another surprise?" I asked.

"You bet. There's something I want to show you."

A few miles later, Eli pulled into the driveway by the barn at the farmhouse. Piles of dirty snow, so typical in an early Wisconsin spring, still sat in mounds along the sides of the driveway to the house and farther down past the house to the barn. It was still early in the day, so neither Georgia or Elliot were there. Eli took my hand and led me across the space where Megan had her flower garden and down a field path along the side of a wide swath of land dotted with snow. We went past the spot where Elliot and Georgia's house would stand, and then along a second path to another field not yet showing signs of the meadow it would become.

"Devin and I made a plan today," Eli said. "And it starts here, on this land."

"Devin, wine…are you going to grow grapes here?"

"Good guess," he said, putting his hand in mine, "but then, I suppose you know a thing or two about grapes."

I laughed. "When your family owns a winery, you pick up a thing or two."

"There's a variety of grapes that have been specially hybridized to withstand our winters up here. Frontenac grapes."

"The name sounds familiar. I probably saw mention of them in journals."

"I told Devin about them, and Devin told me I can learn a lot if I join the Wisconsin Grape-growers Association. The Frontenac type was developed in Minnesota at the university." He gestured with his free hand to encompass the whole field. "So, we start with the grapes and then I'll plant rose bushes at each end of the rows. When the roses have bugs that's a telltale sign that grapes also have them—that's the theory anyway. We'll see."

I threw back my head and laughed. "Just think, we can come out on summer evenings and see how the grapes are doing. Now that sounds like fun."

"It will be," Eli said, "and kind of fits with the history of this land. A couple of generations ago, my grandfather started growing food—mostly vegetables—for the people in town. That idea developed into Farmer Foods. I think of it as a testament to his vision. And this land, right here, is where he started." Eli pointed to the ground.

"And now grapes," I said. "A full cycle."

Eli nodded. "At one point, Granddad had to make a choice. They couldn't keep up with both growing and selling produce, and the town went through various growth spurts. He chose the store. But he kept the land, and my parents and now Megan, Elliot, and I have it. Granddad always had a sense that times could get tough and the land would allow us to stay in the area and not have to leave to survive." He raised his hand to shield his eyes from the evening rays of the sun.

"You're using it well, Eli. All of you are. The flower garden, the horses, a new home for Elliot and Georgia, and now the grapes."

Suddenly, the energy shifted. Eli let go of my hand and cleared his throat, but his nervous energy hung in the air around us.

"What is it?" I asked. "You've got something on your mind."

"Well, in order to avoid issues down the road, Megan and Elliot and I split up the land, with all kinds of provisions, of course, but I own part of this land. But that isn't all. I'm thinking of starting a real winery here."

All along I'd assumed he was growing the grapes for DmZ, but he had bigger plans. He stared at his boots. "I've been thinking of the label—like your Zodiac. How about either Wolf Creek Winery or Homestead Winery?"

An image flashed through my mind. Attractive wine bottles were on my shelves in Square Spirits, some with DmZ labels, and others were blank, just waiting for Eli's label.

"Why not both? It could be Wolf Creek Winery with the first variety called Homestead."

"Yes! That's it." He grabbed me and twirled me around. When he set me down, he stole a kiss and grabbed my hand. And came down to earth himself.

"We'll start small. I think Tracie and Katie know a couple of guys who hire out seasonally, you know, planting in the spring, harvesting later. If they're free, I'll hire them to clear the acres and help with planting. I'll supervise, and I guess we'll all learn together."

We lived and worked close together, now he was linking our families through a common business interest…wine. I laughed to myself. What a day!

Spotting Elliot's truck and Megan's van in the drive prompted Eli to say he wanted to go in and share his plans. That was fine with me.

We went inside the house without knocking, which I guess in their world was okay. The aroma of beef soup and yeasty bread filled the kitchen. The four stood with glasses of wine. Something told me they were waiting for Eli to arrive, but they didn't seem surprised to see me.

The table was set with six red placemats. A vase of red roses sat on the end of the counter. They looked a little sad, wilted, like they'd been there awhile.

Elliot brought two glasses and a bottle to us. "Welcome, Zoe. Always nice to see a pretty face. A glass of wine?"

I felt heat rise in my cheeks, along with a bad case of nerves. I was on display, somehow, maybe needing to pass some kind of test, but I didn't know what it was. "Sure." I needed something to hold.

Eli rested his hand on the center of my back. He wasn't being shy about staking his claim on me for his family to see.

"So, what's up?" Elliot asked, pulling out a chair. Georgia and the rest of us followed suit. "You have to spill it, brother. My wife's radar is on high alert."

"Grapes," Eli said, "I'm going to grow grapes out on the far field. And start a winery."

"In competition to DmZ?" Clayton had entered "we ask/ you answer" mode, obviously interested.

"Not exactly," Eli said. "Zoe's brother is helping me, teaching me their secrets."

I couldn't contain a laugh. "I don't know about that. I don't even know all of Devin's secrets."

"Business? Or is this hobby material?" Elliot reached over and added a little wine to everyone's glass.

Eli shrugged. "Too soon to know. Kind of like the remodeling I'm doing. I had to give it a try."

Georgia got up to retrieve a stack of bowls off the counter. She put them in front of Elliot. "I doubt Eli mentioned this to you, Zoe, but once a month we have a family soup supper—good thing Farmer Foods makes such tasty ones, so it's no fuss."

"We're all so busy," Elliot said, "that if we don't plan, the days fly by without us sitting down together. And Crossroads dinners, while nice, aren't quite like being together as a family. Somehow, even at Crossroads, we always end up taking calls and texts."

"I really don't want to infringe on your dinner." I glanced at Eli, blaming him for putting me in this position.

"I was so wrapped up in the day, I forgot," Eli said, "but you're not going anywhere. Let's have some of our famous soup and our equally famous bread."

"Besides, there's no such thing as infringing," Georgia said, putting a handful of silverware and napkins on the table. "Everyone is welcome in our home anytime."

Megan got up and brought a plate of cut up cheese to the table, and Eli and I moved glasses to make room for a basket of crackers. The kettle and warm bread came last.

That evening, we lingered around the table, giving me a chance to learn more about the Reynolds family and those associated with them. It turned out Clayton and Sadie had been more or less on the run. Clayton's stepfather had been involved in financial crimes that affected both their lives and ultimately led them to Wolf Creek. And I hadn't known that even with their ten year or more age difference, Art and Clayton had known each other in art school.

When there was a lull in the stories, I gathered up my nerve and told an abbreviated version about Tyler and my divorce. "Unfortunately, he has it in his head that I'll go back to him now…a totally foolish notion. But I've told Eli I'm on edge sometimes, almost watching for him to walk into the shop." Eli put his arm across my back, reassuring me.

"If you need any help," Georgia said, "remember Country Law. We can help if needed."

I sighed. "Funny you should say that. Knowing you're on the Square is comforting. For sure, I don't feel alone."

It was late evening when we finished our coffee and cleaned up the kitchen.

In the truck on the way home, I remarked on what a great day it had been. "First my family and then yours."

"You opened up, but none of them will say anything, Zoe. It's your business, but now that you've shared it, you'll see Georgia and Elliot, and probably Clayton more often. You're linked to Megan now, because of the wedding business. But they'll all care about you even more, because I do."

"I've never had friends like the people here. Another casualty of my long marriage to Tyler. Friends were a necessary part of his strategy to stay prominent in the community. I was so busy, I just went along."

Eli laughed, lifting the mood. "Megan and Elliot have been waiting a long time for me to bring a woman home."

"Well, now you have, and I like them. A lot."

Eli drove down the alleyway and left me at my back door, but not before we shared a long, passionate kiss. One I wouldn't soon forget.

APRIL
23

I turned my calendar and laughed when I remembered it was April Fool's Day. I wasn't so happy when the thought passed through my mind that I'd be a fool to believe Eli and his family could protect me from Tyler. They were great people. I didn't doubt that, but there was only so much anyone else could do. Still, it gave me a boost of confidence that I could call on any one of them if I needed help.

I laughed out loud when I realized March had indeed gone out like a lamb. The increasing warmth from the sun's rays boosted my spirits. Winter had retreated as spring made its presence known. On April 1st, three trucks made their way around the Square, with workers picking up snowmen and setting out huge egg-shaped cutouts painted in an array of pastel colors. Large rabbits made in the same cut-out fashion and painted with smiley faces were set at the intersections of the walkways. I watched one of the men break up the remaining piles of snow, and in the bare spots, I saw the first hints of green leaves in the garden beds.

I took a pass on a couple of mornings at B and B after Eli and I had gone to the winery and his family farm. I knew that in order to keep my energy level high and not become embroiled in the constant sad conversation about Doris, I had to take a break. Yes, she had become a friend, and I cared about her future, but I could do nothing to change her circumstances. Sometimes facing the reality of a situation meant getting out of the way and doing nothing. Others on the Square had a much longer history with her.

April meant changing the outfit on the mannequin in my window, and Jessica volunteered to bring over an outfit in my color preference, a soft spring blue. JoAnn and I had tried many names for her, but in the end she became Lady, and it fit.

I had initially dressed the mannequin from Styles in a wintery red velvet dress, but it was time for a change. As I took the dress off of Lady I found a necklace hidden under the scarf I'd tied around her neck. The little jokester spirits were at it again. I'd found other samples of their sprite-like nature lately, including a little pyramid of books precariously balanced on the counter. Sometimes the pendulums would start swinging even when no one was near them. Maybe, like everyone else, Grace and Rose enjoyed the arrival of warmer weather.

I was glad JoAnn was around as I worked on the window. I'd begun to understand Megan and Marianna's complaints about the way window displays drained their time. With Lady ready for her spring outfit, I moved on to taking down more than half the stars and crescent moons I'd hung for the Solstice open house and the holidays. Those I left in place blended with the theme of the shop, but weren't so evocative of holidays and winter. Unfortunately, it also left the shop looking a little bare.

On impulse I took one of the white boxes I had used for wedding-related gifts and put together an assortment of lavender creams, a scarf painted with dancing fairies, and a small sprig of dried lavender. They fit nicely in a nest of violet tissue paper. My first door prize box. I set a notepad and pen next to it and a box for the slips of paper.

My drawing was suspended when my first customer of the day convinced me to sell the box to her. Me, turn down a sale? Not on your life. Since January, customers had been scarce and every sale was necessary to keep the shop open.

When Eli called it was like adding more sunshine on the Square. Sometimes he was in the truck making deliveries and he'd call from the road. If I didn't have customers I picked up the call, but if the shop was busy, I let the call go to voice mail.

That day, I could easily pick up and we…well…*he* talked about the grape project. He'd arranged for the field to be cleared and plowed. Apparently, my brother was coming over to help take soil samples. That was a surprise, but it probably shouldn't have been, given the friendship building between Devin and Eli. He ended the call when he arrived at his destination, always saying, "Sorry, honey, have to go."

His calls always got me thinking, and that particular day, I decided it was time to get rid of that shawl from Tyler. It would make a fantastic door prize to replace the one I'd sold. I ran upstairs and brought it down into the shop. A sharp flurry of air whipped by. Their message was clear. Tyler and anything associated with him were not welcome.

I smoothed out the wrinkles in the fabric that the knots had created at the ends and arranged the shawl in a box, reassuring the girls I was giving it away. Someone else would enjoy it. Mostly, I told them I didn't want any reminders of Tyler around the house. Warm and cool hovered by my side.

Jessica arrived with an outfit for Lady at the tail end of my conversation with the girls. My only comment was, "Wow."

"You like it, huh?"

A blue cotton sweater was matched with a peasant skirt in graduated rows, starting with midnight blue at the bottom and moving up to sky blue at the top. The same concept I used for the walls of my shop. With her experience, Jessica showed me a trick or two about making an outfit attractive on a model. The gold belt cinching Lady's waist was the perfect accent for the line of the sweater.

"Your windows always make me want to stop in and buy what's on display," I said with a laugh. "You do such a fantastic job of choosing your stock and then showing it off."

"That's the idea. It takes a while to learn the tricks. Mimi and I both took a class in New York on marketing clothes. It's a different kind of marketing, because we don't see the clothes as we wear them, but everyone else does. That's why we get nervous sometimes when we're not sure how we look."

Jessica spotted something and when I followed her gaze,

I saw that the journals had caught her eye. "I need to pick up a few of these," Jessica said. "I gave away a bunch as gifts during the holidays."

It didn't take her long to pick out three journals and three pens. I silently thanked the grandmother who asked for pens for her granddaughters when I didn't have them. I'd ordered some that same day. I put Jessica's items in one of my logo bags knowing that others would see my colleague shopped at my store. My spirit was happy.

After Jessica left, I turned my attention to the best way to feature the new crystal bowls, and after some trial and error, I settled on arranging them on one of my display towers and adjusting the LED spotlights so they'd shine. Unable to decide on the perfect place for the crystal candlesticks, I left them near the checkout area.

By the end of the day I was still energetic and my spirits were high. I was looking forward to that evening's call from Eli. I had a lot to tell him, including my decision to use the shawl as a door prize.

Eli also was in a good place when he called later. He'd contacted Liz Pearson to get a jump on the designs for his wine label. He didn't have to wait for his own grapes to grow, but could ship grapes in and get his wine-making started. Most of the wineries in Wisconsin purchased grapes from growers all over the country. Since Devin had offered him the use of DmZ's equipment, Eli had little to lose. If his plans fell into place, he could eventually invest in his own setup to make, store, and bottle the wine.

I suspected Eli knew how exceptional it was for Devin to let what he called smalltime hobbyists use any of DmZ's equipment or supplies.

"I know it's going to be two, if not three years, before I have my own grapes to use," Eli said. "But I'm a patient guy. Sort of. I told Devin I don't have time to wait to jump in and start learning how to make wine."

He kept talking and chuckling, mostly about the prospect of pleasing his brother, who wanted a wine variety named *Georgia*.

"Or maybe Peaches?" I asked, only half joking.

Eli chuckled. "Hmm… I'll have to think about that."

"And you'll have a Megan, too, no doubt."

"Absolutely." I could hear his yawn as he said the word.

"Tired?" I asked.

"Real tired. 'Night, sweetheart."

"With you next door, I can sleep without worrying about Tyler. So sleep well, and I will, too."

It was true. Ever since settling things between me and Eli, I had a sense that Tyler couldn't upset me anymore, no matter how he'd seemed to change. There had been something so off about his voice, though, it was difficult to brush it out of my mind.

***

Rested and still carrying a bright spirit from the day before, I was one of the first to arrive at B and B the next morning. Lily and I both came in at the same time, which gave me a chance to express my sadness about Doris.

Tears instantly filled her eyes, but she stepped back when I offered a hug. "We'd become close, Doris and me. And my emotions are all over the place, the baby, Doris, the new toy order to deal with, and of course, Toby." She waved her hand in front of her. "I don't want to keep crying over this."

"Give yourself time to process all of it," I said, "and if I can help, please call."

Steph handed our coffee cups over the counter. "There's a glow to you, Lily."

Lily managed a smile. "Thanks, Steph, I needed that. You know, with all that's happened."

Steph nodded, acknowledging Lily's sadness.

Lily perked up when Georgia and Megan joined us, leaving Clayton, Nathan, and Jack to be the first arrivals at the men's table. Jessica and Mimi were right behind them.

"I have a favor to ask," Georgia said, opening her purse and taking out magazine clippings and color charts. This wasn't the first time she'd asked for our opinions.

Lily started to spread the clippings apart. "I'll be thrown into the same kind of project soon. Charlie called to tell us he'll be starting our addition next week. With the baby coming, I want it done as fast as possible. We need more space. This winter has been hard on Toby in the little house."

Megan took a sip from her cup and began to finger the clippings. "Sure wish I was building a house."

I was surprised by her pouty tone.

Mimi smiled. "Maybe you should think about a wedding first."

We all laughed when Megan's eyes got large. "Clayton and I are talking about eloping."

"*You*, a wedding planner, eloping?" Jessica teased. "What a funny message to send your customers and those using the Weddings at Wolf Creek concept."

Megan waved off the question, knowing others at the table were thinking along the same line as Jessica. "Clayton and I were talking about all the different kinds of wedding there are these days. You know what I mean. We have destination weddings, or private ceremonies, followed by a reception." She shrugged. "So I mentioned eloping and Clayton said that worked for him."

Before anyone else jumped in, Lily's phone buzzed and then she was off with a quick wave to Nathan, who was sitting at the men's table. I guessed she had places to go and people to see. No time for small talk.

Lily's abrupt departure led the rest of us to check the time and be on our way. When I got to my shop, I walked inside with the perception in mind to see my shop as a customer would. A first impression. I liked what I saw. The crystal stood out, the large amethyst piece a crown jewel, and the wine mixed with other pieces gave the sections a special look. Unique. The scarves flowed over a rack, some hanging high, with light shining through them. Gorgeous.

Late in the slow afternoon, Sadie stopped by. She pointed to the bowls. "No takers yet, huh?"

"No, but I have a new strategy. I think people only saw the stones inside them and didn't realize they were for sale. So I put them in the tower and made bigger price tags for them."

Sadie stared at the display as if considering it, searching

her brain perhaps for a new idea. "It probably only needs time. They'll catch on eventually, once the spring traffic on the Square starts picking up around Easter." She fidgeted with the scarf around her neck. "You coming to the meeting tonight?"

"Sure. Why do you ask?"

"I'm thinking about Sarah. She knew Doris for a long time. We're part of the Square's community," Sadie said, "so good or bad, or sad, we support each other."

"I know. That's what makes the Square such a special place." I wasn't sure what else I could add. It was natural that those who had known Doris the longest would be most affected by her leaving.

Soon after Sadie left, it was time to close. I locked the door and stood looking out onto the Square. The view was so different from what I saw sitting by the window upstairs. The sun was still above the rooftops on the other end of the Square. Longer daylight hours and warmer temperatures meant an increase in the number of shoppers. And sales.

At least, that's what everyone told me.

***

Eli and I had a quick deli supper upstairs before walking over to Crossroads for the business association meeting. This time Jack Pearson had taken a turn handing out the agenda.

Even though small groups of attendees stood at the back of the room and along the far wall, the atmosphere was subdued. When Sarah came in, a hush traveled around the room and what little buzz there had been stopped and people took a seat.

Sarah walked to the front and switched on the microphone. "Let's begin. We'll start with Doris Parker, our colleague and fellow resident of the Square." She stopped for a sip of water from the glass on the podium. "Doris will be moving to a care facility near her sister in Illinois."

Sarah stopped and we could all see her taking hold of her emotions. I glanced around, seeing that others in the room had the same expression on their faces as Sarah. Eli looked grim as well.

"For those of you new to the Square, Ralph and Doris were the first non-residents to buy a building. They stood with the rest of us to fight to save these buildings, which had been scheduled for razing. Why?" Sarah smiled. "To make room for a downtown mall. I have such wonderful memories of Ralph. As much or more as any person born and bred in Wolf Creek, he loved his shop and the people here. Most often customers left with at least one book. He believed in the Square. As we all know, Doris never quite got over losing her husband, but she carried on. She agreed to a new direction when Lily proposed adding toys."

Still holding on to the mic, she stepped to the side of the podium. "Who would like to relate a story about Doris?"

I saw surprised expressions on most everyone's face when Rachel, Marianna's stepdaughter, was the first to stand, nervously wringing her hands. "I first met Doris when I started working for Steph at B and B. Doris made a point of telling me that she didn't approve of me because I had a baby and wasn't married. I was really uncomfortable around her at first because of that. Then one day she asked me what kind of a mother I was. I told her I was a good mother."

Rachel stopped there, but she didn't sit. Instead, she let the silence hang over the room. "It's kind of strange because her question kept coming back to me these last couple of years. I think I'm a better mother because of her question. I'm sorry I never told her that she made me think about my son's future. Now I wish I'd said something."

Alan took one of her hands in his and held it when she sat down. Quite a few people turned to her and thanked her for speaking up. I thought it was a pretty mature comment for such a young person.

"I've got a story," Georgia said, getting to her feet. "I gave Elliot a kiss one day on the steps of Country Law." Shifting to a teasing tone she said, "And Doris came striding all the way across the Square from her shop to scold us for what she called 'carrying on' in public."

The laughter in the room matched her light tone. "At the time, I thought it was very strange, but also kind of funny. I guess she sometimes scared me a little because I never knew what she'd say next." She paused, but her smile remained. "Even with all her grouchiness, she was among the first to come into Country Law on her own to offer her best wishes when Elliot and I announced our engagement. She was a real character, and I'll miss her."

Elliot followed Georgia, taking a similar tone. "When Ralph died, I thought Doris would close the bookstore and move away. Then one day, she asked if I would help her if she stayed. I promised that everyone on the Square would help. All she needed to do was ask." He grinned and looked around. "True, sometimes it seemed she asked a lot, but all that's in the past now. I will miss her calls."

A few others added stories, most often making light of what was universally thought of a gruff disposition, but on the other hand, most appeared to understand that without Ralph, she felt lost and had never fully recovered. Later, Lily brought her back to life.

I thought about adding a word or two, but I didn't know Doris very well, and quite a few people stayed silent, although I could see many nodding along with observations others made.

Sarah stepped back to the podium and offered thanks to everyone for taking the time to remember such a loyal member of the Wolf Creek Square community. She took a sip from her glass before changing the subject. "Doris' apartment is for rent if you hear about anyone interested. Her sister has arranged to take care of her things."

"Can Toby live there?" Lily broke the solemn mood with her question. "He's eight going on eighteen and growing independent. He thinks he should have his own place."

Lily's amusing remark restored the upbeat energy typical for a meeting.

"Oh, you wait 'till the baby arrives," Sadie added.

Lily grinned. "Thanks for the warning, Sadie. Mom says the same thing."

Sarah tapped the microphone to get the meeting moving

along. "So, you'll be happy to hear that Tom Harris is making us a stop on his bus tour next week. And other tour operators are calling to work out the summer schedule. I'll update you when we nail down the dates."

I was in for another surprise when the topic of the Easter Bunny came up. Every year somebody named Red Thompson dressed as the rabbit and handed out candy.

"Everything stays about the same," Sarah said. "We'll put out hidden eggs for the kids to find. Each will have a prize tucked inside. You can decorate your shops as you wish."

"I'll make lots of decorated cookies," Steph said.

I'd quickly learned that Steph enjoyed holidays and the traditions that went with them.

When she ended the meeting, Sarah was quick to leave the room, not her usual style. Eli nudged me and pointed to Richard Connor following her out. Interesting...

24

Warmer weather brought hints of spring. The purple crocuses and white hyacinths, along with the yellow daffodils, added bright spots to the long dormant flower gardens. Snow mounds and melting snowmen were long gone. Patches of green grass appeared in still brown areas.

The few days following the association meeting saw an increase in shoppers on the Square. We all were in a good mood when Tom Harris brought his bus tour to town and the Square bustled with activity. Square Spirits had the advantage of being the newest shop for many of his tour guests and, just like those on his winter trip, they came to buy. The bus tours gave me a new understanding of the term "serious shoppers" on the Square.

At B and B the next morning, I both laughed and groaned about the beginning of another year of holidays and events. I'd survived the holidays, but the constant busy days started around Memorial Day. My seasoned colleagues told of one day blending into the next, and weeks rushing by.

I wasn't shy about asking questions, and they did their best to answer them. When I told Marianna that a customer had bought my first door prize she hooted. "Congratulations! That's never happened to me. Not one time."

Easter Sunday was coming up, and with a new event designed more for kids than for shopping, sales could be slow. Sarah injected her favorite phrase, "Planting the seed," to the conversation.

Meanwhile, Eli was in full remodeling mode. Between hammering and the annoying wood slivers, he called every day to report his progress. But I was never invited to see what he'd done. Apparently, he wanted to surprise me.

We had bright sunshine on Easter Sunday and by mid-afternoon the Square was filled with children and a life-size Easter bunny. The kids shrieked with laughter as he danced and the noise drew me to the front door. It was still too cool to leave the door open, but I enjoyed watching the kids get extra rambunctious when the bunny held up a basket of candy.

Only a few women came into Square Spirits, but none left without at least a small purchase. They all mentioned a return visit, like Sarah hoped they would.

I stepped outside to enjoy the fresh air just as Tracie was leading two lambs past my front door. One sported a blue bow, the other pink. I laughed and said, "Aren't they cute? I didn't know you were bringing special visitors to the Square."

"It was a last minute decision, but we won't stay long. We had to take them away from their mom, and we have to get them back so they can eat. I thought the children would enjoy them."

"I think the grownups are enjoying them as well," I said, pointing to a couple of parents who took pictures of their children petting the lambs. After they left, I stepped forward to pet them as well.

I hadn't seen or heard from Eli all day, so I called to tell him about the day and let him know I was once again peaceful and calm. He had that effect on me.

"You up for burgers again?" he asked. "The kitchen's not quite done yet, but Creekside Pub is close."

"How about Chinese? I saw stir fry on the Crossroads menu. I can call for take-out."

"Bring forks. I don't do chop sticks."

I laughed. "Nothing funnier than me trying to eat rice with sticks. I'll buzz the back door."

"Don't be long, sweetheart."

I hurried to pick up our dinner, then unloaded the bags on Eli's granite counter so I could look around. The basic rooms we'd talked about were in place, but the kitchen was going to be state-of-the-art when it was done. Good enough for a chef.

The fireplace got my attention like a moth to flame. The workmanship was amazing. I rubbed my hand across the wooden mantle, its smooth surface enhancing the rich wood grain. Eli reached around me to light the flame. "I would sit in front of this fireplace every night if it was in my place," I said.

"Glad you approve."

Eli opened the containers and filled the disposable plates I'd ordered to go with the food. He handed me a plate and put a chair in front of the fireplace for me. He sat next to me on the floor and balanced his plate on his knee. "I think I'll need to work on getting some new furniture soon. Not like you and your warehouse."

I jabbed him on the shoulder. "Hey, I still don't have any idea what I want my place to look like, not like I did with the shop. I had a strong vision about it."

"When you're ready, it'll happen," he said.

"Tell me what's going on with your vineyard."

He swallowed before he spoke. "The field's plowed. Devin's waiting for the soil analysis. I might have to add some nutrients to the soil before planting the roots."

"When's that?" I actually knew the answer. I sat through years of my parents' talking and planning, but I wanted to hear it from Eli.

"The ground needs to warm some, yet. You in a hurry?"

"*Me?* Aren't you the one in a hurry?" I shrugged. "Still, I can't wait to see row after row of grapes growing on the Reynolds' farm."

"Me, too. I can already taste the first batch of wine from my grapes."

I tried not to laugh, but in the end it spilled out. "Patience, dear soul. I know with Devin's help it will have a wonderful taste."

Finished with our food, he reached up to take my hand. We sat there quietly, each in our own thoughts, watching the fire. After a few minutes, Eli took my empty plate and set it on the floor next to him.

"The flame doesn't change, does it?" I asked. "Yet it puts out a nice stream of heat."

Eli's soft chuckle sent energy into the room. "Computerized electric flame. With these old buildings, even though they've been modernized, any fire might destroy the Square."

"Oh, that would be devastating." I immediately thought of the two young spirits and their experience with fire.

"We had a small fire in Farmer Foods a while back, right after we opened the new store. One of the new coolers had given us problems since the day we'd installed it. Then one day the compressor started on fire. Scorched the wall, ruined all the produce, lots of clean-up, but no one was hurt and the building wasn't damaged."

"Oh, Eli. I'm so sorry. But what do you mean the *new* store?"

"Farmer Foods used to be where The Fiber Barn is now. We outgrew the space."

"No wonder the store is so bright and shiny," I remarked, "but then I just assumed you'd kept it that way over the years."

Eli knew I was kidding, but, in a way, I wasn't. With the variety of foods Farmer Foods carried and the size of the deli, the store could have competed with any large chain grocery store. They also had pleasant smells filling the store, usually because of one of the soups or stews they made.

Eli stood up and threw our plates into a large garbage can filled with small pieces of wood and sawdust. "Time for us to take a stroll around the Square. The weather's improving and you've mentioned resolving to get more exercise. No time like the present."

As much as I wanted to relax in front of the fire I knew he was right.

Eli held my coat and grabbed his keys. We left by way of the front door, greeted by crisp air that sent a shiver through my body. What a jolt after the warmth of sitting by the fireplace. I pulled up my collar to shield me against the wind.

"Cold?" He reached out and pulled me closer to him.

He didn't need to assure me he'd keep me warm. Every time I was near Eli my body pulsed with heat and energy. Sometimes I laughed to myself that at fifty years old I could feel so vibrant around him. Few men had ever had that effect on me.

We'd walked to the opposite corner of the Square and slowed our pace when we passed Pages and Toys.

"I sure hope Lily keeps the shop going," he said. "Wouldn't want to lose a vital part of the Square, especially now that we've grown so much and draw big crowds."

I nodded. Eli had voiced what I'd been thinking.

We continued along the north side of the Square and stopped in front of Styles. Jessica and Mimi had dressed their windows in mannequins sporting spring outfits. "Oh, I like that one." I pointed to a gold and white pin-stripe jacket on a half-model.

"It's nice, but I like your red outfit better." He twirled me around and we began to do a slow dance to the music in his head. I molded to his body and followed his graceful moves. We stopped dancing when Art and Marianna approached.

Eli continued to hold me as they passed by. "Is there any pie left?" he called out.

"Pie's the last thing on your mind, Eli." Art's eyes sparkled in the glow of the lamp post.

"Oh, leave them alone." Marianna playfully hit Art's shoulder as they kept walking. "You're just the same."

We passed the windows of Crossroads, busy as usual. When we turned the corner, Eli tried to peek into the museum through the small space in the window not covered by paper.

"Sadie told me they're working hard to have some of the new exhibits open this summer," I said. "I don't think it's official yet, though."

"Megan's on the board of directors," Eli said. "According to her, Matt keeps coming up with new ideas to make the renovation the best project he's ever done."

"I didn't know she was involved with the foundation," I said, genuinely surprised. "She's quite the busy lady."

"Too busy. In my opinion, she doesn't have time for Clayton."

I was surprised by his words about Megan and her fiancé. "And how would you know that?"

"I watch. I listen. They're very transparent, those two."

Since I didn't know what he meant, I didn't ask any more questions or contradict his opinion.

The small luminary on the table by the window was on when we came to Square Spirits. I'd come to realize that was the work of the young spirits welcoming me home.

He grabbed me in a fierce hug. I had to break away from him just to breathe. Even my ribs felt the strength of his arms holding me.

Did I mind?

Are you kidding?

I wanted to stay in his arms until we grew old—and beyond.

Eli had other plans. He stepped back, grabbed both my hands and kissed them, first the outside, then the palms. "Time for me to go, my beautiful lady. Doors open again tomorrow."

"Are you always so disciplined?" I wouldn't let go of his hands.

"Don't tempt me." He laughed and pulled free. "Grace, please open the door."

The bolt clicked and the door swung open.

"I'll wait for you to lock up and until I see the light on upstairs," Eli said.

I gave him a mock salute and bent forward to give him one more kiss before going inside and leaving him for the night.

Eli waved when I looked down from my window. I waited for him to get home and saw the glow of the light from his window. I laughed when the phone rang and his name appeared on the screen. "Hi, Eli," I whispered. "Did you have a good day?"

"The best. A beautiful lady told me she loved me."

"Oh, Eli. That's so sweet. What did you tell her?"

"I gave her a kiss." He paused in typical Eli fashion. "And

told her to be safe. I want to be with her for a long time."

Telephones require conversation, but I couldn't find the words. Finally, they came, "Good night, Eli. I love you."

"See you tomorrow, honey."

"Until then."

I settled into my chair, my energy vibrant and surging, yet calm and peaceful. When the girls swirled nearby I told them that I loved Eli and wanted to be with him for the rest of my life. A wave of currents settled next to me.

***

The next morning, Devin called. My first reaction was panic. Something must have happened to Dad. What other reason would Devin have to call? That's why I answered with, "How's Dad?"

"Dad's fine. So is Mom. Why are you asking?"

"*You*...you called." I didn't point out the obvious, that he'd avoided talking to me for many months.

"I called because I looked at the wine sales for the first quarter of the year at your shop. You sold a lot more wine than I expected, each month better than the month before."

"And?" For some reason I was annoyed by this small talk. Devin wasn't telling me anything I didn't know.

"Well, I think you made a good decision to include DmZ wines in your shop. That's all." Long pause. "I'd...I'd like to come and see your shop. Julia has been talking about it non-stop."

"You're welcome to come anytime, Devin."

Another pause, not a disconnect, not a goodbye. I waited.

"Julia and I are coming to Wolf Creek in two weeks. We're meeting with Megan, the wedding planner. We'll be staying overnight at the Inn and we've reserved a table for dinner at Crossroads. We'd like you and Eli to join us."

I'd heard wedding planner and we, we, we. "Wedding planner, huh?"

Devin let out a quick laugh. "Busted. Julia wants to fill you in, so I'll say no more."

Well, well. Julia's instincts were right. Good for her for

waiting Devin out. "Dinner sounds great. Come over when you get to town." Time for me to pause. "Oh, by the way, what did Mom and Dad say about your news?"

"We haven't told them yet, so please don't spoil Julia's surprise."

"I get it," I said with a chuckle. "You can trust me on that. I promise."

Devin had said more words to me in the last few minutes than we'd had in the last two years. And good for him and Julia. I yearned to ask Mom if she'd sensed their deeper connection, but I'd keep my promise and wait.

Devin had sent me an even stronger signal by telling me what was going on in his life. Emotions started to rise in me, making me eager to share my news about my brother coming for a visit. I hurried to dress and leave for B and B for morning coffee. I'd made it out the front door when Richard Connor stopped to introduce me to the woman at his side.

"Hi, Zoe. I'm glad I ran into you. My friend, Millie Harrison, and her granddaughter are visiting Wolf Creek to do some shopping."

"Would you like to come in?" I asked, shaking Millie's hand.

"Oh, yes, I'd love to, but we'll come back when your shop is open," Millie said. "We'll be in town a few days." Her silver-gray hair, stylishly cut, sparkled in the morning sun. Millie looked like the concept of tailored clothes was created just for her. Heeled boots added a few inches to her height and the raspberry-hued, three-quarter length jacket ended mid-thigh. My shop had earrings and scarves that would be perfect for her.

"I hope you come back soon. If I'm not there, my employee, JoAnn, will help you find something unique to take home."

By the time we chatted more about the weather and the Square I noted the morning coffee regulars leaving B and B. My time for sharing had passed that day. I'd have to wait.

I went back inside and called Eli. I couldn't wait to tell him that Devin called and we had a dinner date for Saturday.

"You don't say." Eli's voice became muffled as he responded to someone talking to him in his store. "Gotta go, sweetheart. I've got a customer to help. But, I'll wear my black suit if you wear your red one."

He loved that red suit. I laughed, and then he was gone.

My energy soared all day. I didn't walk around the shop, I danced from shelf to shelf, fixing up displays and feeling so upbeat nothing could change my mood. My interactions with customers were beyond pleasant. I was so excited to help them find the exact item they were looking for. My energy in the store and the energy it gave back to me perfectly matched the visions I'd had for my days in the shop. The hours passed, and with music playing in the background, I told customers the history and folklore about the healing powers of the stones. And many bottles of DmZ wine went out the door with happy customers.

There would be more wonderful days like this ahead.

With Eli.

With Square Spirits.

With my family and community.

The reality I created was quickly matching my visions.

Later, when I locked the door in the afternoon, I noticed small leaves had sprouted on the trees and new growth emerged on the ends of the evergreen boughs. Green grass now covered the lawn areas of the Square. The Connor family stood out as they walked across the Square with Millie and, I assumed, her granddaughter. I hoped both would stop before leaving town.

Such a simple thing, an evening with Devin and Julia and Eli, but it made me so happy that we'd all be together.

That night, Eli called and we chatted and laughed until almost midnight. A perfect end to a perfect day.

***

The next afternoon, Millie came into Square Spirits with a young woman she introduced as her granddaughter, Skylar.

I stepped forward to shake Skylar's hand and then offered the two a cup of tea. "How about peppermint? You can sit at the back table or browse while you sip it."

"Why, yes, thank you. How nice." Millie spoke the words to me, but had her eye on Lady and the clothes from Styles.

Skylar said she'd like tea as well, but she was distracted by the scarf display and ambled toward them.

I planned to use my new clear glass pedestal cups with my logo etched on the side. Millie and Skylar were going to be my first guests for tea, a kind of test case to see if it was practical to offer customers tea in the shop. I stepped into the back room to start the electric kettle.

A few minutes later, I found Millie with three scarves draped over her arm and two journals tucked into her other arm. Skylar had one of the small baskets I provided for necklaces and pendulums balanced on the three books she was carrying.

"Please, let me take these from you," I said, holding out my arms to gather up the items. "I'll put them on the counter while we have our tea."

I soon learned they were an interesting pair, currently living in Minnesota near the Twin Cities. Millie's late husband, an attorney, had worked with Richard Connor on several cases, and Millie and Richard had been friends for many years. A retired book store owner, Millie had lost her husband about five years before. But she and Skylar had suffered another loss when Skylar's parents, Millie's son, Mark, and his wife Carolyn, had died when on route to a conference the corporate jet slid off the runway during a storm and burst into flames. Their deaths had occurred two years before. I could see the anguish in their energy, but I also saw the way the two women had leaned on the other in their grief.

Their energy lingered in the shop after they left. There was something about both of them that intrigued me. I washed and dried my new glass mugs, pleased I'd had a chance to use them.

It was time to ready the shop for the next day. I was about to turn off the lights and lock up when a man entered. He was tall and wore a long coat, much too heavy a fabric for the spring weather we were having.

I went to greet him as I did all my customers. "Welcome to Square Spirits."

When the man looked up, I froze.

Tyler. He'd come. Just as I feared.

I raised my hands and waved them both as a signal to stay back. "Leave, Tyler. Right now." I pointed to the door.

"Hello, Zoe. You're looking well."

I followed his eyes as he pulled his hands out of his coat pocket. Very thin, sun-browned hands.

I took two steps back. "Don't. Come. Any. Closer." My voice was shaky, as if confessing my fear.

Acting like he hadn't heard me, he took a step forward and into a lighter space in the shop. His eyes were sunk deep into his face, but they were glazed and frightening.

"Are you ready to go?" His sinister tone was back.

"*Go?* I'm not going anywhere with you." I took another step backward.

Tyler's gaze moved to the shawl, and he picked up the door prize sign. "You're giving my shawl away?"

"It's not yours."

He dropped the sign on the shawl and fixated on me. "But *I* gave it to you. Because I love you."

"I don't want it, Tyler. I want you to go." I moved my hand across a display counter and put my palm over an amethyst paperweight. The stone in my hand gave me foolish confidence that pushed me an inch closer to him. "It's time for you to leave."

"Not without you. You're mine, and you always will be."

Suddenly, warm and cool air currents swirled around me and whipped through the shop sending papers into Tyler's face. Tyler threw up his arms in a defensive move, protecting his face from the onslaught.

"Leave," I shouted, "or they will send you much worse than a pile of paper."

Tyler spun around full circle batting aimlessly in the air. "Not without you," he screamed. *"Don't you understand?"*

He rushed me. Before I had a chance to react, he grabbed my arm and held on tight. "Turn the lights off and keep quiet." The tone of his voice had become even more menacing.

It worked. My knees went weak. I had to keep my eyes on him, but his eerie stare showed me how crazed he'd become.

I tried to yank my arm away, but, even though he looked thin and frail, Tyler's grip tightened. He struggled to get the paper weight and won.

Frenzied air currents bounced off the walls, first hot, then cold. Grace and Rose were using their maximum energy to help me, and even in the midst of the struggle, I knew they weren't strong enough to defend against Tyler. He was behaving as if possessed. I knew he was ill, and now obsessed with forcing me to do as he wished.

With his free hand he grabbed the shawl and in one motion twisted it around my neck, restricting my ability to move even more. But my energy surged. I still had a free arm and I swung out and caught Tyler's jaw. The fury escalated.

The girls tried attacking him with their energy one more time, but they failed. In an instant they were gone. Defeated, I realized, and unable to help me.

When the image of Eli's face crossed my mind, tears ran down my face. I tried to knuckle them away before Tyler noticed and celebrated his victory.

I couldn't see the front door, but I heard it crash open. Tyler twisted his body halfway around, and I caught a glimpse of Eli in the doorway. Every cell in my body was on high alert, and fear for Eli hit with a rush of hot energy. It was one thing to be Tyler's victim, but now Eli was in danger, too.

"Eli stay away," I said as calmly as I could. "He'll hurt you."

"I don't think so," he said, his voice booming through the shop. "I'm not going to let him hurt *you*, my love." Eli squared his shoulders, rising to his full height and took deliberate, slow steps toward Tyler.

"Your love? *Your* love? Ha! She's mine." Tyler's defiant tone mocked Eli's words.

"Zoe? You okay?" Eli spoke to me but kept his eyes on Tyler.

"Yes…yes, but please don't get involved," I said, as Tyler tightened his grip even more. "I don't want you hurt."

"Stay still, Zoe," Eli said, moving closer and lifting his arms as if in preparation for whatever came next. "This is between Tyler and me now."

Tyler let go of my arm with such force I was pushed backward and crashed into the counter. Before I could stop him, he grabbed one of the crystal candlesticks on the counter and raised his hand to threaten a blow.

"No, no, Tyler. Put it down," I begged, seeing in my mind's eye Eli trying to ward off a direct hit.

Eli took a small step forward, acting as if he barely noticed the candlestick that could easily kill him. "Easy, Tyler. I'm stronger than you. And Zoe has asked you to get out of here. I'm giving you another chance to leave. That way no one gets hurt."

"Not without Zoe." Tyler's voice had weakened. He shuffled back a few inches, giving Eli the advantage.

And he took it. He grabbed Tyler's arm and the candlestick crashed, breaking into tiny fragments scattered across the floor.

With his hand gripping Tyler's arm, Eli hung on and walked a half-dazed Tyler to the back door. "Stay back, Zoe. Just stay where you are."

Like magic, the lock clicked and the door opened.

"Get out of here, Tyler. And never come back. Zoe has made herself clear. She's done with you." Eli shoved Tyler out the door and into the alleyway. He locked the door, ending the ordeal.

I unwrapped the shawl and let it fall to the floor. My heart still racing, I opened my arms and Eli walked toward me and into my embrace. As we held each other, his fast heartbeat slowed along with mine.

Yes, I'd been afraid. But unlike the paralyzing fear that had gripped me during Tyler's phone call, Eli had given me strength. Being there, held in Eli's arms, I was certain I never wanted to be anywhere else.

25

I welcomed the silence inside my apartment, but I shivered from the stress of what had just happened. I flopped on the couch and Eli went to get the comforter off my bed. When he came back with it, I pulled it around me and he tucked one end under my feet, cocooning me in its softness and warmth.

We chose tea over wine, and Eli went to put the water on. He brought back a kitchen chair to use as a table. He started to step toward the comfy chair, but I didn't want him that far away.

Patting the couch next to me, I said, "Come sit next to me."

We snuggled on the couch together, and he drew my hand out from under the covers to rest in his palm.

"We can talk later," Eli said, "but for now you need to rest, sweetheart. I'll be here when you wake up. Elliot's opening tomorrow morning, so I don't have be there at dawn."

"Are you sure?" I asked, letting the tears flow freely.

"Absolutely. We're together now. Right?" He squeezed my hand. "Of course, I want to be near you."

Eli left to fix the tea and when he came back, I wrapped my hands around the mug letting it warm me. I began to relax and took a sip, nestling into the comfort of being safe. I could even feel small bursts of energy returning.

I put my head down on the couch cushion and closed my eyes, stirring only when Eli took my cup and put my hand back under the comforter. The darkness in the room was softened by the glow from the lamp posts outside.

"Go to sleep," he whispered as he bent down and kissed my forehead.

"Hmm…I will. Thank you, Eli."

I got another kiss and felt his presence nearby as he watched over me.

***

I opened my eyes to bright sunshine filling the room. Eli was in the comfy chair, a throw keeping him warm, a soft smile on his face. What a wonderful sight.

"Ah, the princess awakes. Darn. Here I thought maybe the prince would get to kiss her again." A low chuckle followed his attempt at levity.

I pushed back the covers and sat up. I wanted a shower and a change of clothes. "Have you been here all night?"

"Yup. But now we both need to get moving," he said, as he got to his feet. "Another day on the Square is about to begin." He hurried to me and bent over to give me a soothing kiss.

I was able to push the image of Tyler—and the sound of his voice—out of my head most of the day, mainly because the shop was so busy. But first, I had to clean up the mess Tyler had made. How ironic. He was out of my life and I still had to sweep up shards of the crystal candlestick. The handi-vac took care of most it, though. The shawl went into the waste basket, along with other trash and the glass and out the back door it went. No lingering signs of what had gone on in my shop, the place I associated with peace and joy and finding home.

I put on a CD of lively Scottish folk tunes to keep me moving until my energy returned in full force. Then I unlocked my door and the day began.

No matter how I resolved to put Tyler out of my mind, he seeped into it now and again. At first I wrote him off as a bump in the road. Not quite true. His appearance had been a major roadblock for me, scaring me, making me feel vulnerable. But that was over, Eli and I were together, and as the day passed I felt more and more as if I could take on the world. Granted, a small world, but it was so good to murmur to myself, "It's *my* world."

By mid-day, the absence of Grace's and Rose's air currents was conspicuous. I'd been a little surprised they hadn't cleaned up the shop for me, particularly the papers they'd sent flying at Tyler's face.

Late in the afternoon, Eli called to let me know that he was bringing a mix of deli dishes for supper. It was a short call, because he had a store filled with customers, but I wanted to ask him about the girls. Had they communicated with him?

At closing time I locked the door and went upstairs to wait for Eli. I was surprised when he called to ask me to let him in the front door. I'd expected him to use the buzzer at the back, but I hurried downstairs to let him in. Through the door I saw he was carrying a large box.

"I asked Grace to open the door," he said, stepping inside, "but nothing happened."

I relocked the door behind him. "They haven't made their presence known at all today." I was distracted from my train of thought when I peeked into the box and saw a lot of small cartons. My stomach growled.

"You eat today?" Elliot said.

"Sure. Yogurt and a bagel, some cheese and crackers mid-afternoon." I gave him a pointed look. "What? You checking up on me?"

"An independent woman like you? I wouldn't dare. But I don't want my sweetheart falling over from lack of nourishment."

I raised my hands high in the air. "Then by all means, let's eat."

Eli carried the box upstairs and put the small white food cartons on the table while I got out plates and utensils. He wasn't shy about opening the last bottle of Zodiac on the counter and pouring a glass for each of us. He appointed himself the server, and took a dollop of this and a spoonful of that from each carton until our plates were full. We pulled out our chairs and sat at the table.

"Another picnic. I love it." I ate a mouthful of Italian

pasta salad and closed my eyes to revel in its rich flavor.

"While we're alone," Eli said, "I want to tell you what happened yesterday before I got over here."

"Now? I'd rather not talk about yesterday."

He put his hand on my forearm. "It's about Grace and Rose."

That piqued my interest. "What happened?"

He leaned forward, frowning slightly in thought. "Sometimes, we put up new displays or restock the produce in the afternoon rather than wait for morning. I'd just finished building a pyramid of oranges when the whole display collapsed and oranges went rolling across the floor. Well, that happens once in a while, so I wasn't too upset. But then two more displays I'd assembled fell apart making another mess."

The situation was starting to become clear to me, but I kept quiet to hear him out.

He took a sip of wine. "Then I remembered you saying that when the girls wanted my attention, they'd show me. And that's exactly what they did."

I was about to speak when he held up his hand. "Let me finish. Then hot and cold air, and I mean hot and cold, not their usual warm and cool, pushed me out the door and to your shop. And as they say, the rest is history."

Wow. I smiled, picturing the crashing displays and Eli being pushed toward the door.

But that was as far I cared to go. Maybe it was too soon after the scary event, but I was reluctant to become mired in yesterday's events. "Well, regardless, I'm done with Tyler," I said, staring at my plate. "I called Jack Pearson about helping me get a restraining order. I don't think Tyler will come back and, if he does, I—we—will deal with it."

I hadn't responded to Eli's story. Somewhere deep inside I knew my time with Grace and Rose was coming to an end. But on the other hand, I didn't want to keep things from Eli ever again. "If they've been in the building today I'm not aware of it." The loneliness of that thought almost doubled me over.

"They sat on the arms of the chair with me all night," Eli

said. "It's as if they were watching over you, too."

"That must have been comforting," I said, squeezing his hand.

"It was." With a pensive expression, Eli stared into the room. "Lately, I've thought of them as family. Daughters maybe, or sisters. At some point down the road, I'll name a wine for each of them."

That broke me. Tears pooled in my eyes and I let them spill down my cheeks. I grabbed Eli's hand and held it. I knew the girls and Eli had become comfortable together, but I hadn't known to what extent Eli had brought them into his life.

"So, what will you say when people ask how those wines got their names?" I gave him a wistful smile.

"I'll think of something." He winked, then stood and began closing cartons and putting the leftovers in the refrigerator. "By the way, when we see Devin next weekend, are you going to tell him about Tyler?"

"I'm calling Mom tomorrow to tell her what happened, so I'll let her pass it on. I don't intend to make a big deal of it."

"And the Square?"

I took his questions as guiding me along the right path. "I'll mention it at morning coffee tomorrow, too. I won't go into detail about it. You can mention it, if you want. Our colleagues all got the messages about us. They know we're together."

"Good, that's good," Eli agreed, nodding. Then he got to his feet. "Time for me to go. Must be getting old. I can't go another night without sleep."

"Thanks again, Eli." My throat tightened and no more words came.

He smiled at me. "I love you, sweetheart."

"It's such a cliché to keep repeating myself, but I love you, too." And to show him I was serious, I stood close to him so the whole length of our bodies touched. I put my arms around him and kissed him. No words needed.

***

At morning coffee the next day, I brought up Tyler's unwelcome visit and explained Eli's help in getting him out of my shop. I didn't mention the girls. As much as I tried to keep the drama down, once I started to talk a hush fell over B and B. I hadn't planned to be the center of attention, yet I didn't want to keep secrets from the people I now called friends. Especially if Tyler returned.

The conversation pivoted to another topic only after everyone assured me I could call on them for help if I needed it.

When it was time to leave, Eli walked alongside me to Square Spirits. "I'm proud of you, Zoe. I know it was difficult to talk about what happened with Tyler, but it's made *you* even more a part of the Square, not just your shop."

"I like it here, Eli. I think I'll stay," I quipped, filled with joy again.

"Good to know." Eli gave me a quick kiss before running the last short distance to Farmer Foods. He turned and waved before going inside.

Shoppers arrived in small groups and by the end of the day, I faced the reality that Grace and Rose hadn't been in the shop. I worked later than usual restocking some of the inventory. That evening, when Eli and I talked on the phone, I asked him about them, but he kept silent. Finally, I asked what he thought.

His voice was soft, in the tone he used when what he was about to say was difficult for him. "Honey, I think they're gone. I think that when they left your building to come and find me they discovered their freedom, the freedom to move on. They'd been locked in your building for so many decades that they didn't know how to leave. And they were still the frightened girls who hadn't grown up. But coming to get me, when they knew you were in trouble, broke that invisible wall for them."

It was true. I had such mixed feelings. "Way back when they first made themselves known I had a feeling my job, almost a responsibility, was to free them. They need to go to the next realm."

Eli nodded. "We may never know all the answers."

"I'm sure going to miss them—a lot. I may have taken on the job of freeing them, but they were my companions in the shop—and my protectors, too. They did what was necessary to get you in here to help me."

Eli understood my loss on every level. "I'll miss them. Who's going to unlock the door for me?"

His chuckle made this sad revelation easier to accept. Maybe my responsibility to them was over, but I'd wait for them to return and give me a proper goodbye.

For a few days after Tyler showed up, waves of loss and grief crashed over me. Not for Tyler. I was done with him, and would never again waste my time giving him even passing thoughts, although he'd always be part of my past, a chapter in my life story. I had to accept that. No, I grieved for Grace and Rose. The shop felt empty without them swirling about. The biggest sense of loss came in the early evenings when dusk replaced the daylight. Eli's calls were mostly for the purpose of checking in. Sometimes I considered them *check-on* calls, although I knew Eli wouldn't have agreed that he was only calling to see how I was doing. He'd also entertain me with a story or two about his day and I'd talk about my day. Sometimes, he called just to tell me he loved me.

He cared, and that's what I needed most. Especially because of the void Grace and Rose created when they had moved on.

Around closing time on Friday Eli stopped by, a surprise since we hadn't made plans for the evening. I'd just finished with a huge sale and he held the door for the customer as she left with two nearly filled shopping bags.

"Good sale? Must have been. You're smiling." He rested his arms on the counter next to the register.

"Two sales like that every day will keep Square Spirits in the black."

"Well, well, aren't you the businesswoman with all her numbers in a row."

"Those are ducks, Eli. Ducks in a row." I laughed.

"You busy after work tomorrow?"

"Nothing pressing."

"I have a surprise to show you. Come over to my place—and be hungry. I'll feed you."

"Is that all I get? No other hints?"

"Nope." He leaned forward and treated me to a quick touch of his lips. Then he turned and headed through the door, waving as he went out to the Square.

What would it be this time? The man seemed to always have a surprise up his sleeve. I didn't have time to linger with my thoughts, because three women entered the shop only a few minutes before closing time.

"Are you still open? You're the last shop for us today and…" The woman had stopped talking when she noticed the tower display of crystal. "Wow, I see what I want." She touched the outside of the glass display case. "I want this bowl and…and that one." She pointed to one on a higher shelf. "Can you gift wrap them for me?"

"Certainly." I'd have jumped through hoops if she's wanted me to. I opened the display door to gain access to the bowls and said a silent thank you to Sadie.

One of the other women added a pendulum and stones to a basket already filled with necklaces, and then appeared to have lost herself in the bins of note cards and journals. The third shopper carried three bottles of wine to the counter and then went back for three more.

I stood back and watched them browse. It seemed that every area of my shop appealed to these women. Eli would get a kick out of it when I called him later. First things first, though. Sadie would get the first call. I knew who got the credit for those bowls.

On Saturday morning I restocked my necklace display and replenished the supply of stones. I used large amethyst and citrine stones to fill in empty spaces in the crystal display. The tower sparkled with their color. I liked the change.

Sadie dropped in after lunchtime, and I showed her what I'd done with the displays. She circled the free-standing tower. "Looks like you need to order more, lots more. Maybe offer new items—they have lovely figurines. Mystical fairies and angels, things like that."

"I agree. The crystal bowls are on the high-end of what I sell, but they don't take away anything from the smaller stones or the jewelry and even the candles."

"I like the color you've added with the stones. Different." Sadie nodded in approval, but was distracted when her phone rang. The call didn't last long and when it was over she said, "Gotta go. I'm meeting Sarah and some of her family at Crossroads for drinks and dinner." She gave me a hug and hurried out the door.

The bell continued to jingle, because she made a swift turn and came back in. "By the way, I'm sorry you had to deal with an ex-husband. I dealt with a man who cheated his clients—a total fraud. But I survived. I see you're doing the same. You're a strong woman, Zoe."

The bell made its happy sound again when she left the second time.

My thoughts were scattered in the time between Sadie leaving and closing up the shop for the day. I was happy to switch my focus to my evening with Eli. I always looked forward to being with him, but it was more than that. On a more primal level, I wanted to merge our energies, which had steadily aligned since I'd first met him as Madame Zoe last fall.

I checked the screen when the phone rang, surprised to see Eli's name.

"I thought you might be tired of deli food so I've ordered carry-out from Crossroads for supper," he said. "Want to walk with me to get it?"

"Sure, but I'm still waiting for the surprise you promised."

He chuckled. "Patience is the word for the evening. See you in a few minutes."

I ran upstairs and brushed my hair and swiped on a layer of lip gloss. I grabbed a Scottish plaid shawl for the cool evening. When I went back downstairs, he was already waiting by the front door and deep in conversation with Megan and Nora. With a turn of the key, I went to join them.

"Hi, neighbors. Haven't seen you lately." I gave each woman a hug. When Eli held his arms open as if asking for his hug, we all laughed.

"Whatever you are doing to my brother, please continue," Megan said. "He hasn't been the grouchy, lovable curmudgeon lately. We all like the changes."

Eli grinned at his sister, but waved goodbye as he took my hand and we headed toward Crossroads. "Time's a-wasting. Our food will get cold."

His energy bounced against me—happy, excited energy. He was like a young man on his first date. "It can't be only the food that has you so buoyant," I said.

He smiled and shrugged. "You could be right."

That was the extent of his comment. We met others from the Square out for the evening, but Eli didn't linger to chat. Our order was ready at Crossroads and he wanted to get the hot food back to his apartment quickly.

He stopped in front of his apartment door before unlocking it. "Close your eyes and promise you'll keep them closed until I say you can open them. Promise?"

"Yes, of course." I certainly wouldn't peek and spoil his fun.

I heard the lock release and, with him leading me, we went inside. "Okay, open now."

Never will I forget my first look at his finished apartment. All construction remnants were gone, and furniture replaced the saw horses and ladders. Everything was new, shiny, and cozy. The colors were shades of burgundy and green, giving the room enough of a masculine feel, but with a certain neutral touch.

I walked around, exclaiming over the texture of the soft chairs and the coolness of the granite countertop and bright overhead lights.

Eli had created a warm, inviting atmosphere. I could see him in the rooms as he relaxed after a busy day downstairs or coming home from the farm when he'd tended his grapes. "Oh, Eli, you must be very proud. You had an idea and you made this space your own." I swept my arm to take in the entire space.

"Nolan and Reed helped, but I did most everything myself."

"I can see that," I said with a nod.

"You in a hurry to eat? We can reheat it later."

"Good idea," I said.

Eli put the meals into the refrigerator and then took a bottle of wine from the counter and handed it to me. "Liz did a mock-up of my label so I cut it out and glued it over yours."

The label was arched at the top with the lettering below the curve. *Wolf Creek Winery*. A line drawing of an old-style farmhouse and barn filled the rest of the space. In the middle an insert read, *Homestead*.

I held the bottle to my chest. "Oh, Eli, your dream is coming together, isn't it?"

"It wouldn't have happened without you." He took the bottle from my hand and put it on the table. "Later, with dinner."

He guided me to the front window and standing there side-by-side the energy pulsed wildly as we looked over the Square that represented home for us. I reached into my pocket for the amethyst point that steadied me. Eli clicked on the fireplace, although we didn't need it for warmth and stood slightly behind me.

"You know those boxes you haven't unpacked yet?"

With the daylight fading I saw his reflection in the window. "Uh, huh. They're summer clothes and…stuff." I waved my hand in the air dismissing their importance.

"I think it's time I helped you move them."

"Where?"

"Around the corner."

I turned to look at him and saw the blue box from Art&Son in his hand. I'd heard about Art's infamous boxes and the rings that the women on the Square had received. I had a wonderful pin from him myself. But I'd never imagined I'd be part of that other group—ever.

He opened the cover and held it out for me to see. The ring had an amethyst stone set in a crown of diamonds. "I know we haven't talked about this. We've hardly even had a date. But I'm thinking you should go ahead and ask Madame Zoe what your answer should be. Zoe, will you marry me?"

Soft currents of warm and cool air swirled around us,

then disappeared. I took in a quick breath. The girls. They hadn't gone away without saying their goodbyes.

I looked into Eli's eyes. "Madame Zoe is gone, but Zoe Miller says oh, yes."

Eli's response was to pull me close and kiss me tenderly, our energies swirling into one.

Now available from award-winning author
Virginia McCullough...

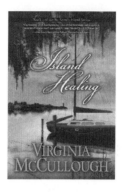

"Beautifully layered, perfectly flawed characters...the kind
of people you'll get invested in...and a few twists that take
the expected down unexpected roads—you will want to
keep reading."
(bluejade, Amazon reader)

Island Healing

Book 1 of the St. Anne's Island Series

Luke Rawley lives aboard *Midnight*, a classic wooden sailboat, secretly preparing to sail around the world. With years of hard-won sobriety behind him, he's ready to set sail. Until he meets Geneva... Geneva Saint returns to her beloved St. Anne's Island, Georgia, leaving her unfaithful husband behind. Back home to stay, she's determined to heal old wounds and help her brother's troubled family. Establishing her one-woman catering company on is all she needs to complete her St. Anne's life. Until she encounters Luke... Now she's torn between her family and taking a chance on love. With the future on the line, Luke is jolted into facing the truth of his dream, while Geneva wonders if she can ever again trust anyone who claims her heart.

Before she began writing novels, **Virginia McCullough** was a ghostwriter for doctors, therapists, lawyers, professional speakers, and many others, and she produced over 100 nonfiction books for her clients. Her award-winning novels that have Wisconsin as the setting include *Jacks of Her Heart,* ***Greta's Grace, Amber Light, The Chapels on the Hill,*** and ***Island Healing****.* Asked about the themes of her fiction, she says her stories always come down to hope, healing, and plenty of second chances. Visit Virginia McCullough's website at: VirginiaMcCullough.com.

From award-winning author of the
St. John Sibling series, another St. John Sibling
contemporary romance,
Craving a Hero by Barbara Raffin...

"Barbara Raffin has created a love story...Kelly and Dane...
both come across as real life individuals with real life concerns
and insecurities... And the internal dynamics of Kelly's family
add an additional reminder of the fact that sometimes events
outside ourselves can greatly affect our own choices."
—Rick Roberts, platinum-recording artist and author of
Song Stories and Other Left-Handed Recollections

Craving A Hero

Book 3 of A St. John Sibling Series

Kelly Jackson believes heroes are just ordinary people who do extraordinary things. Unfortunately, she doesn't believe there is a man out there who would do anything extraordinary for her. Not that *she's* looking for a mate. She is a woman focused on proving herself as a Conservation Officer to the world and her father.

Then Dane St. John shows up in her little corner of Michigan's Upper Peninsula with the looks, the ego, and the charm to take him to the top of his action-hero movie star career. He pays attention to her. He makes her feel like a woman. He is the perfect fantasy tryst.

Too bad he turns out to be a whole lot more substantial than some airhead hunk and Kelly falls in love. Too bad because, in spite of his strong family values, his idea of having a family falls into the *someday* category; and history has taught Kelly, when a man isn't ready for a family, he can't be counted on. So, when she discovers their affair produced a baby, she doesn't tell him because there are no heroes…not for her.

Barbara Raffin grew up a country girl, but loves to visit the big city and live the hurried pace now and then. Blessed with a vivid imagination, she's created stories and adventures in one form or another for as long as she can remember. She wrote her first book at age twelve in retaliation to the lack of female leads in the adventure stories she loved reading. But it is a love of playing with words, exploring the human psyche, and telling stories that keeps her writing. She also loves to make her readers laugh and cry. Whether a romantic romp or gothic-flavored suspense, her books have one common denominator: characters who are wounded, passionate, and searching for love.

She lives on the Michigan-Wisconsin border with her Keeshonden dogs Katie and Slippers and her avid outdoorsman husband who continues to support her love affair with reading and writing. Visit Barbara's web site to learn more about her and her books at www.BarbaraRaffin.com

From **USA Today** *bestselling author,*
Donna Marie Rogers...

"The magical combination of sexy romance and fast-paced
suspense kept me spellbound."
—Stacey Joy Netzel, *New York Times* bestselling author of
Lost In Italy

That Magic Touch

Book 1 of the Lake Shelbyville Series

Once their secrets are revealed, can love heal all?

Living in a small town, Mia Grey has a hard enough time
keeping her own unique healing powers secret, never
mind those of her thirteen-year-old sister, whose powerful
telekinetic abilities grow stronger by the day. Mia's
discovered it's not so easy keeping a moody teenage witch
on the right path while working full-time in her convenience
store/bait shop. And her pre-occupation with their gorgeous
new neighbor certainly isn't helping matters.

Loner Jack Sutton spent seven years behind bars for a
murder he didn't commit. Longing for a family connection,
he heads to Shelbyville, Illinois in search of an aunt he's
never met. Charmed by the picturesque town, he just starts

to settle in when he's stabbed one night in an apparent robbery. He wakes the following morning with a throbbing head, an aching gut, and no memory of the attack. The good news is he's alive. The bad news is he seems to have woken up in an episode of the Twilight Zone—with the mysterious beauty next door cast in the starring role.

USA Today bestselling author **Donna Marie Rogers** inherited her love of romance from her mother, who devoured romance novels like they were Fannie May candies, and never missed an episode of Little House On the Prairie. And though it wasn't until years later Donna would come to understand her mother's fascination with Charles Ingalls, her love of the romance genre is every bit as all-consuming.

A Chicago native, Donna now lives in beautiful Northeast Wisconsin with her husband and children. She's an avid gardener and home-canner, as well as an admitted reality TV junkie. Her passion to read is only exceeded by her passion to write, so when she's not doing the wife and mother thing, you can usually find her sitting at the computer, creating exciting, memorable characters, fresh new worlds, and always a happily-ever-after. Visit her website at DonnaMarieRogers.com.

Acknowledgements

I believe no author is an island with her writing. Yes, she gathers ideas and follows character arcs and deals with the good and the bad people along the way, real and imaginative. It is the good real people authors seek out and strive to emulate with their writing.

Historians, librarians and professionals are our source for accuracy and detail. Two professionals were always available when I needed their help and called. My thanks goes to Laura D. for her natural understanding of stones and their healing powers. Another thank you goes to Virginia M. for her knowledge of energy and spirits. This book could not have been written without your help.

Many thanks to my family. My husband, Gary, and mother, Muriel, have given their support to my dream of becoming an author. I love you both.

Others have been by my side as I travel this journey. Critique partners, Kate Bowman, Shirley Cayer, Virginia McCullough and Barb Raffin are always willing to give their support. Thank you ladies. To the Greater Green Bay Area of Wisconsin Romance Writers of America members, you have been by my side through the ups and downs. I will always appreciate what you have done.

To the team at Written Dreams, including cover artist, Eddie Vincent. Each of you has done your part to put my words together into a book. The team, directed by Brittiany Koren, does the things I don't want to do. Thank you.

Gini Athey
2016

About the Author

G ini Athey grew up in a house of readers, so much so it wasn't unusual for members of her family to sit around the table and read while they were eating. But early on, she showed limited interest in the pastime. In fact, on one trip to the library to pick out a book for a book report, she recalls telling the librarian, "I want books with thick pages and big print."

Eventually that all changed. Today Gini usually reads three or four books at the same time, and her to-be-read pile towers next to her favorite chair. She reads widely in many genres, but her favorite books focus on families, with all their various challenges and rewards.

For many years, Gini has been a member of the Wisconsin chapter (WisRWA) of the Romance Writers of America and has served in a variety of administrative positions.

Avid travelers, Gini and her husband live in a rural area west of Green Bay, Wisconsin.

Square Spirits is the fourth book in her Wolf Creek Square series. *Quilts Galore* is Book One, *Country Law*, Book Two, and *Rainbow Gardens*, Book Three. She is currently working on her next book in the series. Visit her on Facebook or on her website to learn more information.